Praise for

BACK TO BEFORE

"Funny and flirty . . . As refreshing as the North Carolina surf, and just as rewarding."
—Book Page

"A brisk and heartfelt read." —*Publishers Weekly*

"A perfect read if you love romance." —The Reading Cafe

"I'm a fan of small-town contemporary romance and second chances. Tracy Solheim combines the two with heartwarming effect . . . I'm already anticipating my next visit to Chances Inlet."
—The Romance Dish

"A knockout feel-good read." —Talking Books Blog

"I'm definitely looking forward to the next book in the series!"
—Love Between the Sheets

"Everything I look for in a romance." —Smexy Books

Praise for the Out of Bounds Novels

"[An] emotion-driven story." —*Publishers Weekly*

"The sexual tension was off the charts." —The Book Pushers

"A beautiful, fun love story." —Insightful Minds Reviews

continued . . .

"Solid storytelling, sharp dialogue, and genuine, sympathetic characters . . . [An] enjoyable and very entertaining read."

—*RT Book Reviews*

"Purchase this book ASAP!" —Dark Faerie Tales

"Tracy Solheim will have you laughing and cheering and crying." —Rendezvous Books

"Refreshing contemporary . . . A surprisingly deep romance."

—Bookaholics

"*Game On* is a novel that has a lot going for it."

—Book Binge

Berkley Sensation Titles by Tracy Solheim

Second Chances

BACK TO BEFORE
ALL THEY EVER WANTED

Out of Bounds

GAME ON
FOOLISH GAMES
RISKY GAME
A NUMBERS GAME
(A Berkley Sensation Special)
SLEEPING WITH THE ENEMY

ALL THEY *Ever* WANTED

Tracy Solheim

BERKLEY SENSATION, NEW YORK

An imprint of Penguin Random House LLC
375 Hudson Street, New York, New York 10014

ALL THEY EVER WANTED

A Berkley Sensation Book / published by arrangement with Sun Home Productions, LLC.

For more information, visit penguin.com.

ISBN: 978-0-425-28103-1

PUBLISHING HISTORY
Berkley Sensation mass-market edition / March 2016

PRINTED IN THE UNITED STATES OF AMERICA

10 9 8 7 6 5 4 3 2 1

Cover photo Couple on beach walkway © Image Source / Getty Images.
Cover design by Rita Frangie.
Interior text design by Kelly Lipovich.

Penguin
Random
House

For Karen and Howard.
Thanks for raising an awesome son.

ACKNOWLEDGMENTS

It goes without saying that I couldn't do this without the love and support of my family, particularly my husband, Greg, and our two works-in-progress, Austin and Meredith. Love you guys.

As always, thanks to Cindy Hwang at Berkley for your insights and comments—they made this a much better book.

To Melanie Lanham, thank you for always answering the phone and reading what I write.

Thank you to Melissa Jeglinski for your patience.

Thanks to all the wonderful bloggers who've taken the time to promote my books and introduce me to new readers. Many of you have become friends whose kindness I value immensely.

Most of all, I'd like to thank all of you who've taken the time to read one of my books. It's you the readers who make this the best job in the world!

ONE

When he was ten years old, Miles McAlister meticulously and very thoughtfully planned out the remainder of his life. Sitting in the tree house his father had built for him and his four siblings, Miles had put pen to paper and scratched out his future as he saw it: Eagle Scout, All-State track star, high school valedictorian, Duke University, Rhodes Scholar, law school, politics, and most important, President of the United States. Twenty-three years later, he'd revised that list a time or two to include a few things a fifth grader might not have envisioned—like losing his virginity at the national high school debate conference or delaying law school while he backpacked through Europe with his girlfriend. But overall, he was well on his way to executing his carefully mapped out existence nearly verbatim.

Until life had thrown him a curveball. More than one actually.

His two brothers and two sisters—as well as the majority of the people in his hometown of Chances Inlet, North Carolina—hadn't dubbed him "The Ambitious McAlister" without good reason, however. Miles was determined that nothing was going to interfere with the goals he'd set all those years ago. And that's how he found himself on the expansive wraparound porch of his mother's popular bed-and-breakfast stoically enduring the June heat. With its railings draped in red, white, and blue bunting, a dewy pitcher of lemonade on the wicker side table, and his brother's golden retriever snoring at his feet, the Tide Me Over Inn afforded Miles the perfect backdrop for wrestling back control of what he perceived to be his destiny.

The inn had been his mother's pride and joy for four years now. She and Miles' father had painstakingly restored the 1894 Victorian to all its original splendor, turning it into one of the premiere B and B's on the Atlantic coast. Situated among lush gardens and centuries-old trees, the sprawling twenty-room home was also walking distance to the ocean and the historical town of Chances Inlet. The B and B's picturesque location, along with a bevy of championship golf courses in the area, guaranteed that the Tide Me Over Inn's guest suites were booked nearly year-round. Today being no exception. A crowd milled about on the veranda, scrutinizing Miles' every move.

The late day breeze blowing inland off the ocean felt refreshing amidst the wilting humidity so typical of the coast. Miles resisted the urge to tug at his shirt collar as the wind gently lifted the skirt of the woman seated in front of him. Rather than fix her hemline, though, she shifted her long legs suggestively, affording him an unobstructed view of a nicely toned thigh, her skin shimmering with perspiration. The smile she gave him lacked even a trace of innocence, however; instead it was outright daring. But then, she wasn't the one with the television cameras trained on her.

"Just a few more questions, Miles. They'll be painless. I promise." Tanya Sheppard, a blue-eyed, blond former beauty queen who masqueraded as the political reporter from one of Raleigh's affiliate stations, was clearly enjoying her position of dominance in their interview. Miles was sure her antagonistic demeanor was payback for his ignoring the hotel keycard she'd slipped into his tuxedo pocket during last year's Governor's Ball. But he refused to let her rile him up.

Pushing out a breath, he forced himself to relax against the old-fashioned glider he sat in. The guests always raved that the damn things were so comfortable, but to Miles the chair felt like he was contorting his six-foot-one, muscular body into the shape of a paper clip. His dress shirt stuck to his back where it was pressed up against the metal chair. He ignored the discomfort, though, bracing himself for whatever questions Tanya decided to throw at him next. They both knew she had been lobbing softballs for the past fifteen minutes.

His campaign for a vacated U.S. congressional seat certainly wasn't sexy enough to warrant the seven-minute segment on the affiliate's weekly political show. Especially since he was running unopposed in a district located in the county where he'd grown up and where his family was still very much a presence. If Miles was reading the situation correctly, Tanya was here for a bigger sound bite. She wanted revenge with all the trimmings. And that meant discussing the sins of Miles' deceased father.

"How can you expect voters to trust you?" Tanya went right for the most salacious sound bite. "You've repeatedly stated that you weren't aware of your father's efforts to defraud the bank that financed the three-million-dollar loan for this very inn. Even if you didn't know firsthand of your father's thievery, why shouldn't voters assume that the apple doesn't fall far from the tree, so to speak?"

The ice inside the pitcher of lemonade popped, startling the dog at his feet. Brushing a reassuring hand over its head, Miles drew in his own calming breath before launching into the speech he'd been rehearsing in front of the mirror since the mess with his father had been made public the week before. He needed to get ahead of this issue before it compromised his entire campaign.

"*Thievery* is a bit misleading, Tanya." He held up a hand when she began to speak, shushing her before looking directly into the camera lens. "McAlister Construction and Engineering is a privately owned company. If my father moved funds from one account to another, he was misappropriating his *own* money. I don't know what dictionary you use, Tanya, but that's not thievery in my book."

Tanya bristled, uncrossing her thighs and sitting up a little straighter. "There's no *if* about it, Miles. The bank examiner had an airtight case against your father."

And the stress from staying one step ahead of the bank examiner most likely brought on the heart attack that killed Dad.

Miles had to work to unclench his hands and appear relaxed. Donald McAlister had been a larger-than-life role model—a dedicated family man who was also a semipro athlete, an engineer, a small business owner, and a fixture in the community. Apparently, he'd been so devoted to his wife that he'd bought and refurbished the inn for her while playing fast and loose with the books. Miles had no doubt his father would have made good on the loan if the economy hadn't taken a nosedive right when the balloon payment was due. The enormous weight of the financial burden, along with his attempts to conceal it from his wife and children, certainly put Donald McAlister into an early grave.

The emptiness Miles felt in his chest was still raw. All those years ago when he had carefully crafted his life's roadmap, Miles had never taken into account achieving the goals without his father by his side. It was yet another indication of the shortsightedness of a ten-year-old.

Swallowing around the lump in his throat, Miles launched into the rest of his stump speech. "The fact of the matter is this, Tanya, my father isn't campaigning for a seat in the U.S. House of Representatives. *I am*. He died tragically before any of this could get resolved. But I do know this . . ." Miles looked into the camera lens again. "Whatever my father did, it was out of love for his family. Times have been tough financially for many of us these past several years. Washington has forgotten about small businesses and the middle class who are living paycheck to paycheck. When I take my seat in Congress, I plan to be the voice for those people. The same people who would do whatever it takes to ensure their family is provided for and that their dreams can become reality. Just as my father did for his own family."

Tanya covered up an indelicate snort before it could be picked up by the microphone. "And the governor? He obviously wasn't too comfortable with having the stigma that now surrounds you tainting his own reelection bid. Isn't it true that rather than keep you as his chief counsel, he put you on leave without pay?"

It was a chore for Miles to appear unfazed by Tanya's goading question despite the anger that was fueling up inside him, but he miraculously kept his composure. "Governor Rossi's statement was pretty clear on the matter, Tanya. *I* requested the leave of absence. Not the other way around. The leave is so that I can deal with a family emergency here in Chances Inlet. The issue involving my father had nothing to do with it."

At least not in the way she was implying.

She made a show of rustling her notes on her lap. "Of course. Your mother." Tanya brilliantly modulated her voice to sound softer, more serene. Too bad the viewers couldn't see the hard lines still bracketing her mouth. "How is she doing?"

Patricia McAlister had been struck by a hit-and-run driver while riding her bicycle through town ten days earlier. She'd fractured her hip and sustained a concussion along with other minor injuries. But the larger trauma was to her psyche after the secret of Donald McAlister's creative accounting had been revealed on national television.

"She's wonderful." Miles chose to categorize his statement not as a lie exactly, but more as maintaining his mother's privacy. It was partially the truth anyway. Her hip would fully heal. "But it's the summer tourist season, the busiest time of the year in Chances Inlet, and until she's back on her feet, she'll need help running the inn. Since my campaign headquarters is located here in town, it made sense to my family that I be the one to move into the B and B and help her out."

Again, a partial truth. His younger brother Ryan was a professional baseball player whose contract barely allowed for him to visit their injured mother much less take three months off during the season. Their youngest sibling, Elle, had two months left in her Peace Corps service. Kate, the oldest of the five McAlister children, was spending the summer in Chances Inlet. But she and her husband, Alden, were both physicians who operated the beach town's seasonal urgent care clinic. The clinic's hours left them little time to help nurse his mother much less help with the day-to-day operations of the inn. And then there was Gavin.

Miles covertly glanced past the cameras and scanned the sea of townspeople assembled on the inn's sprawling lawn. With their niece perched on his shoulders, his brother was easy to spot standing near the towering black walnut tree similar to the one that had housed their tree house all those years ago. Judging from the deep creases forming in his forehead, Gavin didn't like Tanya's line of questioning any more than Miles did. Guilt, mixed with anger, churned in Miles' gut.

Gavin had single-handedly carried his father's secret for the two years since Donald's death, mollifying the bank examiner with the charm that had everyone in Chances Inlet eating out of the palm of his hand. The middle of the McAlister children, Gavin was a natural peacemaker. He'd devised a plan to pay off the debt and preserve their late father's name with no one in the community—or the family—being the wiser. Miles had to concede that it was a pretty damn good plan given the situation. Too bad Gavin had failed to grasp that people always stab you in the back. *Always.* The past eight years working in politics had taught Miles that.

What peeved Miles the most was that his brother had never thought to confide in him. Born sixteen months apart, they'd grown up in the small town practically in each other's pockets, playing on the same teams, sharing the same bedroom, the same circle of friends. Yet when push came to shove, Gavin hadn't trusted his older brother to help shoulder the burden their father left behind. To help guard the family name and its legacy. He'd made some lame excuse that he'd kept Miles in the dark to protect his political future, but it felt to Miles as though his brother believed he was so blinded by ambition that he couldn't pull his own weight during a family crisis. And that stung. A lot. So, while his mother had still been in the hospital, Miles had taken control of the situation and appointed himself in charge of operating the inn until she was fully recovered. Miles sat taller in his chair. He would take the lead in preserving the McAlister name now.

He refocused his gaze on Tanya. "While I'm in town, I'll have ample time to meet with constituents and take their pulse about which issues are most important to them."

A murmur of approval rose from the crowd and Miles allowed himself to relax slightly. He could do this. Considering the circumstances that brought him back to Chances Inlet, the situation really had worked to his benefit. Not only that, but it afforded him the opportunity to keep an eye on the cast of characters his mother continued to shelter within the walls of the B and B, particularly the stealthy woman his mother had been harboring for the past several months.

Lori—if that was even her name—worked as the inn's maid and cook. While Miles couldn't find fault with her efforts, she was hiding something; he was sure of it. Especially if the smoking hot body she was concealing beneath her baggy clothes and a shield of unnatural-looking, flat black hair was any indication. Shifting slightly in the glider, Miles tried to block out the image of a very wet, very naked Lori all soaped up in one of the inn's luxurious two-person showers. Her body was built for a magazine centerfold, full and curvy in all the right places and very definitely X-rated. It was no wonder she kept it under wraps with castoffs from the Goodwill store. He bit back a groan before his microphone could pick it up. Embarrassment and lust joined the anger that swirled in his gut.

The embarrassment was due to the fact that he'd lingered a moment—*okay, maybe two*—longer than he should have while he surreptitiously admired the view that day when he had unwittingly walked in upon a strange woman showering in a supposedly unoccupied room. Not that anyone would blame him for remaining a few minutes longer than he should have. He was a red-blooded guy and the shower show was one that would have brought a dead man back to life.

The anger Miles felt was fueled by the lust that burned through him then and every freaking time he'd laid his eyes on Lori in the four months since. Miles hated the way his body lit up around a woman who was a mystery—a stranger who was very clearly hiding out under his mother's roof. He worried about what she might be running from and how it could impact his mother, whose heart of gold might not be able to weather another betrayal. Lori was definitely a distraction the McAlister family couldn't afford right now. And yet, she mesmerized him with the things he wanted to do with her. Miles hadn't felt such an intense attraction to a woman since—

"Miles?" Tanya was eyeing him curiously.

He blinked to refocus. *Damn, damn, damn.* Had he missed a question while he was fantasizing about his mother's maid?

Surreptitiously glancing past the television camera again, Miles' eyes landed on the anxious face of Bernice Reed. The elderly woman had managed McAlister C&E for decades and now worked as the office manager of his campaign headquarters. As usual, she was outfitted like a neon sign, today dressed head to toe in bright pink with an oversized necklace to match. She was staring at him through rhinestone-studded glasses, wide-eyed with her hand to her chest and, knowing her, a "bless his heart" on her tongue. Beside her was Cassidy Burroughs, the teenager who operated the Patty Wagon, his mother's seasonal ice cream truck. Cassidy was holding her cell phone aloft, shooting video of the scene while wearing an expression on her face that clearly said, *What the heck?*

"I'm sorry, Tanya." Miles quickly returned his gaze to his other tormentor. "I was distracted thinking of my mother there for a moment." *Jesus, next I'll be invoking apple pie and baseball.* His answer sounded evasive even to his own ears. He needed to wrap up this sparring match with Tanya before he spouted off any more political platitudes.

He looked up to find that Tanya's wide smile had a nasty edge to it. Miles resisted the urge to cross his legs and shield the family jewels. Instead he forced himself to remain relaxed. He was a professional and as such had prepared for anything she could throw at him.

Or so he thought.

"I asked you whether you and your opponent will be debating each other this summer."

Miles could hear the Atlantic Ocean slamming against the sand across the street, the whirring of the ceiling fans above their heads, and even the gentle hum of the LED lights shining on either side of his face, so he knew he wasn't dreaming. He peered over Tanya's right shoulder at Coy Scofield III, the young flunkie the party had dumped on him as a campaign manager. Coy was twenty-five with the political expertise of a gnat, but that hadn't mattered.

Until now.

The kid was talking a mile a minute into the cell phone glued to his ear, his cheeks flushed with what Miles could only assume was excitement. Coy had been very vocal that he wasn't thrilled to be stuck in a campaign where there wouldn't actually be a contest. When the opposing party's candidate had withdrawn after being arrested for alleged racketeering violations just days after this spring's primary, the "race" became a lot less enticing for a young gun trying to make a name in politics. Apparently, however, Miles had bigger problems than keeping his campaign manager happy. He carefully pushed the words past his lips so that the audio wouldn't capture the hint of anxiety in his voice.

"From what I understand, Brian Kendrick is having a tougher battle with the Treasury Department than to worry about debating me. That's why he's no longer running."

"Oh, you haven't heard?" Tanya was practically bouncing in her seat. "Well, I guess that's understandable with your *family crisis* and all. But the opposing party is putting forth another candidate."

"They can't." Miles mentally reviewed the campaign laws. There wasn't a provision. He'd checked. So had the governor and everyone else in the party. The only way they could replace a candidate who'd been put on the ballot via a primary election was if the candidate was ill and could no longer serve the term of the office. The only illness Kendrick had was that of a terminal dumbass and the opposing party was out of luck on that loophole.

Tanya leaned back, seductively crossing her legs again as if to say *checkmate*. There was no mistaking the malice in her grin now. She was obviously enjoying the reaction her bombshell had gotten out of Miles. "Technically the party can't add a name to the November ballot. But the voters can."

Son. Of. A. Bitch.

A write-in campaign. There'd been talk of one during the initial days after Kendrick's arrest, but the pollsters had assured the governor and the national party big wigs that Miles' reputation was sterling enough the opposition wouldn't risk funding another candidate. Instead, they'd spend their time and money on a race that wasn't a shoo-in. Apparently, with all the talk surrounding his late father these past few weeks, some of the shine had worn off Miles' reputation.

"It's funny how these things work, isn't it?" Tanya seemed to be the only one on the veranda who saw the humor in the situation.

Determined not to let her—or any of her viewers—see him sweat, Miles leaned back in the stupid glider and tried his best to look unfazed. "Well, it's a lot better for the constituents to have more than one candidate. A two-party race offers voters greater opportunities to weigh the issues and make sure their interests will be best represented." Miles was pretty sure he'd read that in a political science textbook somewhere, but at this point he just didn't care. He needed to regurgitate enough bullshit to get him through this train wreck of an interview with his shirt still on his back. "Since you have the inside scoop today, Tanya, do you mind telling me who my opponent will be?"

"Of course. We're headed to Shallotte from here for the big announcement. You'll be facing off against Faye Rich."

"Faye Rich as in The GTO Grandma?" Cassidy blurted out from behind the camera and Miles hoped her words and his wince hadn't been caught on tape. The murmur from the lawn rose like a tidal wave as the crowd processed Tanya's bombshell.

Faye Rich was exactly what her name implied: rich as Croesus. She'd inherited a string of car dealerships from her father and married into more. Her commercials were legendary for their low-budget, smaltzy, down-home humor. Not to mention Faye had appeared in all of them since she was three years old. Now somewhere in her mid-sixties, she still was the voice behind Rich Automotive, occasionally even dressed as the Easter Bunny, the Tobacco Queen, or Uncle Sam. She made it a point to appear at events in her souped-up GTO. Her voter recognition would be off the charts. And then there was the fact that her name would be easy to write in.

And just like that, Miles' life plan was broadsided by another curveball.

TWO

"Oh, lordy," Patricia McAlister groaned as she shifted stiffly in the leather recliner. The bulky chair took up most of the small room in the rehab center where she'd been living the past week. With the remote control in her hand, she gestured to the television. "That Tanya Sheppard is a barracuda in designer clothing. Miles can't be happy with this turn of events." Her soft chuckle sounded more like a sigh as she clicked the off button and shook her head. "If there's anything my son hates, it's having his carefully organized life derailed. I don't know if you've noticed this yet, Lori, but Miles can be a little prickly when things don't go his way." She winked just as her lips settled into a resigned smile.

Lori Hunt laughed at her employer's tongue-in-cheek humor while she plumped the pillows on Patricia's bed. "Prickly" was tame compared to the words she would use to describe Miles McAlister. Heading up her list would be words such as: pompous, infuriating, overbearing, and hotheaded.

To the rest of the world, though, Miles was the proverbial Dudley Do-Right. Quick with a smile and a handshake or to help old ladies across the street, he was a true Southern gentleman. In other words, he was the consummate politician. Except when he got near Lori; then a few uncharacteristic flaws in his polished exterior began to show. Miles certainly made no secret of the fact that he didn't trust her. He'd loudly hammered home that point numerous times since she'd been working at the Tide Me Over Inn.

Lori couldn't fault the man for protecting his mother, however. If she were being truthful, "honorable" would be another word she'd use to describe Miles. And she of all people knew firsthand that men with character were hard to come by. But living under his constant scrutiny posed a more serious problem—one to her own well-being. The more attention Miles brought to her existence at the B and B and in Chances Inlet, the more likely she was to be discovered.

Lori's palms began to sweat as she folded the soft throw blanket and placed it on Patricia's bed. She had stayed too long already. Too many people could remember her if asked. She'd planned to disappear two weeks ago, but then the car had clipped Patricia, leaving no one to take care of the cooking at the B and B. She couldn't leave the innkeeper in the lurch. Not when she'd given Lori a safe haven to heal and regroup these past months. Staying put also helped Lori atone for deserting her own mother.

Her plan of sticking to the shadows and keeping her nose buried in her work was becoming more and more difficult with Miles dogging her steps all day, however. It didn't help matters that he was also annoyingly sexy. Dark-haired, blue-eyed, and muscular, thanks to great genes and an addiction to the adrenaline rush of triathlons, Miles' picture could be listed in the dictionary under the phrase "tall, dark, and handsome." Lori's own body practically sizzled whenever he was near. She kept telling herself it was simply a reaction to his irritating personality, but even she had to admit that was a lie more often than not.

"I can't say that I've noticed Miles being anything but a paragon of kindness," she hedged, causing Patricia to laugh along with her. Miles' mother knew exactly how exasperating her son had been these past several months. Lori glanced at the older woman admiringly. Patricia was still elegant and fierce despite being severely injured and left for dead by the side of the road.

"More like a paragon of cockiness," Patricia said. "Don't get me wrong, I love my son. I love all five of my children to pieces. Each one of them is unique and wonderful in their own right, but that doesn't mean any of them is perfect. Miles was born with a hefty dose of self-importance. Fortunately, he's always used it to try and do good in the world." She waved a hand dismissively. "So as his mother, I can't get too upset with him. He's very determined, you know." Her eyes sparkled with pride even as she winced, presumably in pain, when she tried to adjust her injured hip in the slippery chair.

Lori poured Patricia a glass of water from the pitcher beside the bed. "I'm beginning to think that determination is a trait synonymous with the McAlister name."

The older woman gave her a sly smile as she took the offered glass. "And I think that you know a lot about determination yourself, young lady."

Avoiding Patricia's astute hazel-eyed gaze, Lori turned to straighten the pile of magazines on the table. This was a familiar dance between the two women: one where Patricia tried to unearth Lori's secrets while Lori do-si-do'd away. But the reality of Lori's life would only hurt her new friend, and after everything Patricia had done to help protect Lori, there was no way she was going to let that happen. So she deftly steered the conversation into safer waters.

"Do you think this Faye Rich woman is a serious challenger to Miles' campaign?" Despite his tendency to be an asshat where Lori was concerned, she still wanted to see Miles succeed in his congressional bid, if for no other reason than to allow her friend to experience some pride in her oldest son's accomplishment.

Patricia took a sip of the water before picking up the conversation as though she had been expecting a neat deflection from Lori. "Honestly, I don't know. Faye is a bit of a celebrity in these parts, so she has that going for her." She toyed with the tie of her mint green robe. "I've known her for nearly twenty years and this is the first I've heard of any interest in politics on her part, though. Frankly, I'm a little miffed that she'd throw her hat in the ring without telling me. I thought we were friends." Patricia shook her head, her chin-length champagne-colored hair swinging softly from side to side. "Miles won't back down. Politics has been his singular focus for the past decade. I honestly believe his ambitions are what helped him heal after the death of his college sweetheart all those years ago. Although I sometimes think he's become too absorbed in politics. My biggest worry is that he'll marry someone for the wrong reasons."

The people of Chances Inlet were a chatty bunch, and despite the fact that Lori kept out of sight while working at the inn, she'd overheard the story of Miles' lost love several times. The young woman had died in a car crash while studying in Europe. According to the local gossips, her death was the catalyst to Miles' single-minded determination to rule the world.

"I hate the way the media have misconstrued Donald's actions," Patricia continued. "The last thing Miles' father would have wanted was to cast any shadow over his son's campaign."

"The media rarely care about fairness, trust me." Too late, Lori realized that she'd revealed more than she wanted to.

"Why does it sound like you're speaking from experience?"

Lori was saved from having to redirect the conversation a second time when Patricia's daughter Kate swept into the room. Statuesque, brunette, and athletic like the rest of the McAlister siblings, Kate possessed the same infectious smile as her brother Gavin. She was dressed in a bright linen sheath and cute sandals, and her knowing blue eyes sparkled with laughter behind her designer tortoiseshell-framed glasses. Leaning down, she hugged her mother before tossing her bulky medical bag onto the bed.

"Oh my gosh, I can't believe I missed seeing that interview in person. I would have loved to watch Miles sweat through that one," she said with equal parts glee and disappointment.

The sibling rivalry among Patricia's two oldest children was legendary within Chances Inlet, but Lori secretly suspected that neither one would be as successful as they were today without the other one egging them on. A familiar emptiness settled in Lori's stomach. She also secretly envied Patricia's children. Growing up, Lori's family life had been much different than the McAlister clan's rowdy brotherly and sisterly love. Still, she ached to return to the life she once had. *If only that were still possible.*

"That Tanya Sheppard definitely had more than one agenda," Kate continued. "She looked like she wanted to nail Miles—and not in a way he would enjoy." She laughed as her mother rolled her eyes. "Do you think Miles slept with her? I mean, I know my brothers attract pretty much anything with breasts, but I'd like to think they're a bit discriminating. Even 'Practically Perfect Miles'."

Lori quickly dismissed the fluttering in her stomach that the thought of Miles sleeping with the bitchy reporter—or anyone else—produced. Even if he didn't think of her as a petty crook or a freeloader, guys like Miles were no longer within reach for women like Lori. Her past would be more dangerous to him than it would be to his mother. Besides, she was leaving Chances Inlet at the first opportunity she could get. The sooner the better, judging by her overreactive libido.

Gathering up the breakfast menus she'd brought over for Patricia to approve, Lori turned to make her escape back to the inn. "I need to get the tea dishes cleaned up and put away. Miles checked in tonight's guests and everything is taken care of for the rest of the evening."

"Uh-oh," Kate teased. "We're embarrassing poor Lori with talk of the virile McAlister men. Sorry. I didn't mean to interrupt shop talk between you two. The inn looked fabulous on television, by the way, Lori. I'm sure my idiot brother never thinks to mention it, but we're all very grateful for everything you've done to keep the place up and running while Mom is laid up. You're a real saint."

Lori swallowed harshly. Kate wouldn't be saying that if the woman knew even a hint of Lori's past.

"Cassidy has been a huge help," Lori said. Cassidy was

another of the innkeeper's refugees, finding sanctuary at the B and B after her mother had been arrested for solicitation with a few counts of drug possession thrown in for good measure. Lori had become fond of the acerbic teenager these past months. Too fond. The longer she stayed in town, the harder it was going to be to leave when she needed to.

Kate laughed. "But not Miles? I'm sure he's been a huge pain in the ass."

"Kate, stop badgering Lori. Miles has been as helpful as his campaign will allow." Patricia reached out her hand and Lori walked over to take it. "Kate's right, though. I couldn't do this without you." The look she gave Lori told her that the older woman knew she was risking a lot by staying. "Thank you for sticking around."

Nodding stiffly, Lori gave Patricia's fingers a quick squeeze. "I should get back so I can start on those casseroles for tomorrow's breakfast. We have a full house in the morning."

Patricia watched as Lori surreptitiously scouted out the hallway before cautiously slipping out of the room with her head bowed so that her wild halo of hair would conceal her bright caramel eyes. She sighed softly, thankful that the guarded young woman had been put in her path. Whatever she was running from, she knew Lori needed a haven in Chances Inlet more than the Tide Me Over Inn needed a cook and housekeeper. She was grateful beyond measure that Lori hadn't taken off yet. Not until Patricia could find a way to help her as much as she had helped the McAlister family.

"I wasn't kidding about her being a saint," Kate murmured. "I don't care what kind of secrets she's hiding, the woman is one heck of a cook. We're lucky Miles hasn't driven her screaming into the ocean yet. There aren't too many women who would put up with him counting the silver spoons after tea each afternoon."

Squeezing her eyes shut, Patricia let out a heavy breath. She seriously hoped her daughter was exaggerating, but something told her there might be some truth to the statement. Miles was definitely in overprotective mode since his father's death—even more so since Patricia's accident. "Well, hopefully I'll be home soon and things can get back to normal."

"That's the reason I stopped by. Good news," Kate said. "I just spoke with the surgeon and the physical therapists and they all agreed that you could be sprung from here as early as tomorrow afternoon."

Patricia's eyes snapped open. Her heartbeat ratcheted up at the thought of finally getting back to the inn. There was a little trepidation mixed in with her excitement, as well. If Miles was overprotective now, he would be ten times worse when she attempted to take back the reins of her old life.

And if Miles was bad, Lamar would be worse.

She let her lids slide closed again but not quickly enough to hide her troubled feelings from her perceptive daughter, who, despite her jovial ribbing of her siblings, took her duties as a physician seriously. Kate pulled Patricia's hand between her own. "Just because you're going home doesn't mean you still don't have a journey ahead of you. Recovery from this type of injury is a marathon, not a sprint."

"And here I thought Miles was the only one of my children who never met a maxim he didn't put to good use."

Kate chuckled and patted her mother's hand before reaching for her medical bag. "I'm serious, Mother. You still have several weeks before you'll be back to your old self. You need to take it easy. Lori and Miles haven't killed each other yet so your B and B isn't in any imminent danger. And with Miles needing to spend more time actually campaigning rather than having his coronation handed to him on a silver platter, there's less chance of him scaring her off. In the meantime, is there anything I can get you or do for you?"

"Sure, I'll take a big needle and some Botox." Patricia glanced up at her daughter's startled face. "Or any other magic potion that will make me look younger and more attractive."

"Mom, what are you talking about?"

Patricia looked away from Kate and focused her gaze on the garden outside the window. It was no use; her daughter wouldn't understand. "Never mind."

"No," Kate insisted. "Not 'never mind.' Tell me what's going on."

"Isn't it obvious?" Patricia waved a hand over her ravaged body, still painful and bruised. "I'm broken and helpless here. It's not like I was some spring chicken before the accident."

"Wait. Is this about Lamar?"

She sighed in exasperation at her daughter. "Of course it's about Lamar."

Lamar was Lamar Hollister, sheriff of Chances Inlet, and as of a few weeks ago, Patricia's fiancé. She still couldn't for the life of her believe her good fortune at having attracted the rugged ex-soldier's attention in the first place, much less his heart. Patricia was a widow in her late fifties—a grandmother no less—but the younger man didn't seem to mind one bit. He was dependable, kind, and doting to a fault, and Patricia just knew she'd struck relationship gold a second time in her life.

But she couldn't help thinking that the sheriff might be having second thoughts. Her frailty after a broken hip had to be a stark reminder of their age difference, not to mention what the future held. Lamar had been distracted and more stoic than usual since the accident. Patricia needed to get back on her feet as much for her relationship with the sheriff as she did for her beloved inn.

"Lamar will do anything to see you get better." Kate likely intended her words to be placating but they riled Patricia up even more.

"Of course he will. Who wants to be stuck with a decrepit fiancée?"

Kate sank down on the bed across from Patricia. "Oh, Mom, he doesn't feel that way. I'm sure of it. He loves you. If you could see the way he looks at you when you're not paying attention." Her daughter's face softened. "It's really sweet."

"I've got news for you, Kate, 'sweet' isn't what a man like Lamar has in mind when he looks at me. Your brothers aren't the only virile men in Chances Inlet, if you catch my drift."

Her daughter had the good grace to blush. "Oh. Oh . . . well," she stammered. "Uh, I can see . . . um, where you might have some concerns in that area."

"Do you?" Patricia waved her hand over the length of her body once again. "Because healing is apparently going to be *a marathon and not a sprint.*"

Kate dissolved into giggles. "Oh my gosh, I think I've actually used that phrase with Alden in a very different context within our bedroom."

Patricia groaned. "I can't believe we're having this conversation. I blame the pain meds."

Her daughter laughed even harder. "Oh, Mom, you have no idea how much I love and admire you. You're the strongest woman I know. And Lamar loves you, too. No matter what. You'll see. You're worrying about nothing." She glanced at her watch. "I've got to pick Emily up. Gavin is supposed to be watching her, but knowing him, she's running free-range around town." Kate leaned down and kissed Patricia on the cheek. "Everything is going to work out. You'll see."

Patricia let her eyelids fall again, allowing the pain medicine to lull her into a catnap, hoping that when she awoke, things would look very different.

THREE

"Do you think she's really serious about a write-in campaign?" Gavin asked as he repetitively tossed a red rubber ball against the wall of the small back room in Miles' campaign headquarters. The suite of offices was housed in the refurbished old torpedo factory on Chances Inlet's Main Street. McAlister Construction and Engineering had been located in the same space for nearly thirty years. Miles remembered his father building out pieces of the large warehouse, bit by bit, as money became available. The torpedo factory was also home to the Tiny Dancers ballet studio across the hall, as well as his brother Gavin, who lived in the loft space above.

It was Sunday afternoon and the office was blissfully quiet except for the sound of the rubber slapping against the brick, making Miles' head ache. He paused in his pacing of the worn pine floor and snatched the ball out of the air before Gavin could catch it, squeezing it tightly between his fingers.

"Hey!" Gavin complained when Miles tossed the ball out into the hallway that linked the offices to the ballet studio across the hall. Gavin's dog, Midas, scampered wildly after it, his nails screeching on the concrete.

"Oh, she's serious all right. She's already got a website up and running, not to mention over four thousand likes on her campaign's Facebook page. And it's only been live for two hours." Coy barely glanced up from the two laptops he had spread out on the coffee table while he answered Gavin's question.

"Wow." Gavin wrestled with Midas, trying to pull the ball from the dog's mouth. "It sounds like The GTO Grandma is *revving up* for the race."

Miles reflexively smacked the back of his brother's head when he paced by him, making Gavin chuckle even harder. "Dude, you've got to find the humor in this somehow."

"Politics is serious business, Gavin," Coy shot back. "Especially if we want to win."

"Aww, come on." Gavin tossed the ball again and Midas chased after it. "She doesn't actually stand a chance, does she?"

Miles paused in his pacing to glance out the window at the town where he'd lived most of his life. A town he'd always dreamed of representing in Congress. He sighed in frustration. It had all sounded so easy when he was a fifth grader.

"Of course she has a chance," Coy said from behind him. "The opposing party may not get to put their own candidate on the ballot, but they can certainly redirect their volunteers and donors to Faye's campaign. Tanya Sheppard and the rest of the media will try to make Faye's movement sound like a grass-roots effort, but hers will be a highly orchestrated—not to mention well-funded—campaign."

Miles slumped into the chair that had once belonged to his father, settling his body against the familiar creased and worn leather. "We had enough money to run against that idiot Brian Kendrick, don't tell me we have to worry about fund-raising again?" Begging for contributions was Miles' least favorite aspect of campaigning. There was something about it that made him feel bought and paid for.

Coy tucked his cell phone between his ear and his shoulder. "You can never have enough money in politics."

"So how hard can it be to raise some more cash? Just play on the stud factor," his brother teased. "Post some tweets or videos of you running shirtless in a triathlon and sit back and watch the money roll in. Women love your body, man."

Miles flipped his brother off just as their sister Kate walked in, her daughter Emily in tow. "Oh, that's a fine picture for a campaign ad," she scoffed. "And you're one to taunt, Gavin. I seem to recall you pimping your dimpled smile all over the home improvement channels a few months ago just to raise money to pay off Dad's debt."

Gavin tilted the chair he was sitting in onto its back legs, crossing his arms over his chest. "Hey, it almost worked. And I did get a nice consolation prize in a gorgeous woman." He grinned like a fool.

"I'll be sure and tell Ginger you think she's a consolation prize," Kate said, allowing Emily to slip out of her grasp. The six-year-old was draped in pieces of costumes presumably commandeered from the ballet studio. She wedged herself between Miles' chair and the desk before scouring through the contents in the top drawer. Miles ran his hand over the wavy, soft, mahogany hair on his niece's head, breathing in a familiar scent, as the child pulled out a paper clip and began to form it into the shape of a ring.

"Did you take a bath in your grandmother's perfume?" he asked.

Emily giggled. "No, silly. I used the lotion at the inn."

Kate arched an eyebrow at Gavin. "You were supposed to be watching her, not letting her riffle through all the gift baskets meant for Mom's guests."

"Emily, are you still alive?" Gavin asked. "Do you still have all your fingers and your toes? Your teeth?" Gavin's words sounded so much like something their late father would say when he was tasked with keeping an eye on the flighty youngest McAlister sibling, Elle, that Miles' chest seized for a moment.

Emily giggled at the familiar line of questioning from her uncle. "Yes, sir."

Gavin shrugged. "See? No harm, no foul."

Kate smacked their brother on the shoulder before taking the seat next to Coy on the sofa. The younger man turned his back to her and continued to murmur into the phone. Kate shot a wide-eyed look of wonder at Miles before rolling her eyes at Coy's demeanor. "So, I assume we're coming up with a new strategy here?"

Miles bit back an aggravated groan. There was no "we" in his strategizing. As grateful as he was that his annoying siblings wanted to help, Miles needed a few minutes alone to think and regroup. He hadn't had that since Tanya dropped her bombshell earlier that day. His messages to the governor had gone unanswered, making him a bit uneasy. Tanya's slant on Miles' leave of absence had been way off base; the governor had Miles' back both personally and in the campaign. Still, it would have been nice to have some confirmation of that publicly before the interview aired. He needed to get everyone out of his office and get his boss on the line for some one-on-one planning.

"Yes, Governor, I'll tell him," he heard Coy say into his phone, the younger man's words immediately snapping Miles to attention.

What the hell? Was the governor talking to the little pipsqueak legacy instead of returning Miles' calls? The throbbing in his temples became a jackhammer. "Were you talking to Governor Rossi?" Miles managed to ask when Coy began packing up his laptops.

The kid had the decency to blush slightly while he shoved the computers into a backpack. "Yes. He said to tell you he'll call you at eight tonight. We're working on a plan and some new platforms that will better help us to defeat Faye Rich in a head-to-head election."

"*We* are working on a plan?" Miles tamped down on his rapidly escalating annoyance. "Don't you think I should be a part of that process, Coy?" The question was better directed at the governor and the rest of the party staff; Coy was simply the mouthpiece. Still, Miles needed someone to lash out at. Coy might as well learn to take the heat early in his career.

"Um, yeah, of course," he said sheepishly. "I think everyone else wants to present it to you when they have all the kinks worked out."

The dog's panting was the only sound in the room for

several long seconds. Miles scrubbed a hand down his face. Taking out his frustrations on Coy wouldn't solve anything. Besides, once he spoke directly with Governor Rossi, he was sure they'd assign him a new campaign manager immediately. Coy would likely be gone by morning.

"Makes sense." Miles pushed the words out even though nothing about this day made a lick of sense.

Coy nodded and pulled his backpack onto his shoulder. "I'm just going to head back to the inn, where it's a bit quieter, and make a few calls. I'll meet you back here at eight?"

"Sounds like a plan," Miles said and waved the younger man toward the door. Out of the corner of his eye, he saw his sister exchange a worried glance with Gavin. The last thing he wanted was those two feeling sorry for him. Miles wasn't conceding the damn race yet. Not by a long shot.

"Don't you have some tourist's sunburn to treat?" he asked his sister.

She wrinkled her nose up at him. "Funny. The clinic closed an hour ago. Em and I are on our way out to dinner with Alden and some friends. Would you like to join us?"

Ah, a pity peace-offering from his sister. Just what Miles needed to end this shitty day. "No, thanks. I've got a lot to do here." Which was a huge lie, but he really wanted to pace the floor in private, if possible.

She looked as though she knew he was lying, but thankfully, she didn't push him any further. "I spoke with Mom's doctors," she said as she stood up from the sofa and ran a hand over the wrinkles in her dress. "They're going to release her tomorrow at the earliest."

"Well, that works out conveniently," Gavin said to Miles. "You'll likely need to appear at more events now. Mom can start to ease back into taking over the inn, giving you more time to campaign."

"Mom isn't 'easing back' into anything right away," Kate interjected. "She's still got a long way to go in the healing process. We can't encourage her to get ahead of herself." She pointed a finger at Miles. "But you can leave most of the day-to-day running of the inn to Lori. Stop harassing her about every little thing and let her do her job. Mom can supervise from the carriage house."

Miles didn't like the idea of relinquishing control to a woman whose background he knew very little about, but his brother was right; he'd need to hit the campaign trail hard to keep Faye from creeping up in the polls. He'd have to cut Lori some slack if he wanted to make this work. But that didn't mean he'd give her free rein of the B and B. He needed a few questions answered before he'd do that. Not that his bossy sister needed to know his intentions.

"Fine."

Kate narrowed her eyes at his acquiescence. "Just like that? Fine?" She blew out a breath. "Wow. You must be feeling the sting of Faye's announcement. But I'm going to hold you to that. And both of you are going to help me keep Mom from overdoing it. Her emotional state is a little fragile right now, and I don't want her to suffer a setback because of it."

Gavin slammed his chair back onto the floor as both he and Miles went on alert. "What do you mean, she's 'fragile'?" Gavin asked.

Their mother was the toughest woman any of them knew. She'd spawned Kate, after all. Not only that, but she'd survived the sudden loss of her husband while still managing to make her inn prosper, cultivating and maintaining the highest rating her B and B could earn. Even her accident could have been a lot worse had it not been for her iron will. The last word Miles would use to describe his mother was "fragile."

"Is there something you're not telling us about her health?" Miles demanded.

Kate waved a hand as she tugged Emily away from the desk. His niece quietly had taken every paper clip from the drawer and formed a long necklace, which she promptly draped around her neck. "Not her physical health, per se," his sister said. "More like her"—she covered her daughter's ears—"sexual health."

Miles felt as if his head had finally exploded. Gavin was plugging his own ears up with his fingers. "La, la, la," his brother chanted. "TMI, Kate. *T.M.I!*"

"Oh, boys, don't be such prudes. Our mother is engaged to a hot younger man who has needs. Get over it. A broken hip is an obstacle they need to work around. But, hey, where there's a will, there's a way."

Gavin was banging his forehead on the desk now while Miles tried unsuccessfully to rid his mind of the image of his mother and the sheriff practicing moves from the Kama Sutra. "Go to dinner, Kate," he breathed, trying to calm his queasy stomach. "You've just ruined ours."

With a gay laugh, his sister waltzed out the door, Emily skipping beside her.

"We should have let her run away when she was nine," Gavin mumbled, his forehead still resting on the desk.

"Hey, I packed a bag for her," Miles replied. "It was Dad who went after her and coaxed her to come back. I was mad at him for at least a month."

Gavin stood up and dragged his fingers through his hair. "Well, if the sheriff breaks her heart, he'd better sleep with his gun tucked under his pillow. That's all I've got to say."

"If the sheriff breaks whose heart?"

A dopey grin overtook his brother's face at the sight of his girlfriend, Ginger Walsh, standing in the doorway. Petite and blond with unusual green eyes, she was wearing an intimate smile of her own. Gavin reached out and pulled her against his chest, capturing her lips in a scorching kiss.

"Hello, you two! Midas and I are getting grossed out here," Miles said after a few moments passed. "I'd tell you to get a room, but you have one just up those steps," he added. "How about you run along and take advantage of that, hmm?"

Ginger managed to break the kiss and put a sliver of distance between their bodies. "Are you picking on the sheriff again, Miles?" she asked.

Miles had never made a secret of the fact that he didn't particularly approve of his mother's relationship with a man who'd moved to town less than three years ago and was five years her junior to boot. But he had been in the minority within his family—not to mention the entire population of Chances Inlet. Not only that, but his mother had made it abundantly clear that she wasn't much interested in her oldest son's opinion of her love life. Still it was good to know Gavin would likely hold the guy down while Miles beat the crap out of him if Lamar Hollister broke their mother's heart.

Miles held up his hands. "Not me this time." He pointed to his brother.

Ginger looked at Gavin expectantly.

Gavin's sigh was resolute. "My mom is worried that Lamar will lose interest in her while she's recuperating."

Miles snickered at his brother's sugar-coated version of the truth.

"Oh, that's just silly, Gavin," Ginger said. "Have you seen the way the guy looks at her?"

Both brothers exchanged a pained look. They *had* seen the way the sheriff looked at their mother. Like she was lunch. *Damn.* The queasy feeling returned to Miles' stomach.

"You're right," Gavin reassured Ginger like a man bent on getting her naked in the next five minutes. "Mom's just being silly. You can remind her of that tomorrow. Why don't we go up and eat that wonderful dinner you had planned?"

She glanced between the two men. "We can't just leave Miles. Don't be so rude, Gavin." Her elfin face lit up in a smile. "Why don't you join us? I made more than enough."

Miles looked past Ginger and took in the pained expression on his brother's face. Ginger's lack of talent in the kitchen was legendary among the townsfolk of Chances Inlet. Clearly she made up for it in other ways, however, judging by the satisfied smirk his brother wore daily.

"Maybe another time, Ginger, thank you. Lori usually fixes enough dinner for both Cassidy and me. I'm on my way back there now."

Ginger's eyes glazed over briefly and her voice had a bit of a euphoric tone to it. "Oh, I remember those dinners Lori made when I lived at the inn. They were amazing."

"I'm sure whatever you made will be just as delicious, sweetheart," Gavin said. His encouragement was likely born out of the two chili cheese dogs Miles watched him devour at the pier earlier this afternoon. "I'll catch up with you on our morning run tomorrow, bro." And with that, Gavin hustled Ginger up the stairs to the loft, slamming the door behind them.

Midas let out a whimper and flopped to the floor with a sigh.

"Yeah, three's probably company up there, huh, pal?" Miles stood up and switched off the lights. "Come on. You can come hang out with me until my conference call later tonight. Right now, we need to conduct some serious negotiations with the mystery who works in Mom's kitchen."

FOUR

The muted sounds of the grandfather clock chiming the dinner hour floated up from the foyer of the inn. A late-day breeze ruffled the curtains in the window as Lori crouched on the carpet and rummaged through the large duffel bag containing all of her worldly possessions. *Scratch that.* One of her most important possessions was missing: her grandmother's gold wedding band.

Tessa, Lori's Australian sheep dog, breathed out a consoling sigh as she laid her nose down on her front paws. Perched on top of the double bed in the small third-floor bedroom reserved for staff, the dog tracked every movement with her brilliant blue eyes as Lori carefully unpacked and then repacked the bag.

"I know it was in here. I check it every night before we go to sleep."

The dog whimpered softly and Lori tried not to panic. That ring was her talisman—the last remaining piece of the life she'd once had. It was the only article of jewelry she'd taken when she'd made her getaway. Lori hadn't wanted any of the other expensive items—although she could have likely pawned at least one piece, which would have gone a long way toward making her present circumstances not quite so dire. But none of that other jewelry had actually belonged to her. The pieces were all part of an elaborate ruse, just like the life she'd been living the past several years.

The lump in her throat was painful as she dug her fingers through the outside pocket for a third time. "It has to be here."

Tessa's head popped up when the door swung open and a big golden retriever bounded into the room. The dog made a beeline for the open duffel bag, rummaging his snout through Lori's things as if he was looking for a long lost bone.

"Hey! Get out, Midas!" Lori shoved the eighty-pound fur ball away just as Cassidy trounced through the open door.

"That crazy mutt was drinking out of the toilet in the foyer bath again," Cassidy complained. "I mean, he's got a full bowl of water in the kitchen. What's so special about the toilet?"

"Haven't you ever heard of knocking?" Lori's panicked tone shocked Cassidy into silence. The girl froze, her hand hovering over Tessa's head.

Lori squeezed her eyes shut so as not to let the perceptive seventeen-year-old see how anxious she'd become. She was ashamed, too; she had no business barking at the teenager like that. Cassidy had come a long way in the past several months, stepping out from behind the belligerent Gothic personality she'd donned like a shield, finally engaging with kids her own age. But the vestiges of that lonely young girl still hovered just beneath the surface. Lori had no trouble recognizing the look because she saw the same fears whenever she glanced at her own reflection in a mirror.

"You're leaving." The hint of despair in Cassidy's voice cut through Lori, making her feel even more ashamed.

"No." Lori quickly zipped up the bag and stowed it back under her bed before coming to her feet. "I was just looking for something."

Cassidy's amber eyes were shiny as she stroked Tessa's back. "Don't lie. Your bag is packed." The snarky teenager was back in full bloom. "You promised Mrs. Mac you'd stay. Hell, you promised *me*."

"I'm not leaving, Cass." Lori placed a hand on the teenager's tense shoulder and gently squeezed. "I was just looking for something I must have misplaced. That's all."

Cassidy's hard swallow reverberated beneath Lori's palm. "But why haven't you unpacked your stuff? You've been here for what, nearly five months now?" She shrugged off Lori's hand and stalked over to the bureau tucked beneath the dormer window, where she pulled open a drawer, empty except for an old sheet of shelf paper. "If you're staying, why not put your things away?"

Because I'm not staying.

That feeling of the need to flee continued to gnaw at Lori. She was becoming too attached to the inn and these people. The longer she stuck around, the more complacent she became. And she couldn't afford to have her true identity discovered. Not here.

Lori softened her voice and forced herself to relax in hopes of placating Cassidy. "I'm just neat that way. I like to know where my stuff is, okay?" It was as good an excuse as any.

"Is it like one of those OCD things?"

Yanking at Midas' collar when the dog tried to crawl beneath the bed, Lori nodded, hoping that Cassidy would buy the excuse.

"Or are you scared you'll have to make a run for it in the middle of the night?"

Cassidy hadn't graduated at the top of her class for nothing. Lori avoided the girl's glare. In all likelihood she would be found out and would have to make a run for it on short notice. But the last thing she needed was Cassidy's attention and concern. If the teen was keeping a close eye on Lori, then so would everyone else. And that wouldn't do. Taking a deep breath and saying a prayer that she appeared more assured than she felt, Lori looked the girl directly in the eye. "I promised I'd stay until Patricia is better and can run things on her own. From the looks of it, that won't be until you leave for college. I won't go back on my word."

"Are they dangerous?"

"Who?"

Cassidy took a few steps closer. The girl was taller than Lori's five feet six inches and was built with a much larger bone structure. She'd been working out the past few months to lose the pubescent pudginess she'd used as part of her camouflage, but Cassidy still wasn't afraid to intimidate others with her size. "Whoever you're running from. This isn't like that movie where your ex-husband is going to come and burn the B and B down, is it? Do we need to tell the sheriff?"

"There's nothing to tell the sheriff." *Except that maybe there is a thief staying at the B and B because that ring* had *been in the bag last night.* Lori reached for Cassidy's hand and gave it another squeeze. "I'm just a little down on my luck. No one is in any danger because of me." It was the truth. If the mess she'd found herself in could physically harm anyone at the Tide Me Over Inn or in Chances Inlet, Lori would be out of town in a nanosecond. Of that she was sure.

Cassidy looked down at Lori's hand covering hers. The girl was silent a moment before she spoke softly. "Just promise me you won't disappear on me."

Lori's chest constricted. Cassidy was essentially on her own. And Lori knew all too well what that feeling of isolation felt like. But the teenager had the McAlisters and the entire town of Chances Inlet looking after her. She'd be fine in the long run. It wouldn't do for her to get too attached to Lori.

"Oh, please, once you get to college, you won't have to hang out with the hired help anymore." Lori avoided making any promises, quickly changing the subject before Cassidy could call her on it. "I made your favorite: chicken salad. Why don't we grab some dinner while the guests are all at the various restaurants downtown having theirs?"

Cassidy eyed her warily before nodding. Lori breathed a sigh of relief, snapping her fingers for the dogs to follow as she ushered Cassidy out of her room. She'd just have to conduct a more thorough search for the ring later tonight.

"A sandwich sounds good, as long as you leave off all the sprouts and twigs that Ginger insists on putting in everything she cooks." Cassidy stomped down the back staircase that led down to the kitchen area.

Lori bit back a smile. Ginger had spent years training for

a career as a ballerina. Her wholesome eating habits had been widely discussed by everyone in town when she'd first arrived.

"Bernice was just here," Cassidy continued. "She said Kate told her that Mrs. Mac is coming home tomorrow."

Bernice was the queen bee of Chances Inlet's gossip hive. Any information told to or overheard by the woman was spread around town with more efficiency than an Amber Alert.

"But she won't be a hundred percent for a while so you still can't leave yet," Cassidy said as they made their way into the spacious kitchen awash with the late afternoon sunlight that was streaming in from the two large box bay windows. Both dogs scrambled on the hardwood floor making their way to the screen door.

"Who can't leave yet?"

Lori's steps faltered briefly at the sound of Miles' voice. She glanced over to see him resting a lean hip against the large center island. Still dressed in the clothes he'd worn for the interview, charcoal slacks and a crisp white shirt that accentuated his icy blue eyes and summer tan, he paused before taking a sip from a glass of lemonade. A dark eyebrow arched above those keen eyes as he looked right through Lori. He routinely made a point of ignoring her, except she had the niggling sensation he saw her more clearly than anyone else. The feeling put her on edge whenever he was around.

It was as if he knew she couldn't vote in the district and he'd written her off. His disdain riled Lori more than she'd like. Which was ridiculous since her goal was to ensure that her existence in the town of Chances Inlet went unnoticed. It didn't help that the air crackled with tension—and something else she didn't want to analyze—whenever he was near.

Cassidy yanked open the screen door and both dogs sprinted off into the sprawling green grass of the inn's backyard. "Oh, don't worry, Miles. Lori isn't going anywhere." She walked over to the island and poured herself a glass of lemonade. "You can concentrate on beating The GTO Grandma. Lori and I will handle things here at the B and B."

Not surprising, Cassidy had given herself a larger role than necessary. Like Bernice, the teenager liked to be in the thick of things.

"I'm happy you're so willing to pitch in more, Cassidy," Miles said, a trace of humor in his voice. "You've done a great job manning the Patty Wagon and handling the occasional tweet or Facebook post on the inn's social media account."

The teenager pulled a loaf of crusty bread out of the bread box, a slight blush staining her cheeks at Miles' praise.

"I take it you've both heard by now that my mother is coming home?" he asked.

Miles' eyes actually lingered a moment on Lori and she felt their heat burn a path straight to the parts of her that hadn't seen any action in months. This distracting man was the last person Lori wanted her body reacting to. The feeling of needing to flee began to eat at her again. She pulled out a container of chicken salad from the fridge.

"Yep," Cassidy replied. "It'll be good to have her home again. I know she's anxious to get back to her inn."

"Just because she's on the premises doesn't mean she'll be assuming her duties around here right away," a voice said from the back porch.

Lamar Hollister, the sheriff for Chances Inlet, stepped inside the screen door, twirling his campaign hat between his fingers as the two dogs took turns snaking between his long legs. Somewhere close to the age of fifty, the sheriff was ruggedly handsome, like one of those virile guys cast in a pickup truck commercial. The military veteran was taller than the McAlister brothers, with broad shoulders, sandy hair that was graying slightly at the temples, and a very serious chin. His eyes gave nothing away—unless he was gazing at Patricia McAlister. Then the love he so obviously felt for her shone brightly, often making Lori feel like a voyeur whenever she was in the same room with the engaged couple.

Out of the corner of her eye she watched as Miles stiffened defensively. If Miles had reservations about Lori, his mistrust of the sheriff was just as vehement. In this case, though, Lori knew there was at least a reasonable explanation behind Miles' animosity toward Lamar Hollister. Patricia's son was obviously having a lot of trouble adjusting to the fact that his mother was moving on after her husband's sudden death. The fact that the sheriff was a newcomer to Chances Inlet likely didn't help matters. Lori knew firsthand about that.

Miles eyed the older man with a cool, steady gaze. "For once we agree on something, Sheriff."

"Oh, I'm sure there are a lot of things we agree on, Miles," the sheriff drawled. "The least of which is the fact that your mother needs to recuperate fully before she returns to running this place full-time."

"I have no intention of jeopardizing my mother's recovery. You needn't worry, Sheriff. The inn is in good hands."

"I'm not worried about the B and B, Miles. I'm worried about your mother."

"That makes two of us," Miles said stiffly.

The two men exchanged a silent stare before the sheriff glanced over at Lori, who was doing her best to ignore their exchange while scooping chicken salad onto slices of the bread.

"I was wondering if you had anything left over from the afternoon tea that I could take to the rehab center. Tricia hasn't been eating well since the accident and I know she'd enjoy one of your special cupcakes."

"I'll make up a plate." Lori grabbed a paper plate from the pantry, glad to be out of the line of fire between the two testosterone-charged men. Miles had practically vibrated away from the counter at the pet name the sheriff used to refer to his mother.

His hand was steady now, though, when he slid a plastic container along the countertop toward her. "Here, I put some of the lemon ones aside for her. I know she likes those," Miles said quietly.

His gesture was a sweet one and so unlike the man he pretended to be that Lori was momentarily caught off guard. She peered at him from beneath her lashes and for a fleeting moment she watched as a hint of vulnerability flickered in his eyes. But just as quickly it was gone and his mouth formed that familiar arrogant line.

"Any progress on catching the idiot who ran my mother off the road?" Miles asked.

The sheriff shook his head solemnly. "I've scoured the entire county for a car matching the description of the one your mother thought she saw. But it was twilight when it happened. Who knows if her description is even accurate? Chances are the driver never saw your mother on the bike. And all it would take was a slight bump to push her over the embankment like that. Whoever was behind the wheel might not have known anything happened. There likely wouldn't be any damage to the car, either."

"Someone has to know something," Miles protested. "At the very least if they were driving on that road that evening, they should come forward."

"I can assure you, Miles, that I'm following up on every possible lead out there," the sheriff said through clenched teeth. "I want the creep who did this brought to justice just as much as you do. I won't rest until I catch him or her. You can count on that."

A heavy silence settled over the kitchen. Both were used to solving Patricia McAlister's problems. But this time might prove to be the exception.

"Can I go with you to the rehab center, Sheriff?" Cassidy grabbed her own plate and tossed a sandwich on it as she asked. "I've got an hour before I need to open the Patty Wagon for the evening and I'd like to say hi to Mrs. Mac."

Lori tucked some plastic wrap over the plate she'd filled for Patricia. She'd added some fresh fruit and a sandwich along with the cupcakes, knowing her friend would enjoy eating something healthy. The sheriff gave her a nod as he took the plate from her and headed for the door.

"Oh, by the way," he said over his shoulder, "I just heard on the radio that Faye Rich is putting together a write-in campaign. She's been a good friend to the local Fraternal Order of Police over the years, Miles. You're gonna have some ground to make up there."

He was out of the door, Cassidy at his heels, before Miles could respond.

Lori busied herself by opening the industrial dishwasher and filling the kitchen with steam, hoping that when it evaporated, Miles would, too.

"We need to talk."

No such luck apparently. Ignoring his looming presence on the opposite side of the room, she emptied the flatware onto a towel she'd spread on the counter. "Why start now?" In the nearly two weeks he'd been staying at the B and B, he'd barely spared her a word. Not that he'd spoken to her all that much before moving in here.

He chuckled and Lori hated how much she liked the sound of it. "Because it sounds like I may need you to make some of those cupcakes to take over to the station house as a bribe."

She gently stacked the plates onto the counter. "Wow, I can't imagine which one is stinging your pride more, Dudley Do-Right—having to ask me for help or contemplating bribing officers of the law."

Another charged silence settled over the kitchen and Lori glanced over her shoulder to see Miles actually grin at her. "Did you just call me Dudley Do-Right?" His tone sounded as much insulted as amused.

Startled by his demeanor—not to mention what it was doing to her body—Lori resumed her task of unloading the dishwasher so he wouldn't see the pleasure in her own eyes. She heard Miles move away from the counter, his footsteps sounding deliberate as he crossed the kitchen to stand behind her. His distinctive scent teased her nostrils and she could hear his steady breathing as he inched behind her. Lori's own breath caught in her chest, making her words sound raspier than she would have liked. The last thing she wanted was for Miles to know how he affected her.

He chuckled again, the rich sound close to her ear. This time her ovaries did a somersault. "And all this time I thought you didn't respect me."

Lori grabbed a pot out of the dishwasher and walked it over to the cabinet by the stove. She needed some space. Lots of space. "What do you want, Miles?"

When he didn't immediately answer, she turned to face

him. A look of anguished conflict shadowed his face before he quickly shuttered it. Miles raked his fingers through his hair just as an explosive sigh passed through his lips. "I don't have the same blind faith in people that my mother has. And I certainly don't buy in to the bullshit about this town being the haven for second chances."

Reacting to the change in his tone, Tessa walked over and sat protectively on Lori's foot.

"Be that as it may," he continued. "My mother trusts you with her most prized possession: this B and B." Lori wasn't sure, but she thought she heard a hint of disgust in his voice. "It's likely that I'll need to be away from here more than I had originally planned. You do good work. The rooms are clean, the guests are well fed, and I've had no complaints. Keep it that way and don't bring any trouble to my mother's doorstep and we'll get along just fine."

Lori kept her glare level and hard. "It doesn't matter to me whether you're here or not, Dudley. I promised your mother I'd keep the inn running to her standards until she's able to do it on her own. And I'll do whatever it takes to keep that promise." Unless, of course, she had to leave, but she figured knowing that would make Miles even more agitated, given his little spiel about bringing trouble to the inn's door.

"And when she's able to do it on her own? Will you be moving on?"

His eyes bored into her and Lori suddenly wasn't sure what she wanted the answer to be. Too bad she knew what it had to be. She nodded once. "Most likely."

The corners of his mouth turned up slightly. "You didn't happen to pinky swear on that with my mom, did you?"

He was laughing at her, damn the man. She pushed past him to finish putting away the dishes, nearly tripping over the dog that had become a clinging vine. Miles' chameleonlike temperament had her nerves frazzled. One minute he was the arrogant despot and the next . . . the next she was thinking about how it might feel to have him kiss her. She let out an irritated hiss as she tripped over Tessa a second time.

"Sorry," he said. "It's been a long day and I'm feeling a

little punchy. I appreciate your honesty, Lori. You are being honest, aren't you?"

She glared at him over her shoulder. He smirked back at her while he smeared a generous helping of chicken salad onto a slice of bread and took a big bite before closing his eyes. Moaning loudly, he chewed slowly. Lori quickly turned away before she melted into a puddle on the floor.

"Okay, the cooking definitely stays as one of your tasks."

"We're dividing up the work?"

"I think we already covered the part about me having to campaign more."

Lori gave the counter a vigorous wipe with the towel she'd used for the silverware. "How about this: I clean the rooms, do the laundry, prepare the afternoon tea, cook the meals, serve and clean up breakfast, and you"—she turned to point at Miles, who didn't even have the decency to look the least bit chagrined—"can stop coming behind me and counting the bottles of wine, the tea towels, or the crystal? Will that free up enough of your valuable time to schmooze with your future constituents?"

He studied her for a long moment. "It's suddenly not so hard imagining you on the run."

Tears stung her eyes as she turned back to scrubbing the already clean counter.

Miles released a heavy sigh. "That was uncalled for. I apologize."

"You can't afford to piss me off, Miles."

"Believe me, I know that. That doesn't mean I have to like it." Lori tried not to cringe at his words.

"But there's more to be done around here and you know it," he continued. "Let's not forget about the guests. I'll need someone to check them in and out. Cassidy can't always cover for me."

Lori quickly turned around to face him, unwilling to concede this one. "She'll have to because I can't." The less Lori interacted with the guests, the easier it was to preserve her anonymity.

"Can't or won't?" Miles demanded.

"Does it really matter to you?"

His body recoiled slightly, but his gaze never wavered. "Fair enough. We'll work something out." He studied her again; this time it seemed as though his gaze was boring right through her. "You're a fascinating woman, Lori. Definitely tougher than I expected," he said softly. "Truce?"

She glanced down at his outstretched hand debating with her common sense whether to touch him or not. He was a politician. A man who would say or do anything to get what he wanted. His chameleon personality was simply a tool he used to seduce voters—and lonely refugees if the clamoring deep in her belly was any indication. But he was right; she was tough. She had to be if she was going to survive what her life had become.

That sizzle she felt whenever he was around spread up her arm as he wrapped her hand in his much larger one. "I always keep my word, Miles. If nothing else, you can count on that."

He held her hand a moment longer than was necessary and his face relaxed as though he'd just won a hard-fought concession from her. "That's just what I needed to hear." Releasing her hand slowly, he closed the gap between them, coming to within inches of her body. His nearness caused her breath to hitch in her lungs again. Lori was grateful for the baggy cargo pants and long-sleeved T-shirt shielding her skin from the heat radiating off his body. She dug her fingers into her palms to keep from reaching up and stroking the five-o'clock shadow that was forming along his jaw. Miles hesitated, seeming to inhale her scent as he murmured something inaudible. For a moment, she thought he might kiss her, but then he reached behind her, grabbing a leather folio off the counter and pulling out a piece of paper. "Then you won't mind filling out this." The paper floated to the granite. "Tomorrow's payday and I can't write you a check without the proper forms." He took two giant steps back and Lori shivered at the loss of his body heat. "Come on, Midas. Let's head over to the campaign office. We've got some strategizing to do. We have a full house for breakfast tomorrow, Lori. See you then."

As Miles walked over to the refrigerator and pulled out a bottle of water, Lori stared down at the W-2 form. It was all she could do not to cry. Or laugh hysterically. Miles' pleased expression told her he thought he'd won this round. Once she had a word with his mother, however, he'd find that he hadn't.

FIVE

The early morning sun felt warm on Miles' bare shoulders. One of the perks to living back in Chances Inlet was being able to run off some steam along the beach every day. Due to his demanding workload for the governor, his morning jog in Raleigh usually took place on a treadmill, with the occasional weekend run through a local park. Today's run wasn't giving Miles the stress relief it normally did, however, thanks in part to the trio who'd decided to join him.

"It all sounds like some Hollywood B movie." His brother, Gavin, easily kept up with the strenuous pace Miles had set. "A grandmother just decides that selling cars isn't as much fun as it used to be. So she decides to run for Congress because she has some crazy idea that she can loosen the gridlock that is our government. I'm sure some producer is already casting about for an actress with Faye's down-home charm."

"Actually I think the opposing party approached her for a monetary contribution and she decided, 'What the heck, I can do this myself,'" Coy said from just behind them.

Will Connelly, star linebacker for the Baltimore Blaze and the guy who for years had evened out the odd number of boys in the McAlister household, glanced back over his shoulder at Coy. "Who's this guy again?" he asked Miles.

Coy puffed out a breath and sprinted forward in an effort to keep abreast of the other three men. "I'm his body man," he said.

Gavin chuckled. "No offense, dude, but I don't see much future for you as a bodyguard."

"Not a body*guard*, a body *man*," Coy huffed.

This time it was Will's turn to scoff. "The 'man' part is debatable, too. Are you even old enough to vote?"

"Lay off, guys." Miles zigzagged around the foamy brim that clung to the shoreline. Not that his brother and their friend weren't voicing concerns that had already kept him up most of the night. The phone call with the governor hadn't gone as Miles would have liked. His boss had no intention of reassigning the kid. Miles knew that the governor had assigned Coy Scofield III to his campaign as some sort of political payoff. He hadn't minded having the kid as his shadow when there really wasn't much of a race to speak of. But things had changed. Now Miles needed someone with a little more than just a pedigree to help him strategize.

But Coy Scofield II was a sitting federal judge in Lumberton, as well connected to the state party as one could get. And the original Coy Scofield had occupied the very seat Miles was gunning for before being named United States Secretary of Agriculture. The governor had made it very clear last night that Coy Number Three was staying put.

Governor Rossi promised to provide as much support from his own staff as he could, but there was no way to remove the kid and still save face. Not when the governor had his own reelection coming the following year. Making matters worse, the governor didn't seem too concerned about Faye Rich's write-in campaign. And that worried Miles even more.

"Will, is Julianne still hosting her big Fourth of July shindig at the Dresden House?" Miles asked. He was going to need a little grassroots action of his own. Will's fashion designer wife had lots of celebrity friends, as well as a United States senator for a brother. With a little schmoozing, maybe he could enlist the help of a few for personal appearances. Thanks to generous contributions in the early part of the campaign, Miles had a fairly substantial war chest, but some free star power couldn't hurt.

Will snorted. "Of course she is. The baby is due a week after that and you'd think she'd want to settle down and nest, but not my wife apparently."

"Too bad she doesn't design for Betty White," his brother teased. "You probably just lost that demographic."

"On the contrary, Miles scores very well with seniors." Gavin and Will snickered at Coy's statement. "It's true. According to polls, the elderly find Miles' character to be impeccable. A straight shooter. They perceive him to be as trustworthy as a Boy Scout."

Gavin was out and out laughing now. "That's your problem with the ladies right there, Miles. You're too proper. Maybe you need to start carrying a leather riding crop with you."

"Hey, I'm just glad to know you can still score, Miles," Will added. "Even if it's only with geriatric women."

"Oh, Miles scores well with *all* women," Coy said, clearly missing the subtext of the conversation.

"I hate to break it to you, Coy-Boy, but I don't think Miles has scored since high school." Gavin jabbed his brother with an elbow to the ribs.

Flipping them off, Miles jammed his ear buds in and cranked up some Red Hot Chili Peppers in order to drown out the two idiots running beside him. While Miles was close to his siblings, he wasn't one for sharing all the intimate details of his personal life with them. Let his brother think what he wanted, but Miles certainly wasn't a monk by any means. He just needed to be very careful whom he dated, especially now that he was on the campaign trail. A casual hookup was out of the question. And a happily-ever-after gig like the ones Gavin and Will had were not for him. Ever. He'd loved like that once and he still carried the scars.

The song ended just as they reached the stretch of beach across from the inn. Gavin doubled over to catch his breath as Miles yanked out his ear buds. Coy huffed to a stop beside Will and immediately pulled out his phone.

"Awesome, the local affiliate from Wilmington is going to cover our trip to the Sunset Dunes Senior Center today." His announcement sent both Gavin and Will back into peals of laughter.

"Hey, you guys can laugh all you want, but the senior vote is the most critical piece of any election. Do you even know why that is?"

Will and Gavin sobered up quickly, each casting a curious glance at Coy.

"Because they actually *do* vote," Coy continued. "Even in the nonpresidential years, they cast a ballot. Seniors accounted for over sixty-one percent of the vote in the last election and there's no reason to think that will be any different this time. And with Faye Rich in the race, that's going to be our battleground. She'll likely position herself as one of them, saying who better to represent seniors than someone who's walking the same walk. That's certainly how I'd do it. But as long as Miles scores with the trustworthy image of a guy who respects and cares about the elderly, there's no reason we can't beat her."

A small spark of pride flickered in Miles' chest at the emphatic pitch Coy made. The kid certainly was passionate about the race. Unfortunately, it took more than just passion to win an elected office in today's world.

Coy turned toward Miles. "I'll come by the inn to pick you up at ten. Be sure to consult the clothing chart Bernice laid out for you. We need you looking your best in front of the camera."

And just like that, the spark was extinguished.

"Bernice is *not* telling me what to wear," Miles growled. Gavin was doubled over again, but this time not from the effects of the sprint down the beach.

Coy puffed his chest out. "Bernice is consulting with people from Greer Rossi's team. We're lucky to have the governor's daughter working with us on the campaign. She is one of the most respected image consultants in the business right now. And because of her long-standing friendship with you, she's eager to help us out. Don't argue with what works, Miles." With a nod to the other two men, Coy hiked up the steps leading over the dunes and out of sight.

Will's eyes were full of mirth, but he wisely kept the laughter out of his voice. "The kid might be wimpy but he's got some decent brains in that egghead of his." He checked his phone. "Gotta bolt. I have a date with my son and a Tonka truck." He took a step before he paused and turned to face Miles. "Look, Miles, it goes without saying that Julianne and I will contribute whatever you need. And the senator still owes me for his interference in my career last year. So you just say the word and we're there for you. Just don't let The GTO Granny get under your skin. You're a natural politician. The kind that everyone wants to believe still exists. As long as you don't lose sight of that, you'll be fine."

He cuffed Miles on the shoulder and exchanged a fist bump with Gavin before taking off at a jog down the beach to his own house.

"Will's right, you know," Gavin said as they climbed the wooden steps leading them from the sand to the green grass stretching out in front of the B and B. "You've got this. I've known you all my life and you've never backed down from chasing your dream. My one bit of advice: Don't let Bernice dress you in anything orange. It messes with the blue in your eyes," his brother teased.

Miles slammed his shoulder into Gavin's, trying his best to knock his little brother on his sorry ass. But Gavin also carried the McAlister DNA and he proved to be a tough take-down. Before they knew it, they were both grappling on the grass.

"Hey, you two boys quit messin' around and git over here. I need help gittin' your mama's house ready for her to come home today."

Morgan Balch stood next to his pickup, smacking a piece of plastic pipe against his palm as though he was going to knock some sense into the two men. The old coot had worked for their father for as long as Miles could remember. Miles released the choke hold he had on his brother, only to have Gavin hit him with a wet willy as they approached the pickup parked in front of the two-bedroom carriage house their mother used as her private residence.

Built in the same era as the inn, the one-story building boasted the identical gingerbread framework and peaked roof line as well as a smaller version of the inn's veranda. Behind it was an intimate wooden gazebo where Will and his wife, Julianne, had exchanged their vows the summer before. Connected to the inn by a fifty-yard walkway with clematis plants growing over the trellis roof, the carriage house afforded his mother some privacy away from her guests.

"Miles has to go get himself all dolled up for a photo op, Morgan. Sal and Jorge are supposed to be here at nine to put together the ramp for the stairs." Gavin glanced at his phone, presumably to check on the whereabouts of his two employees.

Morgan grumbled something that sounded like "too big for their britches" before pulling down the tailgate to the truck. "I got your mama some of these handicapped thingies that are supposed to make her bathroom safer. I'm just not sure which ones she'd like best."

Miles exchanged a look with his brother. While their mother would appreciate the sentiment, he wasn't sure she'd appreciate the nod to her advancing age, especially given Kate's little confessional bombshell yesterday.

Gavin grinned, clearly happy to throw Miles under the bus. "You've got your finger on the pulse of the senior demographic, bro, so you should definitely pick."

He shook his head in frustration. "Any of them will be fine," Miles said, done with his brother's teasing. "Thanks for taking care of this, Morgan. I'll be back tonight to help with whatever else needs to be done." Ignoring his brother, Miles headed to the inn and a shower.

He heard Gavin say something about calling their sister Kate to help and then his brother's footsteps were eating up the ground between them.

"Dude, wait up," Gavin called. "You know I'm just having

some fun with you. It's so rare to find a wrinkle in that perfect bubble you live in that I have to bust your balls a little when I can."

Miles took the steps leading to the veranda in one stride. "Practice your standup routine on someone else today, Gavin. I have a shitload of work to do."

"Look, I can rearrange my schedule so that Ginger and I aren't in New York next week. That way, we can handle things at the inn if that will help you out. I know this thing with Faye Rich kind of blindsided you."

He turned to see his brother standing at the bottom of the steps with his hands on his hips, eager to jump in and save the day. *Again.* A wave of residual frustration washed through Miles every time he thought of Gavin putting his career—not to mention his life—on hold to protect their family.

"No, you've already done your fair share."

Gavin swore under his breath. "My way may not have been the right way, according to the *Book of Miles*, but I had everyone's best interests in mind. Especially Mom's. At some point you need to let me off the hook for not telling you Dad's secret."

Miles waved his hand. "Water under the bridge, little brother." And he meant it. Miles didn't know what he would have done differently in the same situation, but he could still hate that he'd never gotten the opportunity to try. "Go build your fancy lofts in Manhattan. I can handle the B and B. Besides, Mom will be home today. She can take over the decision making. And with Cassidy and Lori around to do most of the day-to-day work, everything should be fine."

His brother looked like he wanted to say more before shaking his head instead, which was fine with Miles because he wasn't in the mood for a heart to heart. "Yeah, okay. We're lucky to have Lori. I don't know how we could keep the place running without her. She's a hell of a cook and housekeeper."

Lori.

If Miles were being truthful, it wasn't only the campaign's unexpected twist that had him up tossing and turning last night. The B and B's cook/housekeeper had much more to do with his restless night than he'd dare to admit. *Jesus, he'd nearly kissed her.* One minute he'd been negotiating with her and then her hand was in his, skin to skin, and all he could think of was her wet body that day he'd spied her in the shower and he'd become as horny as a sixteen-year-old. It didn't help matters that she smelled like a freshly baked cupcake.

With a groan, Miles wiped his sweaty brow with his shirt.

In his defense, she'd completely caught him off guard with her quick banter and her refusal to be cowed by him. The woman who made it a habit to recede into the shadows most of the time clearly wasn't as timid as she appeared. Lori had a stubborn mouth with a tart tongue and Miles wanted to taste both. Desperately. Even worse, his plan to chase her off had backfired. He should have known she'd go running to his mother.

"Make sure you play nice with Lori, Miles. I don't think we could find someone of the same caliber to replace her in a pinch if we had to. Not without paying a fortune."

"I don't plan on 'playing' with her at all." Miles' answer was more vehement than he would have liked. "And the only reason it would be a fortune to replace her is that Mom isn't paying her a damn thing outside of room and board." His mother had been very forthcoming with that tidbit during her dressing down of Miles when he'd stopped by the rehab center the previous evening.

His younger brother arched his eyebrows at him. "Hmm. I'd say something about you protesting too much, but since I already pinned your ass to the ground not more than five minutes ago, I'll let it go. As for Mom's reasoning behind who she hires as her employees"—Gavin sighed heavily—"I don't think we can fight that battle with her. She's going to do what she's going to do. And that means taking in a desperate stranger or two. All we can do is run interference if something becomes a danger to Mom. I don't like it any more than you do, Miles, but I take some comfort that Mom's got Lamar watching over her now, too. And you can be sure he's already vetted Lori himself."

The mention of the sheriff caused the throbbing in Miles' temple to intensify.

Gavin shook his head as though he knew Miles' train of thought. "Seriously, bro, you've got to let these things go. Focus on the campaign instead, okay? You've worked so hard to get to this point, enjoy it. This is your time, Miles."

His brother was right. Miles' life was back to going as scripted. But that didn't mean he still wouldn't worry about his mother and what trouble might be following the women she chose to shelter. With his mom at least on the grounds of the inn, he needn't sweat the day-to-day running of the B and B. But he would be keeping an eye on Little Miss Stubborn Mouth. A close eye.

Being careful to walk along the periphery of the inn's large breakfast room, Lori quietly checked the contents of each silver chafing dish on the mahogany sideboard. This morning's breakfast consisted of pimento cheese grits, mounds of turkey bacon, hickory smoked sausage, praline and pecan French toast, and seasonal fruit. It was nearly ten o'clock, and Lori took great pleasure in the fact that almost every morsel had been eaten. Cooking had always been her passion. It had also been her downfall, but she couldn't dwell on that right now. Not in a room full of twenty strangers, any one of whom might recognize something about her.

"He has my vote and I don't even live in the state of North Carolina," one of the female guests tittered, stopping Lori in her tracks.

The woman's companion at the table peered over the rim of her coffee cup across the room. Lori followed her gaze just in time to see Miles crouch down to listen to something a guest at one of the other tables was saying.

"Seriously, I wonder how young you have to be to work as a congressional page," the woman whispered.

Both women laughed out loud as their oblivious husbands discussed plans for a day at one of the local golf courses.

Miles was dressed in a light blue shirt that fit him like a second skin, and Lori had no doubt all the females in the room were tracking his progress, paying particular attention as the muscles in his back flexed with every move. Not to mention that when he bent down, his chinos stretched over an ass that had obviously seen its fair share of squats. Putting that body on such an arrogant man was definitely a sin in Lori's book.

He stood up then and his wily eyes swept the room, passing over Lori before quickly flicking back to land on her face. A face she hoped wasn't crimson after having been caught ogling him. His eyes narrowed and he started toward her only to have another guest intercept him. Lori took advantage of his distraction to slip back into the kitchen, where Cassidy sat at the island munching on a banana.

"The dryer is buzzing," the girl said around a mouthful of the fruit. "I'll do most anything around here, but you know I hate wrestling the sheets into neat piles."

Lori headed to the laundry room adjacent to the kitchen, swiftly pulling out a load of towels from the industrial-sized dryer. Snapping each one, she then folded it neatly before stacking them in the laundry basket. The mindless task helped her to regroup after Miles' heated glare in the breakfast room. He was angry and she knew why. But he wouldn't win this round.

Still, his voice startled her when he entered the kitchen. "We need more coffee in the dining room."

Without a word, Lori headed toward the cambro containers at the other end of the room. Rather than make coffee in-house, a local brew was supplied to the inn in the three-gallon containers each morning by the Java Jolt, a coffee shop located in Chances Inlet's downtown. Guests would often wander down to the shop to purchase additional bags to take home with them, making the arrangement a win for everyone.

"Cassidy can do it," Miles commanded. "And while you're there, Cass, please give Mr. and Mrs. Belfield a brochure for Bald Head Island and directions to the ferry."

Both women froze in place.

Miles' hands went to his hips as he aimed his stare at the teenager. "Correct me if I'm wrong, but didn't you say last night that you wanted to help out more around the inn?"

Cassidy nodded.

"Well, let's see you put those words into action."

The teenager silently slid off the barstool and tossed the banana peel in the trash before walking over to fill one of the thermal coffeepots. Lori turned back to the laundry room. Unfortunately, Miles was right on her heels.

"We have to talk."

She kept her back to him while she loaded sheets into the washing machine. "Again? Didn't we talk last night? Surely you don't want to make a habit of this."

He made a sound behind her that sounded like it belonged more to a wild animal than a candidate for Congress.

"You went behind my back to my mother."

It was all she could do not to roll her eyes. "That's a little dramatic, don't you think, Miles? I just asked your mother to explain our arrangement to you, that's all."

"You couldn't have explained it yourself?"

Now she did roll her eyes. "As if you would have believed anything I said."

"In case you've forgotten, I'm trying to spare my mother from having to deal with the day-to-day minutia here. Her method of 'explaining' your 'arrangement' didn't exactly keep her blood pressure low."

"Your mom reams you out, so now you're taking it out on me and Cassidy?" Lori slammed down the lid to the washer. "Cassidy *will* be able to vote in this election, you know."

"Damn it, Lori, this isn't about the election! It's about you hiding out here and whatever fallout is going to ensue when the gig is up."

Lori let out a resigned sigh before slowly turning around. Apparently they were still going to beat the same dead horse. Her breath hitched in admiration when she finally faced him. Miles had both hands bracketing the doorway, eliminating any possible escape route. Not only that, but the pose afforded her a breathtaking view of his chiseled chest where the shirt stretched over it. She jerked her head up before she did something stupid like reach out to trace the ridge between his pectoral muscles.

His hair was still damp from his post-workout shower. If those women in the other room liked what they saw at breakfast, they should roust themselves up at six thirty every morning when Miles took his run. Spying on him out the kitchen window at dawn was Lori's guilty pleasure, her reward for having to rise so early for work.

When Miles wasn't playing politics, he was a world-class triathlete, twice finishing in the top ten of the Iron Man World Championship in Hawaii. Patricia proudly displayed his Iron Man medals—alongside sports memorabilia from her husband and all of the McAlister children—in a trophy case in the B and B's library. Obviously, Miles' ambition wasn't limited to his desire to take over the world, but to keep his body in peak shape, as well. Judging by what she saw as he ran back and forth to the beach every morning wearing nothing but a pair of nylon gym shorts, he was doing an excellent job of it. The man had a beautiful body.

She backed up against the washer and crossed her arms over her chest. "I guess I didn't make it clear enough last night. I'll be gone before there will ever be any 'fallout'."

He wasn't looking through her now. Instead his piercing gaze was bearing down on her face, searching for something. But he wouldn't find anything there. At least not the answers to her identity. If he looked closely enough, though, he might find clues to her desire for him. And that would never do.

"Do you want me to leave now? Is that what this is really about?"

She watched the war of emotions play out on his face. Her breath caught in her throat when she saw what looked like desire flicker briefly in his eyes before it disappeared.

"What I want is irrelevant." He pulled his hands from the doorframe and took a step farther into the room. "But my mother wants you to stay and I'm going to do my best to respect that. It's her B and B."

Lori licked her lips; his steady stare was doing things to her body. "It's only until she's back on her feet. Then I'll be gone from here."

"Mmm," he murmured as he reached out a hand and gently brushed back some of the long hair shielding her face. His blue gaze was still probing, as though he was looking for some tiny clue that would give him the upper hand in whatever it was that was pulling them together. "But what damage will you do while you're here?"

"None," she whispered as she tried to ignore the temptation to lean into his hand. "I would never do anything that could hurt your mother."

He traced his fingers along the line of her jaw, his gentle touch warming her skin. Miles' critical gaze prompted a twinge of vulnerability—and unease. But she knew she shouldn't react. She reminded herself that he was just toying with her, hoping to force her to reveal something of herself. Her eyes drifted to his mouth, which looked quite kissable when it wasn't curled in a frown that he seemed to always be directing at her.

"And what if my mother isn't the one I'm worried about?" he asked softly just as his lips began descending toward hers.

No! No! NO! Too bad her body wasn't listening to her brain. Lori's eyelids drifted shut and she was seconds away from making a huge mistake when Cassidy stomped into the kitchen.

"Hey, Miles, your body man is here. He says you're going to play checkers with the old-timers at Sunset Dunes."

Lori's eyes snapped open and she watched as Miles blinked rapidly before he jerked his hand back from her face. Fortunately, his large body blocked the entire doorway of the laundry room, shielding them so Cassidy couldn't possibly have seen their close encounter of the dangerous kind. He swore quietly, running his fingers through his hair.

"Just see that you don't make any trouble," he said before backing out of the room, leaving Lori to wonder if Miles had directed his warning at her or at himself.

SIX

"I'm so glad to finally be home."

Miles' chest still constricted at the sight of the bruises dotting his mother's cheek, most of them faded to a putrid yellow color. Her accident could have been so much worse. He wasn't sure how he would have survived losing both his parents. Draping a cotton blanket over her feet, he leaned down and kissed her forehead. "No happier than I am."

"Hmm." His mother's smile was dubious. "Does that mean you'll stop harassing my staff?"

Harassing didn't come close to what he'd wanted to do to Lori in the inn's laundry room earlier that day. His carefully maintained control continually slipped its leash every time he was in the woman's presence. This morning, his only intention had been to put her on notice that no matter how much his mother protected her, *he'd* be protecting his mother, so Lori needed to tread carefully.

But like the day before, when he got her alone, that X-rated video of her in the shower kept playing behind his eyes and all he could think about was touching her. His finger was involuntarily reaching for her face before his brain could catch up. When he made contact with her cheek, he was transfixed by the softness of her skin and the vanilla scent that seemed to envelop her.

She'd asked him if he wanted her to leave, and it was all he could do not to pull her against him and show her exactly what he wanted. But kissing the woman silly wouldn't solve either of their problems. As tempting as Lori was, she was also as dangerous as a pocket full of dynamite and he'd already had enough explosions these past few weeks to last a lifetime. He was damn lucky Cassidy had wandered back into the kitchen when she did.

He sat down on the coffee table next to the recliner his sister had bought for his mother's homecoming. Reaching for her hand, he tucked it between both of his.

"You can harass your own employees from now on. I've got a full plate with the campaign. I've worked out the registration duties; Cassidy and I will handle them until you're back on your feet, not to mention taking care of whatever else you need. All you have to do is ask. But don't think I'm not going to come to the rescue if you need it."

With her free hand, his mother reached up to brush the hair back off Miles' forehead. "Why is it that my boys all seem to think I constantly need rescuing?"

"For the record, I'd like to point out that it was Ginger and Midas who rescued you after the accident, Mother," his sister Kate barked as she waltzed into the living room of the carriage house carrying her black medical bag and a tray of iced drinks from the Java Jolt. "*Your boys* are likely feeling a little threatened by the superior sex, that's all."

Miles stood and took the tray from his sister's hands before she could dump the drinks all over their mother. "It never ceases to amaze me that you actually convinced a man to marry you."

Kate laughed. "Alden knows a good catch when he sees one." She bussed her mother on the forehead. "How painful was the drive home, Mom? Do you need something stronger than iced coffee?"

"I'm fine."

He studied his mother carefully while he handed her one

of the drinks. Her face was paler than usual, but then she wasn't used to being cooped up inside for days at a time. The lines around her mouth were a little more pronounced, but she'd never admit to being in pain. Truth be told, the McAlister kids got their stubbornness from their mother. Her hazel eyes lit up at the sound of her granddaughter's voice.

"Gigi!"

Miles scooped the six-year-old up before she could launch herself on top of his mother. "Whoa there, Emily. Don't I get a hug first?"

Emily giggled as she wrapped herself around him like a little monkey. Dressed in a princess gown from one of the Disney characters, she nearly poked his eye out with the plastic tiara on her head. "I'm gonna paint Gigi's nails." She waved a pink bag in his face. "It'll make her feel better."

Miles kissed his niece on the nose. "I think just having you around makes her feel better, Em." The child giggled when Miles dangled her as though he might drop her, before gently letting his niece fall onto the sofa. Emily scampered over to the coffee table Miles had just vacated and began to neatly unpack her little bag.

Kate scowled at him over her coffee. "I hope you didn't manhandle anyone like that at the senior center."

Miles rolled his eyes at his sister. "I wasn't dancing the Nae-Nae with the residents, if that's what you're implying."

"I like when you dance with me, Uncle Miles." Emily handed him a bottle of nail polish to open. He mugged for his sister before sitting down next to his niece and holding the open bottle while she dipped the brush in.

"Still, the word around town is that you were pretty ruthless in checkers today. I mean, you couldn't have gone easy on Mr. Cohen? He's ninety-four and a World War Two vet."

"All the more reason for me not to go easy on him. The man is still sharp as a tack. He wouldn't have appreciated the gesture."

"Too bad the early voting hasn't opened yet," his sister teased. "You'd better hope they all don't forget you by the time November rolls around."

"I doubt that," his mother said as she smiled at Emily, who was meticulously painting powder blue nail polish on her thumb. "Miles has been a fixture at Sunset Dunes since he was a Cub Scout. They look forward to his visits."

"Wait, you go there even when you're not trying to get them to vote?" His sister's look said she might be digging in her black bag for a psychiatric tome.

"Mr. Grimes, my fifth grade social studies teacher, lives there. He's been a widower for eight years and his kids are scattered all over the world." Miles shrugged. "Most of the residents just want someone to listen to them—to validate that they're still worthy of existence. Instead they get con artists who want to take advantage of their naiveté and rip them off. It's shameless."

"Miles, it's not your job to fix what happened because of your brother's investments," his mother said.

A heavy silence settled over the room as the three adults were no doubt thinking of the shame his younger brother, Ryan, felt at the unwilling part he played in a scam that ripped off many people in Chances Inlet. Ryan made millions as a professional baseball player. He gave a great deal to charity and invested the rest. Unfortunately, he'd been too trusting with his financial advisor, who not only ripped Ryan off in a Ponzi scheme, but managed to convince half the town—many of them living on fixed retirement incomes—that "what was good enough for Ryan was good enough for them." His brother had been dumbfounded and mortified when the truth came out. It was just another blemish on the McAlisters' sterling reputation in Chances Inlet.

"Actually it is my job to protect them, and when I get elected, I plan to make it one of my primary goals to make sure seniors won't lose their pensions because of some criminal Ponzi schemer."

His mother gave him a cavalier smile as if to say "good luck with that." But Miles was determined to make this right.

"A good leader can still learn a lot from the folks at Sunset Dunes," he continued. "Their generation represents all that is good about this country. If something needed to be done, they didn't ask, 'What's in it for me?' They just did it. This country can be that way again. I know it."

Miles looked up to see his mother and sister staring at him. His mom wore a soft smile while his sister's expression was more amused.

"Wow, that would have made a beautiful campaign spot." Kate grinned. "I think you should let me hold the Bible when they swear you in. It's only fair since you usurped my status as the only child all those years ago."

His mother laughed. "The only one holding the Bible will be me."

Kate sighed. "Always the bridesmaid."

Emily looked up from her task and beamed at Miles. "Ginger said I can be the flower girl in her wedding to Uncle Gavin. Then I'm gonna be in Gigi and Sheriff Lamar's wedding. Can I be in yours, too, Uncle Miles?"

Both women were staring at him again. Miles carefully set the nail polish down on the table. No way was he discussing his philosophy on marriage with these two. A decade ago, marriage had been all he could think about. He'd found his soul mate in Justine, his girlfriend throughout college, and he couldn't wait to live out his life-plan with her by his side. But when she'd suddenly died, it was as if she'd taken with her that part of his soul that made him want to love. He couldn't imagine himself committing his heart to anyone else. Instead he'd rededicated himself to the goals he'd set all those years ago. Falling in love had never been on that list in the first place. Miles was better off navigating the course of his life alone.

He kissed the top of Emily's head. "If I ever decide to tie the knot, the job is yours, Em." Miles didn't bother pointing out to her that she'd likely marry before he ever would. Neither his niece nor the two hopeless romantics in the room would understand.

As he stood to make his escape, Emily grabbed his wrist. "I can give you a manicure, too, Uncle Miles. Daddy lets me paint his nails."

"Does he now?" Miles gave his sister a look clearly conveying that he needed backup.

Kate grinned mischievously. "You can't paint Uncle Miles'

nails today, honey. You need to check with Bernice first to see what color she wants him to wear."

Both women broke out into giggles.

"And with that, I'm out." Miles kissed his mother's cheek.

"Come back for dinner?"

"Sorry, I get to eat rubber chicken with the Kiwanis tonight. But I know a good place where we can get some breakfast. Can I bring you some tomorrow?"

His mother cupped his cheek and nodded. "I'd like that. And, Miles, whether I believe I need your protection or not, I am glad you're here."

Patricia blew on her tea.

"How is it?" Lamar gently sat down on the bed beside her, as always, careful not to jar her hip.

"It's perfect." And it was. He'd prepared her a cup of Sleepy Time tea with just the right amount of lemon and honey. Everything Lamar did for her was thoughtful and deliberate. And perfect.

She leaned into his warm body and breathed in his familiar musky scent. He tentatively wrapped a strong arm around her shoulders, and she brushed her lips along his jaw, glad that he was finally holding her again. For the past several days, he'd been treating her as if she'd shatter at the slightest touch. Things would get back to normal now that she'd returned home. The distance she'd perceived in him would dissipate and they could go back to planning the rest of their lives together. Patricia let out a contented sigh.

A sigh that Lamar clearly mistook for something else.

He carefully untangled himself from her and stood up beside the bed. "Are you okay? Is the pain very bad?"

The pain was a dull ache, but nothing she couldn't handle. She gave him a bright smile that she hoped was reassuring as she patted the bed beside her. "I'm fine. Really."

He didn't budge an inch and Patricia's contentment faded. "You know what would make me feel better? A kiss from my handsome fiancé."

Lamar's face softened and hope flared in Patricia's belly. He leaned down, gently caressing that sensitive area where her jaw met her neck—the spot that made her body turn to putty—before kissing her soundly. She hadn't lied. His kiss did make her feel better. Everything else faded away except for him and her.

When his lips left hers, she locked her arms around his neck, not allowing him to pull away. Instead, she feathered kisses along his cheek. "Are you sure you don't want to stay tonight?"

He unhooked her hands from his body and cast a glance at the pillows and ice packs he'd placed in the bed around her. "No, you'll sleep better by yourself," he said.

Despite the sting of his refusal, she would never beg Lamar to stay the night with her. If there was one thing Patricia prided herself on, it was being an independent woman. "You're right. I'll probably toss and turn all night." She leaned back against the pillows. "Cassidy volunteered to sleep on the futon in the office tonight anyway. Go to Pier Pressure and get some dinner. Make sure everyone in town is behaving. I'll be boring company anyway."

He did that little growling thing that always made her insides twist up in arousal as he sat back down on the bed. Lamar lifted her chin with a finger and studied her face with his solemn stare. "Tricia, you're always good company. And you always will be." He kissed her gently until her mouth opened beneath his. The familiar passion Patricia felt for him simmered and she thought for a moment that she'd won whatever battle they were silently fighting.

Until he broke off the kiss with a mumbled curse. "I've got a few more leads on a case I'm working that I need to chase down tonight. Promise me you'll get some rest?"

Confused, she studied his stoic face for clues, but none were forthcoming. She hid her frustration behind a sunny smile. "Come by before your shift tomorrow?"

He gave her a look that implied he might say more, but instead he nodded silently. When she heard the sound of the door closing, she counted to ten before hurling a pillow at the wall.

SEVEN

Lori tried to crank the motor by hand, but it was no use. The garbage disposal was well and truly stuck. With a resigned sigh, she looked at the clock on the microwave: ten fifty. Too late to call Gavin to come fix it. Luckily the casseroles were already made and she'd rinsed the fruit earlier. She'd just have to manage without a sink during tomorrow's breakfast.

"It's not the first time I've had a kitchen appliance go on strike during my illustrious career," she muttered as she wiped down the countertops surrounding the deep farm sink in the B and B's kitchen.

She tossed the towel into the washer then nearly leaped out of her skin when she collided with a hard body on her way out of the laundry room. A hard body that smelled like Aramis and the ocean. Her mind drifted back to that moment earlier in the day when she'd almost done the unthinkable and kissed Miles McAlister right here in this very spot. This time, her palms were flat against his chest and she could feel the steady rhythm of his heartbeat beneath her hand—the sound of which seemed to be echoing throughout the small room. Or perhaps that was her own wild heartbeat she heard.

He'd changed out of his casual clothes and was now wearing his buttoned-up politician's uniform consisting of a tailored shirt—soft beneath her fingertips—and gabardine slacks, both of which were doing very little to conceal the finely hewed muscle beneath. Unlike the men Lori had been associated with the past several years, Miles didn't need to cloak himself in designer suits to exude a sense of confidence. His swagger was one hundred percent real and his clothing neither enhanced nor detracted from it.

The dim lighting behind him cast his face in shadows, making it difficult for her to decipher his expression. His hands hovered near her waist, seemingly unsure of where they should be. Parts of her were doing a happy dance at the unexpected opportunity for a second chance, before logic won out and she took a huge step back in order to prevent the idiot portion of her brain from running amok.

They stood in the charged silence a moment before Miles blew out a harsh breath.

"Do you always skulk around the inn talking to yourself late at night?"

"Do you always accost women in the laundry?"

He lowered his chin to his chest, muttering something to himself. Shoving his hands in his pockets, he propped a shoulder against the doorframe.

"Touché." He wore a chagrined expression when he finally looked up at her. "I apologize for earlier. It was never my intention to manhandle you. I wasn't . . . thinking."

His apology pretty much killed whatever happy dancing was still going on inside her. Of course, he would only admit to touching her when he wasn't in his right mind. The connection between them was undeniably hot and she *knew* he felt its potency as much as she did. But Miles would never act on it. She doubted that Dudley Do-Right ever let himself do anything that wasn't carefully planned out in advance. Especially with a woman like her—a woman he suspected the worst of.

Lori crossed her arms over her midsection. "Exactly what was your intention?"

He shook his head slightly. "Apparently, to be an ass."

"Well, you succeeded."

One corner of his mouth twitched. "Are you going to rat me out to my mom again?"

She felt her own smile coming on. "No. I'm pretty sure she already knows you're an ass. Luckily for you, she loves you anyway."

"And I love her. Which means the two of us need to work this out."

Heat surged to her belly just thinking about how she'd like to work it out. But that could never happen. Not while they both were who they were. "I already told you, I'm not filling out any forms."

Miles held a hand up. "That's between you and my mom. As far as I'm concerned, she can handle any legal fallout that might come from that."

"Just as long as it doesn't impact your political career, right?"

He jerked away from the doorframe and Lori instantly regretted baiting him. Miles made no secret of who he was. The fact that he was principled and honest was like a breath of fresh air after the people Lori had known. His integrity was as much of a turn-on to her as was the rest of him.

Lori sensed that perfection wasn't easy for Miles, though. Although she didn't think others noticed—not even his family. Deep down, Miles wanted to stray from his path; he just didn't know how. And as much as Lori would like to be the one to lead him astray, too much danger lay down that road. For both of them.

"Just as long as it doesn't impact my *family*."

She heaved a sigh. "How many times am I going to have to say it? Nothing about who I am will hurt your mother, her inn, or your family. I won't let it."

Miles pinched the bridge of his nose with his thumb and his forefinger. "We need some ground rules."

"Let's start with you keeping your hands to yourself."

His chin shot up. "Wait just a minute there, Sweet Cheeks. You weren't putting up much of a protest this morning. If Cassidy hadn't crashed the party, you would have been fully participating in whatever came next and you know it."

She was suddenly damp at the thought of "whatever came

next." *All the more reason for ground rules*, she told herself. Especially if they included the provision that neither one of them could be in the same room at the same time.

"How about you run off onto the campaign trail and I mind my own business cooking and cleaning," Lori suggested. "That offer has got to be every man's total fantasy."

His hands were back in his pockets again as if he needed to forcibly restrain them. "You clearly don't know what men fantasize about." The rough edge in his voice sent a shiver of arousal through her.

"Excuse me. Miles, is that you?"

The sound of a male voice startled her. Miles spun around, facing the kitchen, his body blocking hers from view. Whether it was conscious or not, Lori appreciated the gesture.

"Evening, Mr. Swanston. Can I help you with something?"

She heard Mr. Swanston step farther into the kitchen. "Sorry to bother you, but my wife has misplaced a bracelet. It was one of those ones with all the charms. The kids have been adding to it every holiday. I was wondering if anyone found it, or turned it in."

Miles glanced over his shoulder at her. Lori shook her head as a trickle of unease crawled down her spine. She'd searched every nook and cranny in her room looking for her grandmother's ring, but still hadn't found it. While she knew she hadn't misplaced the ring, she hated the idea that it might have been stolen.

"No one's turned anything in," Miles said.

Mr. Swanston sighed heavily. "The darn thing probably came unlatched and fell off. It could be anywhere."

Lori stepped around Miles. Mr. and Mrs. Swanston were a kind older couple who were staying at the B and B for a few days on their way home to Florence, South Carolina, following the high school graduation of one of their grandchildren. The odds of either of them recognizing her were slim to none. Mr. Swanston was probably right about the bracelet. Lori wanted to believe that the two missing items were just a coincidence.

"I'll look around for it, Mr. Swanston," she offered. "I can check all the common areas. And Miles will ask around in town tomorrow. He can even check with the sheriff's office. Maybe someone turned it in there."

Mr. Swanston's face relaxed. "That's very kind of you, thank you. Linda has a bee in her bonnet about finding it, but it will put her at ease to know you'll keep looking for it even after we leave tomorrow."

"If it's here, we'll find it." Miles' resolute tone prompted a nod from the older man.

"See you at breakfast." Mr. Swanston waved his way out of the kitchen.

Lori edged out of the laundry room, hoping to make her escape up to her room.

"Nice of you to volunteer my services there, Sweet Cheeks." Miles opened the Sub-Zero refrigerator and pulled out some cold cuts.

"I know how you like to be in charge." She checked the automatic times for the ovens. "Just leave whatever dishes you use on the drain board. I'll get them in the morning."

He stopped in the middle of piling meat on top of a hoagie roll. "You don't have to clean up after me."

"I only meant that the drain is clogged. You can't run the water right now."

Miles shot her a confused look before walking over to the sink and peering down at it. "What's wrong with it?" he asked as he turned on the light above.

"The garbage disposal is stuck. Nothing major. I'll call Gavin first thing in the morning."

He made a sound of disgust before he began unbuttoning his dress shirt.

"What are you doing?" Not that she minded him doing a striptease in the dimly lit kitchen, but she wasn't sure she had as much control of that idiot part of her brain as she needed right now.

"My father believed in raising children who are self-sufficient." He pulled off the shirt in one fluid move and tossed it over a kitchen chair. The muscles beneath his T-shirt flexed as he strode into the laundry room and retrieved a large yellow toolbox. "It doesn't have to be Gavin who fixes everything. I'm perfectly capable."

Lori got the impression that he was aggravated by more than just a clogged kitchen drain. Before she knew it, he was on his back and under the sink with the ease and familiarity of someone who'd been there a time or two before. He pulled a flashlight out of the toolbox and propped it beside him.

"So are you saying Kate could do this if she had to?"

His voice echoed from within the cabinet. "I'm saying even my little brother with the Golden Glove could do this. Although his contract might prohibit it." He blindly reached into the toolbox and grabbed a wrench. "My sisters both know their way around a toolbox, too. If you ever need a piece of furniture from IKEA assembled, they're your go-to girls."

Lori didn't hold back the grin that escaped at the pride in Miles' voice. Not for the first time she thought how delightful it would have been to grow up in a family with siblings and parents who looked after you, instead of ones who sold you out.

There was a clink of metal on metal and Miles swore. "Can you get me a plastic bowl or something?"

She fished into a cabinet and pulled out a bowl. When she crouched down to hand it to him, her thigh brushed against Miles' firm one and she sucked in a breath at the heat that seared through her. Miles stilled for a moment before reaching for the bowl. Lori quickly found her feet and took a few steps back toward the opposite counter and kept her eyes glued to his Cole Haan loafers rather than his muscular legs.

"Here's your problem," he said. "Eggshells in the trap."

"I put eggs down there every day. It's never been a problem before."

"Maybe not since you've been here, but they build up over time. Morgan usually comes to clean out the trap a couple times a year. Looks like the clog didn't want to wait for him." He slid the soggy bowl out onto the floor. "You won't have to worry about this again for a while."

Lori didn't bother pointing out that she wouldn't be there in "a while." It wouldn't do to dwell on her uncertain future.

"You mean to tell me you've never run into this problem at the other restaurants or inns you've worked in?"

His question caught her off guard. He was quiet underneath

the sink awaiting her answer. She knew Miles hoped to trap her into giving up information about herself, but she was wise to his tactics.

"What makes you think I've done this kind of work before?"

Miles snorted. "A person doesn't have to be a Rhodes Scholar to deduce you've had some sort of culinary training. Maybe in the military?" He slid out from under the sink.

Lori laughed. "Why the military?"

"This place has never been cleaner." Miles glanced down at the stains dotting his T-shirt. "Present company excluded, that is."

He got to his feet before reaching behind his neck, tugging the T-shirt over his head, and balling it up to wipe his hands. The sight of his bare chest made Lori light-headed. *Get out, you fool,* her brain screamed, but her feet were glued to the floor. He must have heard her sharp intake of breath—*how could he have not?*—because he stilled in the act of tossing his shirt toward the laundry room. She licked her lips and his eyes locked on to them like a laser missile honing in on its target.

Her hips bumped up against the counter when she took a step back. Miles followed, pinning her there by placing his hands on the countertop, one on each side of her. Keeping her eyes off his face wasn't helping the situation; her lips ached to cover the pulse beating wildly at the base of his neck.

His own lips hovered near her ear. "Tell me your secret, Lori. Tell me something about you that will make me not want you so damn much." His raspy words both shocked and aroused her. The knowledge that she had power over him was thrilling and frightening at the same time. She was wet and wanting and she very nearly did as he asked.

But if she admitted her sins to Miles McAlister, he definitely wouldn't want her. Ever. And that would hurt worse than going to bed unfulfilled.

Lori shook her head, causing Miles to swear violently. He yanked his hands off the counter and turned toward the bay window behind the sink. "Go to bed. Now, Lori. Go, before we break the only rule we've been able to agree on."

She stared at his broad back for a moment before quietly making her way upstairs.

EIGHT

"Oh, for goodness' sakes! It's no use. I'll never be able to do this the way you do, Lori."

Lori looked up from the bread she was kneading to see Ginger wadding up a fitted sheet in her hands.

"How do you make this look so easy?" Ginger asked while Cassidy laughed in the background.

I've had years of experience.

Lori didn't bother admitting that out loud, though. It wouldn't do for either of them to know she'd grown up in a B and B just like this one. She felt that familiar pang of regret she always did when thinking about the way she'd abandoned her mom and stepdad. But Lori had had bigger dreams back then, and they didn't include cooking in the restaurant of a small inn in Oregon. It didn't matter that her mother's dining room had a two-star Michelin rating; Lori wanted her own kitchen. She'd practically had to sell her soul to the devil to get one. Too bad the devil in this case was her own father. Wiping her hands on a towel, she took the sheet from Ginger's fingers.

"For one who's so light on her feet, you'd think she'd be more graceful with her hands," Cassidy teased.

A ballerina by training, Ginger no longer danced professionally because of an ailing Achilles tendon. She'd been working as the makeup artist for the television show *Historical Restorations*, which Gavin had teamed up with to restore Dresden House this spring. The show—and the eventual sale of Dresden House—had been Gavin's plan to salvage Donald McAlister's reputation by paying off his debt. Things hadn't worked out exactly as Gavin planned, but Lori was glad Ginger had stuck around. She was pretty sure that Gavin was, too. Ginger was a great partner for Gavin. She was not, however, great at folding fitted sheets.

"Fold it once lengthwise." Lori demonstrated while Ginger looked on. The pretty blonde pulled her lower lip between her teeth as she watched. "Then tuck one corner into the other. Do the same at the other end and then fold it in half once and then again and"—Lori held the folded square for Ginger to see—"you have a folded fitted sheet."

Ginger let out a resigned sigh. "My arms are longer than yours and I still can't do it like that."

"You're always welcome to practice." Lori winked at Ginger. "I do at least one load a day."

"Here, do it again, Lori." Cassidy pulled out her cell phone. "I'll video it and Ginger can watch it until she gets it right. Oooh, we can even put it up on the inn's website. I'll bet it would get a lot of hits. That would be great publicity."

Lori shoved the folded sheet back at Ginger and turned her back to Cassidy's beeping cell phone camera.

"Turn that off, Cassidy. You know Lori is camera shy."

Ginger had never said anything, but Lori was pretty sure her friend knew at least part of her secret. Diesel Gold, the producer of *Historical Restorations*, and Ginger's best friend, had arranged for Lori's job in Chances Inlet. Diesel and Lori had lived in the same apartment building in New York. Both had traveled in the same social circles and he'd been a frequent visitor to her restaurant. Lori trusted Diesel with her life. She didn't think that trust was misplaced with Ginger, either.

"Besides, I'm sure there's already a video like that on

YouTube anyway, Cass." Ginger gave Lori a reassuring smile before she picked up another sheet from the laundry basket.

"Isn't this a homey scene," Coy said, entering the kitchen through the screen door. "Maybe we should get Greer to film a spot with Miles here in the kitchen. I'm sure he could pull off domestic god." Placing his tablet on the island, he grabbed a leftover muffin and peeled off the wrapper. "Ginger, Miles says he doesn't need any makeup but you know what a television camera can do. Can you maybe work your magic on him?"

"Great, she gets to get out of folding laundry, but I don't get to help at all." Cassidy had been sulking all morning when Coy rebuffed her offer to help with some of the campaign spots.

Coy let out a beleaguered sigh. "You can grab a couple of bottles of water for Greer and her crew if you really want to help, Cassidy."

Cassidy didn't even bother looking up from where she sat at the oval table in the corner of the kitchen furiously typing on her laptop. "I'm pretty sure that falls under your job description."

Lori exchanged an amused glance with Ginger, who grabbed some bottles of water out of the small cooler by the back door and took them outside with her.

"Lunch is being delivered from town, but if you have some of those awesome cupcakes to spare, I know Greer and her crew would appreciate it," Coy said with a shy smile.

"Greer, Greer, Greer!" Cassidy snapped her laptop closed, tucking it under her arm as she stood. "You'd think she was the queen or something. I'm going to check on Mrs. Mac."

Coy chuckled as Cassidy stomped out of the room. "She reminds me of my little sister."

"Yeah, but let's not mention that to her, okay?" Lori was pretty sure the teenager had a huge crush on Miles' campaign manager. "I'll put together a dessert tray for you. Is there anything else you need?" While Coy was easygoing and pleasant to have around, he was also observant and savvy. She didn't need him initiating a game of twenty questions.

"Greer mentioned that she may stay the night. Miles said

you have two rooms open and to check with you which one you want her assigned to."

It figured Miles would send his minion rather than speak with her directly. Since their late-night encounter more than a week ago, he'd buried himself in his campaign, limiting his duties at the B and B to checking the guests in and out. He made his rounds of the breakfast room each morning after grabbing a quick meal with his mother. But other than that, the only sightings of him were through the kitchen window when he was coming and going from his early morning workouts. Miles even changed his own towels and sheets—a fact Lori was insanely grateful for because there was no telling what she'd do when faced with the bed he'd slept in. She couldn't complain about the situation really. It was for the best, especially since both of them had trouble keeping their hands off each other.

"I'll get the Aberdeen Suite ready for her as soon as I finish with the bread."

Patricia had named all the rooms in the inn after cities and towns in Scotland. Decorated in the rich red, black, and yellow colors of the Aberdeen tartan, the suite featured a view of the Atlantic and an antique claw-foot tub. Best of all, it was on the opposite end of the B and B from Miles' room.

Greer Rossi, with her chic wardrobe, her glossy long brown hair, and her even longer legs, had arrived at the inn earlier that morning complete with a worshipful camera crew in tow. From her vantage point within the butler's pantry, Lori watched the affectionate greeting—complete with an intimate smile—the governor's daughter had bestowed on Miles. The image consultant was barely able to keep her hands to herself throughout their breakfast for two, never missing an opportunity to touch Miles possessively. For his part, Miles seemed unfazed by Greer's excessive pawing. In fact, Lori hadn't seen Miles so relaxed and carefree in the months she'd known him. The thought made her stomach clench. She told herself that her jealousy wasn't fanned by Greer's familiarity with Miles but rather that Greer was everything Lori used to be and never would be again.

Ginger came back into the kitchen, Midas at her heels. "Greer talked Miles into some powder. Can I borrow a dish towel, Lori? I don't want to get anything on his shirt. Bernice would probably kill me."

Coy threw the muffin liner into the trash before grabbing a bottle of water out of the cooler. "I figured Greer would convince him. She's a sweet talker."

Sweet talker, my ass. Lori gave the loaf of bread one last whack before tossing it into the bread pan.

"She is that," Ginger said. "They seem to complement each other."

"They would be the perfect couple." Coy's voice was filled with reverence. "A match made in political heaven. Just having her on his arm could gain us five percentage points. Voters like a candidate who's settled and happy. And the male voters would definitely appreciate Greer."

"I seriously doubt Miles is that shallow." Ginger pulled a towel out of the drawer. "If there is something between them, I certainly hope it's not based on blind ambition."

Coy laughed. "There's no room for romance when it comes to politics, Ginger."

Ginger made a face behind Coy's back before they both headed out to the veranda, leaving Lori alone in the kitchen with the dog. Was there actually something between Miles and Greer? Coy was correct; the two were a perfect match. A woman like Greer Rossi would certainly enhance Miles' career. A woman like Lori would only destroy it.

An hour later, Lori stood in the Aberdeen Suite fluffing the pillows on the queen-sized sleigh bed. Voices from below drifted up through the open window. The octogenarian woman who operated the Java Jolt was being interviewed by Greer's team. Lori sat down on the padded window seat to listen.

"When Miles was a boy, we all called him 'Little Mayor,'" the woman was saying. "He was always so responsible and compassionate. Oh, how he did love to organize things, though. And people, too." Lori could hear the smile in the older woman's voice as she recounted a story of Miles circulating a petition to allow skateboards on the Chances Inlet

Pier. "He got all the boys together to come up with and agree to the rules of conduct they had to maintain while on the pier. He even pitched it to the City Council that it would make our town more family friendly if we allowed the skateboarders." The woman laughed. "Of course, Miles broke his wrist the first week after the resolution passed and he had to sit and watch his friends reap the benefits all that summer."

It all sounded so wholesome. Lori wondered how someone would describe her life. They certainly wouldn't use words like "responsible" and "considerate" to refer to the last several years, that's for sure. She possessed as much pride and ambition as Miles clearly did, only hers had fueled a need to feel accepted into a world she had no business belonging to. Guilt gnawed at her as she was reminded of the crimes she had ignored simply to realize her dream of operating her own restaurant.

Lori squeezed the pillow between her hands. Time was running out for her here in Chances Inlet. She had no business tarnishing the image of the B and B and the good people in it. As soon as Patricia was mobile, Lori needed to move on.

"I didn't realize mutilating guest pillows was part of your duties."

Lori's head snapped around toward the suite's entryway to see Miles, leaning up against the doorframe, his arms crossed over his chest. His shirtsleeves were rolled up, revealing well defined, tanned forearms. The blue of his dress shirt deepened the color of his azure eyes. The heat Lori saw in them made her mouth go dry. Before she knew what he had in mind, he was prowling across the room toward her and extracting the pillow from her hands.

"I'm just gonna rescue this little guy before you decompress all of his stuffing, okay?" One corner of his mouth kicked up into that half smile of his. The one he only gave to Lori. Everyone else—Greer Rossi included—got the full-wattage version. Just not her.

Finding her breath and her moxi, Lori stood up and snatched the pillow back. She marched across the room, deliberately putting the expanse of bed between them, and placed the pillow against the headboard before smoothing out the comforter.

"I've put your friend in here. I hope that's okay with you."

He looked a little baffled as he glanced around the room. "I'm sure Greer will love it."

"And will you be doing the turn-down service yourself?" Each night, Lori turned down the guests' beds, leaving a tray of handcrafted chocolates and mints on the pillow.

Miles' hands went to his hips and he shot Lori a hard look. "Is there a reason you can't do it?"

Lori mentally slapped herself for being childish. She had no right to be jealous of any relationship Miles had. There was nothing between him and Lori but a very potent attraction—one that neither one of them had any business acting on. Miles was a good man who didn't need to be saddled with who Lori had become.

"I just thought . . ." she said sheepishly.

"You just thought wrong." Miles' tone was as frustrated as Lori felt. "Greer and I are friends. *Without* benefits." His tone softened. "I think I've made it clear that I'd rather peel back the layers on you."

His statement shocked her and Lori sucked in a breath. "Stay the course, Miles," she whispered. "She's good for you." Her words were meant to encourage him as much as herself.

"And you're not." It wasn't a question because they both knew the statement was true.

"No."

His sigh was heavy as he pulled his fingers through his hair. "It's not working. I need specifics."

"I can't give you those. It's only for another month. Then I'll be out of your life. No longer distracting you."

"And what am I supposed to do until then?"

Lori glanced at the mattress where Greer would be spending the night. "I'm sure you'll think of something."

Miles swore quietly as Lori walked around the bed. Slipping past him, she'd almost made it to the door before his hand shot out, lightning fast, and shackled her wrist. With one gentle tug her body was flush against his hard one. Lori inhaled a ragged breath. He smelled of soap and mint. She made the mistake of tilting her head back to look at his face and the desire she saw reflected in his eyes made her knees weak.

"In case you haven't noticed, I don't give up that easily," he murmured as he released her wrist and cupped her face.

His lips were on hers before she could react. By that time, it was too late. His tongue had insinuated itself inside her mouth and Lori gave in without protest. She fisted her hands in his shirt, opening her mouth wider to him. Lori was determined to enjoy the moment that should never have happened.

The kiss he gave her was raw and hot. Miles explored her mouth as though he was charting it for future excursions. Her body grew restless under the assault as heat shot to her belly. His hands slid from her face to trace her spine before landing on her ass. She felt the groan in the back of his throat as he pressed her hips against his arousal. The room began to spin slightly before Lori reined in her scattered wits.

Miles was kissing her. In the Aberdeen Suite with its massive queen bed and the door wide open. *What were they doing?* She grudgingly pulled out of their kiss and willed her hands to unclench from his shirt. Miles made no move to unhand her. Both were still breathing as if they'd just run a stage in one of his triathlons. Refusing to meet his eyes, Lori smoothed out the wrinkles across his chest.

"Don't pursue this, Miles. Please," she begged softly before stepping out of his embrace.

Apparently he was the gentleman that the older woman and the others were professing before the cameras because Miles reluctantly let her go, sliding his fingers along her bare arm as he did so.

Without looking up, Lori turned on her heel and started for the door again.

"Wait," he called after her. "I had a call from Mr. Swanston asking about the bracelet."

Lori halted at the threshold of the room and looked over her shoulder at him. "Nothing ever turned up in town?"

"No."

She shook her head. "It hasn't turned up here, either." Making matters worse, Lori still hadn't found her grandmother's ring. She could relate to Mrs. Swanston's distress because her stomach knotted up every time she thought of the missing gold band. It was painful to lose a part of her past. The past that she would be proud to have an old woman discussing on national television.

Miles sighed. "I'll tell him we'll keep looking."

Lori nodded before she hurried down the hall.

There was a reason Miles didn't do anything impulsive: spontaneity led to dissonance. And regret. The problem was he didn't regret kissing Lori. What he regretted was not bolting the door and sinking into her right there in the Aberdeen Suite. She would have relented. One more kiss and her body and her mouth would have stopped listening to her brain.

The more he didn't know about her, the more she turned him on, which was just plain idiotic. He'd meant what he'd said about peeling back her layers and discovering her secret. Since Miles already knew the secret of what was hidden beneath her bulky clothes, he was obsessed with knowing the rest. And that obsession continued to be a huge distraction.

"Miles, are you with me?" Coy was drumming his fingers on the old desk in his father's office.

"Yeah," Miles lied. He had no idea what subject the kid had launched into. He looked across the room at Greer, but her face was averted, studying her laptop. No help there. The three were spread out in Miles' campaign headquarters, plotting out his campaign appearances for the next week.

"The polling data doesn't lie," Coy continued. "Faye's campaign is picking up steam."

"That always happens when a new candidate enters a race. It's called the honeymoon period." Greer looked over her laptop at both men. "I really don't think it's any reason to panic. We just need to stay the course."

Stay the course. Lori had used that very same phrase five hours ago. Miles needed to heed both women's advice. Not only was Lori dangerous to his libido, but depending upon what—or who—she was hiding from, she was potentially a danger to his campaign, too. He was wise to keep that in mind. A part of him was grateful to her for putting up some resistance. At least the parts of him above his belt.

"What do we know about Faye's schedule?" Miles asked.

"It's almost a carbon copy of yours. She'll be at every picnic, parade, and fish fry within a hundred-mile radius during the upcoming Fourth of July weekend." Coy scowled at his tablet. "She somehow even wrangled an invitation to the party at the Dresden House your friend Will is throwing."

"Not Will. It's his wife Julianne's party. She owns a design company and manufactures much of the line of baby clothes locally. Julianne is all about women-owned businesses. She would have invited her long before Faye threw her hat in the ring." Miles leaned back in his late father's big leather chair, hoping to channel some sage advice about the campaign. Among other things.

"I think we can work it to our advantage to have Faye there." Both men shot a questioning look at Greer. "I mean it. Your friend Will and his wife are definitely in your camp, aren't they, Miles?"

"Jesus, I hope so." Miles let his head slump back against the cool leather.

"Perfect. Your friends will look magnanimous for inviting her. We can grab some unobtrusive video of you and Faye together. Coupled with what I shot today, we'll be able to paint a portrait of you as a commanding candidate who is gracious to his challenger. A guy who respects older Americans no matter what."

"I'm coming off as Mr. Squeaky Clean in these ads." Miles wasn't sure he was comfortable with the persona, especially since it begged for more scrutiny into his family.

"You are Squeaky Clean, Miles." Greer smiled at him. "Wear it like a badge of honor."

Squeaky Clean. The moniker didn't scream spontaneity, that's for sure. Instead, it felt a little . . . boring.

"I still think we need to find out if there's any dirt on Faye Rich," Coy said.

Miles rubbed his face with his hand. "That's a slippery slope, Coy. I really don't want to run a negative campaign."

"You *can't* run a negative campaign," Greer pointed out. Both men stared at her in silence. Greer let out a frustrated sigh. "We just discussed why not. Miles is squeaky clean. Therefore, a negative campaign might make him look like he's picking on a grandmother who has a recognition quotient that's off the charts. There's no way to go down that road and not reach the other side without smelling like crap."

An image of Lori flashed before Miles' eyes. If voters had access to his thoughts, they'd see he wasn't so squeaky clean. *Far from it.*

Kissing her had been a colossal mistake because it only stoked the fire more. He could still taste her. But any future encounters would be like playing Russian roulette with his freaking squeaky clean image. *Stay the course.* Miles would be wise to make that phrase his mantra while he focused on executing the plan he'd laid out all those years ago.

"She's right," he said, not bothering to elaborate that he was talking about multiple women. "No negativity."

Coy looked as if he might argue the point. Miles shook his head and Coy stood up with a huff. "I've got a happy hour meeting with some of the volunteers at Pier Pressure. If there's nothing else, I'll see you both in the morning."

No sooner had Coy left than Midas bounded into the room heralding the arrival of Gavin. Miles ran his fingers over the dog's silky fur, happy for Midas' distraction. Too bad he couldn't say the same for his owner's wise-ass demeanor.

"Hey, you kids. Working hard?" Gavin tossed a ball across the room and Midas scampered after it, nearly toppling the chair Coy had just vacated.

"We're just finishing up for the day." Greer broke out into one of those rapturous smiles that all women got when they were assaulted with Gavin's annoying charm.

"Excellent. I'm taking Ginger to dinner at the Thai place. We'd love for you to join us."

Miles narrowed his eyes at his brother, who was clearly

up to something. The women in the McAlister family likely wanted answers about his relationship with Greer and they'd sent Gavin as their fisherman.

"Thai sounds great." She shot a questioning smile at Miles. Clearly outnumbered, he shrugged and nodded at the same time. Greer checked her watch. "Do I have time to run back to the inn and freshen up? I also need to return a phone call or two. I can meet you back here in thirty minutes."

"It's summertime. We don't roll up the sidewalks until at least ten o'clock," Gavin teased. "Take all the time you need."

She slid her laptop into its leather case before hefting the bag onto her shoulder. "I won't be long." Greer leaned down to kiss Miles on the cheek before exiting the office.

Gavin watched her walk out, a shit-eating grin on his face. He let out an appreciative whistle when the lobby door closed behind her.

"It's not what you're thinking, Gavin," Miles said with an exasperated sigh.

"Seriously? You're not doing the wild thing with a hot number like that?" Gavin pulled out his phone. "I'm calling Ryan and Will. I think it's past time for an intervention. You're starting to scare me."

"You're the one who needs the intervention. Aren't you practically engaged? You shouldn't be looking at other women."

"I'm very happily practically engaged. But, bro, Greer Rossi is hot. With political polish and connections. You two are perfect for each other. What's wrong with you?"

Greer Rossi *was* perfect for him. Or more correctly, perfect for "Squeaky Clean Miles McAlister." The trouble was, he was beginning to realize that he might have an evil twin: Wild and Dirty Miles McAlister. And that guy? He scared the hell out of Miles.

"Nothing's wrong with me, asshole. Believe it or not, I can have a working relationship with a woman without thinking of her as a sex object."

Gavin snorted. "Hey, so can I."

"Bernice doesn't count."

"Bernice doesn't kiss me on the cheek or look at me like she wants to go down on me right here in the office."

They both were stunned into silence as they processed Gavin's statement. Miles stood up from his chair and shivered with revulsion. "Ick."

Gavin wiped his mouth with his hand. "Yeah, sorry. That's a mental picture I'm going to have to burn out of my brain."

The dog head-butted Miles' thigh, dropping the slobbery ball at his feet. Miles reached down and tossed the ball. "I don't have time for women right now. In case you haven't noticed"—he waved a cardboard yard sign at his brother—"I'm in the middle of a campaign."

Gavin held up his hands in front of his chest. "Jesus, Miles, you've been in the middle of a campaign for something since you were a kid. That shouldn't preclude you from having a healthy relationship with a woman. It may even make the process a little more enjoyable. At the very least, you wouldn't be so damn testy all the time."

"Oh, I get it." Miles tugged at the ball in the dog's mouth. "You and Will are happy with a ball and chain on so everyone else you know needs to be in a committed relationship, too. Let me know how that goes over with our brother Ryan and his harem of groupies in every ballpark. When he falls, I'll fall."

Gavin shook his head. "You're a pain in the ass, you know that?"

Miles blew out a breath. "Look, Gavin, I'm happy for you. I really am. Ginger is special. A girl who loves you like that only comes along once in a lifetime, bro. My advice to you is to put a ring on her finger before she wakes up and smells the coffee."

His brother flipped him off. "Ginger made some appetizers that are surprisingly edible. When Greer gets back, come on up for a drink before we head out to the restaurant. Let's go, Midas. It's dinnertime." The dog trotted toward the stairs and Gavin followed, stopping at the base of the steps. "You're wrong about the once-in-a-lifetime thing, though, Miles," he said over his shoulder. "You just have to stop closing yourself off and let it happen." With that, he was gone.

Miles sank back into their father's chair. Gavin didn't know what he was talking about. No way was love going to 'happen' for Miles a second time. He wasn't about to open himself up to that kind of pain again, no matter how much his brother and Will Connelly sung love's praises. Lust, on the other hand, was a different story. Too bad the woman he was presently lusting over was potentially a ticking time bomb.

NINE

Patricia winced as the physical therapist manipulated her hip. It had been over a month since the accident, and while she was progressing, she was frustrated with the slow pace of her recovery.

"So what's the verdict, Jane?" Patricia was sweating from both the exertion and the agony of her daily workout.

"The verdict is that all women in their fifties should vigilantly do Pilates like you. That way if they ever break something, their rehab will be easy." Jane gave her one of those smiles that was equal parts encouraging and equal parts sadistic. "Just one more set and we can be done for the day."

"Clearly we don't have the same definition of 'easy,'" Patricia panted.

Jane laughed charmingly. "You're my hero, Mrs. Mac. In more ways than one."

The physical therapist had grown up in Chances Inlet under the watchful eye of her grandmother, Connie, while Jane's parents traveled the world as missionary doctors. She'd been friends with Kate when the two were in high school, but Patricia couldn't remember whether Jane had graduated with

Miles or Gavin. With five kids, the high school years had all seemed to run together. Jane had gone to N.C. State—Patricia did remember that—because she'd been working as one of the sports trainers when Gavin blew out his knee playing football for the Wolf Pack.

After graduate school, Jane married a Navy pilot. He was killed five years later in a training accident. Three years ago, she'd returned to the only home she knew, Chances Inlet, to work at one of the premiere sports rehab facilities in the country. The two women had bonded quickly at a support group meeting for recent widows.

"I meant, what's the verdict on me going to Julianne's Fourth of July party the day after tomorrow?" Patricia asked when she'd finished her final set of leg lifts.

Jane handed her a towel. "Not on your own two feet. But I think you'll be able to manage it on crutches. Especially with that big strapping sheriff by your side. No one will dare bump into you."

"Not if they don't want to find themselves locked up for the weekend." Lamar arrived at Patricia's side, a bottle of water in his hand. He unscrewed the cap and offered it to her.

"Strapping" was too tame a word to describe Lamar, especially looking like he did after his workout. Dressed in an Army T-shirt that strained against his muscular chest and shorts that showed off his well-toned thighs, he looked like he was ready to be cast in one of those live-action hero movies. It hadn't escaped Patricia's notice that the eyes of every other female in the large room tracked his movements as he made his way toward her. An obscene burst of pride exploded in her chest; he was all hers. It was followed by a constricting of her heart. *What if he's changed his mind?*

She gulped the water, trying to look anywhere but at his handsome, rugged face.

"How was your session?" His question was as gentle as the hand stroking her shoulder.

Jane answered for her. "Mrs. Mac is tough as nails, Sheriff. She'll be giving you a run for your money soon enough." Jane bundled a large ice pack over her hip area. "Fifteen minutes chillin' and then you're free to go. Keep up those home exercises and I'll see you next week."

The gray-eyed brunette handed Patricia an egg timer and headed across the room toward another patient.

Lamar eyed the ice pack Patricia held to her hip. "Do you want me to hold that for you?" Patricia hated what he must be thinking.

"You heard Jane. I'm perfectly capable. I'm healing just fine." She didn't mean to sound so snappish, but she was getting sick of being treated like a fragile flower.

Lamar patted her hand. "I'm glad."

"Are you?" This wasn't the time or place for this conversation, but the words had already slipped past Patricia's lips. Lamar had helped her discover so much about herself after Donald's death. She wasn't ready to give up on who she'd become. Or on him. But she needed to know if he still felt the same way.

"Of course I am, Tricia." He leaned down and took her mouth in a reassuring kiss that likely had the women who'd been ogling him earlier fanning themselves with jealousy.

"I miss you," she murmured against his mouth.

"Your hip will be better soon."

"I'm not talking about in the physical sense."

He pulled back slowly and she met his unwavering gaze.

"You can count on me, Tricia," he said with quiet determination. "You know that."

She knew without a doubt that she and everyone else in town could count on this man to do what was fair and what was just. That wasn't the issue. Patricia just worried that she might not be enough to keep him happy.

"The natives are getting restless for more cinnamon French toast, Lori." Cassidy came into the kitchen carrying two empty juice carafes. The second hour of breakfast had just gotten under way and the inn was at capacity for the long Fourth of

July weekend. "Everybody decided to eat at once today." She grabbed a carton of orange juice out of the fridge and began refilling the carafes.

Lori pulled a tray of bacon out of the warmer. "It's a perfect day out there. I can't blame them for wanting to get an early start." The weather forecasters promised a weekend of sunny, warm weather, perfect for a holiday at the beach.

"I know. I need to get the Patty Wagon stocked up for the day. I should make some good money over the next three days if I park down by the pier." Cassidy put the refilled carafes on a tray. "Will you be able to handle the rest of breakfast on your own? Or should I ask Miles to come in and help?"

The last thing Lori needed was Miles in the kitchen. Or anywhere within a fifty-mile radius of her, for that matter. Yesterday's kiss in the Aberdeen Suite had been reckless and wild. *Not to mention, enthralling.* Miles McAlister definitely did not kiss like his Dudley Do-Right personality. Instead he'd kissed her like a man who knew how to give a woman what she wanted. And now Lori definitely wanted. She wanted badly.

"No, I've got it covered."

It would mean a few extra trips into the dining room, but Lori hoped the guests would be more focused on their food than on her. She stacked the pan of bacon on top of the pan of French toast and waded out before the prying eyes of the diners. The room was filled with a jovial crowd of retirees who had come to Chances Inlet for the Independence Day boat flotilla, a golf tournament, and some antiquing, based upon what Lori had overheard.

"Oh, bacon!" One of the ladies was helping herself before Lori even had the tray in the chafing dish. "I never cook the stuff because it's so messy. Breakfast is my favorite meal to eat out." Based on her accent, the woman was from the New Jersey, New York area. Lori's pulse began to race. The media in the tri-state area had been relentless with their feeding frenzy about the scandal surrounding her father. And by extension, Lori. Her picture had appeared in every newspaper, blog, and television news show in the area for months. She did her best not to appear rude as she kept her back to the woman.

"You have gorgeous hair." The woman gestured to the long braid that hung down Lori's back. "I own a hair salon in Port Washington, New York. I always do a little ambush makeover when I'm traveling and blog about it on my website. You'd be perfect."

Lori bit down on the panic that was bubbling up inside her. She needed to stay calm and think fast. If she refused, the woman would want to know why, and Lori would be faced with more unwanted attention.

"That's very generous of you." An idea popped into her head and Lori gave the woman a look that she hoped would be conveyed as shy and not anxious. "But there's someone else here at the B and B who deserves it more, a teenager that the innkeeper has taken under her wing. She's struggling with trying to find the right look. Her mom is going through some tough times right now." Lori discreetly left out the fact that Mona Burroughs was in a halfway house at the moment. "I know Cassidy would be thrilled at the opportunity. The whole town would be, as a matter of fact."

The hairdresser bought it hook, line, and sinker. "Oh my gosh, wouldn't that make a wonderful blog post! Her name is Cassidy, you said?" She glanced around the room as if she expected the teen to appear.

Lori let out a relieved breath. "Yes. She operates the Patty Wagon. It's a mobile ice cream stand. Look for her down by the pier today." She'd spoken the truth; Cassidy would be thrilled by the attention. If anything, Lori could take some delight in her subterfuge.

After scooping up several more pieces of bacon, the woman practically skipped back to her table, calling out her thanks over her shoulder. Lori finished refilling the chafing dishes and made for the refuge of the kitchen. Unfortunately, her sanctuary had been invaded by Miles. And his so-called *friend without benefits*, Greer.

"My mind was a little preoccupied last night and I don't

remember taking it off. I might not have even had it with me," Greer was saying as Lori slipped into the kitchen trying not to think about why the woman had been preoccupied while undressing the night before.

"You had it on. I noticed it when we were at campaign headquarters." Miles' tone was agitated.

"I'll make sure I look more thoroughly between the bed and the nightstand before I check out, then." She gave Miles' biceps a squeeze. "Don't worry about it. It'll turn up either here or at home. I'm going to grab a cup of coffee to go. We need to head out to get some footage of you with the Boy Scouts placing flags at the veterans' cemetery." Greer stopped as she passed by Lori. "I seem to have misplaced my Michael Kors watch," she explained. "It's silver with a pink face. If you see it, will you put it aside for me?"

"Of course." Lori nodded. That queasy feeling was back in her stomach. Another piece of jewelry was missing. She exchanged a quick look with Miles. His expression was hard.

"There's a distinct possibility it's sitting on my nightstand at home," Greer said, her tone self-deprecating. "I'm multitasking so much lately, I think I've overloaded my brain."

Lori could relate. Greer ran a business where she had to keep multiple clients happy. Her workload sounded a lot like the one Lori had managed for her father while running the restaurant. She gave Lori a sheepish smile before heading out to the breakfast room.

"What are the chances it will show up with Mrs. Swanston's bracelet?" Miles' question caught Lori off guard. Dudley Do-Right was back and it sounded as though he suspected her of stealing them.

"You heard Greer; she said she might have left it in Raleigh."

"She didn't." Miles' tone was clipped. "I saw it on her wrist yesterday."

Lori turned to the sink, where she busied herself by adding dish soap and water to one of the dirty casserole pans. "Then I'm sure it will turn up."

"Funny. That's what you said about the bracelet."

She spun around to find him standing behind her, his hands

on his hips and that annoying probing look on his face. "What exactly are you implying, Miles?"

He didn't answer right away. Instead he closed his eyes and tilted his head down to his chest. "Maybe it's just a coincidence that we've had two people lose a piece of jewelry. I'm sure there has to be an industry matrix for this sort of thing that would tell us whether that's a normal number based on our occupancy rate."

Technically it was three pieces of jewelry that had gone missing—not that she was going to point that out to Miles. Lori really couldn't fault him for letting his thoughts go in the same direction as hers had gone. But it stung that he immediately thought the worst of her. Especially after the way he'd kissed her yesterday.

"I know you're looking for an excuse to hate me," she whispered. "But I don't steal." *At least not knowingly.*

Miles' eyes snapped open. Hunger and frustration were reflected in them. "Well, at least that's one layer gone." His hand drifted up toward her face. He jerked it back at the sound of voices behind them.

"So this is where the magic happens," a charming male voice said. "My compliments to the chef."

An older couple had wandered into the kitchen carrying their breakfast dishes as though they were going to load them into the dishwasher. Miles hustled over to retrieve the plates.

"We're glad you enjoyed your meal, Mr. and Mrs. Osterhaus. But clearing the table is included in your room rate," Miles joked.

"The wife, here, wanted to take a peek at the kitchen," Mr. Osterhaus said. His booming voice matched his tall body. "The rest of this place is so gorgeous that she figured the kitchen had to be, too." He glanced around the spacious room and gave a little whistle. "Don't get any ideas, Marcy. We aren't redoing the kitchen again."

Marcy took a few steps into the room, her orthopedic sandals squeaking on the hardwood floor. "Oh, Harry, I love that rack." She pointed to the handcrafted iron pot rack that hung above the end of the island closest to the stove. "I'll bet it was custom made."

Harry sighed like a man who couldn't deny his wife anything. "If I promise to get the name of the guy who made it, will you promise not to buy anything else this weekend?"

His wife bristled. "That is not going to happen."

He winked at Miles. "We won a little cash in the lottery a year or so back, and at this rate, we'll have nothing left to travel with."

That certainly explained the stunning jewelry Marcy Osterhaus was wearing. Lori said a silent prayer that the three missing items were just a coincidence. She ignored the fact that she was positive she hadn't misplaced her grandmother's ring.

"Come on, Marcy." Harry hooked an arm over his wife's shoulder and led her out of the kitchen. "I hear there's some nice shopping down in town. Will Connelly's wife and mother each have a boutique there."

"Who's Will Connelly?" they heard her ask.

Harry's laugh drifted back into the kitchen. "A professional football player."

Lori turned back to the sink. "I'll check the Aberdeen Suite thoroughly after breakfast. The common areas, too."

She heard Miles' sharp intake of breath behind her. "Yeah, okay."

The sound of Bernice and Coy's raised voices on the veranda drifted in through the screen door.

"Young man, I've been managing an office since before you were born. I certainly think I can supervise a gaggle of volunteers."

"Look, Bernice, they may be volunteers, but we need them focused on the task of getting Miles elected. I can't have you organizing the Dating Game with them every afternoon."

"A happy staff is a productive staff," Bernice argued.

Lori bit back a smile at Bernice's antics, but Miles ignored them both. She could feel the heat of his body at her back as he stepped in closer. His breath fanned her ear when he spoke.

"You're right about staying the course. I've got to think about my campaign and my future. Neither one of us is in a position where we can act on whatever this is between us. I promise not to cross the line with you again."

They stood like that, inches apart, both seemingly staring out the window, for a few long moments. Lori refused to succumb to the waves of disappointment rolling through her at the thought of his promise. It was best this way. She admired his purpose and drive. At the same time she resented that his ambition forced him to see the world in terms of black and white. There was no room in his life for muted gray Lori.

"Another place, another time," she whispered.

"I hope we get that chance," he replied with a heartfelt sigh. "I'd better go referee those two. Let me know if you find the watch, okay?" He brushed a kiss along the shell of her ear before pulling away and walking out the door.

Lori drew in a few deep breaths, blinking back the tears, before she submerged her hands in the soapy water and got back to work.

TEN

Dusk was closing in as the crowd spilled from the Dresden House terrace onto the grassy bluff overlooking the ocean. Many of the guests had brought lawn chairs or blankets to settle into when they watched the Fourth of July fireworks display later that evening. A trio of musicians had some of the partygoers dancing on the lawn with their cover of a Luke Bryan song.

"Julianne really outdid herself tonight." Miles was standing with his brother Gavin and Will Connelly, their hips resting against the second-floor balustrade overlooking the sea of people milling around below them. The Independence Day party was a fund-raiser for the Children's Center that Julianne had established in Will's name the year before. Judging by the number of people in attendance, the center would be operational for at least another year.

His friend scowled as his eyes tracked his very pregnant wife weaving her way among the guests, a radiant smile on her face. "*Over*doing it is more like it. I'm about ready to drag her out of here so she can go home and rest before she delivers that baby in the butler's pantry downstairs."

"Relax, Will. You act as if she's never had a baby before."

The words were out before Miles realized his mistake. Gavin shot him a look that shouted, *Way to go, dumbass.*

Will hadn't known about his son, Owen, until the baby was several weeks old. Julianne never intended to tell him their one-night stand had resulted in a child. But the baby had been born with a rare blood disorder requiring a transfusion from his father. He and Julianne had obviously worked things out. Not surprisingly, however, Will still carried some emotional wounds.

"Sorry." Miles clapped a hand on Will's shoulder. "I've been spouting out campaign rhetoric and platitudes all weekend. My mouth is moving on autopilot right now."

The big man let out a low growl as he kept his gaze trained on Julianne. "All that's important is that I'm in the delivery room this time. And both Julianne and the baby are healthy." He pulled away from the railing. "It's getting late. I'm going to take her home and watch the fireworks with Owen from our house. I'll see you two on the beach tomorrow morning."

Gavin leaned his forearms on the ornate wooden railing as Will headed for the stairs. "I hope you were more sensitive to your future constituents this weekend, Miles."

"Honestly?" Miles swiped at the tension holding the back of his neck hostage. "I wasn't kidding about being on autopilot. I don't remember half the crap I said during the campaign events I've packed into these last three days." Coy had booked him at thirteen different events from pancake breakfasts to a fish fry at the firehouse and a low country boil over on Bald Head Island. Indigestion churned in his stomach. "Or what I might have eaten. What I wouldn't give for a beer right now."

His brother gave him a discerning look before handing him his own bottle. Miles quickly scanned the room, then took a hurried swallow of the beer.

"You know, it is legal for you to drink alcohol now and then, bro," Gavin said with a chuckle. "You're not running for senior class president."

"Damn it, Gavin, I have an image to maintain."

"Actually, I think your image is maintaining *you*."

"What's that supposed to mean?" Miles demanded of his brother.

Except he'd already guessed the answer: *Damn Squeaky Clean Miles McAlister.* Gavin was right; he was coming across as an egotistical prig in this campaign. Miles took a healthy swig of the beer. He was beginning to really hate his public persona. Especially late at night when he was in bed. Alone.

His brother took back his bottle. "Having integrity doesn't mean you're infallible. You're just as human as the rest of us."

Miles wasn't going to argue. He knew exactly how fallible he was. Twice this weekend he'd ventured down the darkened hallway that led to the stairs up to Lori's room, only to have Squeaky Clean Miles yank on the leash and bark: *Stay the course.* He'd promised to leave her alone, but damn it, whatever was pulling him toward her was twice as loud and equally irritating in the quiet of the night.

While careful not to divulge her secret, she'd admitted that she was dangerous to his career and warned him off. Miles knew her warning wasn't born out of indifference, however. Her body language told him she felt the connection just as deeply as he did. Even worse, despite her caution, he still wanted her. It was costing him to be honorable, to be squeaky clean. For the first time, he felt trapped by the damn list of goals he'd made up as a kid.

"You're not a robot," his brother was saying. "Stop acting like one. It just makes you seem like you're better than the rest of us."

"And we all know he's not." His sister Kate came up beside Miles, playfully nudging him in the shoulder with one of her own.

Gavin calling him out was bad enough, but Kate took way too much satisfaction in pointing out Miles' shortcomings. "Butt out," he warned her, cursing his abundance of know-it-all siblings under his breath.

Kate laughed. "I was sent up here by Coy, the Boy Wonder. He wanted me to tell you—and I quote—that Faye Rich is in the building."

From their vantage point, Miles watched as the stocky, white-haired woman and her entourage made their way through the crowd. Despite the fact that they'd both attended nearly all the same events over the holiday weekend, this was the first time their paths had crossed.

Kate's theatrical gasp was surely meant to irritate him. "Uh-oh, she's going to kiss our mother on the cheek. Are you sure you've got Mom's vote locked up?" Sure enough, Faye embraced their mother warmly.

Miles was worried about a lot of issues where their mother was concerned, but how she voted in the upcoming election wasn't one of them. He stepped away from his siblings and headed for the stairs.

"Better grab a mint on the way down, bro," Gavin teased. "You don't want your opponent to smell the beer on your breath."

Their obnoxious laughter followed him as he descended the wide, grand staircase. Miles tuned it out as Coy intercepted him on the bottom step.

"This technically isn't a campaign stop for her." Coy tried to steer him away from the area where his mother was seated, resting her hip. Lamar loomed over her like one of the giant trees that surrounded her inn. Faye Rich was holding his mother's hand between hers while the two women spoke quietly together. Both women had served as the president of the local Rotary Club and acted as mentors to women operating their own businesses. Miles wasn't sure if their relationship was built on mutual respect or a true friendship, but he was about to take advantage of it either way.

"I really don't think this is a good idea, Miles."

"Well, if it backfires, I'll be sure and tell the governor that you warned me." Stepping around Coy, Miles put a hand on his mother's shoulder and gave it a little squeeze. She looked up at him in surprise. "Happy Fourth of July, ladies," he said.

"Oh, Miles, you look as tired as Faye does." His mother's concern was genuine as she looked between him and Faye. Miles relaxed a bit, picking up the cue that Faye and his mother were, in fact, friends. His strategy just got a bit easier to execute.

"You've both been campaigning at full speed this weekend. Take some time to relax and enjoy the fireworks." His mother gestured toward the other side of the room. "Julianne has a wonderful spread of food in the dining room."

Faye smiled down at his mother, still holding her hand between her own. "I'm going to steal a few of those fabulous cupcakes you serve at the inn for tea, but I'm taking them home to my grandbabies. I promised I'd watch the fireworks with them. I just wanted to stop by and say hello to you. I'm so glad you're feeling better and that you're up and about." She hugged his mother a second time. "My being here is disrupting the party, so we'll just head on out."

Miles glanced around to see that many of the guests had focused their attention on Faye. And on him. He scowled at Cassidy, who was videoing the exchange between his opponent and his mother. "Cass, can you get Mrs. Rich some cupcakes to take home, please?"

Cassidy gave him a startled look before quickly stuffing her phone in her back pocket and heading toward the dining room.

"Thank you, Cassidy. The kids love the ones with rainbow sprinkles," Faye called after her. She lowered her voice and spoke to his mother. "It'll be good to get home. My feet are killing me!"

"I wonder if I can get a minute with you in private," Miles interjected.

His mother's look was skeptical but Faye's smile didn't waver, almost as if she was expecting the unusual request. Miles felt the eyes of everyone in the room follow them to the butler's pantry located next to the front door. There were murmurs about early fireworks, but Miles ignored them. Coy and the rest of Faye's group shadowed their footsteps all the way. As Faye preceded him into the room, Miles held up a hand, stopping Coy and Faye's staff in their tracks.

"We'll only be a minute." Miles gave them all a look that left no room for argument before closing the door behind him.

"I wasn't kidding about my feet," Faye said as she climbed into one of the director's chairs. The cubby-sized room had been used by Ginger as a makeup station when *Historical Restorations* had filmed there earlier that year and the chairs remained as mementos. "I envy you being able to wear sensible shoes all day."

"Can I get you something to drink?"

She raised an eyebrow. "We're not going to be here that long, are we?"

Miles smiled in spite of himself. He liked this lady. She was good for the community. Well connected and well respected, she would make a decent representative. He wasn't sure she knew the first thing about politics, but hell, neither did half the people in Washington. As far as he could tell, she was a woman of character and he was hoping to tap into that tonight.

Leaning a shoulder against the closed door, he crossed his arms over his chest, debating with himself about how to proceed. Coy was right, he probably should have given this conversation more thought. But his campaign manager was wrong about one thing: This talk needed to happen.

"I find it's best to just dive in with both feet," she said softly. "That way we can both be sure to see the fireworks tonight."

"I'm only asking this to protect my mother from more pain." Miles sighed heavily. "It's about my father—"

"Let me stop you right there." Faye held up her palm to him. "This campaign has nothing to do with your father. It's about electing someone to fix what's wrong in Washington. Tanya Sheppard and the rest of the media can try to make it about Donald McAlister, but I certainly won't. Your daddy was a good man. And your mother is a dear friend." She grimaced as she shifted in the chair. "Of course, I probably should hate her for snagging such a virile man for a fiancé, but after all she's been through, she deserves a second chance at happiness."

Miles' gut clenched at the reference to Lamar, but he was going to have to get over his constant visceral reaction to the sheriff's relationship with his mother. He made a mental note to work on that tomorrow. Tonight, he needed to work things out with his opponent.

Faye slid from the chair. "Keep in mind, I can promise only so much. You know as well as I do that the PACs and the party strategists are the ones to go rogue more often than not. But I'll do my best to keep the focus on you and not your family." She reached up and patted him on the shoulder. "The problem is that you have such a pristine image, there's nothing else to go negative on. Help an old lady out, will you? Do something outrageous," she suggested with a wink.

"I have a feeling that you're not going to need any help." Miles extended his hand.

Faye placed her own hand in his and pumped his arm up and down. "Let's give the voters a positive experience."

The crowd was still focused on them when they exited the room. Faye smiled as she took the container of cupcakes from Cassidy. "You're really growing up to be a beautiful young lady, my dear," she said before waving to the crowd and heading out the door.

Miles took a closer look at the teenager. Something was different about her tonight. He just couldn't put his finger on it.

"Well?" Greer appeared at his side, interrupting his scrutiny of Cassidy. "How was your chat with Faye? Did she agree to play nice?"

"Even if she did, it'll never work," Coy said from behind her. "I still say you need some dirt on her just in case."

Greer released an exasperated sigh. "We've already covered this, Coy. Miles is running as a Boy Scout. He can't run a negative campaign."

Do something outrageous.

Faye's words echoed in his head, taunting Squeaky Clean Miles with their idea. He'd always taken the higher road, leading by example while chasing his dream. Up until recently, Miles could honestly say he never minded the path his life had taken. But when Faye had suggested doing something outrageous, Miles had immediately thought of Lori. And all the outrageous things he'd like to do with her.

"Come on." Greer linked her arm through his, rousting him out of his thoughts—thoughts that could only lead to no good. "Let's go line up some endorsements from Julianne and Will's famous friends before I have to head back to Raleigh."

Lori's legs were numb but she didn't dare move. Tessa had finally fallen asleep on her lap and she didn't want to wake her. The dog clearly wasn't a fan of loud noises, which struck Lori as kind of funny given that Tessa had lived as a stray on the streets of New York prior to taking up residence in North Carolina.

The fireworks had ended nearly a half hour ago and guests were wandering noisily back into the B and B. Lori had left a few platters of desserts in the library, which meant she'd need to clean up later. For now, though, she stroked her fingers through Tessa's satiny fur and thought about Independence Day in another small town. Were folks there enjoying the pyrotechnic display over the bay? Had they churned homemade ice cream on the porch? Or waved little American flags as they marched down Main Street behind the fire truck?

Lori's chest ached as she remembered that happy, simpler time in her life. *And how she always wanted more.* She'd wasted all those precious days dreaming of the glitzy, glamorous life her father lived—wanting him to want his daughter to be a part of it.

One of the guests was playing "New York, New York" on the music room's piano, and Lori recalled her first Fourth of July gala on her father's rooftop in Manhattan. The Empire State Building was lit up in red, white, and blue against the night sky as fireworks exploded behind the Statue of Liberty. Lori had been dressed in the uniform of the Hamptons, a chic Lilly Pulitzer dress, while drinking a Cosmopolitan from actual stemware—no red Solo cups at this celebration. The food was served by waiters dressed in white tuxedos, and even the ice cream was some designer flavor made especially for the occasion. Lori had never felt as sophisticated as when her father was escorting her around the rooftop and introducing her to his powerful and wealthy guests. Her sophistication had been a sham, though. She'd been pretending to enjoy herself because that evening on her father's arm was all she'd ever wanted.

Sitting on the dark back porch of the B and B and looking back on that night now, she acknowledged that she'd felt like a fish out of water then. But Lori hadn't been pretending as much as her father had been. His entire life had been a sham.

Tessa jerked back to alertness at the sound of hurried footsteps on the wooden steps.

"Oh my gosh, Lori, I almost tripped over you." Cassidy halted at the top of the stairs. "What are you doing sitting in the dark?"

Hiding. Lori didn't say it out loud. She was so tired of hiding, though. If only she could erase the last years and go back home. Never again would she pine for a different life; that was for sure. But home was out of the question now. Maybe forever. Still, she needed to find a place where she could have a life again. Just not here. As much as Chances Inlet reminded her of home, disappearing in a small town was next to impossible. Diesel had sent word that he had something lined up for Lori in Nashville. As soon as Patricia was healthy again, she'd move on.

Which meant she needed to find her grandmother's ring, pronto.

"I'm just enjoying the night air. Where are you off to in such a hurry?"

Cassidy sat down beside her and Tessa nuzzled the girl's arm. "I just need to get something in my room. I'm meeting some friends down at the pier."

"Showing off your new look?"

A demure smile spread over Cassidy's face. "Isn't it awesome? Thanks for arranging it for me." The hairdresser had spent part of the morning coloring and cutting Cassidy's hair, giving her a softer, more carefree look. Given that much of the teenager's life hadn't ever been carefree, the change suited Cassidy.

Lori reached over and brushed a stray hair off the teenager's face. "You deserve it. Consider it a graduation gift. A new look for college life."

"Hard to believe I'll be blowing this popsicle stand next month. I've been dreaming of getting out of here for so long. But now . . ." She shrugged.

Swallowing down the heartache that had been clogging her throat for the last hour, Lori gently squeezed the girl's leg. "You may be leaving physically, but this place will be with you wherever you go. Small towns are like that. This place will always be your home."

"You could unpack your bags and make it your home, too."

With a shake of her head, Lori tried to lighten the mood.

"Once you've gone, this place will lose a lot of its charm. There's no point in me sticking around."

Cassidy's phone buzzed and she glanced at the screen. "That's Kyle. I've got to bolt."

"There's a lot going on downtown tonight, Cassidy. Make smart choices."

The teenager stared at her openmouthed.

Lori cringed. "I sounded like a mother there, sorry."

Before she realized it, Cassidy had thrown her arms around Lori, wrapping her in a bear hug. Knowing the teenager's history, she'd likely never had anyone care about her whereabouts or the choices she made. Stunned into silence, she peered over Cassidy's shoulder, where she spied Miles in the shadows of the veranda, leaning against the railing.

"Make sure you're home by eleven, Cassidy," he said.

"Eleven?" Cassidy squeaked as she pulled away from Lori and assumed her normal, belligerent posture.

Miles' pose remained relaxed in the face of a blustering teenage girl. "If that's too late for you, we can make it ten thirty."

"No!" Cassidy huffed out a breath. "I'll be home by eleven. I didn't realize I was living in a prison."

She stomped down the front steps, whatever she needed from her room apparently forgotten in her haste to meet up with her friends.

"Oh, by the way," she called over her shoulder. "Mr. Maxwell, the guest in the Glasgow Suite, can't find his pen. It's one of those fancy silver ones. A Montblanc. He's pretty stressed about misplacing it." She shrugged. "I offered him one from the inn, but he didn't seem to want that one. He wanted to talk to management. He's all yours, Miles." With a jaunty salute, she vanished into the dark evening.

Miles swore softly before stepping away from the railing. Bathed in the soft glow of the porch light, his handsome face looked both frustrated and tired. Lori figured after the grueling weekend of nonstop campaigning, he should get an award for still being upright. With a heavy sigh, he sat down on the step beside her. Tessa placed her head in Lori's lap and eyed him warily.

"So what does that bring our total of missing items up to?" he asked. "A bracelet, a watch, and a pen have somehow been 'misplaced' inside the B and B."

"And a ring." Lori hadn't meant to ever mention her missing ring, but the words slipped out anyway. She blamed it on the hot guy sitting next to her. Clearly, her ovaries had overtaken her common sense.

Miles slowly turned his head to look at her. "A ring?"

Lori nodded.

"Whose?" he asked in a tone that clearly indicated he'd already guessed the answer.

"Mine."

He snorted out a breath. "That's convenient."

She tried not to let his statement wound her, but it did. "Because you still want me to be the thief?"

Miles was silent for a long moment as he rested his head in his hands, seemingly contemplating a worm hole in the wooden decking. "I told you before, it would make things a hell of a lot easier," he finally said.

"You mean it would make me less desirable," she whispered.

His head shot around again. "Yes." He forced the word out. Anguish and longing flashed in his eyes before Lori quickly looked away. She knew her own eyes would give her away by reflecting similar emotions. Emotions that she had no business feeling for Miles McAlister.

Miles placed his hands on the wood, the fingertips of his right hand a fraction of an inch away from her own. Arching his back, he shifted his head from side to side. "So if it's not you, then who is it?"

"Well, things started to go missing a couple of weeks ago. Right about the time you moved in."

He stilled, once again slowly turning his face toward hers. Lori raised an eyebrow, letting her accusation hang in the humid night air.

"Two can play at the same game," she said softly.

Miles' long-suffering sigh mingled with the sounds of tree frogs and cicadas before he glanced at the infinitesimal space separating their hands. "So you're saying you have the same desires?"

"I've never denied that I did." Lori slid her hand back an inch. "But that doesn't mean we should act on them."

"Yeah." He shoved his hands through his already mussed-up hair.

Lori wasn't sure how long they sat in companionable silence listening to the sounds of the B and B quieting down around them. But Miles startled both her and the dog when he finally spoke. "I'll check with Lamar in the morning to see if this kind of stuff is going on elsewhere in town. In the meantime, I'd appreciate it if my mom didn't find out about the missing items. It would only worry her. I don't suppose the ring you're missing was costume jewelry?"

Lori shook her head. "It's a gold wedding band."

He stiffened beside her. She almost let him believe what he was so obviously thinking. But something deep inside her wanted him to know at least this one small truth about her. She'd ruined her chances at a future and a happily ever after with a guy like Miles, but that didn't mean she didn't want him to respect her just a bit. Her pride was all she had left.

"Not mine. It was my grandmother's. She died when I was eighteen. It was the one thing she left for me." Lori shrugged. "She said it would bring me luck." Of course, that luck had run out a few months ago. But that didn't mean Lori didn't want it back anyway.

He reached across her lap and stroked Tessa on the head. "Write down a description of it for me and where you last saw it and I'll have Lamar check the pawn shops. Let's just hope that nothing else goes missing."

"Hey, you two." Mr. Osterhaus stuck his head out the screen door. "The missus and I were just wondering if you had any more of those delicious strawberry brownies. She hates to take her bedtime medicine on an empty stomach, you know."

As Lori scrambled to her feet, she immediately thought of Mrs. Osterhaus' ostentatious diamond earrings and hoped that Miles was right and nothing else went missing. "Of course, let me get you a couple."

ELEVEN

"What do you mean, things have gone missing from the inn?" If Lamar had been surprised to see Miles crossing the threshold of the sheriff's office that morning, he hadn't shown it. The guy was as stoic as the Terminator. But he was definitely showing some emotion now. "Does your mother know about this?"

"No." Miles leaned back in the leather chair across from the sheriff's metal desk. A glass wall separated his office from the meager squad room, where two deputies and Valerie Jamison, the receptionist, sat. Valerie liked to remind everyone that she'd asked him to the Sadie Hawkins Dance sophomore year, where she was the recipient of his first kiss. As if having the sheriff engaged to his mother wasn't enough to keep Miles away from the jailhouse, Valerie's detailed, glowing description of their encounter that had appeared in the local paper after he'd announced his candidacy certainly didn't help. Miles was ashamed to admit he couldn't remember the kiss much less it being all that special.

"Good," Lamar was saying. "Your mother needs to focus

on healing right now. She'd be too distracted if she thought someone was stealing from her guests."

He couldn't help bristling at the sheriff's words. "I think I know my mother well enough to predict how she would react. That's why I haven't said anything to her yet."

Lamar squeezed at his brow with his long fingers. "Is this how it's going to be from now on, Miles? You acting like a petulant five-year-old every time your mother comes up in conversation? I'm not some bully who's stealing your lunch money. And I'm not going anywhere. I'm just a guy who happens to think your mother is something special. Considering that you feel she's special, too, I'd think that would give us something to agree on once in a while."

Damn it. Miles hadn't come here to be chastised by the man who had replaced his father in his mother's bed. He stared out the one window in the office, watching as a little boy—four or five perhaps—tried to climb on the old Civil War cannon that stood near the town square. *How many times did I do the same thing while my dad looked on?* The boy sat astride the monstrous weapon, his legs too short to hang over the sides, laughing as his father took his picture. Miles' chest squeezed. His father wasn't coming back. Ever. He needed to embrace that fact and move on.

Lamar was right that he was behaving poorly. He really had nothing against the sheriff. Miles had called in favors and done some digging, and by all accounts the man was a stand-up guy. Except for the part about him having sex with Miles' mother. He suppressed a shudder at the thought. For the sake of his mom, though, he'd overlook that part and stop busting the guy's balls every time he got the opportunity.

"Why don't we start by working together to figure out what's going on at the inn?" As peace offerings went, it was the best Miles could come up with right now. "Nothing major has gone missing, that I know of." He was relieved to check Mr. and Mrs. Osterhaus out this morning with all of her jewelry accounted for. "A charm bracelet, a watch, a silver pen, and a gold wedding band. All of them could have been misplaced somewhere, but

I know Greer had the watch on the night she stayed here. I saw it on her wrist."

"Crimes of opportunity perhaps," Lamar said as he typed on his tablet. "Someone walking by an open room and seeing the item in view."

"Except that doesn't explain the wedding band. Lori said she had it zipped up in her duffel bag."

A quizzical look appeared on Lamar's face at the mention of Lori. *Had he suspected her as well?*

"The wedding band is Lori's?" Lamar sounded as surprised with the notion that Lori was married as Miles had been the previous evening.

"Her grandmother's."

The sheriff's face relaxed. "That makes more sense," he said quietly, almost as though he was talking to himself.

Miles went on alert. Lamar knew something about Lori's past; he was sure of it. Gavin had mentioned months ago that the sheriff secretly checked out all of the inn's employees, just to make sure their mother was safe. For the first time, Miles could see a benefit to having the man sleeping beside his mom. It was only a small benefit in his opinion, though.

"It does seem a little coincidental that she's missing something, too." He tossed the remark out there just to see if the sheriff would bite.

"Coincidence doesn't make someone guilty, Miles. I'm sure they covered that in law school at some point."

"We don't know a thing about her. Who says she isn't a petty thief?"

Lamar glared at Miles over the readers he'd propped on his nose. "Is this a fishing expedition now? Are you trying to find out about Lori's past, Miles?"

Yes! "No. I came here this morning to make you aware of what's been happening at the inn and to see if anyone else in town has reported anything similar that was missing." He stared the sheriff down. "But you do know something about her, don't you?"

The sheriff leaned back against the high back of his leather chair. "I know enough about her to realize that she doesn't need to stoop to misdemeanor theft."

"Maybe she gets a thrill from it." Miles was angry at the sheriff again. He hated that this man knew Lori's secret and he didn't.

"If she did, why start now? She's been in town nearly five months and nothing has been reported missing at the B and B until recently."

"I take it that means nothing similar has been reported missing in town?"

The sheriff scanned his tablet. "Two stolen bikes, a garden gnome, a couple of kites from the outdoor display box in front of the hardware store, and a box of hair dye from the hair salon."

"Jesus, your job must be boring," Miles said without thinking about how degrading it sounded.

"It beats the hell out of being shot at by Afghan kids in the desert."

Miles tucked his chin to his chest and tried to think. "Maybe you're right and these were just crimes of opportunity. We've had nearly seventy guests in the B and B these past few weeks. Any one of them could be a klepto."

"Just in case, why don't you give me the descriptions of the missing items and I'll have Deputy Lovell check the pawn shops in the area. I can't have him sitting around bored on taxpayer's money, after all."

Miles accepted the dig with grace. "You'll let me know if you find anything?" he asked as he slid a piece of paper across the desk.

Lamar nodded. "That goes both ways. If anything else goes missing, give me a call right away."

"Still nothing on the hit-and-run driver?"

It was Lamar's turn to stare out the window. His jaw was clenched so tightly Miles was surprised the sheriff could get the words past his lips. "No. But I won't stop looking."

The fierceness of his answer touched a nerve in Miles. Clearly this man loved Miles' mother deeply if he wanted justice for the accident that vehemently.

"It's not your fault, you know," Miles said with a begrudging respect. "It was an accident and there was nothing any of us could have done to prevent it."

A look of raw anguish shadowed the older man's face before he shuttered it.

"Mom's going to be okay and life will go on whether you find the driver or not. She's happier than I've seen her in a long time and you're the cause of that. Don't let the pursuit of the driver consume you so much that you sacrifice what you've already got."

There was gratitude in Lamar's eyes when he reached out to shake Miles' hand. They likely reflected what was in his own eyes.

Valerie called out a merry good-bye as Miles made his way back out onto Main Street. The little boy was no longer using the cannon as a jungle gym, but the square was crowded with tourists enjoying the early cool before the afternoon heat settled over the town like a heavy blanket.

"The latest polling data isn't good," Coy said without preamble when Miles made his way into his campaign headquarters.

Miles slipped into his father's chair and the feel of the familiar, worn leather relaxed him immediately. "How so?" he asked.

"Faye Rich is up two more points. You guys are nearly neck and neck." Coy shoved his tablet in front of Miles. Colorful flow charts and graphs were displayed on the screen but Miles honed in on a list of questions at the bottom.

"Wait, were these the questions the pollsters asked?"

Coy fiddled with his bowtie. "Yes, Miles. We had to address the issues that have come up. Your father being one of them."

"Damn it, Coy, this campaign isn't about what my father did. It's about me and what I can do for the people of this district. Every time you ask a voter about my father, it just puts the whole damn thing back on the agenda. I want real issues on the agenda."

"We both know the media sets the agenda," Coy argued. "As long as they keep running with this story, we need to gauge how it's impacting your image as a viable candidate. And it *is* having an impact. Just look at the polling data."

Miles squeezed his eyes shut. He didn't always put much faith in polling data. Past experience taught him that those who answered the pollster's questions were the ones who were the most radicalized about a candidate or a cause. Still, he was annoyed that the subject of his father was still hanging around. Blaming Coy wouldn't solve anything, though. The kid was just doing his job.

Opening his eyelids, he saw Bernice standing in the threshold of the office, wringing her hands. Never a good sign.

"Tell him the rest of it, Coy," she said.

"There's a 'rest of it'?" Miles glanced over at Coy just as two pink circles formed on the kid's cheeks.

"It's just a stupid idea she has."

Bernice charged into the room. "It's not stupid. The pollsters put the family question out there. While single women like the idea of an unmarried representative, many voters would prefer Miles to be settled in his personal life. Faye Rich is a happily married grandmother of three. She practically radiates stability."

Miles slid his finger over the tablet to reveal the rest of the questions. Sure enough, Bernice was right. He dropped his forehead to the desk. "How did this get about me and not the issues?"

Coy snorted. "It's almost never about the issues any longer."

He heard the telltale jangle of Bernice's armload of bracelets as she approached the desk. "Don't worry, Miles. We can fix this. I have a plan."

"No, you don't have a plan, Bernice," Coy protested. "I can handle this. Greer and I will come up with a different media strategy to address this issue."

It's not an issue, Miles wanted to scream. At least not one that voters need to be worrying about.

"*Pfft*," Bernice said. "My plan is the only one that will work. Trust me, I've been matchmaking for twice as long as you've been alive, sonny boy."

"Enough!" Miles lifted his head off the desk. He wasn't sure which disturbed him more: having the issues of the campaign diluted or the threat of being the target of Bernice's overzealous matchmaking. It was bad enough the damn woman was being allowed to pick out his clothes. "We're not making this campaign about my personal life."

"Said every rookie candidate everywhere," Greer said from the office doorway.

Miles sighed with relief at the sight of her. Neat, polished, elegant Greer. She looked as if she'd just stepped out of a Junior League meeting with her glossy hair in a sophisticated bun and a string of dainty pearls circling her neck. Her green eyes smiled along with her pretty, pink lips.

Gavin was right to question Miles' man card: Why wasn't he exploring what was beneath Greer's tailored, peach-colored, linen suit? She certainly wasn't hiding anything dark and sinister. He tried to imagine what *was* underneath her clothes. Her body was probably perfectly proportioned and elegant like the rest of her. Too bad even Squeaky Clean Miles wasn't getting turned on by the thought. He sighed. Greer was strictly a friend, but it was good to have her in his camp.

"Greer, thank God you're here. Please talk some sense into these two."

She arched a delicate eyebrow. "Actually, I don't think we can ignore the family issue."

Bernice clapped her hands together. "Now all we have to do is find Miles a suitable girlfriend."

Coy released a beleaguered sigh. "I don't think that's what she meant, Bernice."

Miles pushed away from the desk.

"Where are you going?" Coy asked.

"It's Tuesday. I'm going to the senior center to play checkers with Mr. Cohen."

"I'll get some media on this," Coy said as he pulled out his phone.

"No." Miles had had enough of the media dogging him the past few days. He needed time to think. "Not everything I do is a part of the campaign."

Greer gave his elbow a gentle squeeze as he slipped past. "Your life isn't your own once you enter public office. Trust me. I know this firsthand."

Miles knew it, too. That didn't mean he had to like it.

* * *

Cassidy halfheartedly flung a sofa cushion onto the music room floor. The B and B was blissfully empty for one night and Lori had enlisted the teenager to help give it a thorough cleaning. Not to mention to conduct a methodical search for the missing items.

"I don't see what the fuss is about for a silly old pen anyway," Cassidy griped. "Nobody writes things down anymore. He could just, you know, use a stylus on his phone or his computer."

Lori reached her hand between the creases in the sofa. She found the wrapper to a lollipop and a paper clip, but no silver Montblanc pen. Or any of the other missing pieces, for that matter. "I know you think anyone over twenty-one is a fossil, Cassidy, but as far as I know, pens aren't obsolete yet. Besides, pens like that are more for status than practicality."

"Then why bring a stupid thousand-dollar pen on vacation?"

Crouching down on her hands and knees, Lori peered beneath the radiator. Nothing. "Just to be a show-off, I guess."

The sheriff's voice startled her. "Afternoon, ladies. No tea today?"

"We're taking a day off," Lori said, quickly getting to her feet. "We haven't any guests staying the night so Patricia canceled it."

"Well, that's disappointing. I was looking forward to one of those Coca-Cola cupcakes you make." His eyes drifted to where Cassidy was replacing the cushions on the sofa.

Lori hadn't seen Miles today to confirm whether or not he'd spoken to the sheriff, but the man's body language indicated he wanted a private conversation. "I have a few in the kitchen. Come on back and I'll fix you a cool drink to go with them."

"Great, leave me here to do all the work," Cassidy grumbled as they walked out.

They were silent as they passed through the main hallway trimmed in dark tiger oak wood. Dust motes floated in and out of the sunbeams that were streaming through the stained glass window located high above the main staircase landing.

Tessa looked up from her bed in the corner when they entered the kitchen. She gave her tail a gentle whack before resuming her nap in the sun.

"Have a seat." Lori gestured to one of the stools tucked under the big center island. She pulled out a container of mini cupcakes and placed three on a small plate for the sheriff. Setting them in front of him on the island, she went to the fridge and poured him a glass of milk.

"Uh-oh," he said, a trace of humor in his voice. "I'm becoming a regular if you know my drink preference by heart."

"They taste best with milk. I wouldn't serve them any other way." She handed him the glass. "Did Miles come to see you?"

The sheriff popped a cupcake in his mouth before nodding.

"I don't suppose you have any leads?" she asked. Something about his demeanor told her the news wasn't good, however.

"Deputy Lovell spent the day rummaging through the area pawn shops. Nothing matching the descriptions Miles gave me this morning turned up."

Lori reached for a dishtowel and wiped at the already shiny granite while a fresh wave of disappointment washed over her. Her grandmother's ring was the only tie she had left to her old life. The clock was ticking for her here in Chances Inlet, but she couldn't bear the thought of leaving without the ring. It was beginning to look like she might have to, though.

"Any chance you might have left the ring out somewhere?" he asked. "Maybe you've forgotten that you left it on the counter while you were doing dishes or baking."

She shook her head, fighting back the sting of tears. "I don't wear jewelry anymore. I always kept it in my duffel. In the side pocket."

He reached over and laid his big hand on top of hers, stilling her frantic motion. "Lots of people have been in and out of this B and B these past few weeks. Why don't you give me a list of the guests and I'll check for anything out of the ordinary. Include any deliveries that have been made, as well. Don't give up yet."

Lori nodded and he gave her hand a squeeze before reaching for another cupcake.

"Have you noticed anything else missing? Any of the silver serving pieces? Or the trinkets Tricia has scattered about the place?"

She shook her head before releasing a heavy sigh. "I don't have an exact inventory of every room, but I haven't noticed anything out of place or gone."

"Good. Let's hope it stays that way. With any luck, this was all just an ugly coincidence."

The look she gave the sheriff was meant to convey the message that the loss of her ring was hardly a coincidence. A loud clang came from the area of the house near the parlor, followed by Cassidy's voice. "I'm good," she called. "Nothing broke."

Lori and the sheriff exchanged a look. Concern clouded his eyes. "There have been only three people who've been here consistently when things have gone missing. I take it you've checked her room."

She nodded, hating that she suspected the teen at all. But Lori couldn't take any chances, so she'd carefully searched through Cassidy's meager belongings while the girl was working in the Patty Wagon. "I checked a couple of times," she said, feeling the guilt bubble up inside her. "I don't think she's our culprit."

The sheriff chewed his cupcake contemplatively. "That doesn't mean she didn't hand them off to someone else," he said as he wiped his mouth with a napkin. "But I don't like thinking she's responsible any more than you do. Cassidy has had a tough go of it. Mona isn't exactly a shining example of a mother."

"Still, stealing doesn't seem to be in Cassidy's nature." Of course, Lori hadn't been the best judge of character these last couple of years, so what did she know?

"I agree." The sheriff pushed away from the counter and stood up. "I'll stop by later to pick up that list."

The screen door swung open and Tessa jumped to her feet. Emily skipped into the kitchen carrying a giant stuffed panda bear. The little girl was wearing a long pink veil made from tulle and held in place on her head with a headband of colorful pipe cleaners wrapped with dainty star garland. Plastic bangle bracelets adorned both arms from her wrists to her elbows.

"Tai Chai and I are having a tea party outside," she said as Tessa danced around her. "Do you want to join us, Sheriff?"

The sheriff went down on one knee so that he was eye level with Emily. His features softened and there was a wistful look in his eyes. "I've got to get back to the station, Princess. But maybe you and Tai Chai can come get an ice cream with me later. We'll get some for Gigi, too."

Emily gave him a lopsided smile. "I'll be sure and eat all my dinner."

He tweaked her nose. "Princesses always eat all of their dinner. By the way, you look extra bedazzled today. Where did you get those sparkly earrings and can I wear them?"

Infectious giggles filled the kitchen as Emily fingered the sparkly teardrop earrings she wore. "They're from Gigi's box of sparkly things. She lets me borrow them. And you can't wear these, silly. They're for girls."

Sheriff Hollister stood and adjusted the veil on Emily's head. "I guess they don't really fit in with the uniform. But Gigi will want to wear them when I take her dancing so you make sure you put them back where you found them, okay?"

Emily scampered up on the barstool, placing her stuffed bear on the stool beside her. "Yes, sir."

He shot Lori a look that clearly conveyed he didn't want Patricia's earrings disappearing, too. She nodded. "We'll get them back to Patricia."

"I'll see you two ladies later," he said as he made his way to the door. "Lori, don't forget about that list."

Lori waved good-bye as she pulled out the special princess plates Patricia kept at the B and B just for her granddaughter. "Now, why don't we have our own tea party on the veranda?" she suggested as she arranged some cupcakes on the plate. "Cassidy and I could use a little break."

"Yippee!" Emily shouted and Lori felt her dark mood brighten a bit.

TWELVE

Miles climbed the steps to the B and B's veranda, happy that he didn't have any guests to make small talk with this evening. He'd spent much of the warm July day wandering through Chances Inlet. Idly chatting with the people who'd known him all of his life, eagerly listening to their problems and their concerns. Not once did someone bring up his father—at least not negatively—or Miles' marital status. No one in his hometown seemed to care about either subject.

Coy's stupid polling data still nagged at him, however. The district was composed of more than just Chances Inlet, and that was the problem. He needed to get voters outside the bubble of his hometown to stop focusing on his father and start focusing on the issues. The phone call he'd had with the governor this afternoon had only made things worse. His boss had summoned him back to Raleigh for a discussion on how they should combat the rise in Faye Rich's popularity. Miles had the sinking feeling that the party wanted to go negative. While he figured he could weather the storm, all the negative press about his father was taking a toll on his mother and the rest of his family. Miles just wanted it to go away.

Do something outrageous, Faye Rich had implored. Too bad Squeaky Clean Miles McAlister's life plan didn't have anything on that all-encompassing list that would get voters' minds off his father.

"Uncle Miles!"

Emily's voice brought Miles back to the present. She was seated at one of the small bistro tables surrounded by stuffed animals and the two dogs, Midas and Tessa. His niece was wearing her usual frilly dress-up clothes complete with a flowing veil and pink sneakers adorned with Disney princesses. Eyes so reminiscent of her late grandfather sparkled when he made his way over to her.

"I'm having a tea party," she said.

"So I see." Miles tried his best to sound insulted. "And I wasn't invited."

Emily yanked the giant panda off one of the chairs and hugged it on her lap. "Tai Chai has had too much to eat. He's gonna get a cavity with all this sugar. You can sit in his spot."

Miles bit back a smile as he sank down into the chair. "Thank you, Tai Chai." He eyed the pile of empty cupcake wrappers on the table. "Did you both eat all these yourselves? Tai Chai isn't the only one who's going to get a cavity."

"No, silly." Emily gave him a patronizing smile that she could only have inherited from her mother. "Cassidy and Lori helped. But there's a sprinkle one left." She shoved the plate toward Miles. A small cupcake with garish blue icing, heavily decorated with red and white sprinkles, remained. "I was gonna eat it, but my tummy is full."

While cupcakes weren't exactly his style, Miles had to admit that Lori was an excellent baker. As he peeled the wrapper off, he thought of the many things she did well. Not just related to the B and B, either. He admired how she'd taken Cassidy under her wing—especially with his mother ailing and Ginger now living with Gavin.

Last night, he'd unashamedly eavesdropped on their conversation. Regret and a painful longing had been etched in Lori's voice, but she still cared enough to give advice to a teenager she'd known only a short time and likely wouldn't see again once she left for wherever it was Lori was headed. Her actions and demeanor didn't jibe with the corrupt criminal she wanted Miles to believe her to be. They pointed to a woman of character. The paradox intrigued him. Maybe even a little bit more than her kisses did.

"You have blue lips," Emily squealed with delight.

"Good thing there's no one around with a camera," his sister said as she climbed the wooden steps, Greer by her side. "That would not be a flattering campaign photo."

"Actually, this would have made a perfect campaign ad," Greer commented. "It would have showed Miles' more vulnerable side."

Kate snorted. "Miles has a vulnerable side?" She shot him a cheeky grin. "Emily, honey, grab your things. We have to meet Daddy at the clinic."

"Can't I stay here, Mommy? Cassidy said I could help in the Patty Wagon."

"More like helping yourself to the ice cream, sticky fingers. You've had enough sugar for today." Undaunted by her daughter's impressive pout, Kate reached out a hand to her.

"I have to put my jewelry in Gigi's sparkly box." Rebuffing her mother, Emily slid from the chair, hefted Tai Chai on her shoulder, and shuffled off the veranda. "Bye, Uncle Miles. Bye, Midas. Bye, Tessa."

Kate rolled her eyes at her daughter's theatrics before kissing Greer on the cheek. "See you next time, Greer." She gave Miles a punch in the shoulder. "Check in on Mom later, okay?"

"I always do."

His sister grinned. "I know. You're reliable as a Maytag, Miles. It's what I love about you. And I'd be happy to say that on tape, Greer, if you ever need me to." She waved before following her daughter down the steps. Midas nearly cleared the table with his tail as he chased after them.

"If you ever give my sister an open microphone, I'll fire you," he warned Greer before he scrubbed a hand down his face.

Smiling, Greer took the seat Emily had just vacated. "I envy you having such a big family."

Miles laughed incredulously. "The grass is always greener. I wouldn't have minded being an only child like you."

"That's a lie and you know it. You love your family. They're so much a part of who you are, Miles."

He stared off across the wide green lawn of the B and B. He'd grown up in a house six blocks away, but everything about Chances Inlet was home to him. The town was his family whether he'd grown up with siblings or not. He didn't bother refuting Greer's claim because—as annoying as his close-knit family was—he knew she was right.

"My father and his cronies are going to want you to fight the character issue by going after Faye's character. She's likely done things in the past that she wants kept quiet, too. You don't want to win that way. I know you think Bernice's plan is crazy." Greer held up a hand when Miles turned to her dumbfounded. "Hear me out. There's no way to distance yourself from your family, of which your father was a big part. And you shouldn't have to. But Bernice's idea of creating a little buzz about your personal life is pretty genius."

"What exactly are you suggesting?"

She shrugged. "Scroll through your contacts and ask someone out. Take her someplace where the media will surely see you."

"Wait, you want me to use a woman as chum for the sharks in the media?"

Greer scrunched her face up. "Well, it didn't sound that disgusting when Bernice was proposing it."

Miles glanced over toward Tessa, still lying quietly on the porch, that world-weary look in her eyes. "I'm running on my own merits, Greer. I don't want to get elected because someone thinks the woman I'm dating is hot. Just as I don't want people to *not* vote for me because of something my father did."

Her sigh was resigned next to him. "Someday you'll have a wife and kids and you won't be able to avoid their being a part of the campaign."

"No, I won't."

Greer was silent for a moment. "Some woman is going to blindside you when you least expect it. I can't wait for that day, you know."

He shook his head. "There's no room for that in the plan. Besides, growing up in that life, would you wish that on another woman or children?"

She shuddered beside him. "Okay, you've made your point," Greer said as she got to her feet. "We'll just have to come up with another plan. I'll see you in Raleigh tomorrow. It'll be you and me against the old guard, but I'll try and have your back."

"That's what I'm paying you for."

Her heels clacked against the wood of the porch as she made her way to her car. For the second time that day, he wished he felt something more than friendship for Greer.

"You're seriously going to be a monk all your life?" His brother's voice startled him. Gavin pushed through the screen door and whistled for Midas. "That doesn't sound very fun."

"My life isn't like that of most people."

"Probably because most people are having sex."

Miles shot his brother an annoyed look.

"It was ten years ago, Miles. Don't you think you've grieved long enough?"

"I was done grieving Justine months after it happened." It was true; the ache in his chest had faded long, long ago. "But I'll never love anyone like that again. That kind of soul mate only comes around once in a lifetime. I'm focusing my life on other goals now."

"You're forgetting where we live," his brother said. "Those second chances have a way of biting you on the ass when you least expect it."

Cassidy charged through the door just as Miles was giving his younger brother a one-fingered salute. "Julianne's in labor! Come on." She grabbed each man by a hand and tugged them toward the steps. "Everyone is already at the hospital."

"She's beautiful, isn't she, Lori?" Patricia slid the iPad across the kitchen island.

"Absolutely precious," Lori said as she glanced at the photo of a beautiful blue-eyed baby already with a halo of dark hair and a satin rose headband circling her perfect head. "Ava Rose fits her."

"Rose was my grandmother's name," Will's mother, Annabeth, explained proudly.

Patricia patted her best friend's hand. "Your grandmother was a great lady. Everyone in town respected her. She'd be very proud right now."

Lori refilled both their coffee cups before turning back to the cupcake batter she was mixing. She tried not to think of the lovely happily ever after Will and Julianne Connelly were experiencing right now. It wasn't so long ago that Lori had dreamed of that kind of life with a husband who was prominent in his field, a career of her own, and babies, lots of babies. But that's all it had been: a dream. She'd been living in a parallel universe built on a house of lies.

Patricia signaled for her to stop the mixer. "You're off somewhere far away." The look she gave Lori was quizzical. "Everything okay with you?"

Lori nodded.

"The Keenans have arrived." She hobbled across the kitchen on her crutches. "Is the Edinburgh Suite ready for them?"

"I set it up last night. I'll text Cassidy to come check them in."

"No, you finish what you're doing. It's about time I start earning my keep around here," Patricia joked.

"She has a formidable will," Annabeth said after her friend had navigated her way out of the kitchen. "If I know Patricia, she'll be fit weeks before the doctors predicted she would."

Lori's stomach fell. She'd always known her days in Chances Inlet were numbered. The original plan had been to move about until everyone forgot. *Or forgave.* She'd already stayed in Chances Inlet too long, but the inn felt safe, like a comfortable shoe. Now the thought of starting over somewhere else scared the crap out of her.

"Are you sure you're all right, Lori?" Annabeth asked. "You look a little pale."

Pasting on a reassuring smile, Lori waved her off. "I think the hot kitchen is getting to me," she lied. She gestured to her oversized green T-shirt, emblazoned with the Ron Jon Surf Shop emblem, and her khaki cargo pants. "Will you excuse me a moment? I'll be back in time to set up the tea."

Not waiting for an answer, Lori made a beeline for the screen door, Tessa at her heels. She crossed the lawn in long strides, headed for the secluded gazebo, hoping that a quiet moment alone would calm her anxious nerves. Sliding into one of the rocking chairs, she stroked Tessa's head. Was this how she was destined to spend the rest of her life? Moving from place to place, leaving behind friends and giving up her dreams? It had all seemed so doable before, considering the alternative. Now she wasn't so sure.

"There has to be a solution out there," she said softly as the dog solemnly stared back at her.

"When you find it, let me know."

Lori jumped out of the chair with a squeak. She turned to find Miles with his back propped up against one of the wide posts and his long legs stretched out on the bench in front of him. He was facing away from her, his body obscured by the honeysuckle plants that surrounded the pillar. She stepped around her chair to get a better look at him. Dressed in navy slacks and a pinstriped shirt, he'd neatly draped his suit jacket on one of the Adirondack chairs next to him. He didn't bother turning around, instead continuing to seemingly contemplate the B and B's garden shed located behind the gazebo. A bottle of beer dangled from his fingertips.

"I thought you were in Raleigh for the day."

"The day is almost over, Sweet Cheeks," he said before taking a pull from the beer.

Something wasn't right. She could sense it in Miles' demeanor. The anxiety Lori had been feeling moments earlier ebbed into concern for Miles even as her brain was telling her to ignore it.

"So what problem are we trying to solve today, Lori? How to make the sheets softer? Or maybe your cupcakes more addictive?" His questions had an edge to them as he swung his feet over the side of the bench and finally turned to face her. A maelstrom of emotions swirled about in his eyes, the intensity forcing Lori to take a slight step back. "Or maybe you're trying to solve that dark secret you're hiding behind?"

Something told Lori this wasn't about her or her secret. The same voice was telling her she was already in too deep in this town and not to get wrapped up in anything more with these people, particularly anything having to do with sexy Miles McAlister. Her eyes darted to the inn, but Miles looked as troubled as she felt and her feet didn't listen to her brain when it told them to flee.

"I'm not the only one who's hiding, apparently," she said, ignoring her grandmother's sage advice not to poke the bear.

The laugh he gave her was menacing. "Even I get tired of Squeaky Clean Miles McAlister once in a while." He took another swig of his beer. "Oh, wait, it's Dudley Do-Right to you, isn't it?"

Lori leaned her bottom against the back of one of the Adirondack chairs. "He's not such a bad guy," she said softly. "Trust me, the world needs lots more people with a conscience."

"I'm pretty sure life in politics is going to totally obliterate my conscience."

Her chest squeezed at the cynicism in his voice. It was so unlike the Miles she'd watched from the shadows these past few months. "That must have been some meeting with the governor."

He snorted. Then he looked across the manicured lawn at the B and B, grand and peaceful in the sleepy summer afternoon. "Oh, it was. Greer was correct. I was blindsided all right." He gulped from the beer bottle in his hand. "Essentially, I've got two choices: Smear Faye Rich by revealing a youthful mistake she made. Or divert the media's interest in my father by marrying the governor's daughter."

She dug her fingernails into the wood of the chair at her back while trying to draw breath through her lungs. *Miles married to Greer.* Just another reason why she needed to hightail it out of this town. She didn't want to be around to celebrate Greer's good fortune.

But the idea made sense. What had Coy called it? A match

made in political heaven. They would certainly make beautiful babies. Her mouth went dry at the thought.

"And how does Greer feel about being bartered off?" Stupid question. *The woman would be a fool not to want to marry Miles*, Lori thought to herself.

"She'll do anything to please Daddy. Whether she agreed with his tactics or not."

Lori's stomach rolled with nausea. Apparently she and Greer had a lot more in common than either of them knew.

"She was eager to throw herself on the mercy of the campaign," he continued. "Apparently I missed her subtle hints yesterday."

"Well, um, congratulations, I guess."

He sprung off the bench and began pacing the gazebo. "Seriously? Does everyone think I'm that blinded by ambition? That I'd let the governor coerce me into a freaking marriage of convenience just for some political gain?"

Lori gnawed on her bottom lip, feeling guilty that she felt a twinge of happiness that he might not marry Greer. "Are there other options?"

"None that I've found yet, but I'm only two beers into this six-pack, so give me a half hour."

"I'm sorry." The words sounded lame as they left her lips, but Lori sincerely meant them. She of all people knew what it felt like to be out of options.

"Oh, don't feel sorry for me. The thing is, marrying Greer makes perfect sense. She'd be a solid partner in my career. Having grown up in the public eye, she's no rookie when it comes to politics and the media. That flawless skin of hers is very thick. We'd be very compatible together. It's a brilliant tactical move." His tone didn't sound the least bit sarcastic.

Lori's stomach bottomed out. "I don't understand."

He placed the empty beer bottle into its cardboard carrier with the others before sitting back down on the bench. "I don't like the idea that her father practically has his shotgun out. He's supposed to be helping me get elected, not trying to get some sort of leverage over me. I don't want to be in anybody's pocket." Miles dragged his hands through his hair. "Hell, I don't know why I'm telling you all of this."

"I'm a good listener." She wasn't really. Had she listened to her mother, she wouldn't be in Chances Inlet right now lusting over a man she could never have. A man who apparently was just like her: willing to sacrifice his integrity for his ambition. *Even if he doesn't want to admit that truth to himself—yet.*

His laugh sounded a bit manic as he stood up and began pacing the gazebo again. "Faye Rich dared me to do something outrageous. This wasn't exactly what I had in mind, but it beats the alternative."

Damn, is he actually considering it? "You said you two were friends without benefits," she blurted out.

Miles shrugged. "I'm sure the benefits part will have to be reevaluated. She'll want kids, no doubt. But we'll never be more than friends."

Lori's fingers were gripping the chair so tightly she thought it might snap in two. Would he kiss Greer with the same passion he'd kissed Lori with in the Aberdeen Suite? The thought made her angry, even though she knew she had no right to be. He'd been honest with her that day, just as he was being painfully honest with her now. "That's a pretty bleak way to start a marriage," she challenged.

"It's the only kind of marriage any woman is going to get from me."

"You can't be serious?" Lori needed to get back to the B and B. She was giving too much of her inner feelings away.

Miles stopped his pacing and propped a shoulder up against one of the columns supporting the gazebo. He stared out over the lawn again, his gaze seeming to look for something far off on the distant shoreline. "You're missing a vital part of the story, Sweet Cheeks. I already had my one great love of a lifetime."

"Your college sweetheart who died in a car accident."

Miles glanced over his shoulder at her, a bemused smile on his face. "I'd ask if you were some sort of spy, but this is Chances Inlet. Nothing is sacred in this town." He turned back to his perusal of the shoreline before continuing his tale.

"Justine was my girlfriend all through college. She was the one I was going to spend the rest of my life with. Until she wasn't. We were backpacking in Europe. I came back a week before she did to register for law school. She and some friends were in a car accident. The others survived. Justine didn't."

Tears stung the backs of her eyes as she watched him swallow harshly. She ached for his loss—and for hers, as well. They were kindred spirits, she and Miles. Even if she wanted to, Lori could never allow herself to fall in love, either. She'd never want to burden another with the guilt shadowing her. *Another place, another time.* How she wished things could be different. For both of them.

His voice had become raspy with emotion. "Greer and I would be compatible, but Justine was my soul mate. There won't ever be another."

"Does Greer know this?" she whispered around the boulder in her throat. Lori found herself sympathizing with the other woman. From the few encounters she'd witnessed, Greer clearly had feelings for Miles.

"Her father does. Imagine a dad who would knowingly use his daughter for his own gain?"

Lori's stomach rolled and she gripped the chair even tighter in order to stay upright. She didn't have to imagine.

Miles refocused his attention back on her. He took a step closer, then another, while his eyes continued to study her as if she were a cell beneath a microscope.

"Not that I have it any easier. Every choice I make seems to result in some sort of collateral damage. Tell me, Lori, are you someone's collateral damage? Or the instigator of it?"

She swallowed painfully as he closed the distance between them, intense scrutiny still in his eyes. There was no way she could answer that question honestly so she kept her mouth closed.

"Still hiding behind your secret, huh? Even after I've just bared my soul to you," he said as he fingered her long braid. His fancy loafers were parked on either side of her white Keds, essentially pinning her to the back of the chair. Miles' other hand found its way to her waist, where he bunched up the fabric of her T-shirt and gripped it in his strong fingertips. He smelled of hops and summer and aroused male, and Lori put her hands on his chest to push him away.

Something happened when her fingers made contact with his muscled chest, however. Her body seemed to drift toward him of its own accord. "Knowing my secret won't make your decision any easier, Miles. Rely on your integrity." She desperately wanted him not to give up on love so easily. Almost as desperately as she wanted her own destiny to be different.

He growled low near her ear. "By tomorrow I might not have any integrity left." His lips nuzzled that sweet spot on her neck, the one that always made her knees weak. "Tell me something," he murmured. "Just give me a clue as to what's behind the mystery of Lori. Anything."

She moaned when his teeth nipped at the shell of her ear. His hand crept beneath her T-shirt and his warm fingers pressed into the small of her back. Desire made her a bit woozy.

"I . . . I . . ." Lori sucked in breath when Miles' fingers slipped beneath her bra. "I . . . I snore!"

His hands and his mouth stilled and Lori nearly wept when he lifted his lips from her skin. She felt his body begin to shake beneath her fingers. The sound of his laughter had her burying her head against his chest.

"That must be a really nasty snore if it has caused you to hide out in the depths of my mother's B and B," he said, still chuckling.

"I'm told it's pretty deafening," she murmured against his shirt.

He laughed again as he lifted her chin with his fingertip. She was relieved to see that his face had relaxed, allowing the sexy laugh lines to fan out from his eyes. "I guess I should be thankful that you sleep on the third floor."

Lori nodded, mesmerized by the desire starting to cloud his pupils. This was madness. Miles pulled in a ragged breath. "Damn it," he said before his mouth seized hers.

Any thought of resisting never entered Lori's mind. His confession made her feel even more lost and helpless and her body desperately craved physical contact. Not to mention, Miles was a damn fine kisser. He kissed like he did everything else: with a confident self-assurance. At least Greer wouldn't be disappointed on all fronts. Taking his time to make sure they both enjoyed the experience, he slowly explored her mouth as though they weren't in full view of anyone who walked by.

Her common sense began screaming and Lori started to pull away, but Miles had other ideas. His fingers pressed into her back, bringing her flush with his hard body. Heat shot to her belly as she sighed into his mouth. That was all the invitation he needed. The kiss that had felt reassuring and comforting became greedy and intoxicating. Miles slid his tongue over hers and Lori's knees would have buckled had she not been clinging to him with such need. He delved deeper into her mouth, still looking to uncover her secrets, she was sure. Another few minutes of his lips and hands on her body and who knows what she might confess to him. Certainly that she wanted him, wanted this, as much as he seemed to want her.

The sound of a train rumbling through town shook her loose. Lori forced her fingers to unclench from his shirt as she pulled her mouth from his. He was breathing as hard as she was, but he didn't try to pull her back. Instead he reverently traced his lips along her hairline while he pulled his hands from beneath her shirt.

"What will you do?" she asked.

"Damned if I know." His sigh sounded more like an anguished groan. "But I know what I'd like to be doing and it involves the both of us naked."

She smiled. His words were a definite boost to her confidence right now. "You say that in the heat of the moment, but it would be reckless and stupid. And you're neither of those things, Miles." He snorted and she bit back a laugh. She patted him on the chest. "We're going in different directions, you and I. Don't forget that." Stretching up on her toes, she kissed him on the cheek. "Don't ever give up on who you are."

Slipping out of his arms, she headed for the B and B and the afternoon tea that needed to be prepared and served. She felt his eyes on her back, watching her as she crossed the lawn. But she didn't dare look back. Lori wasn't sure how many more times she could resist Miles McAlister. As much as she dreaded having to move on from Chances Inlet, it would be better to sever the connection between them once and for all as quickly as possible.

THIRTEEN

"I couldn't be happier." Patricia hugged Ginger as she fought to keep the tears from her eyes. "Now, let me get a look at that gorgeous ring."

"Ooo, I need to take a picture of it so I can tweet it out." Cassidy pulled out her phone. "You're gonna want all his fans to know he's off the market, Gidget," she said, calling Ginger by the nickname Cassidy had given her when she'd first arrived in Chances Inlet.

Gavin groaned. "I really wish you'd shut that Twitter account down, Cassidy. The show's over."

"It had better be a gorgeous ring," Kate said. "A girl's got to have some consolation prize for agreeing to marry this goofball." She kissed her brother on the cheek before clapping him on the back. "And your tens of thousands of Twitter stalkers need to see it."

Patricia shook her head. Some things never change. Still, she loved that her children continued to engage with one another. They teased and bickered, but when push came to shove, they had each other's back. Her kids had been her rock these past few years and Patricia was grateful for their love and support. She was also thrilled to add Ginger into the mix.

Ginger and Gavin—along with Kate, Alden, Miles, Cassidy, and Lamar—had crammed into her small sitting room in the carriage house to make their announcement. Alden was pouring champagne into flutes and the mood was festive and happy, which was a boon to Patricia's sagging confidence.

"I know I wasn't always supportive of you two as a couple," Patricia tried to get out but the lump in her throat was painful. "And for that I apologize. I'm proud to have you as my daughter-in-law, but I hope you'll know I'm always your friend, too."

Ginger's eyes were damp as she leaned down to kiss Patricia on the cheek. "Thank you."

Gavin smiled over his fiancée's shoulder. "Great, now they're forming an alliance against me." He leaned in to deliver his own kiss. "You'll always be my girl," he whispered in her ear. The words caused Patricia's heart to skip a beat. His father had always said the same thing to her. It made her feel good to know that Donald would live on through his children's mannerisms.

"Have you set a date?" she heard Kate ask.

"We thought we'd wait until the baseball season is over so that Ryan can be here," Gavin said.

"Maybe a Christmas wedding?" Ginger gave Gavin a wistful look before he kissed her on the forehead.

He wrapped an arm around his fiancée. "Whenever you want, just as long as it's soon."

"Aww." Kate took a flute of champagne from her husband. "Remember when you were that whipped, honey?"

"I still am. Emily's sleeping over at her friends' house tonight." Alden winked at Kate. "Remind me to show you later."

Miles heaved a sigh before waving his glass. "Are we going to toast or sit around and share TMI with each other?"

His harsh tone quieted the jovial room. Patricia eyed her oldest son carefully. He'd been withdrawn and moody since he arrived at the carriage house earlier. His mouth was drawn in a formidable line, so unlike the easy smile he normally wore.

She knew he liked Ginger, so Gavin's decision to marry her couldn't be the problem.

From where he stood behind her, Lamar lowered a hand and gently cupped the back of her neck. "Miles is right, we need a toast."

Patricia searched Miles' face. He wouldn't be happy to have Lamar insinuating himself on a family event in such a way, but her son's eyes remained distracted and distant. That concerned her even more.

"To Ginger and Gavin." Lamar saluted the couple with his glass. "Wishing you both a happy, healthy marriage."

"Here, here," Alden and Kate called out.

She watched as Miles downed his champagne in one swallow. *Oh, dear.*

"Congratulations, you two." His movements seemed a bit wooden as he placed the empty flute on the table before kissing Ginger on the cheek. He reached out a hand to Gavin. "I've got some stuff to take care of down at campaign headquarters."

Patricia cursed her injured hip when she tried to stand too quickly.

"Tricia!" Lamar grabbed for her elbow when she winced.

"Mom, please be careful," Miles commanded as he sank down on a knee and took her hand between his. "Are you okay?"

"I wanted to ask you the same thing." She cupped his cheek with her free hand.

A look of sadness flickered in his eyes and her breath caught in her throat. He wasn't okay. Thirty-three years of staring into those eyes told her he wasn't.

"I've just got some hard decisions to make involving the campaign, that's all." Miles paused as though he wanted to say something more. But then he was kissing her on the cheek and trying to make his escape. Since he was a child, he'd always shouldered his burdens alone. Even when his fiancée had died in a car accident, he hadn't wanted to share his grief with anyone. Yet he was always the one to want to solve the problems of others. He still was that man.

Patricia heard everyone else in the sitting room teasing Cassidy about not liking the champagne, but she kept her gaze locked with her son's. "You'd stop doing this political stuff if it wasn't what you wanted, right?" Miles' pride was a lot like his father's: stubborn and deep.

He gave her what he surely meant to be a reassuring smile. Instead, it seemed a little hollow. "It's what I want, Mom. It's what I've always wanted." He squeezed her hand.

All she could do was nod and hope that he'd confide in her at some point. "Oh, by the way," she said, remembering something she'd meant to mention to him before Gavin and Ginger had made their announcement. "You haven't moved things around in the guest rooms, have you?"

Miles slowly got to his feet. "No. Why do you ask?"

"I was in the Edinburgh Suite today and I noticed that the Swarovski crystal paperweight wasn't on the secretary desk. I thought maybe you'd moved it somewhere."

He exchanged an uneasy look with Lamar. "No, I didn't. But I'll check with Lori. She might have rearranged things."

Patricia shook her head. "I asked her. She said she hadn't. Of course, I might have moved it into one of the other rooms before the accident and I just don't remember. All this pain medication has made me a bit dopey. Once I'm back on my feet, I'll be able to search a bit more thoroughly." She waved Miles off. "You've got enough on your plate right now. Don't worry about a silly piece of crystal."

"You don't worry about it, either," he said. "I'm sure it's in that big house somewhere." Miles called out a good-bye to the rest of the room and then surprised Patricia by extending his hand to Lamar. "Take care of her." His words choked her up again.

"Be right back," she heard Gavin murmur to Ginger before he followed Miles out the door. Patricia felt a sense of relief that Gavin, the most intuitive of her five children, might be able to get to the bottom of what was troubling his brother.

"Hey, Miles, wait up!"

Steps from a clean getaway. Miles stopped in the middle of the breezeway connecting the carriage house to the B and

B and waited for Gavin to catch up. He'd hoped to escape the impromptu celebration before his sour disposition spoiled the whole thing. Unfortunately, he hadn't been successful and now he felt like an ass.

Gavin came up beside him, a concerned look on his face. "Everything okay?"

Miles looked everywhere but at his brother, who possessed the freakish ability to read everyone in the family. Instead, he glanced toward the inn's kitchen window, where he caught a glimpse of Lori moving about. Damn it, he'd been an ass with her earlier, as well. He shouldn't have breathed a word about Governor Rossi's stupid bargain. And he sure as hell shouldn't have kissed her. He told himself it was because she was convenient and he'd been searching for a diversion from the disastrous meeting he'd had earlier that day.

But that was a lie. The truth was he'd been curious to know if the kiss in the Aberdeen Suite last week had been a fluke. When she came up to the gazebo looking lost and alone, he took advantage of her, breaking his earlier promise not to. But now he had scientific proof their first kiss wasn't a fluke. Worse, along with being frustrated and peeved about the campaign, he was now horny as hell.

Miles wasn't worried about Lori revealing his secret, however. He knew she'd keep their discussion to herself. He couldn't say how he knew; he just did.

The missing crystal paperweight did worry him, though. Was it possible his mother had simply moved it somewhere else and didn't remember? Miles didn't think so. That meant something else had gone missing. He wondered if Lori had already begun checking other rooms. Or if he was really being a sucker by believing she wasn't the thief. His temple began to throb and he wished he'd finished the rest of that six-pack of beer. A good buzz would really take the edge off this shitty day.

"Miles," Gavin was saying. "You've been a million miles away all evening. What gives?"

He returned his gaze to his brother, forcing a relaxed smile on his face. "Nothing, man. I just have a lot going on with the campaign."

"Anything I can do to help?"

"Nah, just the usual bullshit. It's nothing that needs to overshadow your big moment."

Gavin donned his shit-eating grin as he looked back at the carriage house. "I'm pretty sure my big moment ended with the proposal. The rest of the wedding is for the bride."

Miles leaned up against one of the posts holding up the trellis overhead, letting his brother's happiness seep into his own bones. He was glad for Gavin. Ginger was a keeper. "I'm happy for you, Gav. I really am. I'm just a little surprised you didn't give this relationship a little more time to take root, that's all. Although I don't get the vibe that she's going to be a runaway bride like Amanda."

Gavin's fiancée had ditched him and Chances Inlet days before their wedding once she found out they wouldn't be returning to New York right away due to Donald McAlister's death. Since Miles never really warmed to the girl, he figured his brother had dodged a bullet. He was pretty sure Gavin felt the same way.

"Amanda walking out on me was the best thing that ever happened." Gavin leaned a shoulder against the opposite post. "Ginger and I talked about just enjoying being together without the stress of worrying about what came next. No expectations, you know?" He shrugged. "I don't know, though. When I held Will and Julianne's baby last night, something sort of hit me. I could picture myself with a kid of my own. Ginger's baby."

"That's your first mistake, asshole," Miles warned him too late. "Never, ever hold a baby. Especially not in front of the woman you're sleeping with."

"Says the politician who's supposed to be kissing every baby he sees." Gavin chuckled. "Hey, there's something I wanted to ask you before you run off."

"As long as it has nothing to do with babies, ask away."

His brother hesitated briefly. "I'd like for you to be my best man again. I mean, it's not like you got the chance the first time."

"Seriously?" Miles gripped the back of his neck. "What if I'm bad luck? Maybe you should ask Will."

Gavin's look was incredulous. "He's not my brother."

"But he's your best friend."

"Jesus, Miles, if you don't want to do it, just say so. I'll ask Ryan." Gavin pulled away from the post and headed back toward their mother's carriage house.

A tide of emotions welled up inside Miles, nearly choking him. Yet he still managed to call after his brother. "Gavin. I'd be honored to be your best man."

Gavin's eyes were cautious and his mouth pissed off when he turned around. "Are you sure? Because if you're still gonna bust my balls over the whole thing with Dad, you can forget it."

Miles took a step toward his brother. "It's not that." He looked back at his mother's inn, the catalyst to his father's demise. "I mean, it might be a little of that. But I get where you were coming from with Dad. I really do. You made a hard choice. Life is full of them. A lot of them suck."

"Are we still talking about Dad?"

No, Miles wasn't. But in hindsight, he didn't begrudge his brother for taking matters into his own hands any longer. He wasn't even angry about being kept in the dark. Miles wished there was a way he could keep his family in the dark regarding his looming decision, but he didn't see any way to make that happen. He only hoped Gavin—and the rest of the McAlisters—would respect him afterward.

"It doesn't matter," Miles said. "All that matters is we're good. And I'm happy to stand up for you at your wedding."

The corners of Gavin's mouth turned up slightly and he nodded. "Thanks, bro."

Miles clapped him on the back and suddenly they were locked in a man hug.

"I think this calls for some nachos and a beer," Gavin said when they pulled apart. "Let's go to Pier Pressure. We'll tell Jolene we're celebrating the baby and to put it on Will's tab."

With a quick glance back at the B and B, Miles agreed. After all, there were guests staying in the Edinburgh Suite, so he couldn't do any snooping tonight. It was no use stewing at campaign headquarters, either. Nachos and a beer with his brother sounded better than anything else he had planned.

* * *

Lamar stood at the sink rinsing out the champagne flutes. Patricia sat next to him, her hip propped on one of the tall stools from the breakfast bar.

"Thank you," she said as she carefully dried the crystal that had once belonged to her grandmother.

"You know I don't mind helping you out, Tricia." He slipped his hands back into the soapy water.

"I'm not talking about the dishes."

He turned to face her and those solemn gray eyes of his were so intense they made her heart flutter. "I know you're not talking about the damn dishes." He swallowed roughly. "I'm sorry I wasn't there for you that night," he whispered. "What I wouldn't give for it to have been me and not you lying beside the road suffering."

She licked her lips. "I love you, Lamar. I truly do. But I need to know you still love me, too," she whispered.

He sighed heavily. "There's something romantic about a husband wanting so badly to make his wife's wish come true that he sacrifices everything to achieve it. I don't know how I can compete with that." He took the dish towel from her fingers and wiped his hands with it. "I didn't know Donald, but I feel like I know him through your children. And he'd want me to do whatever it took to protect you and keep you safe."

Tears stung her eyes and she wrapped her arms around his waist, pulling him in closer. She could feel the steady beat of his heart when she rested her cheek against his solid chest. "But what if I don't want to be protected like that?" she asked. "Donald kept a secret that surely killed him. How did that help me? I don't expect you to wrap me up in bubble wrap. I just want you to be there to help me up if I do fall. And I want to be the one who does the same for you."

"I love you, woman. All of you. Your crazy kids, your hapless strays, and your gorgeous body. But most of all, I love your beautiful soul." He leaned down to kiss the top of her head, but Patricia pulled back. She cupped his face with both hands and pulled him down for a deep kiss. A spasm of arousal flared deep inside her as she twined her tongue with his.

"Doc said you're not ready for that yet," he murmured against her mouth. "But I can do amazing things with an ice massage."

She laughed in spite of her herself. "I bet you never thought you'd ever use that as a pickup line."

Lamar gently scooped her up off the stool. Wrapping her arms around his shoulders, Patricia buried her face in his neck.

"It's a first, but it comes with the territory for our generation." He carried her into the bedroom and laid her on the bed. "I'll get that ice."

"When you get back, you can fill me in on what's going on with Miles."

Her words stopped Lamar in his tracks. Framed in the doorway, he turned to face her, his stoic mask firmly in place. "Why would I know what's going on with Miles?"

"He was very distracted earlier. When I asked him about the paperweight, he looked to you before he answered. Why would he do that?"

Lamar walked back to the bed. "I think you're misreading things. He's doing two jobs right now: campaigning and managing your B and B. More than one of us has questioned his ability to do both. Perhaps even a bit unfairly. Miles doesn't want to let you down."

His excuse made sense, up to a point. "Since when did you start defending my son? He's been barely civil to you since he met you. Not that I'm complaining, mind you. It's nice to see you two get along."

He sat down on the bed beside her. "We had a Come-to-Jesus meeting the other day. It seems we have something very important to bond over: We both love the same woman."

Patricia took one of his bigger hands between both of hers. A renewed sense of calm ebbed through her body when she made contact with his skin. "You'd tell me if something was wrong?"

"Of course," he said without hesitation.

Tears stung her eyes again but this time they were happy ones. Things were starting to go her way; she just knew it. "It's going to be all right, isn't it? We're going to be okay?"

"We are going to be better than okay," he said before leaning down and taking her mouth in a searing kiss.

Patricia relaxed into his comforting embrace, letting the worries of the day fade away.

FOURTEEN

The grandfather clock chimed its final chords announcing midnight. The B and B settled into a peaceful quiet around Lori. It was midweek and only three of the inn's suites were booked with guests, all of whom were presumably fast asleep. The sounds of the waves crashing against the shore seeped in through the closed windows. The only other sound Lori heard when she slipped out of her room was Tessa's gentle snoring.

Careful to skip the stair tread that squeaked, Lori made her way down from the third floor to the guest room level. She maneuvered quietly through the darkened hallway before slipping into the empty Paisley Suite. Closing the door until all but an inch remained open, she settled her shoulder against the wall and peered out the crack. Moonlight streamed through the stained glass window, giving her a bird's-eye view of the landing at the top of the main staircase.

Lori's heart told her Cassidy wasn't responsible for the recent thefts, but her heart had been wrong before. *So very wrong.* Someone was stealing from the B and B. Since Lori could rule herself out, that left only Miles and Cassidy as the likely culprits.

Not that she believed for a minute that Dudley Do-Right would steal anything, much less something from his mother or her guests. Of course, she also knew firsthand that Miles wasn't exactly the man he wanted everyone to believe him to be—especially when he had his hands beneath her bra and his tongue down her throat. She shivered slightly, remembering their kiss in the gazebo earlier. The only thing Miles was guilty of was making Lori want things she no longer had any right to. Things like a normal life and a normal relationship. None of that was going to ever happen for her and she needed to face that fact and move on. *Except she couldn't move on without her grandmother's ring.* And if that meant staking out the hallway to capture whoever was stealing things from the inn, Lori was going to do it. *Desperate times called for desperate measures and all that malarkey.*

Of course, if neither she nor Miles was the culprit, that left Cassidy. Lori felt guilty even considering it, despite the fact the teenager had grown up with no boundaries. According to Patricia, Cassidy not only parented herself but, more often than not, had to parent her mother, too. These past few months, Lori hadn't seen any evidence that Cassidy was anything but a teenager hiding her tender heart behind the façade of a belligerent Goth. The girl was smart, industrious, and devoted to the McAlister family. She made as much sense as the thief as Miles did. But while Lori hated to believe Cassidy was guilty, she also knew what it was like to be alone with an uncertain future. A girl could do anything under those circumstances. Stealing a few trinkets here and there was just the tip of the iceberg.

She sighed softly, leaning her head against the doorframe. Lori hadn't quite thought this plan through. With her luck, she'd stand here all night and no one would venture through the B and B's halls.

She felt the heat at her back nanoseconds before a large hand covered her mouth. Her skin tingled when a second hand landed on her stomach, pulling her body in contact with a muscled chest. A very familiar muscled chest judging by the way her insides were heating up. She tried to jab an elbow into Miles' stomach, but his reflexes were quicker. With his hand still plastered to her mouth, he pinned her arms with his other hand. Shifting her body to his side, he pushed the door closed with his knee.

"Fancy meeting you here," he whispered as he pulled her toward the back of the suite. Moonlight bounced off the pale duvet that covered the four-poster bed. The moon's brightness illuminated much of the bedroom. Lori turned her head to glare at Miles. He was dressed in a dark blue T-shirt and black running shorts. *All the better to blend in with the darkness.* His hair was wet and Lori caught a whiff of his mother's trademark shampoo in the air. The cucumber scent should have made him seem less manly, less threatening. It didn't.

"What are you doing up so late, Lori?" His tone wasn't quite as menacing as it had been earlier in the day, but she still sensed the tension coiled deep within him.

She tugged a hand free and peeled his fingers off her mouth. "I could ask you the same question."

His eyes were probing her again; she could feel it. "I'm looking for a crystal paperweight that seems to have found itself missing from the Edinburgh Suite."

Lori relaxed a little against his hold and she heard Miles' breathing hitch. "Don't waste your sleep. I already checked this room four hours ago." She huffed out a frustrated sigh when he showed no sign of releasing her. "It's not here. Or in any room of the B and B, for that matter. I checked them all. Well, all except yours," she challenged.

Miles' eyes narrowed and his grip on her tightened. "Let's remedy that right now, then, shall we?" He led her toward the door. Lori debated protesting but a small part of her wanted a peek inside Miles' bedroom. Of course, she'd seen the Dundee Suite hundreds of times before, just not since Dudley Do-Right had taken up residence. *It was the only way to rule him out as a suspect once and for all*, she tried to justify to herself.

After manacling her wrist with his long fingers, he quietly pulled the door open. Miles checked down each of the long hallways before he ventured out of the suite. She followed behind him, the thick carpet muffling the sounds of their footsteps. Glancing down, Lori noticed that Miles' feet were bare.

Her stomach did another one of those somersaults. There was something intimate about Miles and his bare feet. After their kiss that afternoon, did she really want to be alone with him in his bedroom? Her body was screaming yes while her brain was demanding that she get a grip. She needed to stay the course, which meant catching the thief, getting her ring back, and moving on. Lori began to hesitate, but Miles tugged her along.

In a few short strides they'd made it to the Dundee Suite. Miles opened the door soundlessly and quickly propelled Lori into the dimly lit room. He released her wrist and she heard the telltale click of the lock sliding home. Still, she relaxed as she took a few steps into the sitting area. The corner suite was one of Lori's favorites in the inn. Decorated in the Dundee tartan colors of red, green, black, and white, the room always reminded Lori of Christmas.

Miles had been living in the suite for more than a month now, yet with the exception of his laptop and some papers spread across the sofa, there was not a single trace of him anywhere. Lori glanced into the adjoining bedroom. The bed was made and the pillows neatly stacked against the sleigh-style headboard. She peeked into the bathroom, where her suspicions about his recent shower were confirmed by the moisture wicking over the tile floor in the large shower. The only item evident in the room was a tube of toothpaste, which was, of course, neatly crimped on the end where he'd rolled it up.

A little disappointed not to find out more about the real Miles, she wandered back into the sitting area. No crystal paperweight—or any of the other missing items—was visible. Not that she ever thought they would be. Miles was leaning against the closed door, his arms crossed over his chest and those same sexy bare feet crossed at the ankles.

"Satisfied?"

Not hardly. At least not in the way he was talking about. She shrugged. "I never seriously considered you as a suspect, Dudley."

One corner of his mouth twitched. "I'll remember that if I need additional campaign endorsements."

"Glad we got that cleared up. Can I go now?" Cassidy could be on the move and neither one of them would know it.

"Why? So you can take something else?"

Mirroring his pose, she narrowed her eyes at him. "We both know I'm not the thief, either."

He sprang away from the door. "Actually, *we* don't. That whole story about your grandmother's ring is likely a ruse just to throw everyone off. What other reason do you have for skulking around the B and B at night if you're not the thief? And *for the love of Pete*, do you sleep in that ridiculous outfit?"

His last question caught her off guard. Lori wasn't sure whether to be embarrassed or aroused by the fact that he had bothered to notice her clothing. She looked down at her faded, oversized T-shirt and her pink Victoria's Secret sweatpants, both of which she'd picked up at the local thrift store. The wretched outfit was a far cry from the designer clothes she'd donned in her previous life. She was sick and tired of the necessary guise, but her options were limited. All she could do was make the best of it.

"This old thing? It's a vintage Hootie and the Blowfish concert shirt. There's nothing ridiculous about it." She decided to brazen it out. "Not a Hootie fan, Dudley? The shop had some Backstreet Boys T-shirts as well. Maybe that's more your speed?"

He let out a low growl as he took a step closer. The air in the room crackled, forcing Lori to draw in a tight breath. Miles' nostrils flared at the sound. "You shouldn't be wandering the inn at night, Lori. Not even dressed like that."

His words brought an appreciative smile to her face, but Lori bit it back before he could see it. Encouraging him wouldn't do either of them any good. "I was hoping to catch Cas—the burglar in the act."

Miles took another step forward so that their bodies were only inches apart. "So you think it's Cassidy?"

Tears stung Lori's eyes at the thought of saying it out loud. "I don't know who else it could be," she whispered. "It's not you. And it's not me." He arched an eyebrow at her, but Lori ignored him. "If it is her, I'm hoping she has a good excuse. But more importantly that she still has my ring. I don't want to leave without it," she said around the lump in her throat.

He reached up a hand and cupped her face. "So you're leaving soon, then?"

She leaned into his hand and nodded. "I have to." She didn't tell him that her imminent departure had as much to do with her desire not to be discovered as it did with her growing attachment to the B and B and everyone in it—including the arousing man standing before her.

His other hand found her hip and he pulled her in closer. His fingers began a gentle assault of her bottom, causing her body to arch into his. She sighed at the contact with his arousal.

"Tell me who you're hiding from." His lips began a slow exploration of her neck and Lori's breathing began to fracture.

She slid her hands beneath his T-shirt, allowing her fingers to explore the smooth planes of his chest. "It's complicated."

Life was about to get a lot more complicated if they didn't stop what they were doing. But whatever they'd begun in the gazebo was burning out of control again and Lori didn't seem to have the willpower to resist any longer.

"All the good things are." He palmed her breast while his tongue traced the shell of her ear. "Are you married?"

"No," she moaned as he rolled one of her pebbled nipples between his fingers.

"Then it's not that complicated."

Lori wanted to argue with him, but his mouth quickly covered her own and she was too busy accommodating his demanding tongue and lips. She eased her hands between the waistband of his shorts. Her panties grew damp when she came in contact with warm, bare skin. She felt him gasp when she wrapped her fingers around him.

He pulled his mouth from hers. "Remember what you said earlier about me not being reckless? I'm feeling very reckless tonight, Lori. If you're not feeling the same, now's the time to go back to your room."

It was so very Dudley Do-Right of him that Lori nearly

laughed. The sad part was Miles knew nothing about being reckless. At least not like she did. Apparently she hadn't learned her lesson, though. Instead of hightailing it back to her room and locking the door, she began toeing off her Keds.

Miles breathed a relieved-sounding sigh as his hands began shoving her sweatpants down her legs.

"You'll regret this in the morning," she warned him. Her heart constricted at the look on his face. She desperately wanted him to deny it.

"I probably will," he said instead.

Lori should have been angry and hurt, but the fact of the matter was, this was their reality. She wanted this as much as Miles did. If she couldn't have a normal life with someone like Miles, then she was going to take whatever she could get and bank the memories for her lonely future. This was all they'd ever have and she intended to make the most of it.

He crouched down on his haunches, allowing her to step out of her sweats. His eyes were dark with desire when he looked up at her. Lori slowly dragged the T-shirt over her head, obscenely glad that she'd managed to take a decent supply of her La Perla lingerie with her when she made her escape from New York. A slow, appreciative grin formed on Miles' lips at the sight of her molded bra and matching panties. Both were made up of delicate sheer mint green fabric with matching bows in all the right places.

"That's more like it," he said as he rocked back on his heels.

Miles groaned as his fingers spanned her waist and he pulled her body toward him. Lori buried her hands in his thick hair while his lips trailed along the low waistband of her panties. His mouth cruised over her belly button, eliciting a sigh from Lori. She felt him smile against her stomach before his lips moved lower, grazing her skin through the silk of her panties. Lori's breath hitched and she dug her fingers into Miles' skull.

"Is this what you want?" he asked as his tongue flicked between her legs. The sensation of the silky fabric rubbing against her tender skin made her body throb. Miles took a breath, inhaling her scent. "Oh, yeah," he said. "This is definitely what you want."

Before she could reply, he was shoving the fabric of her panties aside and burying his tongue inside her. His hands were kneading her bottom as he licked and sucked. It didn't take much before her muscles were convulsing. She squeezed her eyes shut, trying not to scream when the powerful orgasm nearly took her out at the knees.

He smiled against her skin again and Lori didn't have to see it to know it was a smug one. He'd given her satisfaction—intense satisfaction—in under two minutes. Lori wanted to attribute it to the recent drought in her sex life, but she had to concede that Miles had a way with her body. He kissed the inside of her thigh before righting her panties and slowly coming to his feet. His hands skimmed over her bare skin reverently.

"Are you ready for the good stuff?" he breathed into her ear as he pulled her hips against his very aroused body.

"That wasn't the good stuff?"

He let out another one of those toe-curling growls before sweeping her into his arms and carrying her to the bedroom. Lori bounced once when Miles tossed her on the big sleigh bed. "Don't move," he ordered her.

Through the screen of her eyelashes she watched as he yanked his T-shirt over his head and neatly folded it before placing it on the bench at the foot of the bed. Lori bit back a smile when he shucked off his shorts and folded them up also. Her amusement died, though, when he turned and marched into the bathroom. The sight forced her to catch her breath. *That ass has definitely seen some squats.*

Miles returned to the bedroom carrying a handful of foil packets, which he tossed down on the nightstand. Lori propped herself up on her elbows, eyeing the condoms. She arched an eyebrow at Miles.

He crawled up onto the bed. "I believe if you're going to have regrets, it's always better to make them worth it."

Considering the appetizer he'd just given her, Lori had no doubt tonight would be worth it. She reached behind her back to unclasp her bra, but Miles beat her to it. His warm body brushed against hers as he used his fingers and his mouth to divest her of her meager clothing. He whispered how, for weeks now, he'd fantasized about unwrapping her layers and exposing her body to him. Then, he told her all the things he'd been dreaming of doing to her—with her. None of it was characteristic of his Dudley Do-Right persona. Lori had never been so turned on. Miles was thorough in his exploration of her body, leaving her flushed and writhing beneath him.

When at long last he covered her body with his, she sighed with relief before nipping him on the shoulder. In response, he slid into her, filling her completely. Lori's breath seized in her lungs at the sensation. His body hovered above hers. He'd left the lights beside the bed on low and she watched as his face relaxed into a satisfied smile. His blue eyes were determined behind his long, inky lashes. She was relieved that she didn't see regret in them. *At least not now anyway.*

Reaching up, she threaded her fingers through his hair, pulling his mouth down to hers for a deep, drugging kiss. Tongues and teeth collided until neither one of them could take it any longer and Miles began to move within her. Lori anchored her feet over Miles' calves as she matched his rhythm. She whispered words of encouragement and sighs of pleasure as he carried her body back to the edge again and again, before finally giving her what she wanted. Arching her neck, she squeezed her eyelids shut as a million lights exploded behind them. Her soft cry of pleasure whispered through the quiet bedroom, making Miles still yet again.

When Lori opened her eyes, he had the familiar deep probing look on his face. She didn't want him thinking about who she was or what she might be. Lori just wanted this night with him, this moment filled with pleasure. Their moment. It would likely be the only one they ever had—especially if he was foolish enough to marry Greer. She clenched her muscles, squeezing around him as she slid her nails up and down his back.

"Don't think, Miles," she pleaded with him. "That will only lead to regrets."

Thankfully, he slammed his eyes shut and began to move again. Growling next to her ear, he came in a rush, his body shaking with release. A peaceful bliss settled over Lori as they lay there waiting for their breathing to return to normal.

* * *

Miles shifted onto his back so as not to smother Lori, yet not wanting to put too much distance between their bodies, which were still flushed with passion. He'd waited months to get his hands on her, and he still had some exploring left to do. Her soft brown eyes had little flecks of gold, which sparkled when she was aroused. That stubborn chin had a little dent in it. And a small scar, white with age, bisected her left eyebrow. Her sassy mouth was not quite symmetrical, but talented nonetheless. Miles was growing hard again just thinking about where he wanted her to put her lips next.

"I should be keeping an eye on the hallway." Her voice sounded sated and she made no effort to move any part of her body. "Is it wrong that part of me hopes it's not Cassidy, but another part of me wants it to be her so I can get my ring back?"

Something fluttered in Miles' belly at the mention of her ring. He felt absurdly guilty that he was glad the missing ring was keeping her in Chances Inlet. Miles told himself it was because he needed her help at the inn, but one part of his body was calling him out as a liar: the part that wanted to be back inside Lori again. If she found her ring, she'd be gone tomorrow. He was sure of it.

"I don't like the idea of Cassidy taking anything from anyone. Especially since I had to pull a shitload of strings to keep her out of foster care when Mona went to jail."

Lori rolled over onto his chest. "It would break your mother's heart."

Given the tears he'd seen in Lori's eyes earlier, it would break her heart, too, even if she did manage to get her ring back. He nodded, distracted by her long hair brushing against his chest. Its dull black color was obviously a part of her disguise given that other parts of her body were covered with rich, russet hair. He brushed a silky strand of it off her face. She flattened her hands on his chest and laid her chin on top of them, releasing a contented sigh.

"I've checked her room multiple times. She doesn't have much and she's pretty much an open book about what she does have." She gnawed on her bottom lip, the sight making Miles hard and tight.

He groaned. "I checked the Patty Wagon yesterday. Nothing."

Her eyes grew wide. "I never thought to check there. And if she was going to steal, wouldn't she just take the cash from the register?"

"Yep. But I've gone through the books. Everything adds up."

She sighed again. "I may never find my ring."

He dragged his fingers through her hair. "We'll find it." Miles had no idea what possessed him to say the words. Well, aside from the fact that Lori was sexy and naked in his bed and he'd do and say just about anything to keep her there.

Her eyes grew wide and the corners of her lopsided mouth turned up. "You'll help me?"

Finding who took her ring meant that Lori would be leaving sooner rather than later. Miles wasn't sure how he felt about that right now. But he didn't want anything else to go missing from his mother's inn, either. "Sure."

Her eyes were damp as she crawled up his body. "Thank you, Miles," she said before kissing him softly on the corner of his lips. She kissed the other side. "I know you've got a lot on your plate right now."

Miles didn't want to think about what was *on his plate* right now. He didn't want to think about the campaign, Faye Rich, Greer, the governor, Cassidy, his mother, or anyone else. That was for tomorrow. Tonight was for escaping into the soft confines of a sexy body and he was done wasting time talking. He nipped at Lori's lips before taking her mouth in a greedy kiss. She responded by straddling his body and giving him the ride of his life.

FIFTEEN

When Miles' alarm rousted him awake the next morning, Lori was already gone. He rolled over and buried his nose in the pillow. It smelled of her minty shampoo and sex, the scent making Miles instantly hard enough to pound nails. He jumped out of bed, yanking the sheets off as he did so. Tossing them in the hamper, he made his way to the bathroom, where he spied a piece of paper tucked beneath his tube of toothpaste. He snatched it up.

No regrets.

Miles smiled at the elegant handwriting on the paper. Glancing in the mirror, he realized that his only regret was that the night was over. Lori had been everything he had expected her to be. And the sex? That had been even better. As much as Miles hated to admit it, his brother Gavin had been right about him needing to get laid. Despite the meager amount of sleep he'd gotten, Miles felt more relaxed and ready to face the agonizing decisions that loomed before him. He had Lori to thank for that. Miles grinned just thinking about the ways he wanted to repay her for the favor.

Just as quickly, his grin faded. She wasn't sticking around.

Hell, she might already be gone. His pulse sped up at the thought. He shoved the note into the top drawer of the dresser and began furiously brushing his teeth. Miles knew the reality of the situation. Theirs was a one-night stand months in the making. Their relationship could never be anything more. Still, he wasn't ready for Lori to take her secrets and vanish into thin air.

And those secrets bothered him. There was no way she was some nefarious criminal. Not judging by the way she cared for Cassidy, his mother, and this B and B. Clearly she was running from someone and that thought stirred up Miles' ire even more. He spit into the sink, swearing as he did. He knew people. People who could help. Just look what he was able to do for Cassidy. Miles could protect Lori, too. If she'd only let him in on her secret.

His phone beeped with a text message. That would be Will alerting him that he was beginning his run. He'd be on the stretch of beach in front of the B and B to meet up with Miles in ten minutes. He pulled on his running clothes, eager to get down to the kitchen before he had to meet Will.

The smell of bacon greeted him at the threshold of the room. He blew out a relieved breath when he spied Lori, standing at the counter with her back to him, filling a chafing dish with grits. She was dressed in her usual garb of baggy cargo pants and a long T-shirt. He'd known for months that she was hiding a hot figure beneath her clothes, but now that he'd touched—and tasted—that body, Miles appreciated the drab outfits she used to blend in. They kept other men from fantasizing about the secrets she kept concealed beneath them.

Coming up behind her, he pressed his lips to the freckle he'd discovered on her neck the night before. Lori jumped away from him, nearly spilling the contents of the tray.

"Miles!" she hissed as she quickly glanced around the empty room. "You can't do that."

The muscles clenched in his jaw. He wanted to kiss her and do a hell of a lot more, but she was right. *Damn it.* The last thing he needed was his mother, Cassidy, or—God forbid—Bernice walking in on them. He didn't know how to explain what was going on with Lori to himself, much less to anybody else.

Placing a hand on her lower back, he guided her into the laundry room, out of the line of sight of anyone who might happen into the kitchen.

"The breakfast room opens in ten minutes, Miles." Lori licked her lips and her gaze roamed his face, an uncertain look in her eyes.

"This will only take five," he said before he sealed his lips over hers. Thankfully, she didn't resist. Instead, she rocked her hips into his as she wrapped her arms around his neck. That was all the encouragement Miles needed. He plundered her mouth, kissing her like some greedy frat boy who was totally out of control. She tasted like strawberries and cinnamon. Miles' body grew hard and his head grew light with every little breathy sound she made.

Lori's common sense was obviously working more effectively than his because she pulled out of the kiss before either of them did something stupid. Miles leaned his forehead against hers, waiting for their breathing to return to normal.

"I just came down to tell you, no regrets."

She pulled back and a look of faint wonderment spread over her face followed by an effervescent smile. Those golden flecks sparkled in her caramel eyes again, and Miles swore she seemed brighter.

"I'm glad," she whispered. "So very glad."

Miles slid his hands up and down her back, continuing to study her. She was definitely not a hardened criminal. Not with lips and eyes like that.

"Let me help you," he whispered.

"There are only six people in for breakfast," she said, misunderstanding his intent. "I think I can manage."

"That's not—"

The screen door slammed, followed by the sound of scratching on the kitchen floor before his brother's damn dog appeared complete with a piece of driftwood in his mouth. The dog got hung up as it tried to ram the oversized stick into the doorframe in an effort to greet Miles and Lori.

"Careful, Midas," Lori said with a laugh as she stepped out of the laundry room. She stopped a few steps into the kitchen at the sight of Will Connelly. Will eyed both her and Miles shrewdly before pilfering a piece of bacon out of the warmer.

"I'll call the help line about the dryer later today. I'm sure it's an easy fix," Miles lied, saying the first thing that came to mind. He knew that look on Will. Despite the lie, there would still be questions. In many ways, his friend would be harder to fool than Bernice. The only thing Miles had going for him was the fact that the big man looked exhausted. Hopefully, he was easily diverted.

Lori nodded before picking up a chafing dish and disappearing into the breakfast room.

"How'd you end up with Midas?" Miles asked as he grabbed a bottle of water out of the cooler. "You've already got your hands full with a new baby in the house."

Will reached in behind him and pulled out a bottle of his own. "Gavin headed back to New York for the rest of the week. I told him I'd run the mutt every morning to wear him out. Ginger is teaching a dance summer camp so she won't have much time to keep Midas entertained." He shrugged. "It gives me an excuse to escape the house and get my run in."

They headed toward the beach, the dog frolicking at their heels. Gavin had probably told him all this the night before, but Miles had been distracted by the governor's ultimatum—among other things. He needed to get his head back into the campaign and regain control of his life.

The two ran in companionable silence for the first mile while the dog bolted in and out of the surf, zigzagging between both men.

Miles decided to leap right in with both feet. "Can I ask you a personal question?"

"As long as I get to ask what was going on in the laundry room this morning," Will answered.

"Nothing was going on in the laundry room. Just a problem with the washer."

"Funny, you said it was the dryer before."

Miles cursed the Ivy League–educated jock.

Will just laughed. "Don't worry. I'm not going to tell

anyone you're fooling around with the maid. There's no crime in that. As long as you're both willing and single."

Miles stumbled before catching himself. Will wouldn't be so flippant if he knew Miles was considering ending his single status. "About that . . ."

His friend eyed him with that astute look again before pulling up to a walk. "She's not single?"

"No!" Miles paced the shoreline. "I mean yes. But I'm not talking about Lori. I'm talking about me."

Will took a long pull from the bottle of water. "You're not single?" he asked sarcastically after he'd swallowed.

"Can I just get to my damn question?"

"Sure." Will tossed a stick out into the ocean and Midas scampered after it. "Ask away."

"It's about your marriage."

His friend shot him one of those icy looks that had the rest of the NFL nicknaming him William the Conqueror. "There's personal and there's none-of-your-damn-business, Miles. What goes on with my marriage falls into the second category."

This was going to be more difficult than Miles thought. He needed to talk to someone about the governor's proposal. Miles didn't feel comfortable talking to anyone in his family about it. With his luck, the governor had already informed Coy of his proposition and Bernice would have all of Chances Inlet making wedding plans before noon. Miles cringed, picturing his mother's reaction. She would be disappointed and his siblings would no doubt accuse him of being overly ambitious yet again. But Will had originally married Julianne for convenience, as a way to share custody of the son he hadn't known about. At least he'd understand Miles' dilemma.

"I'm not interested in the intimate details," Miles said. "I want to know about your first marriage. When you married Julianne as a formality. You didn't love her, but you married her anyway."

Will stared at him in silence. Miles knew he wasn't making any sense. Frustrated, he yanked off his T-shirt and swiped at his sweaty face. Better just to spit it out, he figured.

"The governor is worried about my campaign. All this

bullshit about my father is making my approval ratings tank. Faye is a happily married woman with a family. Apparently, voters like settled." He pushed out an aggravated sigh. "The governor thinks it would be best if I got married."

"What?" Will looked as if Miles had just told him they were going to run to New York and back. "That's the stupidest thing I've ever heard. People just don't get married to improve their image."

"You did," Miles fired back at him.

"That was different and you know it. I married Julianne to protect my *son's* image. I didn't want him growing up labeled a bastard like I did." Midas dropped the stick at Will's feet. Will angrily chucked it past the waves. They both stood there silently, watching the dog leap through the water before Will spoke again. "You're not actually considering it, are you?"

"I might not have a choice. The party will make the campaign negative if I don't."

Will snorted. "You have more integrity than that, Miles. Besides, you aren't even dating anyone. Unless you're planning on marrying whoever tattooed your back with their fingernails?"

Miles swore as he pulled the T-shirt over his head.

"Washer and dryer my ass," Will mumbled.

"The governor wants me to marry his daughter."

Will whistled. "The plot thickens. At least she's gorgeous. And smart. There's also that whole politically well-connected part. At the risk of sounding like a dumbass, what's there to be conflicted about here?" he asked condescendingly.

His friend clearly didn't understand. Miles kicked off his shoes and waded out into the surf. The dog barked excitedly, weaving between Miles' legs. How had everything gotten so complicated? His life plan had never included Justine and his father's deaths and his mother's subsequent financial woes. Or an arranged marriage. Not to mention a distracting stranger who made him want to abandon his squeaky clean image for a night. Or two.

Will waded in to stand beside him. "What's really going on here, Miles? I know you and Greer are friends and you respect her, but you're the most honest guy I know. The lie of the relationship would eat at you." Will rolled his shoulders. "If you're asking me whether or not you'd learn to love Greer, I have no idea what to tell you. I blackmailed Julianne into marrying me the first time because I didn't want her taking Owen away. But in truth, I wanted her, too. We started with a pretty potent chemistry. Love became a part of the game plan later."

Miles sighed. "That's not the case here. I think of Greer like I do my two sisters. And you know I'm not planning on falling in love again."

Will mumbled something that sounded a lot like *dumb ass*. "And this thing with Lori? What's that about?"

"Lori has one foot out the door. We were just scratching an itch." Miles hated how the words sounded as they left his lips. Yet he didn't want to analyze why last night felt like something more than a one-night stand. "Would it make me an ass if I said despite what happened between her and me last night, I'm still considering marrying Greer? It seems the lesser of two evils."

"Is what they have on Faye that bad?"

The governor claimed to have evidence that Faye Rich had had an abortion when she was seventeen. According to his source, the baby's father was one of the mechanics at her father's car dealership. The man was also fifteen years her senior and married. Miles cringed just thinking about it. True or not, he was in no position to judge Faye for a youthful indiscretion. The woman had made a huge success of her life and her business. It had no bearing on whether or not she should serve in Congress.

He shook his head. "It's not worth repeating."

Will blew out a resigned sigh. "Well, then what would make you an ass would be if you went into this without letting Greer know the score up front."

Miles nodded. If he went through with this marriage, the one thing he could give Greer was his honesty. She'd likely take that as a challenge to secure his heart, but she'd only be disappointed in the end.

"One more thing, though," Will cautioned him. "Even when I married Julianne for convenience, I gave her my word

I'd be faithful. If you decide to go through with this madness, you can't go around *scratching any more itches*. You'd better hope Lori really does have one foot out the door."

"She does." Ironically, with everything he faced, that thought troubled Miles the most.

"Careful with the sprinkles, sweetheart." Lori caught the bottle of rainbow-colored sugar before Emily accidentally knocked it off the counter with the oversized sleeves of her princess costume. Patricia's granddaughter was piling the sprinkles on the heart- and star-shaped sugar cookies that Lori had rolled out. "Maybe we should use a little less on each one so we have enough for all of them," Lori suggested.

"I have to make these stars extra sparkly." Emily pushed out her bottom lip, giving Lori that look that said she wasn't going to be denied. Lori glanced across the kitchen for reinforcements, but Kate was on her phone talking about a patient. Patricia had hobbled into the library where guests were enjoying afternoon tea.

"Those are lovely, Em," Ginger said over Lori's shoulder. Emily beamed at her future aunt, her smile shouting, *I told you so*. "Even if they are extra cavity-inducing," Ginger whispered to Lori. Both women shared a smile.

"What are you doing out of the studio?" Lori asked. "I thought Audra had you teaching camp all week."

Ginger snitched one of the cookies, discreetly dusting off the excess sugar into the sink.

"They're watching *Cinderella* this afternoon. It's the dance they're breaking down in camp."

She lowered her voice so that only Lori could hear. "I ran up here because something came in the mail for you today. It's from Diesel."

Lori's pulse skipped a beat. She'd been waiting for the letter from her friend for days now. It likely contained the details of her next job. It also meant that as soon as she found her grandmother's ring, she could move on. The thought made her nauseous.

She took the envelope from Ginger. "Will you keep an eye on her for a minute?" she whispered.

Ginger nodded and Lori made her way out to the sunny veranda. Thankfully, it was empty of guests. She tore open Diesel's letter and read his carefully laid out plans for the next phase of her life. He'd gotten her a job as a personal chef to a country singer. The position came with a small apartment. Diesel had thought of everything, including sending ample money for her to buy a bus ticket to Nashville. The whole process would be easy.

Too bad it wouldn't be painless.

When Lori had left Oregon, she'd felt little remorse at breaking her mother's heart. She'd been a callous, reckless teenager wanting the life she figured she'd been denied. Wealth and independence were waiting for her with a father she'd barely known. The only emotion she'd felt was the thrill of the glitzy life and excitement for the career that awaited her.

Eight years later, when she'd escaped New York, panic and anger were the emotions weighing her down. Those were tempered by the relief she'd felt when she'd found a safe haven in Chances Inlet, and the Tide Me Over Inn. Despite her best intentions, she'd become attached to the people here. It would hurt not to be a part of their lives any longer. There was no way for her to repay Patricia's kindness. Lori would miss the ease of Ginger's friendship and Cassidy's quirkiness.

It's for the best, she told herself. Once they found out who and what she was, they wouldn't want her working here any longer. Worse, they wouldn't want her in their lives, period. Their rejection would be even more painful than slipping off in the middle of the night without so much as a good-bye.

And then there was Miles. A flush warmed her body just thinking about the things they'd done to each other between the sheets of his big bed. Last night had been a one-night stand for the ages—hasty and wild. But like Miles, Lori had no regrets. Except that the circumstances of both of their lives meant their relationship could never be anything more. They'd just been using each other to escape the real world that was closing in on both of them. She squeezed back the tears building behind her eyes.

"Hey."

Lori jumped at the sound of Miles' voice. She shoved the letter into her pants pocket.

"Everything okay?" he asked.

"Sure," she lied.

He made a noise that sounded like he didn't believe her. Leaning a hip against the railing, he crossed his arms over his chest. Miles was casually dressed in a pair of well-worn jeans and a faded Duke T-shirt, which stretched nicely over his muscled chest. Lori's eyes roamed over him and her mouth went a little dry. She'd never seen this version of Miles. It was almost as appealing as the naked version. *Almost.*

"Casual dress at work today?" she asked, hoping to distract him from probing.

The corners of his mouth turned up into a grin. "Still avoiding any direct questions, I see." Miles shook his head. "At least you're predictable." He looked down at his Sorel work boots. "Not so much casual as necessary. I was helping the local housing authority restore one of the older houses for a family in their system."

Of course he was. "That had to make a fantastic campaign photo op. I hope Greer captured you showing off your McAlister skills with a tool belt. The video should definitely gain you some rating points."

Miles dropped his chin to his chest and reached around to squeeze the back of his neck. Lori immediately felt guilty for accusing him of manipulating his image. It was in Miles' DNA to help others, regardless of whether he was running for office or not. He genuinely cared about people despite the decision he had to make. Unlike her father, who wore a false persona like a cloak and used everyone around him.

"Sorry," she said. "That was snarky of me."

"No. It was fair. Especially after everything I told you yesterday."

She didn't want to ask, yet the not knowing was killing her. "Have you come to any decisions?"

He lifted his chin so that his eyes met hers. She nearly shivered at the intensity in them. "I'm still weighing my options."

Lori wasn't sure which aggravated her more: that Miles would marry Greer without loving her or that he'd once loved another woman so much he'd closed off his heart to everyone else. Rationally, she knew she had no claim to him, even after last night. But that didn't stop her from wanting to see one of them happy.

"Midas, no! Bad dog," Ginger shouted from the kitchen, followed by a wail from Emily.

The screen door shot open and the golden retriever came bounding out. He trotted over to Miles, wagging his tail and sporting a snout covered in rainbow sprinkles.

"Oh, Midas, what did you do?" Lori got to her feet, shoving the dog away as he made a beeline for her crotch. "I should go clean up whatever disaster he made in there."

She headed for the door, but as she passed Miles, he reached out and gently wrapped his fingers around her upper arm. The warm feel of his skin on hers made her catch her breath. He stroked his thumb in a slow circle and heat shot to her core. Staring down at where his fingers brazed her skin, she slammed her eyes shut so he wouldn't see the sadness building in them.

"I'm leaving soon, Miles," she whispered. "My plans have been firmed up." She skimmed her fingers over the letter tucked in her pocket.

"Have dinner with me tonight, then."

Lori's eyelids snapped open at his words. A refusal hovered on her tongue but she couldn't seem to make the words come out.

He leaned in closer so that his words rasped against her cheek. "I know you said yesterday that we're both going in different directions. But right now our paths have intersected. I'm not asking you for any promises and I'm sure as hell not making any. I just want to be with you for however many moments we can carve out together. Tell me you don't feel the same way?"

However many moments we can carve out together. Her common sense was telling her that she should be satisfied with the moments they'd spent together last night; that it would be risky to get any closer to Miles. But he was right—they might not ever get to another time or another place. When she opened her mouth, she was as surprised by the recklessness of her words as he was. "I guess dinner would be okay. I can make something here."

He shook his head. "I have a better idea."

Panic raced through Lori. She wouldn't risk going out in public. Not even for Miles.

"Don't worry," he said, rubbing his fingers up and down her arm to calm her. "I have someplace very private in mind. Meet me at the garden shed at seven thirty."

The sound of Emily crying filtered through the screen door. Lori gave him a quick nod before hurrying back into the B and B.

SIXTEEN

Lori was late. Miles glanced at his phone again. Seven forty-five. He kicked a tuft of grass with his sneakered foot. Sure, he was the Rhodes Scholar, but Lori was probably the smarter one tonight. She was wise to stay away. Miles clearly hadn't been thinking with the correct body part when he'd invited her to dinner. But she'd looked so forlorn and worried sitting on his mother's veranda earlier that he said the first thing that had come to his mind.

Not that he didn't want to have dinner with Lori. Hell, he wanted to do that and a whole lot more with her. The zipper on his jeans became painfully tight recalling how gorgeous she looked the night before with her hair spread out on his pillow, her face relaxed with rapture when she came. She'd been a welcome and willing distraction.

But Lori was also practical and forthright. She'd probably come to her senses minutes after returning to the kitchen this afternoon. *I'm leaving soon*, she'd said. Miles' gut clenched just thinking about it. Her words had sounded so desolate. So final. Whatever she was running from guided the direction of her life and Miles was a jerk to want to use the chemistry between them for his own diversion. He needed to focus on the mess his campaign had become.

The governor had given him a stay of execution of sorts. Miles had until the next set of polling data was released to make a decision about how he wanted to proceed. That meant he had five days to come up with an alternative plan. While marrying Greer wasn't the most abhorrent idea, Miles would be damned if he'd let the governor dictate his campaign. Or his career. Miles lifted up the picnic basket he'd had prepared at the gourmet market in town. He'd just take it over to the office and munch on its contents while he pondered a new strategy.

Tessa suddenly rounded the corner of the garden shed followed closely by Lori. At least he thought it was Lori. The white Keds were familiar but the rest of the outfit didn't jibe with the mousy woman who worked in the inn. She was dressed in a pair of Capri jeans that hugged her ass so well Miles had to adjust his own jeans again. Instead of her usual baggy cast-off T-shirt, she was wearing a sleeveless blouse decorated with little anchors. It showcased her lean arms and was all tied up at the waist, making Miles want to tug at the bow to get at the body beneath. He stifled a groan just thinking about the sexy underwear he hoped she was wearing. Her hair was in a high ponytail beneath a worn baseball cap that likely belonged to his brother Ryan at one point. Dark sunglasses shielded her from being recognized. Not that any red-blooded male wouldn't do a double take with her in that outfit.

Miles playfully lifted the ball cap back from her face. "Lori? Are you in there?"

She yanked the hat back onto her head. "Sorry I'm late. I had to wait for the McDaniels to leave for dinner so I could finish the turndown service in all the suites."

An unexpected shot of pleasure burst within Miles. She hadn't been waffling on whether or not to meet him tonight. Lori had only been doing her job.

"Thanks," he said.

Lori's face had a bemused expression on it.

"For always being on task at the B and B." He slipped his empty hand into hers. "And for agreeing to have dinner with me."

She looked around at the shed. "We aren't eating in there, are we?"

Miles pulled her fingers up to his lips. "No. You seem to be a pretty brave woman, but even I don't want to have dinner with spiders."

Lori's laugh was guileless but he felt the potency of it in his groin, nevertheless. Miles led them along the bramble path that snaked through the trees behind the inn. Tessa ran on ahead of them, circling back to check on her master every ten yards or so.

"Why do I get the feeling that I'm Little Red Riding Hood and you're the Big Bad Wolf?"

Miles smiled at that. "You're about to pass a very famous landmark in our town. See that live oak tree over there?" He pointed to her left. "The one with the intertwined trunks?"

"It's in the shape of a heart," she said wistfully.

"Legend has it, that if you walk by it with a beautiful woman, you have to kiss her or risk never knowing true happiness in your lifetime." Miles was pretty sure Will had made the whole thing up to score with Allison Baker back in high school, but he wasn't sure if he could hold out until they got to their destination without a quick taste of Lori's lips.

Her expression was dubious when she lifted the sunglasses off her face before securing them on top of the baseball cap. "Is that so? Well, we don't want to risk eternal unhappiness, do we?" She stretched up on her toes and brushed a chaste kiss over his mouth. "Hmm. We'd better not take any chances," she whispered. Suddenly her whole body was pressed up against Miles and she was opening up his lips with her own. He growled low in the back of his throat, depositing the picnic basket on the ground with a thud so he could sneak his fingers beneath the cute little top she was tied up in. She sighed into his mouth when his fingers came in contact with her skin.

Miles took control of the kiss then, walking her backward toward the nearest tree trunk. She arched her body into his and he had to suck in a deep breath in order to maintain his composure. Lori was practically crawling up his body and he gave her ass a firm squeeze with both hands. She wrapped her arms and legs around him, plunging her tongue deep into his mouth. He slid his erection back and forth against her core.

Lori tossed her head back with a gasp, dislodging both her hat and her sunglasses. "Please tell me that basket is full of condoms," she begged.

He nipped at her exposed collarbone and she thrust her hips forward, nearly shattering his control.

"I like the way you think but we're not doing this here."

"I thought you were a Boy Scout, Miles," she moaned.

Miles untangled her legs from behind his back and let out a harsh breath as she slid down his body. "I am," he said through clenched teeth. "An Eagle Scout, in fact. But we're still not doing this here."

"Why not?" Her question was practically a wail.

"Chiggers."

Lori jumped away from the tree trunk at the mention of the bugs and Miles bit back a smile. He grimaced when he leaned down to retrieve her hat and sunglasses. His body needed time to recoup from their heated exchange. Tessa was sitting quietly guarding the picnic basket, circumspectly eyeing Miles as he approached. "Good dog," he said. "Midas would have devoured everything inside by now."

The dog swiped her tail over the ground as Lori scratched her behind the ear. She returned her hat to her head and Miles reached for her hand. His body twitched again with the contact and Miles set an urgent pace out of the woods. They emerged facing a row of backyards along one of the residential streets in town. Lori hesitated, pulling her hat down lower on her head.

"Don't worry, no one will see you," Miles reassured her. "We're going in the back way." He led her through a very familiar gate into a fenced backyard. Tessa sniffed around the rosebushes and rhododendrons lining the fence. Miles surveyed the landscaping and shook his head. "My mother would be disappointed with how this place has been maintained."

"This is your mother's house?" she asked as he led her up the flagstone steps he and his brothers had installed one hot weekend while his father shouted out directions.

"Technically, yes. It's the house I grew up in."

He reached beneath an old planter attached to the laundry room window and pulled out a key.

"Does someone live here?"

Miles shook his head. Placing the key in the lock, he opened the door, gesturing for her and the dog to precede him inside. He guided her through the laundry room and into the spacious eat-in kitchen. The sunny yellow his mother had painted the room had been covered up with heavy floral wallpaper. Miles set the basket on the white Corian countertop his mother had been so proud of all those years ago. Tessa wandered through the great room with its wide pine floors. He smiled at the memory of his family camping out in the backyard for three days while his father meticulously laid the tongue and groove planks.

Lori trailed her fingers over the keys of the antique carved upright piano in the corner of the room. The piano was too delicate to be moved, so it had remained in place. It was the only piece of furniture in the house. "Did you play growing up?" she asked.

"My mother insisted that we all take lessons. Evil Mrs. Dickerson came over every Thursday to teach us." Miles shuddered at the memory.

"You didn't like it?"

"Music wasn't my thing. Ellie is the gifted one. Kate mastered it so she could be better than me at something and Gavin is actually a passable player. I'm a little tone deaf and Ryan wouldn't sit still long enough."

She smiled coyly. "So there is actually something you're not good at."

He leaned a hip against the island in the center of the kitchen. "It's a short list."

Lori meandered toward the front of the house. "Has it been empty since your father died?"

Miles swallowed roughly. "No. We've had a couple sets of renters come through. The last ones moved out at the end of the month."

"Will your family keep it?"

"Gavin's talking about renovating it. The loft won't be big enough for them to live in once they start a family."

She looked over her shoulder at him. "You'll need a place for your family, won't you?"

And with that, the elephant had arrived in the room. One of them, at least.

"I told you, I haven't decided what I'm going to do yet."

Lori eyed him astutely. "You'll do what's right, Miles. You always do."

Something about her innate trust in his judgment irked him. He didn't want to be Squeaky Clean Miles McAlister this evening. Miles didn't want Lori being the stealthy, secretive mystery woman, either. Instead he just wanted them to be the two people they'd been last night: erotic and intimate without all the damn pretense.

He stalked over to where she was studying the craftsman door his father had made as a Mother's Day present one year. "Do you want the grand tour?"

She spun on her heel and placed her palm on his chest. Gnawing on her bottom lip, she dragged her fingernails along his shoulder. "As long as it starts in your bedroom."

Miles' cock jumped at her words. He wasn't one to look a gift horse in the mouth. Grabbing her hand, he headed for the stairs, leading her upstairs after taking a quick detour through the kitchen to grab the blanket he'd brought along for their "picnic." Lori's steps slowed when they reached the landing. Miles breathed in a few disappointed gulps of air before he realized she was just busy taking in the rooms at the top of the stairs. His sisters' room was still painted the delicate pink with its random Hello Kitty border. A Jack and Jill bathroom stood between the girls' and boys' bedrooms.

"One bathroom for five kids. That must have been cozy," she said.

"Especially when we got into high school. Gavin, Ryan, and I lived to torture Kate by taking all morning in there." As fun as those memories were, Miles was eager to make new ones with the sexy woman next to him. His body was telling him just how eager it was as all the blood rushed to his crotch. He tugged her toward the room he once shared with his brothers.

No trace remained of the three rambunctious boys who'd

shared the space for most of their lives. Miles thought briefly how that was probably a good thing. Especially since the room had smelled like a locker room for most of those years.

Lori stepped inside. "So Miles, did you ever bring a girl up here?" she asked as she slowly began unbuttoning her blouse.

Miles reached over and yanked on the bow tying it shut. "No," he answered. It came out more as a groan when he caught sight of the candy apple red bra she was wearing beneath her clothes.

"Of course you didn't, Dudley Do-Right." She kicked off her shoes and shucked the blouse.

His zipper had grown excruciatingly painful again. "I'm pretty sure Ryan had Tracy Waterman here a time or two," he managed to say despite the fact that his mouth was suddenly dry as the Sahara watching her shimmy out of her tight jeans. *Damn.* The panties—at least what there were of them—matched the bra. He wanted to take a big bite of them.

"Well, I think I can help you remedy that tonight."

Miles stepped out of his sneakers before stripping his shirt over his head, all the while saying a silent prayer that he wasn't in some crazy dream. Lori reached out and slid her fingertips along his chest. A little puff of air escaped her lips when she did and Miles grew painfully hard.

A flush stained her cheeks and she hid her eyes from his. "You must think I'm very forward."

He gripped her waist in his hands and pulled her body in contact with his. "Forward works for me," he managed to say despite the fact he was feeling a little light-headed with her warm skin rubbing up against his.

Lori laughed and Miles was awed by the raw delight in her voice. She'd closed herself off from everyone since arriving in Chances Inlet. Finally, he was getting to see the real woman beneath her fortress of layers.

"It's just that I don't know what my future holds," she whispered. Her wistful words made something squeeze inside Miles' chest. "And when I'm with you, I can forget that for a little while." She finally lifted her eyes to meet his. They were flooded with desire, but there was something else there, too—honesty. "I know you're using me for the same thing and that's okay."

It's not okay! Miles felt like a jerk for being called out by her. Except he couldn't argue because what she accused him of was the truth.

She flicked her tongue over his nipple and all coherent thought left his brain.

"Thank you for dinner," she said. "But if it's all the same, I'd like to start with dessert."

Miles watched as she unbuttoned his jeans and carefully pulled down the zipper. He groaned when her greedy fingers slid between his boxer briefs and his skin. Lori lingered there a moment, gently stroking her thumbs along his raging erection.

"Lori," he hissed when she pulled her hands away to shove his clothes over his hips. She shot him a coy smile before flicking her tongue over his nipple again. He stepped out of his pants and underwear and kicked them aside. Lori spread her hands on his chest and traced her tongue lower, circling the inside of his navel before she reached nirvana. Miles threw his head back with a heavy sigh when she sank down on her knees and circled him with her very skilled tongue.

A soft hum escaped her as she took him more fully in her mouth. Miles grabbed hold of her ponytail just to keep upright. He guided her head back and forth with it as she pleasured him with her mouth. One of her hands kneaded his sac while the other slid along his thigh. Miles was seconds from losing control when he pulled her head back, easing her mouth off him. She tilted her head up and the sight of her wet lips and unfocused eyes wrecked him.

"I want to be inside you. Now."

She nodded, reaching around on the floor for his jeans. He took them from her and dug into the back pockets to retrieve the condoms he'd stuck in there earlier.

"Let me do it," she said. Her breathing was still raspy and it was doing crazy things to Miles' body. After she'd rolled the condom over him, she gracefully got to her feet. Miles backed her across the room to the wide desktop he and Gavin had installed in the room's alcove. Lori eyed it carefully then tested it for sturdiness.

"Tell me, Dudley Do-Right, is this where you did your homework?" She shot him a wicked smile.

"Every night."

She slipped her bra straps off her shoulder then reached behind her back and undid the clasp. "Did you ever think of doing this when you were doing that homework?"

Miles pulled the bra from her fingers and tossed it on the pile of clothes on the floor.

"Every night," he growled as he slid a finger beneath her panties. "And it looks like I'm not the only one thinking about it now."

Her eyes drifted shut when he traced his thumb along her wet seam. He yanked the panties over her hips before nudging her deeper onto the desktop. She balanced herself on her hands, letting her legs hang open over the side.

"I've been thinking about it all day, Miles," she confessed breathlessly.

"Who am I to deny such an industrious girl her dessert?" Stepping between her legs, Miles leaned over her lush body. She looked more appetizing than any dessert he'd eaten before. Miles took a pink nipple in his mouth. With a contented sigh, she arched her body to give him better access, stroking her foot over his hip. He traced a finger through her curls before thrusting it deep inside her. Lori's eyes flew open as she bucked off the desk.

"What happened to you wanting to be inside me *now?*" she demanded.

Miles smiled to himself as he gave her pert nipple one last tug with his lips. Wrapping his hands around her hips, he stood up tall. She chewed on her lip while she watched raptly as he slowly slid inside her. A sweat broke out at the back of his neck at the eroticism of their pose. He groaned with satisfaction when her warm, wet body wrapped around him. "Damn," he said as he pulled her body closer. "You feel so good."

Threading his fingers beneath her ass, he lifted her up so he could slide deeper inside her. Lori wrapped her legs around his hips and draped her arms over his shoulders. She threw her head back again when he filled her to the hilt. Her moaned "yes" was like a benediction to his ears. Miles stilled so that he could slow things down and savor the moment, but Lori had other ideas. She clenched her muscles around him and he was lost. They moved together at an urgent pace, her little breaths fanning his ear.

"Yes," she moaned. "Just like that. This is what I need." She nipped his collarbone and he could feel her muscles growing tighter. He wanted to watch her find her bliss again. Slowing the pace, he leaned her back against the desktop and maneuvered a finger between their bodies. Her head rolled from side to side.

"Please, Miles," she begged. "Make me forget." Something about her words was unsettling at the back of his mind, but the sight of her writhing before him pretty much obliterated any rational thought. His brain told him to give her what she wanted and to follow her over the edge. He dragged his thumb over her sweet spot and circled once, twice, three times. The third time was the charm. She convulsed around him and Miles barely had time to take in the gorgeous picture of her as she came before he was pumping into her again, his powerful release making him swear like a sailor.

SEVENTEEN

They were each sitting cross-legged, the picnic basket between them on the floor in front of the pretty stone hearth. Miles had brought along several wide candles to place in the fireplace and the candlelight danced on the bare skin of his chest every time either of them moved. Lori had dressed before they'd moved downstairs, but Miles had only gone so far as to pull on his jeans. She was distracted by his sexy body until he'd opened up the basket and started pulling out the food. Suddenly Lori was ravenous.

Miles should be the poster boy for Scouting. He'd definitely come prepared this evening. The basket contained not only candles and wine, but a delicious dinner of sandwiches and salads. The only thing missing was the dessert, but since she'd already enjoyed a thoroughly satisfying one upstairs, Lori wasn't going to complain.

Miles ripped off a piece of bread and tossed it over to where Tessa was lying. The dog caught the morsel in midair. Lori smiled. "You're going to spoil her."

"She's really very sweet. Have you had her long?"

"Actually, she's a stray who used to hang out in the alley

near my apartment. Diesel and I would take turns feeding her. I was worried about how she would survive when we both left, so I brought her with me."

Miles' body went still at the mention of Diesel and she quickly realized her mistake. Pursing her lips, she swore silently.

"Diesel?" His voice was low and ragged. "You two knew each other before you came to town?"

"Yes, we lived in the same apartment building. In New York." Of course, he'd likely already figured that out on his own.

He turned to face the fireplace and Lori cringed a bit at the hard set of his jaw.

"So Diesel knows who you are?" he asked without bothering to face her. "Does he know your whole freakin' back story?"

Lori reached over the picnic basket and gave his knee a gentle squeeze. "He and I are friends, Miles." She waited until he swung his eyes back around to meet hers. "We've never had *dessert* together, though."

"Good to know," he said as he tossed the remains of his sandwich back onto his plate.

She didn't know whether to laugh or cry over the fact that Miles was miffed. "Miles, this"—she waved her hand between them—"is all you need to know. We're just two people enjoying each other, helping each other through some rough times. My back story and *your future* aren't important. The woman sitting here right now, the woman you made love to, is who I really am. Truth."

He swallowed roughly before he eventually nodded. "At least I know where you lived before you came here. Although I don't think you grew up there. Your accent is too flat to be a native New Yorker."

Lori smiled. "You're right. I grew up on the other side of the country. In a small town very similar to this one." She was safe in giving him that much information. The media had thankfully never connected her father to Lori Hunt of Logan, Oregon.

Miles took a sip of his wine then stared at her over the rim of the glass. "Brothers and sisters?"

"Only child." She was splitting hairs, but technically it

wasn't a lie since she was the only child her biological parents had together.

"Favorite color?"

Lori always hated that question. She never really gravitated toward one color or the other, preferring whichever one fit her mood at the time. Glancing across at the serious expression in his eyes, however, there was only one answer she could give. "Blue."

He crooked an eyebrow as though he knew he was being played but he continued with his questioning. "Dogs or cats?"

It was Lori's turn to raise an eyebrow. She angled her chin toward Tessa.

Miles grinned. "Okay, favorite subject in school. And don't say home ec."

"I didn't take home ec, thankfully. I was a band kid. Piccolo." She swallowed a mouthful of wine, basking in his admiring smile. "But my favorite subject was always science. I loved doing the experiments."

He gave her an approving nod. "Favorite music then, band girl?"

"Oh, wow, that's not fair. I like all music. Although being in North Carolina, country music is really starting to grow on me."

Miles set his empty glass down on the hearth, then he moved the picnic basket to the side. "How about North Carolina? Is it really growing on you?"

She tried and failed to fight the smile forming on her lips as he prowled across the blanket toward her. "Some of the people definitely are." A lump formed in her throat at the truth of her statement.

Taking the wineglass from her fingers, he set it next to his on the hearth. "Favorite flavor of ice cream?" he asked as he gently leaned her back against the blanket on the floor.

Lori stretched out her legs beneath his muscled thighs, which were pinning her down. "I have to go with chocolate."

He ran his tongue along her nape and the fluttering began deep in Lori's core. "Really," he said between nibbling her neck. "All thirty-one flavors and you pick something as boring as chocolate?"

Lori slid her hands beneath his loose jeans, skimming her fingertips over the firm globes of his ass. "Vanilla is boring." She leaned her neck to the side, giving him better access. "And I told you I was easy."

"Easy enough that you won't object to a second helping of dessert?" he murmured in her ear.

Miles' hands were circling her tender nipples, eliciting a long sigh from deep within her. "A real woman never refuses a second helping of dessert," she managed to get out before his mouth took hers. His kiss was achingly slow and tender. Lori's hips flexed beneath his in an effort to try and spur him on. But Miles ignored her message, taking his time savoring her mouth while his fingers unfastened the buttons of her blouse. He stroked his tongue against hers in a slow, deliberate rhythm. His unhurried movements were having the opposite effect on Lori as she grew wet and wilder beneath him. Pulling out of his kiss, she rolled her head to the side. The aroused flush covering her body made her breathless.

"Please." She might have been ashamed that the word sounded more like a sob, but at the moment, all she could think about was how much she needed Miles inside her.

Stretching up to a plank position, Miles chuckled as he watched her peel off her clothes. He jumped to his feet and took care of his jeans and the condom efficiently before pinning her body back to the floor with his.

"Please what, Sweet Cheeks?"

"Please take me," she whispered.

The words were barely out of her mouth and he was thrusting into her with one swift movement. Lori cried out from the sheer pleasure of it. Miles shifted so that with every move he made he was rubbing against the part of her that needed it the most. He moved a few strokes and stars began to form in front of her eyes.

"Favorite position?" he growled against her neck.

Lori laughed out loud and Miles stilled as if to listen as it echoed off the bare walls.

"Hmm, I'm pretty adventuresome," she said, nipping at his chin. "But right now, this one's working really well for me."

He thrust again and Lori moaned with pleasure.

"Let me help you," he said.

"You are helping me." She clenched her muscles around him and he moved deeper.

"That's not what I meant." He sounded as impatient as Lori felt.

She dragged her nails down his spine, hoping to urge him to move. "I know what you meant, Miles, but you can't help me with anything else but this." Lori arched her back so she could take him more fully. "This is all you can ever give me. And all I can ever give you."

He growled something obscene before rocking into her at a pace that had them both breathing heavily with the exertion. When the world started to splinter, Miles captured her shout of pleasure with his mouth. His tongue mimicked the thrusting of his body until, moments later, he came with a long jerk of his hips.

Lori wasn't sure how long they lay intertwined on the floor. A sense of wholeness enveloped her body, warming her from her fingers to her toes. Her heart and her mind were still racing at a frantic pace as her body came back from its sensual stupor. Was this really all they could ever have? *Would ever have?* Tears burned the backs of her eyes and she wanted to rail at the younger version of herself for making such stupid choices—ones that had forced her on the road she was now traveling. All she and Miles would ever have was this little intersection along the divergent paths of their lives. She needed to get a grip and soak up everything he was willing to give her for the short time they had left.

Thunder rumbled off in the distance. Darkness had settled over the quiet street. Lori traced Miles' ear with the tip of her tongue. "I have to get back to the B and B soon," she whispered. "I need to get the breakfast dishes organized."

"Mmm," was all he said before he eventually stirred.

They dressed in the quiet as the thunder crept closer. Miles extinguished the candles before repacking the basket. He led her out of the house, locking the door and returning the key to beneath the flowerpot. Pulling a flashlight out of the basket,

Miles used it to illuminate the path through the woods. The sky opened up just as they emerged near the garden shed. Tessa yelped as she ran ahead to the safety of the inn.

Miles' face split into a wide grin. "Let's make a run for it," he said as he twined his fingers through hers and pulled her toward the house. Both of them were soaked when they reached the kitchen. Fortunately the B and B was quiet and settled for the night. Miles handed her a towel from a stack in the laundry. Then he helped her carry the necessary plates and silverware into the breakfast room. Lori returned to the kitchen to set the timers on the warming trays. She shivered when Miles came up behind her and pressed his damp body against hers.

"Let me warm you up," he whispered against her neck.

She never considered denying him. Miles turned off the lights and led her up the stairs to his room, where he proceeded to do more than warm her under the spray of the large shower in his suite.

"You weren't kidding about the snoring," Miles teased Lori as he carried the heavy cambro container of coffee the Java Jolt had just delivered into the B and B. It wasn't quite seven in the morning and the kitchen was empty except for the two of them. He needed to get out the door and hit the beach for his run, but he seemed to be getting later and later with his training every morning.

The past four nights spent with Lori had been diverting and relaxed. Despite the heavy decisions weighing them both down, they'd managed to carve out more time together—most of it in bed, not that Miles minded. But he could feel reality hovering, waiting to strike, like the storm clouds that currently blanketed the sky above the beach. Inexplicably, that only made him want to spend more time with her.

She blushed prettily as she piled the muffins into a basket. "I did warn you, Dudley."

Will stomped up the porch steps, making Miles abort the kiss he wanted to give her. His friend stopped at the screen door and reached around it to grab a bottle of water from the cooler. "The clouds are looking ominous out there," he said. "Let's run into town and grab a treadmill at the gym instead. You can kill two birds with one stone and press the flesh with some of your adoring future constituents."

Lightning flashed behind Will's head and Midas scrambled between his legs into the kitchen, seeking refuge beneath the back stairs. The dog had the right idea. Miles would much rather stay at the B and B and spend more time with Lori than work out at the crowded Ship's Iron gym. His friend eyed him discerningly as though he knew the way Miles' thoughts were tracking.

Miles blew out a resigned sigh. "Let's get moving, then, if we're going to beat the rain." He grabbed his own bottle of water. "Can you keep an eye on Midas?" he asked Lori.

Glancing at the dog cowering in the corner, she gave him a soft smile. "I don't think he'll give me much trouble." With a quick wave, she carried the muffins into the breakfast room.

His gut clenched as he watched her disappear through the doorway. Whenever they parted, Miles found himself constantly wondering if he'd see her again. That needy feeling working its way through his body was starting to concern him.

"Earth to Miles," Will said. "Let's go or we'll have our shower before we get to the gym."

He hesitated a moment longer before following Will out the door. They started off at a slow jog in an effort to cover the half-mile trek into town before the sky opened up.

"So, what happened to Lori having one foot out the door?"

They hadn't even gotten down the drive yet and Will was already asking questions. Miles felt defensive about revealing any details of his relationship with Lori—even to his close friend. "My mother is only at seventy-five percent. Lori won't leave until she feels my mother is ready." There was that rolling in his gut again. Miles wasn't exactly sure of what Lori would do—especially if whatever it was she was running from backed her into a corner.

But she still hadn't found her grandmother's ring. Her eyes always clouded with emotion whenever she mentioned it. Lori wouldn't leave without it. At least, he hoped not.

"That's sweet of her," Will said as they rounded the corner onto Main Street.

"It is sweet of her," Miles argued. "There's no reason for you to be such a dick."

They stopped at the corner across from the Java Jolt and Will gave him a sharp look. "I wasn't being a dick, Miles. I meant what I said: It *is* sweet. The woman even gave you a genuine smile a few minutes ago. Hell, I didn't even think it was possible for her to make eye contact, much less grin. Whatever you two have been up to, it seems to be good for her." The light changed and they both started across the street. "I'd say it's been good for you, too, but that stick is back up your ass again, so never mind."

Big raindrops began to splatter on the pavement and they both picked up their jog. Miles pondered what his friend had said. The last few nights with Lori had been good. *Damn good.* Miles chocked it up to the fact that Lori was a willing and very accommodating distraction. They were just scratching an itch until their paths dissected again. So why then did he feel so anxious about her slipping away?

Will was right that Lori was starting to come out of her shell. She was still stingy about the details of her life before she arrived in Chances Inlet, but certainly not with anything else. Her dedication to his mother's B and B went above and beyond even that of a paid employee. Not to mention that she went out of her way to be a lifeline for Cassidy, a kid that might have stolen her grandmother's ring. And she was certainly not stingy with her body. Miles' junk tightened up in his shorts just thinking about what she could do with her hands and her mouth.

"I know you're considering this thing with Greer." Will's words were like a slap upside the head, refocusing Miles to the dilemma that he'd been avoiding these past few days. "But I wish you'd factor your own happiness into the equation. You think achieving your life's goals is the only thing that will fulfill you, but trust me, there's more out there that can make you happy. Politics is stressful enough. Your relationships shouldn't be."

The rain began falling in earnest as they stopped under the

long awning leading to the entrance to the gym. The three-story brick warehouse formerly housed an iron works for local shipbuilders, but its name was the only indication of its previous life. A group of former trainers for professional athletes had reconfigured the building to accommodate a state-of-the-art fitness center—complete with an Olympic-sized swimming pool. The Ship's Iron attracted visitors from up and down the East Coast with its spa vacations and wellness boot camps. Miles' mother even offered a temporary pass to the gym with many of her B and B guest packages.

Miles stood on the sidewalk, hands on his hips. "I told you, Connelly, I'm not interested in a relationship. I'm not like you and Gavin. I never will be again."

Will shook his head in disgust. "For such an educated jerk, you really can be an idiot sometimes. Your feelings aren't something you can turn on and off with a switch. Take it from one who tried and failed. All I'm saying is that maybe a spontaneous *relationship*—like the one you have with Lori right now—makes more sense than the arrangement you're dooming yourself to with Greer." He yanked the door open. "But you're going to do what you're going to do. Just because you're compartmentalizing your actions under the guise of keeping some integrity in politics doesn't make it the right decision."

His friend stormed into the gym, leaving Miles standing alone on the sidewalk. He stared down the street as the rain beat out a steady rhythm on the canvas above his head. Will was way off base. What he and Lori had was *not* a relationship—spontaneous or otherwise. It was just sex and fun for both of them and he was confident she felt the same way. The feeling of unease he felt whenever he left her was just concern for her circumstances, that was all. Miles was worried that whatever she was hiding from could hurt her somehow. Their relationship—or however a person defined it—was as innocent as that. Will didn't know what he was talking about. The big lug was just trying to flex his brain before he hit the gym.

Still, Miles wondered whether there was a way to protect Lori. He wanted to solve her problems for her. After all, when their fling was over, she'd still be a woman he respected. Miles would do the same for any of his friends, whether he was sleeping with them or not, he told himself. All he needed was for her to open up to him and then he would do whatever it took to help her.

The rain came down harder and Miles made a silent vow that no matter how crazy his campaign schedule, he'd find time to help Lori. Because that's what he was in the business of doing: helping people. He'd just have to be extra persuasive with her tonight so that he could ferret out her secret. His shorts got tight just thinking about it and he bit back a smile as he headed toward the door of the gym.

"Miles!"

Son. Of. A. Bitch. The sound of Governor Rossi's voice was enough to douse Miles' lightened mood, not to mention his burgeoning hard-on. Coy held a giant golf umbrella over the governor's head as they both made their way from the gubernatorial Town Car toward the gym.

"Governor." Miles strode to the end of the portico to meet his boss. "I thought you had a breakfast in Wilmington?"

The governor extended a hand. "Not until nine. I thought that since I had to be up before the birds, I'd leave a few minutes earlier and try to catch a private word with you. Coy tells me you have a full schedule today."

Not full enough that he couldn't have met the governor in Wilmington, especially since he had a Rotary luncheon there later that day. Miles shot Coy a look, but the little shit didn't back down from his stare. His cocky body man had likely lied to the governor just to get more face time. Miles wondered if he'd been that bold when he was starting out in politics. *Probably.* He was beginning to realize that ambition was a pretty potent drug.

"Why don't we head over to the campaign office?" Miles said, gesturing toward the torpedo factory located catty-corner to the gym. "Bernice won't be in yet, but I'm sure Coy wouldn't mind running over to the Java Jolt and getting us some coffee."

"That would definitely hit the spot," the governor said, taking the umbrella from Coy. The kid had the nerve to spear Miles with a look, but he was smart enough to take the hint and do what he was told, sprinting up the two blocks to fetch some coffee.

Miles punched in the code on the lock to the office door and ushered the mayor into the large open room, littered with campaign posters and yard signs. Several desks were lined up in rows for the volunteers who came in to do whatever needed to be done that day. He gestured to the smaller office in the back—the one that had belonged to his father. "I don't know who'll be arriving when, so if you want this conversation to actually stay private, why don't we talk back there."

The governor immediately headed for Miles' father's chair as Miles pulled the door closed behind him. Miles bit back a protest and leaned a hip against the credenza instead. At least standing, he could maintain as much power in what he sensed would be a confrontational *private chat.*

"Sorry to interrupt your run," the governor said. "I know how you competitive athletes get a high from that. Never understood that concept myself, though." He leaned back in the chair. "Golf is much more my speed. And don't underestimate how much you can get accomplished politically out there on the course."

At sixty-one, Bob Rossi was in adequate shape, despite a thickening midsection. The guy was nearly six feet tall with a full head of dark hair, sprinkled with some gray. He commanded a room when he entered it with his deep baritone voice and his unique Mediterranean coloring. Governor Rossi had been called a "man's man" but he was definitely a favorite with the ladies, too.

Miles wasn't sure where the governor was heading with this "chat." "I've played golf with you before, sir," he said, trying to keep the conversation light. "You're as competitive on the links as you are in the political arena."

"I'm competitive in everything I do, McAlister." He propped his feet up on the desk and Miles tried not to cringe. "And so are you. We're a lot alike, you and I. We're both goal-oriented and very driven to succeed. We do whatever it takes."

Miles' breath stilled in his lungs. He wasn't sure he'd describe himself as doing "whatever it takes," especially if it meant harming others along the way. "Not if it means taking this campaign negative."

"Grow up, Miles," the governor said. "This isn't Cub Scouts. You're playing with the big boys now. You can't control every aspect of this campaign. Faye Rich's party is taking your father's story national with a few well-placed blogs this weekend." He raised his eyebrows when Miles flinched reflexively. "Yeah, the local media will continue to pick at the story as long as it's a part of the news cycle. Do you think that won't keep your polling points from free-falling?"

Miles' temples began to pound. He dropped his chin to his chest. This whole process was insane. Why did people care about something hasty his father had done with his privately held company? The creative bookkeeping hadn't hurt anyone but the McAlister family. "Whatever happened to the issues?" he argued. "I'm a huge advocate for the small businesses in this region and for fair pay for workers. Voters care about that; I know they do because I've freakin' asked them."

The governor laughed sardonically. "People don't vote on the issues any longer. They want leaders with personality. Faye Rich has got personality in spades and the voters are eating it up." He dropped his feet to the ground. "The way I see it, you've got two choices: Go on the offensive and attack Faye's integrity or do something to refocus voters on something other than your father. Let Greer help you, son."

The governor's use of the word "son" made Miles' chest squeeze and he felt as though he was suffocating. He wanted to open the door to the small office, but he could see through the window that Coy was making his way inside. The governor stood up, tugging at each sleeve of his suit jacket.

"She's been groomed for this all of her life," he continued. "Hell, if she had any political aspirations of her own, I'd be backing *her* for this seat. But she'd rather be the woman behind the man, just like her mama. Don't get me wrong, Greer will be an asset to your career. She has an agenda she'd like to pursue to make this country better; she just needs a platform to do it. You're not the only one riding my coattails to higher office, McAlister, but you're the one she picked. You should be flattered."

Miles felt anything but flattered. He suspected Greer chose him because she was being forced by her father to marry and he was the only one she trusted. But this was getting ridiculous. "Governor, I respect your daughter tremendously, but I don't love her. And I never will."

"I know you like women, McAlister. Believe me, I had that checked out years ago and I had you vetted again before we embarked on this campaign."

Bile rose up in Miles' throat at his boss' words. He'd heard whispers of the governor checking out his opponents, but never people on his own staff.

"Greer's mother and I married for political advantage," he continued. "Hell, Hillary and Bill managed to stay married while they each pursued careers in politics. Stop looking at me like I'm proposing something from some damn Gothic novel. You could do a lot worse than my daughter. I've invested too much energy into shaping you as a contender to let this campaign be pissed away because you want to rest on your honor. That doesn't work in politics today. This campaign needs to change its direction to something voters will be interested in. Talk to Greer. And for God's sake, make a decision about this before it's too late to recoup from your slide."

He reached up and squeezed Miles' shoulder as he passed by him.

"I need you in Congress, son. Hell, I need you in the White House. Let's win this."

Miles wasn't sure how long he stood there, breathing deeply in through his nose and out of his mouth, trying to get his heart rate under control. It took him several long moments before he could step away from the credenza. Unfortunately, he worried it might take him a lot longer to regain control of his political career. But he was determined not to let the governor—or the media—dictate his campaign. Staring at his father's empty chair, Miles prayed a silent promise to his dad that he would win this election on his own terms.

EIGHTEEN

"You look different," Ginger said before taking a sip of lemonade.

The storms from earlier in the day had passed through town, leaving behind a thick, muggy sky. Rather than meander along Main Street, many of the guests had returned to the B and B for afternoon tea. Lori tried to appear normal in front of Ginger's prying eyes as she frantically arranged cupcakes on a tray bound for the library and the demanding crowd.

The truth was she did feel different: lighter, more carefree. She hadn't been this relaxed in months—maybe even years. And she owed it all to Miles. The past few nights spent with him had been like a balm to her cynical soul. Just when she'd given up on men, along came her very own Dudley Do-Right with his justice-for-all character.

She should have listened to that voice deep inside her and run from him as far and as fast as she could before the muck that followed her tarnished all that was good about him. Except her body was sinfully glad that she'd ignored that voice. She felt the heat of the blush staining her cheeks. Miles was anything but a mild-mannered Boy Scout when it came to sex. Her body responded to his like it had to no other man. The feeling was heady, arousing, and confusing.

Lori needed to move on, to stay one step ahead, yet she was lingering in Chances Inlet longer than was wise. She kept telling herself it was because of her grandmother's missing ring, but she knew better. This thing with Miles made her long for a second chance at the life she'd thrown away. That second chance could never be with Miles; she knew that. Even if she wasn't tainted by her past, he'd vowed never to love with his heart again. In a sudden burst of clarity, Lori wanted it all: love included.

"Diesel wants to know what's taking you so long," Ginger said softly.

Lori glanced around the kitchen. Patricia was in the library with the guests. "Patricia still needs me."

"Cassidy and I can handle afternoon tea for the next couple of weeks. The guests will have to settle for baked goods that aren't homemade. And I'm sure Patricia can find someone to come in and clean."

"Wow, good to know I'm so indispensible."

Ginger sighed. "You're not. I'm sorry. That sounded awful. But you're my friend and I want to see you somewhere you don't have to hide. Where you can just be happy."

She couldn't be angry at Ginger. Lori wanted those things, too. She just wanted them here in Chances Inlet now.

"Oh, there it is," Patricia said as she hobbled in using one crutch. She picked up Emily's steeple hat with its sparkly pink cone and long veil of tulle. "That child leaves a trail of her things all over this place." She shook her head. "They're at Duke University Hospital already, and of course, she just remembered her *crown*. Emily is beside herself. Kate doesn't need that kind of stress right now."

Lori glanced at both women. "Is everything okay?" She'd just assumed that Kate was going to Durham to see a patient, but from the looks Ginger and Patricia were exchanging, she wasn't so sure.

Patricia hesitated before breaking into a nervous grin. "Kate is having in vitro fertilization tomorrow. She and Alden want a second child and the usual way just wasn't working this time. She doesn't want everyone in town to know," Patricia explained. "Just in case . . ."

Ginger patted her future mother-in-law's hand. "Soon you'll have lots of grandchildren leaving their toys all around the B and B."

Patricia smiled at Ginger before turning her attention back to Lori. "But there's no reason you shouldn't know. After all, you're practically family."

You're practically family.

Patricia's words ricocheted around in Lori's head, making her dizzy. She reached for the counter to steady herself.

"Lori, are you okay?" Ginger's voice sounded as if it were coming through a tunnel. She found herself being edged onto one of the high stools at the island.

"Here, drink this," Patricia was saying, wrapping Lori's fingers around a damp glass filled with cool lemonade. Lori swallowed the sweet drink and the spinning in her head began to recede.

"You poor thing." Patricia gently rubbed a hand up and down Lori's back. "You've been working too hard since the accident."

If only that were it, Lori thought to herself. The truth was, she'd become comfortable in Chances Inlet. While the reminders of her previous life hovered in the recesses of her mind, here she could be that woman she was before the mess with her father. Living and working in the inn was like slipping on a familiar pair of shoes, ones she could be herself in. This time when Lori slipped off in the middle of the night, she'd be leaving people who were "practically family" behind. *Running kept getting more and more difficult.*

"Ginger, would you mind taking those cupcakes into the library?" Patricia leaned against the stool beside Lori while Ginger carried the tray out of the room. "Tell me what I can do to help you," she said.

"I need to leave soon."

Patricia let out a heavy sigh. "I figured that was coming. Will you be all right? Do you need money? References? Anything?"

Lori shook her head. "It'll be better for everyone if no one finds out I was ever here. Promise me you won't tell anyone."

"Of course not." Patricia took Lori's hand and gave it a squeeze. "You're safe here. You always will be. I just wish there was something more we could do so you didn't have to go. Maybe Lamar could help you? Or Miles? He knows people who are well connected."

"No!" She was already too tangled up with Miles.

Patricia studied her face. "Diesel promised me that you weren't in any physical danger from anyone. I hope that's still true."

"It is." Lori nodded. "The only thing in danger is my reputation—and yours if anyone finds out you allowed me to stay here."

"Ha," Patricia laughed. "It seems my family's reputation is going to be dragged through the mud no matter what—especially with Miles running for Congress. A little more dirt certainly couldn't hurt too much."

It was the impact on Miles' campaign that had Lori worried the most, not that she mentioned that to his mother.

"I might not get the opportunity to say thank you," Lori said around the tightness in her throat. "You've been so kind and generous to me. The only way I know to repay you is to go before anyone finds out I'm here. I wish I could do more. I really do."

"Oh, honey, you've already done so much. I don't know how I would have gotten through the last two months without your help. It's almost as if you were born to run an inn like this."

Lori couldn't help smiling. "That's because I was."

Patricia looked at her questioningly. Lori had trusted this woman for nearly seven months now. She knew she could trust her with a snippet of the truth.

"I grew up in a place very similar to this," Lori explained as the tightness returned to her throat. "You remind me a lot of my mom."

"Is she . . ." Patricia didn't finish her sentence before Lori was shaking her head.

"She's alive and well." Lori drew in a harsh breath. "All I can tell you is that I made a rash decision years ago and left, thinking that I wanted more for my life. I was stupid and immature. Unfortunately I looked to the wrong person to help me. And now I'm paying the price. I let my mom down. Twice. I couldn't let you down, too. Not after all that you've done for me."

The older woman's eyes were shiny as she pulled Lori into a tight hug. "Mothers can forgive a lot of things, Lori. I'm sure she'd welcome you back."

"It's too late for that. I'm protecting her by staying away. Just like I'm protecting you by leaving."

They stayed locked in an embrace for a few moments longer. "You'll always have a home here," Patricia said softly. Her words caused Lori's body to wilt in sadness. She'd never have a home like this again. The choices she'd made were irrevocable. Now she had to live with the consequences. And she'd likely be living with them alone.

The sound of the screen door slamming startled both women. Bernice stormed into the kitchen, her face flushed. "Is Miles back yet?" she asked breathlessly.

Lori sensed Patricia stiffen beside her. "No. His Rotary lunch was in Wilmington, so he stayed up there to pick up Gavin at the airport. Is something wrong?"

"I'll tell you what's wrong." Bernice slammed her pocketbook down on the counter and began digging through it. She pulled out her phone and checked its screen. "That little snot-nosed Coy won't answer my calls. He thinks I'm just there to make his coffee." She let out an indelicate snort. "I've known the candidate since he was in diapers."

Lori watched as Patricia bit back a smile at Bernice calling Miles "the candidate."

"That she-devil Tanya Sheppard called campaign headquarters looking for confirmation of an outrageous rumor," Bernice said. "And Coy doesn't have the decency to call me back."

"I'm sure Coy's just in a meeting or something, Bernice." Patricia tried to placate the woman. "What's the rumor?"

Bernice blanched and Lori suddenly had a very bad feeling in the pit of her stomach.

"Oh, Patricia, honey." Bernice's lip began to quiver. "She said that Miles is engaged to Greer Rossi."

"Thanks for the ride." Gavin reclined in the passenger seat of Miles' Audi. "Although if I had called Faye Rich, I'd be riding in a souped-up GTO right now."

Miles shot a glare at his brother before returning his eyes to the road. "I can still drop you off in the taxi line, smart ass."

Gavin chuckled. "How are things in campaign land?"

Things in campaign land sucked. Miles had spent most of the day schmoozing with local business owners, discussing potential tax incentives that would promote more growth in the economy. The conversations had been stimulating and issue focused—exactly how Miles wanted to interact with potential constituents. Yet he couldn't stop reliving his conversation with the governor earlier in the day. His gut churned at the way his former boss thought he could manipulate his campaign—not to mention his life.

"That bad, huh?" Gavin asked.

Miles gave his head a little shake to refocus his thoughts. "Sorry. I'm just a little disillusioned right now."

"Uh-oh. Things *are* bad when the actual politicians are using words like 'disillusioned.' You wanna talk about it?"

He did want to talk about it, but the one person he wanted to bounce ideas off of was no longer around. Sadly his father stood to be hurt the most by his campaign right now. "Despite everything I've tried to do, things are going to get nasty."

"They always do," Gavin said with a cynical laugh. "You've been at this game long enough to expect that."

"I just didn't expect I'd have to drag our family through the mud with me."

"I thought Faye agreed to play nice?"

Miles sighed. "I'm beginning to think that Faye and I are just pawns in something bigger here." While waiting at the airport for Gavin, he'd checked in with his contacts at various media outlets. It seemed the governor was correct when he said Faye's campaign was taking the story of his father's money issues national. They were going so far as to call it a 'scandal.' Miles gripped the steering wheel tighter in annoyance. The woman had given him her word, damn it.

Gavin sat up a little straighter in his seat. "Are we talking about something other than the mess with Dad?"

Of course his perceptive brother would sense there was more to the issue. But Miles didn't want to go into detail about the governor's machinations. Not when Miles didn't know how he was going to cut the governor's puppet strings yet. He sure as hell wasn't going to tell Gavin about the man's proposal that Miles marry his daughter. There was no telling how his brother would react to that news. Besides, Miles still hadn't decided how he was going to handle that situation. It irked him that he might actually need Greer to stay in the race.

"Let's just say the governor and I disagree on how to respond to Faye's claims," was all Miles said.

Gavin paused a long moment before speaking. "Miles, whatever you decide, you know we're with you."

Miles blew out a breath as emotion clogged up his throat. He hadn't realized how much he needed to hear those words. With a brisk nod he navigated the car onto the highway leading south to Chances Inlet. "Let's talk about something else," he said. "What's Ryan up to?"

Gavin talked about their brother's lavish New York apartment and his crazy antics with the baseball groupies that seemed to follow Ryan everywhere. "Seriously, a woman was hiding in the trash chute of his building just to meet him," Gavin said. "I almost clocked her on the head with a bag of garbage." They both shared a laugh.

"For a guy who lost a shitload of money in a Ponzi scheme, he sure has landed on his feet," Gavin said.

"Yeah, but unfortunately, most of the other people conned in the scheme aren't professional athletes with a salary that rivals some school districts' budgets." Miles tried to keep the disgust from his voice. It wasn't his brother's fault he was talented enough to earn outrageous sums of money for playing a game. Or that he'd been duped by his business manager into a bad investment. He hated that there were unscrupulous individuals out there who would prey on innocent people like that. "Lots of senior citizens lost everything they had in the deal."

"Trust me, Ryan is aware of that. I know he's proud that you're proposing legislation to stop these crimes as part of your platform, but I think a part of him would just like to see the subject die. He's still carrying around a lot of guilt."

"Do you think that's why he doesn't ever come back to Chances Inlet?"

Gavin shrugged. "Partly. But he's also living the life in New York as a celebrity, superstar jock."

"I'm not sure having women crawling out of my garbage is 'living the life,' but whatever."

Gavin laughed. He went on to explain progress in the loft renovation his firm was designing. By the time Miles pulled into the sandy parking lot off to the side of the B and B, he felt a little more relaxed about his predicament. As much as he hated how his campaign for Congress was damaging his father's reputation, he knew that ultimately his dad would be proud of the men he and his brothers had become. Miles just needed to continue on and not lose sight of that.

"That doesn't look like a very happy welcoming party," Gavin murmured as he lifted his bag out of the trunk of Miles' car. "I know they'd never turn on me. What did you do?"

Miles looked over to the veranda where his mother, Bernice, Cassidy, and Ginger were seated. Gavin's pesky dog bounded down the steps, followed quickly by Ginger. His brother's fiancée threw him a bewildered look over her shoulder before flinging her arms around Gavin's neck. Bernice's mouth was set in a grim line when Miles climbed the stairs up to the veranda. His mother's expression pretty much mirrored Bernice's.

"You got some 'splaining to do, Miles," Cassidy mumbled.

Panic coursed through his body as he immediately thought of Lori. Had she left? Did his mother blame him for her leaving? He let out a breath he didn't know he was holding when—through the kitchen window—he caught a glimpse of her at the sink. As shitty as this day had already been, he wasn't sure he was ready to say good-bye to Lori yet. Not that she'd give him the chance.

"Mom, is everything okay?"

"That depends. Were you planning on telling your family that you're getting married?"

Son. Of. A. Bitch.

Patricia watched as her son slid into one of the gliders on the porch, the expression on his face a mixture of betrayal and rage. She hadn't for a moment believed Miles was engaged to Greer Rossi. Still, it was a relief to see him just as shocked by the news as she was.

"Where did you hear that?" he demanded to know.

Bernice snapped to attention. "Tanya Sheppard. She called the office for confirmation. I've been trying to get ahold of Coy all afternoon to have him refute it."

Miles waved her off. "Don't bother. He's way too deep in the governor's pocket. Hell, he's likely the one the governor had leak it."

Patricia stared at her son. "Are you saying what I think you're saying?"

He tucked his chin to his chest and dragged his fingers through his hair. "Things are getting complicated, Mom."

"Is this what you meant before when you said you and the governor weren't seeing eye to eye?" Gavin asked.

Miles nodded at his brother. "Faye Rich's campaign is going on the attack against Dad. They're taking it national, too."

Patricia closed her eyes and took a deep breath. She'd finally come to terms with how and why Donald did what he did. She knew her husband wasn't guilty of any wrongdoing. The only thing he was guilty of was trying to protect his family—and she would love him forever for that. But it was time to move on. She was getting on with her life with Lamar. Just like Miles needed to move past this and get elected. The opposing party could try to pull apart the McAlisters but her family—Donald's legacy—was tougher than anyone thought.

"What does any of that have to do with you marrying Greer?" Bernice asked.

Miles was staring at Patricia when she opened her eyes.

Ever since he was a baby, he'd been the easiest of her children to read. "The governor wants to hit back," she said, meeting her eldest son's stare. "But Miles doesn't want to. Am I right?"

He nodded once.

"Whoa, so he wants you to marry his daughter instead?" Gavin shook his head in disbelief. "And you made me feel like a jerk for suggesting that you and Greer hook up."

Ginger elbowed Gavin in the ribs. "Shouldn't Greer be able to make up her own mind? I mean, what father does that?"

"One who wants to make sure he can keep me under his thumb." Miles had that dejected look on his face; the same one he'd worn when he found out his favorite teacher had allowed students to cheat on an assignment all those years ago.

"Are you running for Congress so you can be beholden to another man, Miles?"

He contemplated her words for a moment before his eyes grew determined and his mouth turned up at the corners. "No, Mom, I'm not."

"I didn't think so." She reached out and wrapped her fingers around his larger ones. "Don't compromise who you are for this campaign. If this family is going to take a beating in the media, then at least let it be worth it. Your father wouldn't have wanted it any other way."

Miles leaned across her lap and brushed a kiss on her forehead. "I love you, Mom," he whispered.

"What do I tell Tanya Sheppard?" Bernice wanted to know.

"Don't tell her anything yet," Miles said. "Just let her simmer. We'll draft up a statement tonight and release it in the morning."

Bernice snorted in disgust. "Good luck with that. Your boy Coy is AWOL."

He patted Bernice on the knee. "I think you and I can handle writing this one ourselves, Bernice."

The older woman's lips quivered. "Really? Hallelujah!" She jumped up from her chair. "I'll go get my laptop."

Gavin cuffed Miles on the shoulder. "I meant what I said earlier. I've got your back. The whole family does."

Patricia's heart skipped a beat as she watched her sons share a quick embrace. There had been a lot of hard feelings between the two the past several months and she was glad to see them finally resolving things. "Gavin's right, we're all here for you, Miles." Using the back of the chair for leverage, she stood up.

"Good, because I'm going to need you to do a favor for your friend Faye," Miles said. "I can't stop the party from going negative. I'd like for you to give her a heads-up."

"Wait." Cassidy stood up, too. "Her campaign gets to say what they want about Mr. Mac and you're going to give her a warning? I don't get it."

Ginger wrapped an arm around the teenager. "You're seeing integrity at its finest, Cass. Watch and learn."

The teenager shook her head. "I hope I'm not seeing a sucker."

NINETEEN

The sunlight was fading when Lori finished the turn-down service in the seven occupied suites. Tessa trotted ahead of her as they both climbed the two flights of stairs to her bedroom. She'd have to leave the dog behind. The woman at the bus station was adamant about the no-pets-on-board policy. Her eyes burned at the thought, but she knew Patricia would keep Tessa safe and happy.

Using the money Diesel had sent her, Lori bought a ticket for the 6 a.m. bus to Raleigh. From there, she'd get on another bus to Nashville. In less than twenty-four hours, she'd be starting over. *Again.* This time without her grandmother's ring.

But staying until she found it had become too perilous. Lori couldn't risk being detected here in Chances Inlet. For once in her life, she wasn't thinking about the implications her discovery would have on her, but rather on those she'd come to love. *Both here and elsewhere.* From what she'd overheard in the kitchen this afternoon, the McAlisters were gearing up for another major assault on their reputation. If word got out they'd been harboring her here at the B and B, it would be devastating to the family. Even worse, it would be destructive for Miles' campaign. She couldn't do that to them. She couldn't do that to *him*.

Lori squeezed back the tears as she pulled out her duffel from under the bed. Of all the stupid things she'd done in her life, falling in love with Miles McAlister had been the dumbest. She'd known up front that any kind of relationship with him would be doomed. Aside from the fact that she wasn't here for the long haul, he was all that was good in a person and she . . . wasn't. Miles was the light to her darkness. After everything she'd done, she didn't deserve a life with a man like him. And yet she'd fallen in love with him anyway. Obviously, her common sense and judgment still needed a good alignment.

The fact that he vowed never to love again should have given her some consolation. Except it didn't. She wanted Miles to know love one more time. And, silly woman that she was, she wanted him to love *her*. Disgusted with herself, she tossed her extra shoes into the duffel bag.

"I take it you found your grandmother's ring?"

Miles' solemnly asked question made Lori's chest squeeze. She took a moment to compose herself before turning to face him. He was gripping the frame of the door with both hands as if to keep her from escaping. The long day had left him looking rumpled and tired but there was still that sense of energy about him humming just beneath the surface. Miles was a bit of an adrenaline junkie, whether it was training for a triathlon or running for Congress. She had no doubt he'd survive whatever the opposing camp threw at him. Lori was disappointed that she wouldn't be around to watch him succeed.

She sat down on the bed in order to keep from embarrassing herself by jumping into his arms. "Still no ring."

"But you're leaving anyway?" His fingers were white knuckled against the dark tiger oak doorjamb, almost as though he was holding himself back, too.

"I have to."

Miles swore viciously. "Let me help you." His words were spoken softly, but it was a demand nonetheless. Dudley Do-Right, the ultimate Boy Scout, couldn't stand not being able to make things right.

The tightness in Lori's chest grew stronger. This was why she should have left days—make that weeks—ago. "You can't. Don't you see?" she whispered.

"No." Shaking his head angrily, he stepped into the small room, slamming the door closed behind him. "Try me, Lori. Tell me what it is you've done. You can trust me."

Trusting him was no longer the issue. Lori was more afraid of the disgusted reaction she knew would come when he found out who she was. Who her father was. She didn't want him to know that woman. Instead, she wanted him to remember the woman he'd been sleeping with the past several nights. *The woman who loved him.*

She tried to deflect the focus back onto him. "Have you broken off your engagement with Greer yet?"

His blue eyes narrowed and he gave his head a little shake as if to refocus his thoughts. "You know as well as I do there never was a real engagement, Lori. But I'll show Greer the same courtesy I would any woman and discuss it with her in private. Not via that witch Tanya Sheppard."

"Of course you will," she mumbled. "You're the quintessential gentleman."

Miles plopped down on the bed beside her. Tessa gave him a guarded look from her perch on the upholstered chair in the corner of the room.

"Am I detecting a touch of jealousy, Lori?"

She swallowed around the knot in her throat. "I'm not jealous of Greer Rossi." Her next words weren't meant to be cruel, but they would do the trick of getting Miles to back off. "I'm jealous of Justine."

He flinched beside her. His eyes darkened and his mouth formed a grim line.

"When she died," Lori continued, "she took your heart with her. That makes me jealous as well as sad because now there's nothing left for the rest of us."

"What exactly is that supposed to mean?"

She watched as recognition dawned on his handsome face. He shook his head violently.

"You knew better," he growled.

Lori's laugh was hollow-sounding. "That seems to be my life's mantra."

"Damn it, Lori." He plowed his fingers through his hair.

"You don't need to worry, Miles. I've packed my heart up with the rest of my stuff and I'll be taking it with me."

He reached over and traced a finger along her cheek. "I'll still worry about you."

She leaned into his palm and covered his hand with hers. "I know you will, but I'll be fine."

He pulled her in closer so that his lips brushed over hers. "Promise?"

Lori knew enough not to make him a promise she had no idea would hold up, but she wanted to reassure him. Instead of speaking a lie, she pressed her lips to his, opening his mouth with hers and delving inside. She felt the low rumble at the back of his throat as she wrapped her fingers around his skull and pulled him in closer. Miles' hands slid beneath her T-shirt to cup her breasts and suddenly Lori was frantic to have him inside her one last time. She yanked at the buttons of his dress shirt, eager to get at the smooth skin beneath it. Taking control, Miles used his powerful body to push her back onto the bed.

"No," he said as he nipped at her neck. "If this is going to be our last time, we're not going to be hasty. We're doing this slow and thoroughly."

His words, delivered with such fierceness, made her core ignite. Lori's fingers trembled as they undressed each other but Miles' expression was unwavering. His mouth and hands roamed over her body as though he was trying to commit her curves to memory. Lori gasped when he finally slid home.

"Look at me," Miles commanded. Lori forced her eyelids open and stared into the blue depths of his resolute eyes. "This is our truth, Lori. Right here. Right now." He rocked his hips into her and began a slow, deliberate thrusting, his eyes never leaving her face. Lori picked up his rhythm and they moved as one until both were falling headlong over the edge.

* * *

Heat lightning flashed beyond the veranda of the inn. Patricia carefully navigated the wooden stairs leading up to the B and B. In all the excitement this afternoon, she'd left her reading glasses somewhere—hopefully on the kitchen counter of the inn. Flipping on the light switch, she breathed a sigh of relief when she spied her glasses on the desk in the corner. The kitchen was quiet; Lori had likely finished for the night, but she heard guests in the common area down the hall. She was debating whether to check in with them to make sure their rooms had everything they needed when Cassidy barreled through the screen door.

"Are you okay?" she asked.

"I'm fine, Cass. I was looking for my glasses, but I found them." She held them up for the girl to see. "What's got you so riled up?"

Cassidy leaned against the island, trying to catch her breath. "I was downtown with the Patty Wagon when someone said there was an emergency call into the sheriff's office from the inn. I was worried it was you."

Patricia gave Cassidy a puzzled look. "There's no need to worry about me, honey. I'm fine. No one here has called the sheriff."

A knowing smile broke out on Cassidy's face. "Oh, I get it. You and the sheriff are just fooling around and you don't want anyone to know he's come over here." She winked at Patricia. "Don't worry, I won't tell."

A blush warmed Patricia's face. "That's not it at all, Cassidy. Lamar is on duty tonight. There's no 'fooling around' when he's working."

The teenager's face sobered. "Then why is his cruiser out front?"

She stared at the teenager a moment before realizing she heard Lamar's voice among the chatter in the common rooms. Pivoting on her crutch, she shuffled toward the foyer with Cassidy at her heels. Sure enough, Lamar was standing in the entrance to the music room taking notes on his phone. Several guests were clearly eavesdropping on the conversation he was having with Mr. and Mrs. Benson, who were staying in the Perth Suite.

"Is there a problem here, Lamar?"

He wore a resigned look when his eyes met hers and Patricia's stomach dropped. What was going on here and why hadn't someone informed her? Her own expression must have conveyed her questions because his stance grew defensive. *Damn.* She was being coddled and protected yet again. Patricia hobbled closer, nearly smashing Lamar's toe in annoyance.

"Yes, there is a problem here," Mr. Benson was saying. "My wife's diamond tennis bracelet is missing."

"Uh-oh," Cassidy murmured.

"I took it off this morning before we went on our bike ride," Mrs. Benson said. "And now it's gone." She gulped and Patricia wasn't sure whether it was for real or for the benefit of those watching.

"When exactly did you last see the bracelet?" Lamar asked. It was a good thing he was doing the talking because Patricia was furiously reviewing her insurance policy in her head. There was always a chance a guest could lose something while at the B and B. She just hoped the diamond tennis bracelet wasn't as expensive as it sounded.

"This morning, around nine. That's when I put it in my jewelry roll with the rest of my pieces."

"You didn't think to put it in the safe provided for you in your suite?" Lamar seemed to be trying his best not to sound accusing, but Patricia had to concede that he was failing miserably.

"Given the reputation of this B and B, I had assumed that we didn't have to." Mr. Benson's tone was every bit as condemning as Lamar's. "But I can see we were wrong about that."

Patricia's head was throbbing as much as her hip now. Most of the guests were taking in every word as though this were a planned entertainment for the night. "Perhaps we should take this into my office. We'll need a description so that we can begin searching the inn for it."

Cassidy groaned. "Lori made me tear apart this whole

hotel earlier this month looking for that guy's thousand-dollar pen. Are you telling me we're going to have to do it all over again?"

Two of the guests stepped closer at Cassidy's words. Patricia's stomach dipped a little lower. "What 'guy's thousand-dollar pen'?" She intercepted the quelling look Lamar shot Cassidy, and a lick of panic crawled up her spine. What else had gone missing that her family and staff had forgotten to mention?

Probably realizing that she'd said too much, Cassidy licked her lips. "Mr. Maxwell. He lost a silver Montblanc pen."

"Do guests' belongings often disappear from your B and B, Mrs. McAlister?" Tanya Sheppard's voice was like nails on a chalkboard. Patricia turned to see the television reporter and her cameraman standing just inside the B and B's front door.

"Not any more than they do in any other establishment in town," Lamar interjected.

Patricia could have kissed him for his quick defense of her and the B and B. But that would have to wait until after she shooed Tanya and her camera crew off the premises; dealt with the Bensons and her other guests; and chewed her fiancé out for acting like her late husband and shielding her from things she ought to know.

She turned to Tanya with what she hoped was a serene smile on her face. "Can I help you, Ms. Sheppard?"

Tanya glanced around the crowded foyer. "I was looking for Miles. I've been trying to get a comment from him all day."

"He's at a campaign function." It was a lie, but she figured it was a mother's prerogative to buy her son some time before he debunked the rumors tomorrow. "We don't expect him back until later. Much later."

The reporter smirked as if she knew she was being played, but she got the message regardless. She nodded to her cameraman to head back to the veranda before she thought better of it and stopped herself midway out the door. "Perhaps you'd like to tell me what you think about your son's rumored engagement to the governor's daughter?"

Excited tittering and gasps echoed among her guests and

Patricia tried to keep the exasperation from her voice. "Right now, I'm *not* thinking about it. I'm taking care of my guests. I'll happily discuss it with you tomorrow." That was an interview Patricia was definitely looking forward to. "Now if you'll excuse me, Mr. and Mrs. Benson need my attention right now."

Tanya looked as if she might say something more, but Lamar was wearing his intimidating military policeman's face. With a smirk and a wave to the crowd, she closed the front door. Lamar gestured to the Bensons to lead the way down the hallway to Patricia's office located in the corner of the kitchen.

"Y'all have a good night now," Patricia said to her guests as she limped behind the Bensons. "If there's anything you need, just let Cassidy know." She shot the teenager a look that clearly said: *Stay here*. Cassidy's shoulders slumped, but she remained in the foyer.

"Would you mind if I had a look around your room?" Lamar asked once they'd reached the kitchen.

"It won't do you any good." Mr. Benson had become quite defensive. "I checked everywhere."

Lamar nodded patiently. "All right, then I'm happy to file a police report."

Patricia swallowed harshly. This had the potential for negative publicity for the inn. The Bensons were avid golfers who traveled frequently. The word of mouth alone could damage the Tide Me Over Inn's reputation.

"You'll need the report to file a claim with your insurance," Lamar continued.

"The insurance company will demand an investigation," Mr. Benson said. "That bracelet was insured for twenty-five thousand dollars."

This time when Patricia went to swallow, nothing was moving. Lamar didn't flinch at Benson's declaration, however.

"If you happen to have a photograph, that's helpful, too," he said. "I'll have my department check the area pawn dealers to see if it turns up."

"It still may turn up somewhere here in the inn," Patricia interjected. "As I said before, we'll conduct a thorough search for it."

Mrs. Benson gave her a pitying look. "I know I put it away with my other jewelry, Mrs. McAlister. It didn't just walk off on its own."

"But none of your other jewelry is missing, is that right?" It was Patricia's turn to be defensive. One of Lamar's eyebrows rose up slightly, but he let her continue. "If someone were going to steal it, why not take the entire jewelry roll?"

Mr. Benson clicked his teeth together. "This is getting us nowhere. My wife's bracelet is missing. It might be somewhere in this inn or, more likely, in somebody's pocket. I suggest you check with your staff, Mrs. McAlister. Sheriff, we'll stop by your office on our way out of town in the morning. I'll have my insurance agent fax you a photo of the bracelet then. Nicki, let's go up to our room now."

Patricia opened her mouth to say more but the warning look in Lamar's eyes stopped her. She let the Bensons leave the room without so much as a good night. Lamar held up his hand, allowing for the couple to get some distance down the hall before he spoke. They stared at each other in the quiet room for a full minute until Patricia couldn't take it any longer.

"What else is missing?" she hissed.

Lamar sucked in a deep breath and Patricia knew she wasn't going to like what was coming. "The pen, Greer's watch, a silver charm bracelet, your crystal paperweight, and a gold wedding band."

Patricia stumbled to the closest chair and sank down into it. "How long has this been going on?"

"Since your accident."

"And no one thought to let me in on the secret?"

"Your hip was mending. Miles and I were handling it."

"You and Miles?" Patricia was incredulous wondering how things had gotten so out of hand. "Lamar, when I asked you two to get along, I didn't mean for you both to gang up against me! This is still my inn."

"Damn it, I know it's your inn, Patricia." Lamar tossed his campaign hat onto a nearby chair and rubbed his hands over his head. He took a step closer and knelt down before her. "And nobody is 'ganging up on you.' You need to face the fact that the men in your life are going to protect you. It's what we were bred to do. You can fault your husband and your sons all you want, but they're just doing their jobs. Because they love you. And so do I." He took both her hands in his larger ones, bringing them up to his lips for a gentle kiss.

Tears gathered behind her eyes. "It seems I'm destined to fall in love with men who'd rather be white knights."

He looked up at her with a solemn expression. "It's who I am, Tricia. I'm too old to change now."

She leaned down and kissed him on the nose and then on the lips. Lamar slowly stood up, gently lifting her so her body was flush against his. Patricia wrapped her arms around his neck as he deepened the kiss.

"If we're going to move forward with this relationship, we need to be able to work this out," Patricia said as his lips grazed her collarbone. "I'll agree to let you protect me, if you'll agree that protecting me doesn't mean keeping secrets."

"Deal," he murmured against her neck.

Patricia met his lips for another deep kiss.

"Hey," Cassidy interrupted them. "You said he wasn't here to fool around."

Lamar mumbled something unkind about teenagers before he lowered Patricia back into her seat. "Cass, you wouldn't happen to know anything about these missing items, would you?" he asked.

Both women stared at Lamar in astonishment. "Hey! You don't think I had anything to do with this?" Cassidy asked with a huff. "I'm not my mother."

"Of course not," Patricia answered quickly while shooting Lamar a pleading look.

He was silent for a moment before shaking his head. "No, I don't think you're guilty of anything, Cass. But you are a very perceptive young woman and you seem to know everything that goes on in this town. I was just wondering if you'd heard anything. Or if you had any other theories."

The teenager went from belligerent to preening at the sheriff's words. "My theory is that the pen and the bracelet rolled into a nook or cranny in their room. Maybe under the radiator."

"We're missing more than a pen and diamond tennis bracelet, Cass. It seems a gold ring, a charm bracelet"—Patricia glanced over at Lamar before continuing—"Greer's watch, and the crystal paperweight from the Edinburgh Suite have all disappeared from the B and B the past few weeks."

It was obvious from the look on Cassidy's face that she wasn't the culprit and neither did she have any idea who might be. Patricia was relieved and frustrated at the same time.

"And nobody told me?" Cassidy asked incredulously.

"Join the club." Patricia stood and gave Lamar a reassuring pat on the chest. "But we're all going to work together to solve this mystery before any more damage is done to the B and B's reputation."

There was a knock on the screen door and Deputy Hayden Lovell walked into the kitchen. "Sorry to interrupt, Boss, but something's come up."

Lamar looked at the deputy quizzically. "You could have reached me by radio."

Deputy Lovell glanced at Patricia and Cassidy before turning back to Lamar. "I didn't think this was something the whole town should hear."

With a nod, Lamar and the deputy stepped to the opposite side of the kitchen. Patricia was still able to make out the gist of their conversation.

"The FBI is in town," Deputy Lovell said. "They've commandeered the station house as their command post."

She watched anxiously as the tension gripped Lamar's body. Deputy Lovell handed him a folded-up piece of paper.

"They've been using facial recognition cameras in bus stations to track down some of their most wanted," the deputy explained. "They got a hit today here in Chances Inlet. I played dumb with the feds. I wasn't sure how you wanted me to handle it."

"Damn," Lamar said grimly before turning to face Patricia.

She knew instantly who he was talking about. "Lori."

"Is she still here, Tricia?"

"No!" Cassidy said from behind Patricia. "I'm sure she's already left."

“The ticket she bought was for tomorrow morning’s bus,” Deputy Lovell said.

“She’s not a criminal,” Cassidy cried. “You’re not going to turn her in, are you, Sheriff?”

“I think for now, I need some answers. We’ll figure out what to do from there. I’d like to check her room, please, Tricia.”

“Not without me you don’t.”

He nodded, albeit reluctantly.

“Everything is going to be fine, Cassidy,” Patricia tried to console the worried teenager. “You just need to make sure the guests stay out of this side of the inn.”

Cassidy nodded as Lamar helped Patricia up the two flights of stairs to the loft room Lori occupied. A sliver of light shone through the door and Patricia wasn’t sure whether she was relieved that the woman she’d come to admire was safe or frightened that she hadn’t already made her escape.

Patricia knocked on the door. “Lori, it’s Patricia. I need to speak with you.” She looked over at Lamar’s grim face. “It’s an emergency.”

They could hear the sound of urgent movement in the room, but it took a moment before the door was flung open. The wind rushed out of Patricia’s lungs at the sight of Miles, shirtless with his pants barely on, standing in the entryway. Lamar huffed in frustration behind her.

“Mom?” Miles’ eyes were wide with worry. “What’s wrong? Are you all right?”

“Get dressed, both of you,” Lamar ordered. “We need to talk.”

Patricia leaned against the wall, her head spinning, hoping the last half hour was all a dream she was going to wake up from soon.

TWENTY

The sound of Patricia's startled intake of breath spurred Lori's sated muscles to move quickly as she pulled on her clothing. Miles blocked the doorway, shielding her from view with his body. Still, a sense of foreboding settled deep in the pit of her stomach. Tessa jumped from the chair, wagging her tail, as she tried to squeeze out the door to greet Patricia.

"What the hell is going on?" Miles demanded. His demeanor had quickly gone from concerned to defensive.

"I'd ask you the same thing," his mother countered sharply, "but we haven't time."

Lori slipped on her shoes, dreading the next few moments. She knew precisely what was going on. She'd lingered too long. She grabbed her backpack off the dresser and draped the strap of her duffel bag over her shoulder. "I'm leaving now."

Miles turned to her then, confusion and alarm etched on his face. His blue eyes narrowed. "You're not going anywhere until someone answers my question."

"I'll be happy to tell you what's going on," a familiar voice said from the hallway behind the sheriff.

Lori froze as her heart sank at the sound.

"He just barged in!" Cassidy said with a huff and Lori felt the tears begin to form behind her eyes. It seemed she was to be humiliated in front of everyone she'd come to love here in Chances Inlet.

"Who the hell are you?" Miles demanded.

"Special Agent Matt Kovaluk of the FBI's Organized Crime Unit."

The flinch in Miles' torso was slight, but given how in tune she was with his body, Lori had no trouble detecting it. Miles pulled on his shirt, his rigid frame still filling the doorway. She wished she could freeze time and stay like this forever, with Miles still respecting her and Patricia and Cassidy still caring about her. But the truth would inevitably come out. It was better to just rip off the Band-Aid now. She blinked back her tears—she knew firsthand how Agent Kovaluk preyed on weakness—and gently squeezed Miles' arm before stepping out from behind him.

"Hello, Mallory." Matt Kovaluk was leaning a shoulder against the wall wearing a cat-ate-the-canary grin on his face. His mossy green eyes were alight with the thrill of victory. She'd trusted those eyes once. Her body trembled with disgust now. Kovaluk was fit and muscular like Miles, but with sandy blond hair and a surfer's demeanor. The agent had used that sunny, laidback personality to insinuate himself into her life in order to unveil her secrets.

"Hello, Matthew," she said. "At least you didn't lie about your first name."

"Now, Mallory, that would be the pot calling the kettle black here, wouldn't it?" His face sobered suddenly. "Matthew Everett *is* my name. I just left off the Kovaluk part. My excuse is that I was working undercover. Do you want to share with these fine folks *your* reason for concealing your true identity, Mal?"

Lori shivered.

"That's enough," Miles snapped. He wrapped his fingers around her biceps and pulled her body next to his warmer one. "Don't let him badger you, Lori. Perhaps you should explain yourself, Agent Kovaluk."

Matt's eyebrow arched when Miles referred to her as

"Lori" and that insufferable grin returned to his face. "Going back to your humble roots, I see, *Lori*." He shook his head before he squared off in front of Miles. "Your . . . *friend's* real name is Mallory Dykstrom. If the name sounds familiar it's because she's the daughter of Leonard Dykstrom. The same Leonard Dykstrom who stole millions from unsuspecting investors."

The air seemed to still in the hallway and Lori was having trouble drawing a breath. Miles' grip tightened on her arm before his body recoiled and his fingers slid away from her skin. She gulped down a sob before it could escape her lips.

"That's not possible." Miles' tone was disbelieving, yet the inches separating their bodies now felt like a gulf. "That can't be."

Patricia's cheeks were damp and Cassidy gasped in surprise. Lamar's face was stoic but his eyes were calculating. Lori didn't dare look at Miles. She didn't want to see the regret that was surely in his eyes. Grabbing her by the elbow, Miles didn't give her a choice as he spun her around. The revulsion she saw on his face was worse than she imagined and her knees grew weak. Were it not for his fingers digging into her skin, she'd be on the floor.

"Tell me he's lying, Lori." Miles jerked her body back and forth before Lamar reached over to pull her from his grasp. "Leonard Dykstrom stole millions from innocent people. Elderly people who have nothing left to live the rest of their lives on. Defeating cheating bastards like him is one of the focal points of my campaign." His voice rose in frustration. "Hell, he stole money from my brother, Ryan, and dozens of people in this town!" He stepped closer to her. "Tell me he's lying. Please," he demanded.

Lori blew out a ragged breath, unable to meet his eyes.

Miles unleashed a string of obscenities as he ran his fingers through his hair. "Damn you!" His eyes darted to the bed. "How could you? Jesus, how could you hurt so many innocent people?"

I didn't! she wanted to scream. But she remained silent. It was no use protesting. Her father had used her, just like he used everyone else in his life. She'd suspected for months that something wasn't right, but she'd been enjoying her new life too much to question the flow of money through her restaurant. Just as Miles was being tainted by the sins of his father, so would she. In her case, she was culpable simply for turning a blind eye.

"Well, kids, this has been fun," Matt interjected. When Lori shot an angry glare at him, she thought she saw a touch of remorse in those green eyes before he donned his mask again. "I've got a jet waiting to take us back to New York. We've got a lot of catching up to do, Mal, starting with where dear old Dad is hiding out."

Patricia looked at Sheriff Hollister anxiously.

"Not so fast," the sheriff said when Matt reached for Lori's duffel bag.

The agent arched an eyebrow at the sheriff, who was pulling his handcuffs off his belt.

"I got here first." The sheriff gently guided Lori's hands behind her back. "Lori—Mallory Dykstrom, you're being taken in for questioning regarding felony larceny. It seems a twenty-five-thousand-dollar tennis bracelet and other assorted items have disappeared from this B and B while you've been working here. You're not leaving Chances Inlet until this case is cleared up."

The sound of the handcuffs clicking shut echoed off the walls.

"Oh, no you don't, Sheriff," Matt protested. "I've been chasing after her for nearly seven months now. She's wanted on eighty-seven counts of fraud. A federal warrant trumps whatever you've got in your pocket."

Lori heard a little squeak escape Patricia's lips.

"Mmm," Lamar said. "Correct me if I'm wrong, Agent Kovaluk, but I thought Leonard Dykstrom was the only person indicted on those charges?"

"Mallory is being charged as an accessory," Matt growled. "It's only a matter of protocol for me to get the warrant."

"Then get your warrant. For now, she's coming with me."

Matt stepped up closer to the sheriff, his jaw tight. "Don't be a hero, Sheriff. I know you think you're doing the right thing here by protecting her. But this is bigger than both of us. You do realize she stole money from a lot of people in this town, including half the city council. You're risking your job by interfering."

"Again, her father is the only one indicted for stealing that money," Lamar said, and Lori wanted to wrap her arms around his neck and hug him for defending her when no one else ever had. "And the way I see it, I'm doing what I was elected to do."

Matt huffed out an explosive sigh before he plastered his boyish grin back on his face. "I'm not letting her out of my sight. Mal and I can catch up with each other just as easily in your quaint little jailhouse as we can in the New York Regional Office. Lead the way, Sheriff."

Lori risked a last glance over her shoulder to see if Miles had any reaction to the tug-of-war going on over her fate. His chin was dropped to his chest in that familiar pensive pose. She wanted to say something to him; what, she wasn't sure. An apology was in order for the way her presumed guilt would damage his campaign. Lori opened her mouth to speak just as Patricia gave her elbow a soft squeeze. The older woman shook her head slightly before her mouth turned up in a supportive smile.

"Everything is going to work out," she mouthed as Lamar guided her toward the stairs.

"I'll take care of Tessa," Cassidy called after them. "Don't worry, Lori. Okay?"

A single tear found its way down Lori's cheek as she gave Cassidy what she hoped was a reassuring nod. They'd made it to the foyer when she heard Miles' voice behind them.

"Wait!"

Lamar halted at the door and Lori turned to see Miles running down the stairs in his bare feet, his shirt unbuttoned and billowing open to reveal the muscled chest she loved to run her hands over. His blue eyes were blazing with his Dudley Do-Right determination. Unfortunately, he was looking through her again; just as he had all those weeks ago. Lori swallowed another sob.

"Lamar, you do everything by the book, you hear me?" Miles trained his fierce stare on Matt. "Make sure that Special Agent Kovaluk does as well."

None of them saw the television camera until its light blinded them. Before she knew it, Lori was safely out of view in the back of the sheriff's cruiser. Miles was left standing on the veranda, vulnerable and exposed to ruination, thanks to her. She didn't bother holding back the tears this time.

"Congressional candidate Miles McAlister got caught with his pants down tonight, quite literally. It seems the thirty-three-year-old special assistant to the governor was doing more than just helping to run his mother's bed-and-breakfast while he was in Chances Inlet." Tanya Sheppard smirked at the audience during her live broadcast on the eleven o'clock news.

"Jesus, she should get fired for making such a ridiculous double entendre like that." Gavin balled up a dirty sock and threw it at the television screen. His goofy dog scrambled from its bed to retrieve it. An hour earlier, Miles' brother had rescued him from the B and B following an urgent phone call from their mother. Ginger stayed behind to help Cassidy with the breakfast the next morning.

Tanya continued reporting from the lawn of their mother's inn. "The Tide Me Over Inn behind me was the last stop in a nationwide manhunt for Mallory Dykstrom, daughter of Leonard Dykstrom, the man who orchestrated one of the largest Ponzi schemes on U.S. soil."

The screen was suddenly filled with a picture of a very glamorous Lori, wearing a designer gown and enough jewelry to require her own armed guard. She was smiling brightly, her rich auburn hair shimmering like a new penny as she stood with her father on the red carpet at some charity event. The repeated stabbing that kept assaulting Miles' chest for the past two hours continued to plague him.

Gavin let out a little whistle before he mumbled under his breath. "Damn. She's a redhead."

Miles clenched his fingers into fists as Tanya droned on.

"It seems the elusive daughter of one of the country's most wanted criminals was hiding out in Chances Inlet, where she was working as a cook and housekeeper at the fashionable B and B. Apparently, however, she was doing more than just baking and cleaning. Before the FBI could take Ms. Dykstrom into custody, Sheriff Lamar Hollister escorted her to the station house for questioning regarding a series of thefts, including a twenty-five-thousand-dollar diamond tennis bracelet. These revelations apparently came as a shock to local congressional candidate, Miles McAlister."

The video of Miles chasing Lori and her armed entourage onto the veranda played on screen again, making Miles groan with embarrassment.

"Nice abs," Gavin joked.

Miles flipped his brother off as he took another swallow from his bottle of beer.

"Aw, come on, bro. I'm trying to lighten the mood here. You need to cut yourself some slack. None of this is your fault. And none of it is life or death."

"Tell that to Mom as Tanya trashes the B and B's reputation on the air," Miles said.

"I think Mom's more worried about Lori than she is about her inn right now."

"You mean Mallory," Miles corrected him. He had to force his tongue to spit the name out. Miles couldn't seem to wrap his head around the events of this evening. A conflagration of feelings churned in his gut, the strongest of which was betrayal. Everything he'd heard about Mallory Dykstrom seemed to contradict the woman he'd come to respect and desire these past few weeks. Obviously, he'd been letting the wrong body part act as his guide.

Tanya wrapped up her segment, throwing it back to the anchors. "Chances Inlet is famous for second chances. It's safe to say that Mallory Dykstrom won't get one. The question is, will Miles McAlister?"

Gavin swore as he changed the channel to ESPN. "Don't listen to that bimbo, Miles. She doesn't know what she's talking about."

His brother's placating words weren't effective in this instance. Tanya Sheppard was likely correct about second chances. Miles knew he could count on his hometown to overlook whatever his father had done in the past, but his involvement with the daughter of the man who'd ripped so many people off would be a harder sin for voters to overlook.

A knock sounded at the door, followed by Will strolling into the loft wearing some sort of harness on his chest. A soft wail echoed off the high ceiling and the dog began sniffing at Will's chest.

"What is that you have on?" Gavin asked. "And is there something alive in it?"

Will rolled his eyes. "It's a Baby Björn, and yes, my daughter is in here." He gently jostled the contraption and the wailing faded to heavy breathing. "She's a bit colicky so we thought we'd go for a walk. The movement soothes her."

"You sure she's not suffocating from your stench?" Gavin teased.

Will's face was impassive as he glared at his best friend. "If she's a bit fussy, it's because we had to traverse a swarm of media just to get inside the building." Still, he peeked in on his daughter, presumably just to make sure. "They looked like they're going to settle in for the night."

"Fuck 'em," Miles said. He took another pull from the bottle of beer.

Gavin exchanged a look with Will before getting to his feet. "Why should Deputy Lovell have all the fun tonight? I'll go scare them off. If I'm not back by morning, assume the vultures ate me."

Will chuckled. "If you're not back by morning, we'll assume you're reliving the days when you snuck into Ginger's room at the B and B." He made his way over to the kitchen and grabbed a beer out of the refrigerator.

"Make sure he doesn't give that to the baby, Miles. Come on, Midas, let's go scare the paparazzi."

"You okay?" Will asked once Gavin and his dog were out the front door.

With a heavy sigh, Miles leaned his head back against the

leather sofa he was sitting on. "I'm pretty sure this is what a quarterback feels like when you blindside them."

"Nah." Will paced around the room, jiggling the baby each time she whimpered. "When I hit a quarterback, he's usually sipping through a straw for several days. You're handling that beer just fine."

"The funny thing is, she tried to warn me off. I just couldn't seem to help myself."

"I told you before, you can't always fight chemistry. Or your heart."

Miles sprung off the couch. "And I told you, my heart was never engaged here. It was just a fling."

"Really?" Will asked. "If that's the case, then why are you up here licking your wounds and not downstairs spinning this with the media?"

"Screw you!"

"Hey, I let the first one slide, but try and watch your language in front of the baby."

Miles kept his back to Will and his now quiet daughter. Staring out the large window behind Gavin's drafting desk, he peered off toward the point at the end of Main Street where the shore met the Atlantic. A buoy bobbed in the darkness, its light blinking to warn sailors of the rocky shore. Too bad Miles hadn't paid attention to the very clear warning signs Lori had thrown off. It was unfair to blame her. He was angry at himself for being so blind with lust. And he was angry at Lori for being Mallory Dykstrom.

"You asked me about my marriage with Julianne," Will said softly. Miles turned to find him slumped on the sofa, the little pink baby asleep on his massive chest. "Desire to possess our son—and Julianne—led me to do some crazy things. To believe some crazy things. I never considered that there was another side to the story. Another perspective that was so different from what I believed, yet that was also correct." He stroked his fingers over the wispy hair on the baby's head. "People you love disappoint you, Miles. Hell, I'm sure your mother could give you a whole dissertation on that subject right now. But that doesn't mean that your father or Julianne or Lori didn't do what they did for a really good reason. Don't you owe it to her to find out what that reason might be?"

Miles snorted. "Greed probably tops the list."

"You're a better judge of character than that."

"What's that supposed to mean?"

Will had a disgusted look on his face. "You've slept with the woman. More than once, if the cocky grin you've been wearing the past few weeks is any indication. You both looked different afterwards—transformed and relaxed. I haven't seen you like that since Justine." Anguish coursed through Miles but Will held up a hand when Miles opened his mouth to speak. "Fine, I won't go there, but your crap detector is more finely honed than anyone else I know. You believed in Lori. And not just with your crotch. Every fiber of you believed in her. All I'm saying is that there's a chance she could be the person you thought her to be. There's no reason to beat yourself up until you know for sure."

Gavin and Midas reappeared. "Bernice is driving them all away with her bad coffee," Gavin joked. "Coy just arrived and he looks like he just flunked out of hell week in his fraternity. I told them all you went back to Raleigh. Cassidy hid your car over at the old house. That should throw them off the trail for the night. They were packing up and heading to the station house to join the media throng there. Luckily, people are more interested in Leonard Dykstrom's daughter than in you right now."

"Somehow, I don't feel very lucky," Miles muttered as he turned back to the window. In fact, he was convinced his luck had run out hours ago.

"Blech," Matt said after taking a sip from the Styrofoam cup. "What I wouldn't give for some Starbucks dark roast." He took another swallow before setting it back down on the table. Lori and the FBI agent were crammed in the small interrogation room at the Chances Inlet sheriff's office. If she had to guess, it was getting close to midnight, yet there was still a larger than usual crowd milling about the station house. She suspected they'd all come to catch a glimpse of her.

"If you left now, I'm sure you can grab a cup in New York before morning."

Matt tipped the chair he was sitting in onto its back legs and leaned his head against the cinderblock wall. "Nice try, Mal, but I can wait the twenty-four hours before Sheriff Robin Hood has to release you. Then we can get a cup of coffee together, just like old times."

They'd first met in a Starbucks on Manhattan's west side. It was late on a hot August afternoon and she'd stopped in to grab a caramel Frappuccino, hoping the drink would reenergize her for the long evening she had ahead. Matt had bumped into her, spilling an iced coffee on her dress. In hindsight, she realized the scenario had been a ploy to meet her. He'd insisted on paying for her dry cleaning, and after a few moments of his persistent charm, she'd forgotten she'd been miffed at him in the first place. When she ran into him at a gala later that evening, she'd thought it was serendipitous. Little did she know their chance encounter had also been premeditated.

Matt told her he worked as an accountant for an international construction firm that was rebuilding the World Trade Center. He was interesting, fun-loving, and good-looking. Best of all, he wasn't one of the stuffed suits her father always seemed to be foisting her way. They'd dated casually for a few months, often meeting at her restaurant/bakery after it closed in the evening. Matt seemed genuinely interested in her work, he enjoyed her cooking, and he was always willing to help with any problem that came up.

That last part proved to be her downfall.

Taking a large swallow from the bottle of water Sheriff Hollister had given her when they arrived, Lori glared at Matt. "I'm fine with my water, thanks."

He closed his eyes, still leaning up against the wall. "I know you hate me, but it could have all gone down differently."

Lori slammed the water bottle down onto the table. "The only way it could have 'all gone down differently' is if I hadn't trusted you." When she'd begun to suspect her father, she'd stupidly asked *her friend*, Matt the accountant, to take a look at the books. She'd been a naive sap who'd played right into the FBI's hands. "I'm sure you and your special agent friends enjoyed a good laugh at how gullible I was."

He lifted the lid of one eye. "That's not what I'm talking about, Mal. And for what it's worth, I always had the utmost respect for you. I still do."

"Don't bother, Matthew, because the feeling is not mutual."

The legs of the chair slammed down onto the concrete floor and the table shook when Matt thumped his elbows down. His green eyes were agitated and his mouth was set in a grim line.

"Why did you do it?" he demanded.

She rolled her eyes in annoyance. Lori was done confiding in Matthew Everett what's-his-name.

"Damn it, Mal, your father used you," he snapped.

"Well, he wasn't the only one who used me, now was he?" she shouted at him.

Matt had the good grace to look away.

"And you can spare me the *I-was-just-doing-my-job* speech," she said. "I really don't want to hear it."

Sheriff Hollister poked his head in the room. "Everything okay in here?" He directed his gaze and his question at Lori, not bothering to look at the FBI agent.

Lori nodded.

"Are you going to book her or not, Sheriff?" Matt asked.

"Do you have that warrant yet?" the sheriff countered.

Matt swore under his breath as he checked his phone.

"You don't have to answer any of his questions without an attorney," the sheriff said. "We just got word that a team is headed down here from New York. They've asked that you not be questioned in either case without them present."

Lori nearly groaned out loud. The "team" was made up of her father's associates. They were tools, all of them. None of whom she'd trust to represent her for jaywalking, much less eighty-five counts of fraud. But she could use them just as well as she'd been used in this little drama.

"Well, I guess this is good night then, Matthew." She stood up.

Matt was on his feet at the same time. "Why did you do it, Mallory? You tipped your father off. I just want to know why."

Nausea rolled through her stomach. The sheriff stiffened beside her. He hadn't anticipated that last gem of information. Truth be told, neither had she until she'd actually done it.

She shook her head and Matt sucked in a breath. "Then I hope your boyfriend and the sheriff here can protect you, Mal, because unless you tell me the truth, I can't help you."

"I asked you to help me before and look where that got me." Lori spread her arms out as if to say "this." "I won't misplace my trust in you again."

Patricia was waiting outside the small jail cell. She pulled Lori into a tight hug.

"You shouldn't be here," Lori said despite the fact she didn't want Patricia to let her go. "You shouldn't be seen associating with me. The B and B is your livelihood, your dream, and I destroyed its reputation by staying. I'm so sorry for everything."

"*Pfft.*" Patricia laughed. "Are you kidding? Cassidy has been on social media all evening. She has us completely booked until October. Folks want an up close and personal look at where the scandal took place. Some are even requesting that they stay in your room."

Lori hesitated, unsure whether she wanted to know the answer to her next question. She asked it anyway. "And Miles? How is he?"

Patricia seemed to be considering her words. "Tanya is doing a number on him in the media, but she's been after him from the get-go. I'm not going to lie, she's making him look like a fool."

"You have to tell them the truth," Lori pleaded. "Or let me talk to Tanya. I'll tell her."

The look Patricia gave her was laced with pity. "I don't think that would be a good idea."

Tears of frustration leaked out of Lori's eyes as she nodded.

"What is the truth, Lori?" Patricia asked softly. "Can you at least tell me what the truth is behind your relationship with Miles?"

Lori tried to compose herself by taking a deep breath. "Your son is a good man. He's compassionate and driven to do great things." She swallowed. "Miles is dedicated to his family and to his principles. I respect that in him. He doesn't deserve to have his future destroyed by someone like me. If I could go back and do it again, I would have left after that first night."

Patricia brushed Lori's hair back off her face. "You love him that much?"

"Yes," she whispered. "I know I shouldn't. But I do."

TWENTY-ONE

Slipping out of his brother's loft at daybreak, Miles made his way down to the beach for a much-needed run. Sleep had evaded him all night and he was hoping a quick jog would calm his racing nerves. The night before, Gavin and Will had made arrangements to go with him—just in case the media was still lurking about—but Miles didn't want to listen to any more of his brother's teasing or Will Connelly's philosophical blubbering on love. He wanted to be alone with his own turbulent thoughts.

He wondered how Lori—*Mallory, damn it!*—was faring. Had the FBI agent already whisked her off to New York? Or had Lamar's delay tactics worked?

The sheriff's actions had surprised Miles. The FBI agent hadn't been wrong when he'd reminded Lamar who elected him. Lots of people in Chances Inlet had taken his brother Ryan's endorsement of Dykstrom's investment to heart. The irony was that Ryan had no idea what he'd been investing in. It was his crooked agent who'd faked the endorsement. Ryan was as much a victim as the rest of those caught up in the Ponzi scheme.

Miles kicked at a strand of seaweed that had washed

ashore. The sun was rising over the ocean, painting the water a bright orange. Seagulls and pelicans were dive-bombing the surf in search of breakfast. Dawn was always Miles' favorite time of the day; a time when new possibilities still seemed endless. Today, however, only controversy loomed. He needed to right his campaign and that included damage control where his personal life was concerned. Yesterday morning's dilemma seemed mild compared to what he'd been embroiled in last night. Dealing with Faye Rich and refusing an engagement with Greer Rossi had taken a backseat to handling the character explosion that resulted from his relationship with Lori. The carefully worded press release he and Bernice had crafted the previous afternoon would need to be revised to address this morning's headlines. The problem was, Miles had no idea what he wanted to say.

His only coherent thought was that he was going to have to tread carefully and not appear to be a hypocrite. For months now, he'd been espousing campaign rhetoric about how he would defend against the lowlife who would take advantage of innocent people by luring them into fake investments. The elderly at the senior center had anointed him their champion on the matter and how did he repay their trust? By sleeping with a woman who took part in one of the most abhorrent schemes in the books. Miles forcefully kicked another glob of seaweed. She'd duped him just like she'd duped everyone else.

There's a chance she could be the person you believed her to be.

Will's words had been tormenting Miles all night. Did she have a reason for doing what she did? Or was that just wishful thinking so that he could absolve himself for being a horny idiot and getting involved with her in the first place?

Not finding the answers he was looking for on the beach, Miles made his way back to his brother's loft and showered. Thirty minutes later, he slid into his father's comfortable leather chair hoping for some divine intervention. Instead, all he got was an interruption.

"It would be nice if your brother was a little more forthcoming with your whereabouts, Miles." Coy stormed into the room, bringing with him a cardboard tray of coffees from the Java Jolt and a sour disposition. "I was halfway to Raleigh when I got your text last night. Gavin may think it's funny to send me on a wild-goose chase, but I've got work to do. The wheels are coming off this campaign and it's going to take everything I've got to save it."

Miles wanted to deck the little egomaniac, but he was suddenly distracted by Coy's companion. Greer was standing in the doorway, looking a little sheepish as she rolled her eyes at Coy's tirade. She'd never returned his phone calls from the day before, yet here she was, dressed in a conservative blue suit and an elegant strand of pearls, looking for all the world as if nothing had changed.

"How are you?" she asked.

"He's resilient," Coy answered for him. "The finest politicians are made of Teflon. Nothing sticks to them." He nodded to Greer. "Your father has one of the best suits of armor. Let's hope that translates to this guy, as well. If we can salvage this mess without anything sticking, you two will be well on your way to living in the White House one day."

Coy busied himself with setting up his laptop on the opposite side of the desk. Greer gave Miles a demure grin, but she didn't bother to refute his statement. Miles swore under his breath.

"Greer, can I have a word with you?" Miles stood up from the desk. "In private."

"No need," Coy interjected. "Greer and I have worked on the preliminaries for the press conference you'll have this morning. We've scheduled it for ten. With luck, we can lure some of the national media circling the sheriff's office to come down here for some Q and A."

"I've got an edit bay reserved in a postproduction studio in Wilmington for this afternoon," Greer said. "If we work quickly, we can have new thirty-second spots up and ready to air tonight. At the very least, I'll be able to float them on the website before the national news. By the way, is there any chance Lori—I mean, Mallory—still has my watch?"

"The girl had her own vault at Tiffany's," Coy mumbled.

"Clearly she's got a disease if she still felt the need to steal your watch."

Indignation surged through Miles. "She didn't steal the watch," he said through his tightly clenched jaw.

Greer looked at him curiously. "I thought she was arrested for stealing it?"

Miles tucked his chin to his chest in exasperation. "That was all just a smokescreen. She didn't steal anything."

"Uh, she's facing eighty-five counts of fraud, Miles," Coy said. "Whether or not she stole Greer's watch is just a technicality."

"I said she didn't *steal* anything, Coy."

There's a chance she could be the person you believed her to be. Will's words rattled around in Miles' head. *Don't you owe it to her to find out what that reason might be?*

Whatever Lori's reason was, Miles knew it was a good one. His chest tightened at the realization.

"You sound awfully convinced." Greer crossed her arms over her chest in a move that was clearly defensive. It was the first signal she'd given that she was less than confident in her situation.

"I'm positive."

"Well, get un-positive," Coy ordered. "Our strategy paints Lori as a guilty, conniving seductress who threw herself at you in order to gain asylum if she was ever found out. We're even prepared to say she was blackmailing you into keeping her secret."

"You can't be serious?" Miles felt as if he were grinding his teeth to dust.

"This is serious, Miles. Your campaign is tanking. You need to take action now before you get caught up in the tsunami of news coverage Mallory Dykstrom's arrest has brought with it. The media will run with just about anything involving her right now. She won't be in a position to refute it."

Greer's face was impassive when Miles looked over at her. "Are you in on this?"

She drew her lips into a thin line. "I've told you numerous times that the first priority is to get you elected."

Coy pulled two pieces of paper out of the printer and laid them on the desk in front of Miles. "Here are the prepared remarks. Greer will cut off any questions that might lead you to contradict your statement."

Miles scanned the documents. Not only did the words on the pages vilify Lori, but they made him look like a total dick. He glanced up at Coy and Greer. "I'm not saying this."

Greer sat down on the sofa with a huff.

"Jesus, Miles, presidents have admitted to more than you confess to here," Coy argued.

Bernice strolled into the room, a plate of doughnuts in her hand. "Good morning, Mr. Candidate. I thought you'd be at it early so I brought you something to make the morning a little sweeter." She winked at Miles.

He handed her the papers Coy had printed out. The tips of Bernice's ears turned pink as she read it. "Can you take care of that for me, Bernice?"

"My pleasure," she said as she walked over to the shredder.

"Hey! I worked all night on that. You can't ignore this, Miles. You're going to have to address it. Face it, your numbers are taking a nosedive. Faye Rich's supporters have already jumped all over this."

"Let them."

Coy snapped his laptop closed. "Fine, if you don't want to go on the defensive, we'll just go on the attack. News of Faye Rich's teenage indiscretions will be of interest to the media coming to the press conference."

"Oh, sweetie, I think you missed the boat on that one," Bernice said. She pulled up Faye's campaign website on the desktop computer. The headline announced the disclosure of her teenage abortion. Miles' stomach was queasy just reading it. But he couldn't feel guilty. It would have likely come out sometime in the campaign. He took some consolation that she was able to prepare her family and get ahead of the story.

Coy unleashed a string of expletives that had Bernice red-faced again.

"You were my ticket, McAlister," Coy hissed. "The up-and-coming Congressman who'd been practically green-lighted into the White House by the party. They called you smart and upstanding, an all-American guy that the heartland would love. I've got news for you, Mr. Squeaky-Clean-Miles-McAlister: Nice guys don't finish first. It's the candidates who are willing to do what they need to do who get elected." He shoved his laptop into his bag, nearly spilling the tray of coffee. "Good luck trying to ride your morals into the Capitol, Miles. I'm out of here."

He stormed out of the office, slamming the door behind him.

"If that boy had a lick of sense, he'd realize that Faye's admission actually just helped our campaign." Bernice picked up a blueberry doughnut.

The corners of his mouth turned up at Bernice's use of the word "our." He was in the race until the end, and if all he had was his hometown to carry him, so be it.

A phone rang in the front room and Bernice wandered off to answer it. Miles sank back down into the security of the leather chair.

"Let me help you, Miles," Greer said softly.

"My image could use all the help it can get right now, Greer. But I'm not going to fall on my sword. I'm in this campaign for what I believe are the right reasons and I'm sticking to them. If you still want to help me, it's going to be on those terms."

"I admire that about you, Miles. And you know how much I respect you." She leaned forward, scooting to the edge of her seat. "We'd make a great team, you and I."

"Jesus, Greer, you can't be proposing what I think you are."

A pink flush spread over her face as she slumped back against the sofa. "Is it that horrible of an idea?"

She sounded a bit peeved and genuinely hurt. Miles moved from his father's chair to the leather sofa beside Greer. "Greer. You have to know that I respect you, too. I care what happens to you, but as a dear friend. That's why I can't go through with a marriage of political convenience." He paused in an effort to search for the right words. "I've known a great love in my life. And there's nothing that beats that feeling. You deserve that, too. You deserve to spend the rest of your life with someone who's going to revere you and not look at you as a political asset."

Greer snorted. "Love is overrated, Miles. It can destroy you if you let it. Trust me."

Miles' gut clenched. He'd had no idea that his friend might have suffered heartbreak like he had. He reached for her hand and laced his fingers through hers.

"My father has used me as a political pawn all of my life," she said quietly. "Did you know I hate politics?"

He shot her an incredulous look.

"Mmm." She smiled. "I hate everything involved with it. I only stay in the 'family business' so that my mother and father will take me seriously. They never gave me the time of day when my documentaries were about real issues. It was only when I moved into the political image consulting business that they saw a use for their grown-up photo op."

"And you thought marrying into politics just to appease them would make you happy? You can't live your life for your father, Greer."

"If it's any consolation, you were the only one I actually considered. My father's other protégés are all . . ." She shivered, leaving the rest of the sentence unspoken.

"Thanks, I think." Miles gave her hand a reassuring squeeze. "Selling out to please Daddy seems to be the theme of the day."

The media had been busy all morning, portraying Lori as a spoiled rich girl who'd do anything to win her father's affection. While Miles still couldn't quite square up that image with the woman he'd been sleeping with this past week, Greer's admission made the scenario seem more plausible. After all, he'd known the governor's daughter for nearly five years and he'd never suspected she'd been living a lie all this time.

Greer pulled her hand from his. "I'm not sure I want to be lumped in with Mallory Dykstrom."

"I'm not sure all the facts are out yet," he challenged. "You and she may not be that far apart in what motivates you."

She sighed heavily. "But it is a fact that you slept with her."

Miles didn't bother acknowledging her statement. He'd never understand what motivated jealousy among women.

"Does she know you'll never love her, either?"

Her question baffled him. While he'd been friends with Greer for years, he didn't feel the same distress at losing her as he felt about the possibility of never seeing Lori again. He chalked it up to chemistry and lust, once again cursing the fact that he couldn't feel that same attraction to the woman sitting next to him. It would have made life so much easier.

"It was just a fling, Greer—one of those 'heat of the moment' events that just happened."

She smiled slyly. "You keep telling yourself that, Miles. But I know you're not a 'heat of the moment' guy. If you were, we'd be announcing our engagement." Greer stood up from the sofa, smoothing her skirt. "So what's the plan from here on out? I'm assuming you didn't know who Lori was before last night?"

Miles nodded.

"Okay, so we need her to go on the record saying that. Maybe to apologize, also. We'll keep going with the integrity ads that we have. We can portray you as being as human as the next guy while you use this as an example that it's even more imperative that we pass legislation to get these types of crimes stopped."

He stood as well. "Are you sure you want to keep your wagon hitched to my campaign? It could very well be a blow to your own credibility in this business. Not to mention your relationship with your father."

She shrugged. "You'll be my last hurrah in politics. I told you, I respect what you stand for. Once we get you elected, I'll have plenty of time to decide what I want to be when I grow up. And you're right; it's time I cut the apron strings from Daddy. Watching what Mallory is going through has given me enough motivation."

Lori sipped from the coffee Deputy Lovell had brought her from the Java Jolt. After months of serving it every morning, she'd become used to the unique blend. Cassidy had come by the station house after helping with the morning rush at the inn. She'd brought Lori a change of clothes, a toothbrush, and a breakfast of leftover muffins Lori had made yesterday.

"I'm going to search the entire B and B from top to bottom," the teenager said. "I'll find that stupid pen and bracelet if it's the last thing I do. Sheriff Hollister can't keep you here forever."

Lori smiled at Cassidy. The fact was the sheriff could only keep her for another ten hours. After that, she'd be in Matt's custody. The idea of Sheriff Hollister holding her in the cozy Chances Inlet jailhouse indefinitely was certainly more appealing.

"Are you really who they say you are?" Cassidy asked quietly. "I mean they're saying you're this greedy girl who just wanted her father to love her so you helped him steal from all those people."

Lori tried not to cringe at Cassidy's description of her. "Part of that's right," she admitted.

"You're forgetting who I grew up with. I know the difference between a generous person who cares about others and one who . . . doesn't."

Reaching across the small table in the interrogation room where they were having breakfast, Lori linked her hand with Cassidy's. "Thanks for believing in me. I'm glad you don't let your past experiences cloud your relationships with others."

"Is your dad the one you were hiding from?"

"Not exactly," Lori explained. "I'm sure my dad is living quite comfortably somewhere."

"He just deserted you?"

Lori's lips formed a grim smile. "My dad is pretty good at that."

"Yeah, I always thought my mom would change, you know? She'd disappear for a few days or sell my laptop for money to buy some blow and then beg me to forgive her. 'It's the last time,' she'd say." Cassidy snorted. "I believed her. Every time."

"I never knew my dad really. My mom divorced him when I was two. But he was always this larger than life romantic hero to me." Lori smiled in remembrance. "The gifts he would send me were amazing. He always seemed so important when he came to visit. I would get angry with my mom and stepfather every time he left." Tears stung the backs of her eyes. "I'd beg for him to take me with him. But he always told me my mother wouldn't let me live with him."

"Sounds like your mother had some common sense," Matt said from the doorway of the room.

Cassidy pinned the FBI agent with her belligerent glare. Matt was unfazed, shoving a mini lemon poppy seed muffin in his mouth. "Mmmm," he said when he'd swallowed. "Your pastries are truly one of a kind, Mal."

He'd showered and shaved somewhere after spending the night in the holding cell across from hers. Matt had refused to leave her despite the sheriff's assurances that she wouldn't disappear from the jailhouse. Clearly, the FBI agent didn't trust anyone in Chances Inlet.

Matt gestured toward the lobby. "Your legal team has arrived. Since there are six of them, we'll have to adjourn to the sheriff's office."

Cassidy stood. "I should get back to the inn and help change over the rooms. I hope the Bensons have left already. I don't think I can be nice to that lady right now." She hesitated before quitting the room. "You'll still be here this afternoon, right?"

Lori met Matt's eyes. *Not if he has his way.*

"We'll stop by the inn before we leave," he surprised Lori by saying.

Cassidy visibly blanched. "Promise?"

He nodded solemnly.

With one last agonizing look at Lori, the teen slipped out of the room. Matt sat in the chair she'd vacated.

"I hope you weren't just placating the girl. She's had a pretty crappy life," Lori warned him.

Matt scrubbed a hand down his face. "I'm not a monster, Mal. I'm the same guy who was your friend."

"Ha!" Lori choked out a laugh. "'Friend' is laying it on a bit thick, isn't it?"

The FBI agent looked genuinely upset. "I was doing my

job. Contrary to what you think, I don't go around picking on innocent people."

"Until me."

"I truly believed you were innocent, Mal. Right up until the point where you ratted me out to your old man. Then you ran. I would have helped you." He leaned across the table. "Let me help you now."

"That would involve me trusting you, Matthew, and I think we've already covered that."

He gave her a resigned look as he stood up again. "As much as I'd like to stall all morning so those stuffed suits can bill your father up the ass, I'd rather get you back to New York tonight. I've got tickets for the Yankees game tomorrow."

"It's not going to matter whether I'm here or in New York," she said. "I'm still not going to cooperate with you, Matthew."

"I wish you would, Mallory. Things are going to get ugly from here on out." His charming smile was gone and his lively green eyes were determined as he lowered his voice to speak to her. "Believe it or not, I do care what happens to you. And when I get my hands on your old man—and I will find him with or without your help, Mal—I'm going to make sure they throw the book at him for the way he's treated you."

Lori swallowed painfully. She wanted to trust someone. And Matt was definitely one of the good guys. He'd been that way even when he was pretending to be her friend, she reluctantly realized. But the need for self-preservation was greater than her need for reliance and comfort right now. Keeping her own confidences, she led the way down the hallway to the sheriff's office.

Matt wasn't lying when he said a team of lawyers awaited them. Four men and two women were seated around the conference table. Two of the sharply dressed people were talking quietly on their cell phones. One of them Lori recognized from his visits to her father—Daniel Thomlin—who was likely the ring leader. He shot to his feet at the sight of Matthew at her elbow.

"Don't say a word, Mallory," the lawyer ordered. "Agent Kovaluk, you don't have permission to speak with our client at this time." He turned to the sheriff. "Sheriff, we'd like to meet with Ms. Dykstrom in private, please." No one in the room was fooled by the word "please"—it was a command, pure and simple. The lawyer's demeanor made her recoil, but the sheriff seemed to take it all in stride.

Sheriff Hollister stood up from his chair, indicating to Lori that she should take his place. She shot him a look of relief as she slid into the position of power within the small room. The sheriff gestured for Matt to precede him out of the office. "If there's anything you need"—the sheriff directed his remark at Lori—"don't hesitate to let me know."

The door had barely closed when Mr. Thomlin began speaking. "This is a fine mess here, Mallory. If you had just remained in New York like you were told, we could have avoided all this nasty publicity." Not waiting for her to respond, he turned to the lawyers at the table. "What have you got, Eric?"

"The sheriff hasn't located the missing items. Apparently, he's been searching the area pawn shops for at least a week and nothing has turned up," one of the younger minions said.

"Have you disposed of the items yet, Mallory?" Thomlin asked her.

The breath left Lori's lungs in a whoosh. "Excuse me?" she managed to choke out. *Wasn't her own lawyer supposed to assume she was innocent until proven guilty?*

He huffed disapprovingly. "The stolen items. The sheriff won't find them today, will he?"

"I have no idea," she said incredulously. "Since I didn't steal anything, I can't possibly tell you when and where they'll be found."

Six sets of eyes stared at her as if she'd just said the earth was square.

Anger swelled in her stomach. The jerks all really did think she was guilty.

Mr. Thomlin cleared his throat. "If you say so."

"I do say so!" She slammed her palm down onto the desk.

He looked at one of his other minions—one of the two who had a cell phone glued to his ear. "Where are we with the plea deal, then?"

"Plea deal?" Lori's chest squeezed in panic. *Surely he wasn't talking about a plea deal for her?*

"Yes, Mallory, a plea deal," Mr. Thomlin said condescendingly. "Your father doesn't want this to even reach the courts."

Lori was taken aback that her father was even in communication with this blowhard, much less that he would help defend her. "But I just told you, I didn't do it."

The lawyer eyed her as if she were a recalcitrant toddler. "Not the theft. The money laundering."

"I didn't do that, either."

He all but rolled his eyes at her. "The deed to the restaurant was in your name. It will be impossible to prove you had no knowledge. A plea is your best bet. It will also appease the feds for the time being, which will give your father some peace."

A roaring began in her head and her face grew painfully warm. *Which will give your father some peace.* Her father was selling her out. Again. He was going to let her take the fall for something she didn't do.

"It's for the best, Mallory," Mr. Thomlin was saying—most likely in reaction to the look on her face. "Your father has asked that we pursue a deal that would get you to a minimum security facility—most likely the same one where Martha Stewart was incarcerated." He spoke as though they were booking her a vacation at a resort, not sending her to prison. Lori's head felt like it might explode any second.

"Sheriff!" she shouted as she jumped to her feet.

The door burst open a second later as Sheriff Hollister stormed back into his office. She was relieved to see Matt standing behind him. Surely this team of morons couldn't strike a deal without the FBI agent's backing.

"I'd like to go back to my cell," she said, biting back the tears that threatened. "And these people"—she waved an arm at the room at large—"do *not* represent me. Do you hear me, Matthew? I'm not making a deal with anyone."

Matt gave her that cocky grin she was used to. "Atta girl."

"You heard her, ladies and gentlemen," the sheriff said. "You're off the case. Now get out of my office."

Mr. Thomlin blustered while his entourage watched in

stunned silence. "Don't be churlish, young lady. Not after all your father has done for you."

The air in the room seemed to crackle as she turned to face the buffoon who represented Dykstrom. "You tell your client, I know exactly what he's done *for* me and *to* me. And from this moment on, he doesn't have the right to call himself my father."

"You can't just dismiss us," he continued. "You don't have a dime to your name. Everything you owned came from your father."

"I'll take my chances on a free public defender rather than let him or you idiots steer my life."

Mr. Thomlin began to panic. "You may not discuss this case with anyone else, Mallory."

"Is that a threat?" The question came from outside the small room.

Everyone turned to the doorway to see Miles filling up its frame, his blue eyes snapping with anger. Lori swallowed a relieved gasp at the breathtaking sight of him, his posture ready for battle and his mouth dogged.

"Just exactly who are you?" Mr. Thomlin demanded.

Miles' eyes met hers for a brief moment before he shocked the heck out of her with his words.

"Her new attorney."

TWENTY-TWO

"Have you thought this through?" Lamar asked under his breath.

Hell no. Miles hadn't thought anything through. Not since last night when the man had led Lori out of his mother's B and B in handcuffs. He certainly hadn't been thinking when he left his campaign headquarters a few minutes ago and strolled down to the sheriff's office practically making the walk of shame in front of a barrage of national media camped out on the street. Ignoring the questions reporters threw out at him, Miles told himself that his purpose was to see if he could get more details on Lori's arrest in order to prepare a defense against the character attack that was being waged against him. If he caught a glimpse of her in the process, so be it. But the overwhelming feeling of relief at the sight of her was like a sucker punch to his senses.

She was dressed in her usual drab wardrobe, yet she looked different somehow. Despite the telltale shimmer of tears in her eyes, she held her head high and kept her back ramrod straight. Her long hair was pulled back in a sleek ponytail, where it could no longer disguise her determined chin and model-worthy cheekbones. There was a tremor in her voice, but she managed to keep her composure in spite of the bullying from her supposed attorney.

Miles planned on telling the assembled media that he had only ventured to the sheriff's office to get the details of his employee's arrest, but the sight of Lori valiantly fighting her battles alone made something snap inside him. Perhaps she was right after all and he was Dudley Do-Right at heart. The fact remained, however, he couldn't let her fight this battle alone.

The team of stuffed suits eyed him incredulously as they passed by him while exiting Lamar's office.

"You'll be sorry that you got involved with this, young man," the older guy warned.

"Again with the threats," Miles said, keeping his tone mild. He wanted to tell the man he'd grown up with four siblings and his words were like a dare that only spurred him on.

"What are you doing?" Valerie mouthed behind the attorney's back before she turned and led the team toward the building's foyer. *Committing professional suicide*, he very nearly said out loud.

Lori stared at him, her eyes wide and her shoulders squared. "You shouldn't have done that," she said. "You shouldn't even be here."

Resisting the urge to haul her into his arms, he wisely kept the desk between them as he wandered into the room. "It's a little late for that, don't you think?"

"No! It's not. You need to tell them you didn't know who I was; or that I tricked you somehow. Anything so this doesn't ruin your campaign. Please, Miles," she pleaded. "Don't jeopardize the political career you've dreamed about your whole life. Not for me."

Her last words were said with such anguish that Miles' breathing hitched. "I'm here to get the truth, Lori. If you want to help me, don't push me away. Just tell me what really went down. Because I know you're not guilty of anything."

A puff of air escaped her lips before she sank down limply into Lamar's chair. "But I suspected it," she whispered. "And I looked the other way. That makes me guilty."

Miles barked a sarcastic laugh. "Using that logic, half the world would be guilty of something."

The sound of a throat clearing made them both turn to the doorway. "Agent Kovaluk's superiors are on their way in from Washington. I can certainly stand in for a lawyer while they question her if need be, Miles."

Out of the corner of his eye, Miles watched Lori blanch at the sheriff's words.

"Can you give us a second, Sheriff?" he asked.

With a silent nod, Lamar closed the door behind him.

Miles placed his palms flat on the desk and leaned down to meet her wide-eyed stare. At the risk of his dream, he was going to rescue a second woman today from selling out for her father. Except Lori hadn't been willing to sell out, he realized. She'd all but told those high-priced defense hacks where to go. Unlike Greer, she never considered bowing to her father's pressure. Which meant she was protecting someone else and that thought made his gut burn.

"You can save face with the media by telling them you came to make sure charges were pressed," she said. "But you need to go now, Miles."

He was getting a little sick and tired of her trying to get rid of him. Especially since he was trying to do the chivalrous thing here.

"Why didn't you tell me who you were?" He asked the question that had plagued him the most since last night. "You had to have known you could trust me. But you didn't. You're still hiding from me now." He shoved away from the desk, breaking their stare. "Damn it, after everything we shared between us, even knowing who I am, you're still keeping secrets from me. You're prepared to go to prison for someone. The least you can do is tell me who it is."

Lori shot from the chair and circled the desk. "How dare you! I'm trying to help you."

"And I'm trying to help you!" Miles reached for her elbows, pulling her body flush with his.

"I told you before, you can't help me." She smacked her hands on his chest. "Of all the people in this world, Dudley, I would have confided in you. Now all that's going to happen is I'm going to hurt you. And that's the last thing I wanted, you idiot." Tears were streaming down her face and Miles couldn't help himself any longer. He wrapped his arms around her and pulled her in for a kiss. Lori's body melted against him as she opened her mouth to his more demanding one. Her hands reached up to grip his skull. She kissed him as though she were trying to hide inside him. Miles would have let her if it were the only way to keep her safe. His hands slid beneath her T-shirt, roaming the familiar soft skin beneath. One of them—he wasn't sure which—moaned deep in their throat when Miles used his body to guide her back against the wall. She arched her hips into his and all coherent thought left his brain for other more demanding parts of his anatomy.

"Hey! Before you two get any further along with that, you might want to alert Deputy Lovell so he can kill the security cameras," Lamar said, startling them both apart.

Reluctant to be separated from her, Miles traced the flush along Lori's neck while both tried to regulate their breathing back to normal.

"I'm sure that's an image neither of you want Tanya Sheppard and her cronies to air on the evening news tonight," the sheriff continued.

Miles continued to contemplate Lori. "Then I guess it's a good thing my mother is sleeping with the sheriff. He wouldn't want to upset her by leaking any video."

Lamar harrumphed as he took his seat. "We're running out of time here, kids. I can't legally hold Lori in the station house past nine o'clock tonight."

A throbbing began in Miles' temple. The woman before him was stubborn and loyal to a fault. He told himself it didn't matter who she might be protecting. Their relationship wouldn't be anything more than friends with benefits. Miles was peeved because he was risking his career to help her and she was still withholding the truth, not because he was jealous of some mystery person.

"Lori," he said, gripping her shoulders. "We can't help you if you don't tell us the truth."

Her chin jutted up and she crossed her arms beneath her ample breasts. "I told you the truth. I suspected my father was up to something wrong, but I ignored it. For all the reasons the talking heads on the news channels are citing. I was selfish and I wanted to be a part of my father's rich lifestyle."

There was more to the story; he understood her well enough to know that. But pressing her further wasn't getting them anywhere. "Fine," he snapped. "Then let's just bring the FBI agent in here and tell him that. I'm sure he's never had a suspect say she's guilty of ignorance before."

Lori narrowed her eyes at him. "Matthew already knows all this."

"And that's another thing," Miles continued, his voice rising in volume. "How come you and this guy are so cozy?"

The sound of a deep chuckle had Miles spinning on his heel and coming face to face with the shit-eating grin of the FBI agent.

"I've got to hand it to the guy, Mal," the agent said. "He clearly has a set of stones to brave the paparazzi. But I really don't want to find myself on the other end of Lover Boy's fist, so can you please set the record straight about us?"

With a roll of her eyes, Lori shoved past Miles and moved between him and the FBI agent. "Matthew claimed to be an accountant," she explained, her tone a mix of condescending and exasperated woman.

The agent shrugged innocently. "I did take an intro class in college."

Lori groaned. "I confided my suspicions to him about my father and showed him the books from the restaurant." She shot the agent a glare. "I played right into his undercover ploy."

"What can I say?" Agent Kovaluk grinned unabashedly. "I'm good at what I do."

"You took advantage of a woman," Miles accused.

The FBI agent's face grew hard. "That's not how I operate, McAlister, on or off the job."

"Play nice, boys, or I'll throw you both out of my office," Lamar warned from behind his desk.

Miles blew out a breath, trying in vain to cool his growing frustration. "Either way, you know she's innocent."

Kovaluk shot a resigned look at Lori. "Anyone who gets to know Lori like I did knows she couldn't have perpetuated this kind of crime against unsuspecting people."

The agent's words made Miles' fists clench. "Exactly how much getting to know her went on?" Just imagining Kovaluk's hands on Lori's body made him furious.

He hadn't realized he'd advanced on the agent until Lori grabbed his arm and yanked him back. "Miles, stop it." She turned him so he was facing her. "Matt and I never had *dessert*."

It took a moment for her words to penetrate the haze of anger that enveloped him.

"We had lots of dessert together," Kovaluk interjected, making Miles' pulse ratchet up again. "You're one of the best pastry chefs the city has. Well, had. I used to bring your cupcakes back to the bureau and the rest of the team would devour them. They'd beg the agent in charge to take me off the op and let them take the assignment just to get a taste of your baked goods."

Miles' whole body tensed. Lori dropped his arm, putting both her hands on her temples. "That's not what I'm talking about, Matthew."

The agent looked from one to the other before recognition dawned. "Oh." He grinned as he leaned a shoulder against the wall. "Is that what they're calling it these days?"

Lori blushed and Lamar simply shook his head. "I'm glad we got that all sorted out," the sheriff said. "Now if you two boys are done beating your chests, perhaps we can solve Lori's dilemma?"

Miles glared at Kovaluk. "You're wasting a lot of energy on an innocent woman. Why?"

The agent studied Lori with a desolate look in his eyes. "After I had the evidence we needed, I revealed my true identity. Mallory was offered immunity in exchange for her testimony." His mouth formed a grim line. "Instead, she tipped her father off."

A feeling of trepidation danced down Miles' spine. That couldn't be right. There was no way Lori would condone her father's actions, much less help him flee the authorities. Miles turned to Lori but she wouldn't meet his eyes.

"The game changed that night," Agent Kovaluk continued ominously. "And then they both disappeared."

"I don't understand," Miles said. Had he been wrong about her?

"That makes two of us," Kovaluk added.

Lori was wearing a belligerent mask she'd obviously borrowed from Cassidy.

"Damn it, Lori. The man just tried to use you as a scapegoat for his crimes," Miles yelled. "He's not worth protecting and he's definitely not worth giving up the rest of your life for."

"I'm not protecting him!" Lori shouted back.

Miles' gut clenched at the thought that she might be protecting another man. "Then who is it?" he demanded.

"Ian," said a female voice from the doorway.

Miles turned to see a woman who looked like the Earth Mother version of his own mom, with her long silver hair and her makeup-free face. The stubborn set of her mouth and her light brown eyes were very much like Lori's, however.

"And the cavalry has arrived," Kovaluk said.

"Mom!" Lori cried before launching herself into the woman's open arms.

"I'm so glad you are all right," her mother, Diana, murmured as she held Lori tightly. They'd moved in tandem to the small sofa in the corner of the sheriff's office. Lori was afraid if she let go, her mother would slip away and the last few moments would have just been a dream. A hand squeezed her shoulder and she looked up to see her stepfather, Bruce Hunt, smiling above them. Tears flowed down Lori's cheeks when Bruce leaned down to kiss the top of her head.

"We got Diesel's message that you were somewhere safe," Bruce explained. "But we were a mess not knowing where you were and if you needed help. We came as soon as we saw the news."

"I'm sorry," Lori said through her tears. "I'm so sorry about everything."

Her mother pulled back, and with the pads of her thumbs, she gently wiped the tears off Lori's cheeks. The smile she gave her was one Lori never thought she would see directed at her ever again. There wasn't a trace of disapproval in it.

"Stop blaming yourself. Your father is the villain here, not you," she said.

"I should never have left you like that. Not for him, that's for sure."

The sound of her mother's rich laughter was like a balm to Lori's battered soul.

"You aren't the only one who was a rebellious nineteen-year-old," her mother said. "Nor are you the only one who fell for Leonard Dykstrom's charms. I guess I got the biggest consolation prize, though." She cupped Lori's chin in her hand. "I got you out of the deal and I will never regret that part of my rebellion."

Lori leaned her head on her mother's shoulder. "Still, I never should have left. I can't believe how stupid I was to think that life with him would be better than life with you. I know I gave you a lot of grief whenever he came to visit and you wouldn't let me leave with him. Thanks for showing more common sense than I did."

Bruce and her mother exchanged a distressed look. Lori understood its meaning without them having to explain.

"He didn't want me to come with him, did he?" The realization should have been a shock, but after everything she'd learned about her father, it wasn't.

Her mother shook her head sadly. "Half the time he didn't remember your birthday or Christmas. Bruce and I would buy you gifts and say they were from him."

Tears clogged the back of her throat. "And you two would give me some token gift because you couldn't afford anything more." Lori gulped back a sob. "Why would you do that for him?"

"We didn't do it for him." Her mother pulled her into another hug. "We did it for you. So you'd feel loved."

"It might have been better to let me feel unloved. I would have appreciated you two more and I could have enjoyed a stress-free life in Oregon."

Her stepfather laughed. "Oh, I don't know about stress-free," he said. "We would have put you to work full-time and traveled around."

She looked from her stepfather to her mother. "That would have been perfect."

Miles cleared his throat. "I hate to break up this little reunion, but who is Ian?"

Lori would have laughed at Miles' apparent irritation had she thought he was actually jealous. Since she knew he didn't love her the same way she loved him, jealousy likely wasn't the cause. In all probability, Miles was just anxious to get the situation resolved so he could fulfill his Dudley Do-Right obligation and get back to saving his campaign.

"Ian is my half brother," she explained. "He has Asperger's." Her throat grew tight just thinking of the young teenage boy. How frightened he must be to have been uprooted from everything he was familiar with—the things that kept him stable—and dragged someplace where the people might not even speak the same language.

"Our reports indicate the nanny went with them," Matthew said.

"Of course she did," Lori said. "She's sleeping with my fath—Leonard."

"What about the child's mother?" Lamar asked.

"Carole?" Lori scoffed. "She's ashamed of Ian and much more concerned about her status among the elite than about how her son is faring."

"She was in on the whole Ponzi scheme, wasn't she?" Matthew asked.

Lori shrugged. "She had the connections. He told me he couldn't have carried it off without her."

Matthew pulled away from the wall. "So he admitted it to you? When exactly was that?"

Miles took a step into the center of the room, putting himself between her and the FBI agent. "Is this a formal interrogation?"

"Time is running out, McAlister," Matt growled. "I won't be able to help her once she moves up the chain of command."

Her mother squeezed her hand. "Bruce and I are here now. We'll protect you. You just have to tell the truth."

"But who is going to protect Ian if both his parents are in jail!" Lori bounced up from the sofa and began to pace the room. "I was livid when I found out Leonard had been using my restaurant to launder money—money he had stolen! But I was hurt and angry when I found out *you*"—she shot a menacing look at Matthew—"had used me, too. I didn't know what to do, so I went to his office and begged him to turn himself in. For his son's sake. I told him I'd take care of Ian." She turned to her mother and Bruce. "I was going to bring him home to Oregon. He'd love living at the inn on the farm." Lori had told her younger brother about the barn with its horses and kittens, the free-range chickens and the ducks in the pond. Ian had grown up trapped in a New York high-rise because his mother was embarrassed by her less-than-perfect son. The idea of being in the country both intrigued and frightened him, but Lori knew he would be happy there.

"What did Dykstrom say when you confronted him?" Matthew's face mirrored Miles' in its lethal intensity.

Lori's heart sank remembering that January night. "He told me to go back to my apartment and wait for him. He was going to call his lawyers and draw up the papers to make me Ian's guardian. Or so he said." She wrapped her arms around her midsection to stop her body from trembling as she recalled what came next. "His lawyers showed up early the next day, but Mr. Thomlin was only interested in what I had learned from the FBI and what I might have said in return. Ian called me to say they were going on a trip and would I bring him some purple Skittles because he didn't like plane rides. By the time I got to the penthouse, they were already gone. The story broke that day and I was named as one of the suspects. I never even knew I was under suspicion." She glared at Matthew again.

"You said Ian called you." Matthew was quick to hone in on that one minor detail. "That call didn't show up on your cell phone records."

Lori's stomach lurched. "You were tracing my calls? Were you listening to them, too?"

Matthew's face remained impassive. He ignored her question. "There wasn't a record of a call coming from any of Dykstrom's lines that morning, either."

Seething, she squeezed at her temples. "How dare you!"

"Mal, focus," Matthew commanded. "You can rip me a new one for doing my job later. Right now, I need you to tell me how you and Ian communicated."

Her mother nodded with encouragement. Lori let out a resigned sigh. "We have a set of Captain America burn phones that I gave him for Christmas. He liked the idea of us being superheroes who communicated on our special phones."

She could feel the tension ratchet up a notch in the small room. Even the sheriff was now sitting on the edge of his seat. Lori swallowed harshly.

"Please tell me the kid still has his phone," Matthew pleaded. "And it still has minutes left on it."

"He still has it," she said quietly. "I try and talk to him for a few minutes every Sunday."

Matthew took a step forward, but Miles blocked his path.

"Hold on there, Kovaluk," he said. "What does Lori get in exchange for the information?"

A heavy silence settled over the room. Matthew puffed out a breath as he seemed to consider Miles' question. "The original deal was she'd walk if she testified against Dykstrom. Ian wasn't ever factored in." He paused again before meeting her eyes with his solemn green ones. "I'll make the case with the DA that you were only looking out for your half brother. None of the evidence points to you being involved in the overall Ponzi scheme. No one was happy about Dykstrom being tipped off, but they can't put you in jail for that."

Guilt squeezed at Lori's stomach as she realized how much trouble Matthew must have been in when she had warned her father. Again, she hadn't taken into consideration all the consequences for her impulsive actions. No wonder he'd been searching high and low for her.

"I'm sorry for ruining your undercover operation," she said, really meaning it now.

His lips curved up into a wolfish grin. "You know how you can make it up to me."

Miles tensed beside her and Lori put a hand on his chest to keep him from presumably decking the FBI agent.

"I have two conditions," she said.

Hanging his head, Matthew unleashed a string of expletives.

"I won't leave Ian unprotected," she told him.

Matthew nodded. "I figured as much."

"He can't go into foster care."

"Fine, that will be part of the deal. What else?"

This part was going to be a lot harder to pull off. She risked a peek at Miles' stony face. He needed to be protected as much as Ian did right now. Lori loved both of them too much not to make sure they got through this unscathed. Dudley Do-Right wouldn't like what she was about to do, but it was for his own good.

"I want to talk to Tanya Sheppard. To make a statement that exonerates Miles from all of this."

The room erupted as Matthew and Miles both tried to outdo each other with the obscenities.

"I don't think that's a very good idea, honey," her mother said.

"You can't talk to the media! The agent in charge will have my ass if I let that happen," Matthew yelled.

"I'd pick someone other than Tanya Sheppard," the sheriff muttered.

"Quiet!" Miles shouted and the room went still. He turned to Lori. "As your attorney, I can't let you do that. The feds can take your statement and use it against you."

"Oh," she said. "I guess I really had three demands. You can't be my lawyer, Miles."

Those blue eyes she'd fallen in love with were stunned before he narrowed them at her. "Don't be ridiculous. Who else is going to defend you in this town?"

"Certainly not the man whose dream it is to represent the people of Chances Inlet."

"They'll get over it."

She shook her head sadly. "No, Miles, they won't. I know you're just trying to help and I love you for it, I truly do."

His head jerked back a fraction at her declaration of love.

"And it's because I love you that I'm going to have to insist on this," she continued before turning to Matthew. "I won't give you Dykstrom unless those three things happen."

"Fine." Matt yanked his phone from his pants pocket. "I'll make some calls." He was already barking into his phone as he left the small office.

The sheriff cleared his throat. "Mr. and Mrs. Hunt, can I buy you both a cup of coffee? We may not be in the Pacific Northwest, but the Java Jolt brews a decent blend."

Bruce nodded. "We've been up all night, so a cup of coffee sounds delicious."

Her mother gave Miles a discerning look before kissing Lori on the cheek. "We'll be right back, sweetheart."

Lori pasted an encouraging smile on her face. "I'm not going anywhere."

An awkward silence settled over the room when the three departed. Miles dragged his fingers through his hair. "You need to be careful. They could still arrest you. I know some attorneys in New York. At least let me have one of them help you."

"If it comes to that, I'll find someone myself. You need to distance yourself from me. Starting right now."

He grabbed her arms and pulled her against him. "As long as you promise to come back when this is all over."

Her chest grew tight at his command. "As what?" she whispered. "Your mother's cook and maid?"

Miles' mouth descended on hers. His kiss was angry and demanding and Lori let him have his way while she soaked up as much of him as she could, storing up her memories for the lonely days ahead.

"We could still have this, you and I." His voice was raspy as his lips cruised her jaw. "This works for us."

"Are you offering me what you considered giving Greer?" The question was unfair and Miles stiffened at her words. But Lori asked it anyway despite the fact she knew the answer. "Are you proposing a loveless relationship?"

He jerked away. "Damn it, Lori, you knew the score up front."

She pulled in a deep breath to keep the tears at bay. "I did. And you've been nothing but honest with me. I fell in love with you anyway. But, hey, I've got a track record for being impulsive and making bad decisions. I'm trying to rectify that situation now."

Miles was incredulous. "I'm not a bad decision."

Lori couldn't help the smile that formed because Miles was one of the best decisions she'd ever made. She couldn't even regret falling in love with him. Her only regret was that he could never return the feeling.

"No, you're not," she reassured him. "You're what this town and this country needs, Miles. Being elected to represent the people of Chances Inlet is all you ever wanted. I can't let you throw that away for me. You may think your integrity makes you invulnerable, but the other party will destroy you. And deep down, I think you know that."

He stood there with his hands on his hips and his chin on his chest.

Lori reached up to cup his cheek. "I know you can't love me, but if you care anything about me, you'll let me do this for you."

Miles opened his mouth to speak, but Lori silenced him with her lips. The kiss she gave him was soft and comforting. She lingered, savoring his taste and feel, committing all of him to memory for when she left him.

"What we had was amazing and I thank you for it. But our lives are diverging now, Miles," she whispered against his cheek. "We both need to go on and do the things we were meant to do. And that starts with you walking out that door and getting back to your campaign. Please, do it for me."

She felt his chest rumble beneath the palm she had flattened over his pectoral muscles. "Another place, another time," he murmured before his lips found hers for one last thorough kiss that had her toes curling and her body quivering. She pulled away before she did something reckless like reconsidering her plan. Wrapping her arms around her middle, she tried to appear resolute. Miles swore under his breath. Without looking back, he left the sheriff's office.

Lori sank down on the sofa and let the tears silently fall, knowing another place or another time could never be.

TWENTY-THREE

The nightly newscasts were all abuzz with the details that Leonard Dykstrom had been arrested while in bed with his child's nanny.

"The man who orchestrated one of the nation's largest Ponzi schemes was captured today, in a Caribbean villa where he and his family were hiding," one network news anchor reported. "When agents stormed the home, they found Dykstrom's wife, Carole, recovering from plastic surgery she claimed was to disguise her appearance. Her husband was enjoying some extracurricular activities with the nanny charged with caring for the couple's special-needs son. Dykstrom's arrest comes after his daughter, Mallory, was detained in Chances Inlet, North Carolina, last evening."

Lori's image filled the screen for a second day, but this time the video wasn't of the glamorous socialite, but rather the woman who'd been hiding out in his mother's B and B for the past six months. At Miles' request, Greer had helped prep Lori for the interview with Tanya, not that she needed any assistance. It turned out Lori was adept at handling the media all on her own.

"No one in the McAlister family knew who I was until last night when Special Agent Kovaluk arrived," Lori told the world. "I never intended for them to find out. Their family is very caring and community driven and I in no way wanted to diminish their reputation by associating with me. They're good people. The best people, in fact."

Tanya pasted on one of her snarky smiles. "But you did have a relationship with Miles McAlister, the candidate for United States Congress."

Lori matched her smile. "I'm not going to sit here and kiss and tell, Tanya. But what I will say is that Miles McAlister is an incredible person with an abundance of integrity. His compassion for others is boundless. Whatever did or did not go on between Miles and myself is private and has no bearing on his campaign."

Tanya pulled no punches. "Do you love him?"

Miles choked on the sip he'd just taken from his bottle of beer. Cassidy reached over and slapped him on the back while Bernice muttered a "bless her heart" at the television propped in the corner of the campaign office. *Damn it, what was it with women and love?* Lori had pushed him away all because she claimed to love him. He'd been up front with her, telling her at the beginning that his heart was not in play and it never would be again. She'd been more than okay with that; at least that's what she'd said.

The camera zoomed in and Lori licked her lips. Miles' throat wasn't the only body part constricting at the image.

"I have the utmost respect for Miles as a person and as a politician," Lori declared. "Voters should, too. That's all that's really important here, Tanya."

Greer was sending Miles glowing texts about how Lori's confession was a boon to his campaign, but Miles ignored them. His body still ached in the region where his heart used to be every time he saw Lori through the lens of a camera and not his own eyes. *She'd said she couldn't leave without her grandmother's ring yet she walked away and wasn't coming back all because she loved him. How mixed up was that?* He took another pull from the beer in hopes of washing the sting away.

The screen changed to a video of Lori being reunited with

her brother, Ian, as the news anchor spoke. "Ms. Dykstrom has not been indicted on any charges and she cooperated fully with federal officials once she was assured her younger half brother would be safe."

Matt Kovaluk mugged for the cameras next. "Mallory Dykstrom spent the past few months living in fear for her younger brother," he told reporters. "She was invaluable in bringing Leonard and Carole Dykstrom to justice. There is no evidence linking her to the crimes committed by her father and stepmother. She was as much a victim as the thousands of people Leonard Dykstrom conned money from."

"Well, that's quite a different tune than they were singing last night." Bernice clapped her hands. "Greer is a miracle worker at image makeovers."

Miles nearly choked on his beer again. Bernice was only half right; Greer and Lori both had one common goal and that was to make over *his* image. The fact that Lori came out smelling better than she had yesterday was just a happy coincidence. Still, Miles was relieved Lori wouldn't be tainted by her father's crimes. He'd hated the way she wanted to take on the media in defense of him. Knowing she'd done so out of some misguided love for him only made it worse.

"I'm glad she has a family to help her," Cassidy said from her place on the sofa beside Miles. Her tone was a bit melancholy, however.

"I'm sure you'll see her again," he tried to reassure her.

Cassidy's face brightened. "I know I will. She said she'd fly me out for fall break so I can see Oregon. I've never even been on a plane. Isn't that cool?"

"Oh, sure, desert us during crunch time in the campaign for a sightseeing trip across country," Bernice said, crossing her arms beneath her bosom.

"Ever since you kicked Coy out, she's acting like she's in charge," Cassidy groaned.

"She is in charge," Miles said as he gave Bernice a wink. "Of the office and the staff." He'd already hired a campaign coordinator who didn't have a connection to Governor Rossi. Despite the negative publicity of the past few days, Miles had people jumping at the chance to right his campaign. There were still three months left in the race and he was grateful that the man he'd hired had already sweet-talked Bernice and charmed Greer. Miles wasn't out of the woods yet, but at least his integrity was still in one piece.

"While I don't agree with the adage that any publicity is good publicity, I'm glad Greer was able to turn things around for you today, son," Governor Rossi said from the doorway of Miles' office. "Although it looks like you're a little light on campaign staff." He gestured at the empty outer office.

Miles worked to unclench his jaw. Bob Rossi was the last person he expected to see today. Or any day from here on out, for that matter.

"The office is closed for the day," Bernice informed the governor in an indignant tone. "But we are certainly not 'light' on campaign staff."

She wasn't lying. Bernice and Cassidy had spent a good portion of the day wrangling up locals to work the phones and pass out campaign literature. Some were leery at first, still angry at Miles' association with Lori, thinking she was a part of her father's scheme. But Bernice could be persuasive and Miles had no doubt he'd have the manpower to help get out the vote when the time came.

Respect had been ingrained into Miles' personality at a young age, and he stood reflexively when the governor entered the room. Bernice shot the man an evil look from behind his back before clicking off the television. "Come on, Cassidy. They're serving shrimp and grits at the diner tonight and I'm buying. I doubt you'll get anything decent to eat with Ginger in the kitchen at the B and B."

"Ugh, she made tofu hotdogs for lunch," Cassidy groaned as she followed Bernice to the door.

"Look at it this way, the cafeteria food in college won't look so bad after a few weeks of Ginger's cooking," Bernice said. She lifted an eyebrow at Miles as if to ask if he'd be all right with the governor. Miles gave her a confident grin and waved them both out the door. Truth be told, he might need her to come back and mop up the mess after their conversation was over.

Governor Rossi slipped into his father's chair as if he owned it. Miles' throat burned at the sight. "What can I do for you, Governor?"

"You can zip up your pants and calm down, for one thing."

Miles clenched his fingers into fists, but he wisely kept his mouth shut.

"Just because you showed some indiscretion with a notorious woman doesn't mean you throw out half your staff. Coy's family is miffed at you and frankly, son, so am I."

"Let's get one thing straight here, Governor. I'm not, nor will I ever be, your *son*. There are only two people in the world who call me that and you are not one of them."

"I think you're forgetting who you're talking to, McAlister. I made you who you are today."

"Actually, Governor, the man whose chair you're sitting in made me who I am today. So did my mother, my family, and the people of Chances Inlet."

The governor shot to his feet. "I gave you a job and inroads to some of the most powerful people in this state—in the country, in fact."

"Yes, sir, you did, and I worked my ass off to do the job justice. I didn't do it so that I can be your puppet on a string, however."

Governor Rossi actually laughed. "Oh, so now you think you're better than me, is that it? You're so rich with integrity? We all start out that way, McAlister, before politics jades us. Then we learn to play the game. Politics isn't pretty and even squeaky clean Boy Scouts like you will have to wallow in the muck to get anything accomplished."

"There's 'wallowing in the muck' and there's playing dirty, Governor. I can do one, but I refuse to do the other."

The governor narrowed his eyes at Miles. "You're playing with fire, McAlister. I can destroy you just as easily as I made you. Don't ask me for any more political favors. You're on your own in this election. And should you find yourself actually winning, you're going to discover you crossed the wrong man." He stalked over to the door.

"One more thing, Governor," Miles said quietly as he unlocked the top drawer of his desk and pulled out a file folder. "I have to ask you if you have any knowledge into the case against my former opponent?"

Governor Rossi stopped in his tracks, his face dark red as he turned to face Miles. "Just what the hell are you accusing me of?"

Miles studied his former boss carefully. Bob Rossi knew exactly what he had done.

"I have sworn testimony from two individuals stating you orchestrated the entire thing, including the man's indictment."

"You son of a bitch!"

"I can 'wallow in the muck' with the best of them, Governor. After all, I had an adept teacher."

"What are you going to do with that?"

Miles sucked in a deep breath. "Leave me alone and these will never see the light of day." He meant it, too. While Bob Rossi would use the evidence to curry political favor, Miles just wanted the man out of his life.

The governor swore under his breath before turning to leave.

"One more thing," Miles called after him. "I'm giving a copy of this to Greer. Treat her right or this goes public. Understand?"

"You two would have had it all." He shook his head in frustration. "You're both ungrateful and I'm glad to be rid of you."

The slamming door shook the small office. Miles sank down into his father's chair and rested his head back against the soft leather. Closing his eyes, he said a silent prayer of thanks for everything his father had taught him.

"She'll be okay, won't she?" Patricia asked. Her head was nestled on Lamar's bare shoulder. The two of them were lying in her bed watching the late-night newscast with details of Leonard Dykstrom's arrest.

Lamar gave her shoulders a squeeze. "Lori's pretty tough. Agent Kovaluk was very protective of her, though. I don't think he'll let anything happen to her."

"He did seem to care about her to some extent."

"Mmm. He's got a decent reputation and his mother is a federal judge, so there's always some help there."

Patricia rolled onto his chest. "You checked the agent out?"

He arched an eyebrow at her. "I wasn't just going to let her go with anybody."

Smiling, she leaned down to press her lips to his.

"You don't think Lori and Agent Kovaluk were ever, you know, an item?"

Lamar's rich laugh bubbled up from his chest. "Your son already covered that this morning. I thought I might have to break up a fight between an armed federal agent and a congressional candidate. I'm telling you, Tricia, I don't think this town could take any more publicity this summer."

Patricia rested her head on his chest. "I must have been very preoccupied not to have seen Miles and Lori's affair. I never saw that one coming."

"I doubt they did, either." Lamar chuckled. "I'm sure neither one of them counted on falling in love."

She straightened her arms so she was looking down on him from above. "In love? Lori admitted to me she had feelings for him, but what made you suspect she loved him?"

He sobered up and traced a finger over her shoulder. "Lori told him so, right there in my office. Right before she demanded the interview with Tanya to set the record straight."

Stunned, Patricia rolled on her back and propped herself up against the headboard. "She did it for him. Oh, the poor girl. Miles is determined never to love again."

"Someone should tell him that love doesn't work that way," he murmured as his hand found her breast beneath the sheet.

"You're absolutely right. They don't call this town the Home of Second Chances for nothing. Miles is just avoiding the obvious. It'll have to be up to the women in this family to make him see reason."

His hand stilled and he looked over at her with his solemn eyes. A slow smile spread over his face. "I almost feel sorry for the guy, except that he was such a pain in the ass all those months."

"Good." She leaned over and kissed him on the corner of his mouth. "My son deserves as much happiness as we have. We just need to see that he makes it a priority."

"He's a good man, Tricia. But he's also a McAlister. And I know firsthand how difficult it is to convince one of their kind to let go and fall in love." He had the audacity to wink at her.

Patricia harrumphed at him. "Oh, yeah? Well, I'm his mother. There's no end to what I would do to make my children happy."

Lamar laughed as his lips nuzzled her neck. "How 'bout I make you happy, hmm?"

And he proceeded to. Thoroughly.

"Sissy, will Tessa go to Oregon with us, too?"

Lori looked across the hotel suite at Ian, seated on the floor with Tessa curled up on his lanky legs. It was late in the evening and both boy and dog were dozing off and on. The dog had always been a favorite of his when he came to visit her at her apartment. Ian had talked her and Diesel into caring for the stray. It was Ian who named the dog after a horse he'd ridden once when Lori had taken him riding in Central Park. He loved animals and they seemed to love him back.

"Tessa goes wherever you go from now on, Ian." She walked over and ruffled his wavy brown hair. "I told you I was just keeping an eye on her for you."

"She'll have fun with the other animals on the farm," Bruce said. Lori smiled gratefully at her stepfather, who had taken Ian under his wing since they arrived in New York five hours ago. The FBI was footing the bill for Lori, Ian, and her parents to stay in a boutique hotel on the West Side. All she had to do was testify against Leonard Dykstrom and his wife, sending them both to prison for the rest of their natural lives. She shivered at the thought.

"How you holding up, honey?" Her mother wrapped an arm over her shoulders.

"I'm fine. I'm so happy you both came with me. I wasn't looking forward to doing this alone."

"You're not alone, Lori. You never were," her mother said. She nodded at Ian and Bruce. "He's going to be a lot of responsibility."

"I know. But he's a sweet kid. He won't be any trouble, I promise."

"It's not him I'm worried about. It's you. Having another person to take care of can tie you down."

Lori studied her mother. "I told you, I'm through with thinking the grass is greener everywhere else. Oregon, the inn, and the farm are everything I need. Ian and I will be content."

"And Miles McAlister, how does he fit in?"

Her heart skipped a beat at the mention of Miles' name. He'd honored her wish—just as she knew he would—and stayed away from the sheriff's office and the media circus that surrounded her trip out of Chances Inlet. Matthew had also honored his word by letting her say good-bye to Cassidy, Ginger, and Patricia. She'd vowed to keep in touch with all three of them. Her mother had invited them all out to her B and B and Patricia promised to visit soon. Ironically, the last sight Lori had seen as they pulled out of town was a MCALISTER FOR CONGRESS sign. Lori had said a silent prayer that Miles would be able to restore his campaign and achieve his dream.

"He doesn't," she told her mother.

"Because he's running for Congress?" Her mother had that determined look that said she wasn't going to be satisfied until she got all the answers. As a teenager, Lori had hated that look. Tonight, she was grateful to have her mother looking at her at all. "You're not the one who's guilty here. Leonard and Carole are. As far as everyone else is concerned, you did the right thing by thinking of Ian before everyone else. He should be proud to have a woman like you love him."

Lori kissed her mother's cheek. "Thanks for defending me, Mom." It was easier to let her mom think what she did rather than tell the truth: Miles didn't love her and he never would. Still, she had no regrets. She just had to convince the tears threatening at the backs of her eyes.

"I found rainbow sprinkles," Matthew called as he entered the suite.

"Yay," Ian and Bruce cheered.

Her mother began dishing out the vanilla ice cream she'd ordered from room service in hopes it would cheer Ian up.

He hadn't once asked about his parents, but Lori knew her mother wanted to keep him distracted. Unfortunately, Ian didn't eat ice cream without rainbow sprinkles. Matt had saved the evening by locating some at the corner bodega.

"You bought two containers?" Lori asked.

Matthew shrugged. "Hey, he's a growing boy. I didn't know how much he'd eat." He checked his phone. "I've got to stop by the Bureau and brief the agent in charge. Do you have everything you need?"

She watched as Ian shoveled more sprinkles than ice cream into his mouth. "We do now."

Lori walked him to the door.

"Try and get some rest. Tomorrow could be a long day."

"Thanks for everything, Matthew. I mean it."

He eyed her critically. "You know, I can find a reason to go back to Chances Inlet and rough the guy up."

"What guy?"

"McAlister. The candidate."

She felt her cheeks grow warm. "You're very sweet, but it's totally not necessary."

"Mmm. The guy's an idiot. But then most politicians are these days."

"Hey! Don't say that about Miles. He's one of the good guys."

"You sure about that? Because a good guy wouldn't have let you go."

Lori couldn't find the words to answer him because her mouth was suddenly dry.

Matthew leaned over and kissed her softly on the cheek. "You're one of a kind, Mal—I mean, Lori. Remember that." With that he was gone.

"Sissy, is my mouth purple?" Ian called to her.

Lori pushed away from the door, refusing to let Matthew's words get to her. She'd won. Ian was safe and Leonard Dykstrom would face the penalty for his crimes. So what if she'd left her heart in a small town in coastal North Carolina? She could be like Miles and live a perfectly normal life without it.

"Hey, save some for me!"

TWENTY-FOUR

A crisp, November breeze blew off the Atlantic Ocean, ruffling Miles' hair as he hurried through the torpedo factory's door. Little girls were clambering into the dance studio for a ballet class, all of them dressed in red, white, or blue leotards. Ginger grinned at him as she hustled the girls inside.

"We have a theme going today in your honor. It was actually Emily's idea. Although she was disappointed that members of Congress don't actually wear tiaras." She kissed him on the cheek. "The kids are so excited to share in your special day."

"I'm pretty sure they're just excited because Election Day is a school holiday," he said as he waved to his niece, who was in fact wearing a patriotic crown.

"Okay, maybe a little of that, too." Ginger winked at him. "I'll see you at Dresden House later."

He watched for a moment as the little girls followed Ginger into the studio. His brother's fiancée was right: It was a special day for Miles. One he'd been waiting for most of his life. Despite a bumpy start to the campaign, the pollsters predicted he would beat Faye Rich by a nine-point margin. He was actually going to be a United States Congressman just as he'd planned all those years ago. It was heady stuff.

Still, Miles was battling a sense of hollowness that had been dogging him most of the campaign. He told himself it was because his father wasn't here to share in his accomplishment. It was a feeling he was going to have to get used to apparently.

Cassidy poked her head out of the campaign office. "Hey there, Congressman-elect. A reporter from one of the Wilmington television stations would like a quote. Are you available?" She gave him a cheeky smile and Miles couldn't help returning it.

The campaign office was bustling despite the fact it was nearly five o'clock on Election Day. Cassidy had brought along a crew from college to help with the last-minute campaigning and the room had a festive vibe going. Miles pulled off his jacket and gave it to Bernice.

Greer handed him a cell phone. "This is the fun part, Miles. You did it. Enjoy these interviews."

Bernice smiled broadly as she passed him a sheet of talking points. Spurred on by everyone's enthusiasm, Miles took the call. Surely this feeling of melancholy would go away when he stepped into his new role.

Hours later, surrounded by friends and family celebrating his victory at Dresden House, Miles still felt disconnected and out of sorts, however. A band was playing on the patio and a stream of well-wishers queued up beside him for a handshake and a selfie. Keeping a smile plastered on his face, Miles worked the room before seeking some sanctuary in the area of the big house his family was occupying.

"Congratulations, Miles." Will Connelly, sporting a splint on his wrist after a punishing victory over the Pittsburgh Steelers, clapped him on the back. "You did what you said you would do. Not that any of us ever doubted it. You'd just better not become a Redskins fan like all those other politicians, you hear me?"

His brother, Ryan, sporting his own splint after a mishap at second base late in the season, draped an arm over Miles' shoulder. "The same goes with baseball. I can't have you cheering for those Nationals when your brother plays for the opposing team."

"Pish-posh," Bernice interjected. "When are you boys going to learn? Miles McAlister is his own man. He'll cheer for whichever team he wants to."

Miles leaned over and grabbed Bernice in a bear hug. "You sure you don't want to come to Washington and run my office?"

She shook her head. "And give up my bridge club? No, I've had my fun. I'll hold down the fort in the district office, thank you very much. But I still want invites to the inaugural balls. I've already got my dress picked out."

His sister, Elle, grinned as she linked an arm through his. "So when do I get my in-depth interview with America's hottest new Congressman?"

Gavin snorted. "Hey, there's only room in this family for one *Cosmo* Bachelor of the Month and I'm not giving up the title."

"And here I thought you were embarrassed by that distinction," Ginger teased as the rest of the family laughed.

Pretending to ignore them all, Gavin pulled the wrapper off a cupcake he was carrying. He took a bite before making a face.

"Man, I miss Lori's cupcakes," his brother complained.

The unsettled feeling intensified. Miles had worked hard to keep thoughts of Lori contained to late at night when he was alone in his bed. Otherwise, he'd be distracted all day wondering what she was doing and how she was faring. Of course, everyone in town knew the answers to those questions. Cassidy and his mother frequently reported she was successfully working as the chef and manager of her mother's restaurant on the Oregon coast. She'd navigated the trial and the media with grace and humility. By all accounts she was content with her old life—enjoying it even.

So why then couldn't Miles enjoy his? Especially now that he'd gotten all he ever wanted.

"Miles." Greer grabbed his arm. "This is it. Faye is on the phone. She's calling to congratulate you. Do you want it on speaker?"

"No." Despite being beholden to the people of Chances Inlet, there were still some conversations he wanted to keep private. This was one of them. He took the phone from Greer and headed to the small butler's pantry, where he and Faye had first spoken all those weeks ago.

"How are you, Faye?" he asked when he'd closed the door behind him.

Faye sighed. "I'm in need of a spa vacation that starts with a two-hour bubble bath."

Miles chuckled at her candor. "Would you believe me if I said the same thing? Substituting the bubble bath for a few beers, of course."

She laughed out loud. "I'd say we both deserved it. But in all seriousness, congratulations, young man. If I hadn't voted for myself, I would have definitely voted for you. I'm happy to have you representing me and our community, Miles. I know you'll do us proud."

He swallowed around the lump that had formed in his throat. "I hope that means you won't mind serving as an advisor when I need one. I'm serious about protecting the rights of seniors. I know people in Washington would take me more seriously if I had some bipartisan support."

"I'm available for whatever you need me for, Miles."

"I appreciate that. Especially after everything that happened in the campaign."

"We both did our best to keep the nastiness out, Miles. I can't blame you for what other people said and did. Just as I hope you don't blame me. I told you how much I respected your father and what a dear friend your mother is to me. It was never my intention to go after them."

"I know and I appreciate that. I even helped things along by doing something outrageous just like you asked," Miles joked.

"*Pfft*," Faye said into the other end of the phone. "You call that outrageous? You're both single and attractive. Who could blame you? *Outrageous* would have been if you'd gone and married Leonard Dykstrom's daughter. Although she's turned out to be America's favorite, so even that wouldn't be that outrageous any longer."

Miles wasn't sure what else he'd said to Faye before hanging up. He'd been on autopilot after she'd mentioned the subject of marriage. The idea of him marrying Lori was preposterous. Just the thought was making his heart race and head feel light.

"Here you are," his mother said as she slipped into the butler's pantry. "The natives are getting antsy for your speech."

Miles shook his head slightly in order to realign his thoughts. He'd been planning this speech for most of his life. He needed to get his game on.

His mother smiled broadly at him. "Such a wonderful day. All my children are in one place. Kate is growing another grandchild. Gavin is getting married. And my oldest son just got elected to Congress. I don't know if I can get any happier." She adjusted his tie. "Your father would be so proud of you, Miles. Not just because you've been elected, but of the man you've become. You didn't change who that was to achieve your goal."

He leaned down to kiss his mother on the head. "Thanks, Mom, for everything."

Her eyes were shining when she looked up at him. "Are you happy, Miles? You look a little strained."

"Just tired, that's all. It's been a long few months. I'll be fine once things settle down."

"You should take some time off now that you have the chance. After all, your life will be busy once you get to Washington. Maybe you can go on a little vacation."

Miles studied his mother's face. She was up to something; he just couldn't figure out what. "Did you have someplace specific in mind, Mom?"

"Well, now that you mention it." She dug through the large purse on her shoulder. "I don't really want to send this through the mail." His mother opened her hand and a worn gold wedding band was resting in her palm. "You could take this to Oregon and give it to Lori. I know she'd love to get it back."

He blew out a ragged breath as his pulse beat faster. "Where did you find it?"

His mother rolled her eyes. "It seems my granddaughter is a bit of a kleptomaniac. She's been 'collecting' things and stashing them in a box in my bedroom where I keep the costume jewelry for her. I was looking for a bracelet I'd let Emily borrow, to play dress-up, and lo and behold, there it all was, right there in the sparkly box. Apparently she'd been picking up a few extra trinkets when she followed Cassidy around the inn while Cassidy was restocking the bathrooms each day." His mother gripped his arm, pleading. "Please don't tell Kate. She and Alden would have the child in therapy or something. Emily and I had a long talk about it today. She seemed to think that everything in the inn was hers to play with. But she knows now what she did was wrong. It's bad enough I'm going to have to grovel to former guests."

Miles barely comprehended what his mother was saying as he stared at the delicate ring in her hand. *Lori's ring.* It was supposed to have brought her luck, according to her grandmother. She would want it back. His mother was right—the mail was unpredictable and he couldn't take a chance at it being lost again. The campaign was over. His heart felt like he was in the home stretch of a triathlon, it was beating so quickly. Miles could certainly fly out to Oregon and return the ring in person. All that stood between him and seeing Lori again was a rousing campaign speech he'd been rehearsing since he was ten.

"I'd be happy to deliver it in person." He pocketed the ring and wrapped an arm around his mother's shoulders, feeling like he was having an out-of-body experience when he agreed to run his mother's errand. "But first, I have some people to thank."

The ragged Oregon coastline was spectacular as the sun dipped toward the sea on the late autumn afternoon. Lori had forgotten how much she'd missed the gorgeous sunsets of her hometown. The sprawling three-story inn sat on top of a bluff overlooking one of the many inlets along the Pacific coast. Unlike the Victorian-style Tide Me Over Inn, the Towering Peaks Inn was covered entirely with redwood shingles, from its roof to its foundation. Nearly all of the ten guest rooms featured a patio overlooking the bay. There was even a turret with a large sitting room at the top featuring a spectacular 360-degree view of the ocean and the surrounding forest. The interior of the B and B was decorated in the cozy French provincial style with fresh flowers from Bruce's nursery adorning every room.

Lori had been back in Oregon, cooking at her mother's inn, for nearly three months. True to her word, her mom had relinquished complete control of her restaurant to Lori. Now, her mother and Bruce spent part of their time traveling and touring other B and B's around the country, giving seminars to inn owners about their successful farm-to-table approach.

Unencumbered by the disguise she'd been forced to don in Chances Inlet, Lori felt free in the kitchen. She reveled in the ability to create unique dishes and bake delicious desserts for her mother's guests. In addition, she'd instituted a daily tea similar to those Patricia hosted, as well as the weekly wine flights she'd perfected at the Tide Me Over Inn. Given the vineyards surrounding the inn, Lori had quickly been able to work out a partnership with most of the wineries in the area. At long last, Lori had everything she ever wanted.

Most everything anyway.

"Sissy."

Lori looked away from the dining room's panoramic view to see Ian hesitating in the doorway of the kitchen. He'd stopped asking for his parents weeks ago, and as long as Tessa was by his side, the boy was content and adjusted. Lori felt a rush of pride that her mother had taken her ex-husband's child into her home and her heart as if Ian were her own. A tutor came each morning to help with schoolwork, and in the afternoons Bruce or her mother took the boy fishing or on a nature hike looking for animals. Ian was even asking if he could join her mom and Bruce on their trip to Arizona later in the month. While Lori would miss her brother, she was glad that he had adjusted to the transition in his life so seamlessly.

"Hey, Ian. How are the kittens doing?" One of the barn cats had just had a litter and Bruce tasked Ian with checking on them throughout the day. Her stepfather had been incredibly empathetic to the boy, finding things at the inn to keep Ian engaged and happy.

"The black one with the three white feet scratched the gray one," Ian said. "But the momma cat swatted the black one with the three white feet. Then she licked the gray one all better. She's a good momma."

Lori's throat grew tight. She wasn't sure how Ian could differentiate between a good mother and the one he had, but somehow he did. "Most mommas are good, sweetie." She kissed the top of his head. "It's a Wednesday night, you know what that means?"

"Family dinner!"

The inn was typically closed in the middle of the week during the winter months and Lori's mother had always insisted on a family dinner out that night, just so they could reconnect. She was glad her mother had thought to continue the practice for Ian.

Ian's smile suddenly fell. "Can he come, too?"

Perplexed, Lori stared at the boy. "Can who come?" She hoped he wasn't asking about one of the kittens.

"Your friend Miles."

Lori's stomach dropped to her feet. "How do you know about Miles?" she croaked.

"He's here," Ian answered earnestly. "He's in the barn. He likes kittens, too. I told him I was coming to get you."

Miles is here? In the barn? With the kittens?

Lori glanced into one of the small antique mirrors her mother had scattered about the walls as part of the décor. She anxiously smoothed back a strand of hair, now back to its natural fiery red color and cut into waves. Running a hand over her cashmere sweater and black denim jeans, she followed Ian out to the barn, her Steve Madden boots loud on the slate walkway.

"I found her," Ian called as he ran into the barn.

Lori's stomach took another nosedive while her eyes took a moment to adjust from the afternoon sunlight to the dark confines of the barn. When finally she could see, her breath halted in her lungs, forcing a gasp past her lips. Sure enough, Miles

McAlister was in the barn looking sexy as ever. He was sitting on the straw as a trio of kittens crawled over his legs. His blue eyes met hers and Lori thought her knees would surely buckle at the impact of his slow, appreciative smile.

"These little buggers have sharp claws," he said as he lifted the black one with three white legs by the scruff of the neck so it couldn't do further damage to the leather bomber jacket Miles was wearing. Lori licked her lips. Miles looked nothing like a newly elected Congressman. Dressed in worn jeans, dark Sorel boots, and a light chambray shirt, he looked like he belonged on the small farm rather than the marble halls of Washington, D.C.

"That's Chester," Ian was saying as he took the kitten from Miles. "He can be a bit precocious."

Miles arched an eyebrow at Ian. "Can he now? I bet you can handle him, though."

Ian's chest puffed out, making Lori's own heart swell.

"I'm good with animals," Ian said proudly, parroting a phrase he'd heard often throughout his lifetime.

As if to validate Ian's comment, Tessa wandered into the barn. She gave an excited yip at the sight of Miles, before brushing up against Ian's leg.

"Good to see you again, too, Tessa," Miles said as he got to his feet, wiping straw off his jeans. Tessa gave a contented groan when Miles scratched her behind an ear. "Midas says hello, by the way," he murmured. When he looked up, his eyes came to rest on Lori. Her stomach fluttered again.

"Hello, Lori."

"Miles. Wh-what are you doing here?" she stammered.

"He came to see you," Ian answered for him. "Didn't you, Miles?"

"I did." Miles shoved his hands in his pockets.

His easy grin was doing things to her body. Lori wiped her damp palms on her jeans.

"I don't understand. You just won your election. Don't you have things to do? Important things?" She was babbling like an idiot when all she wanted to do was throw her arms around his neck and kiss him before she woke up from the wonderful dream she apparently was having.

"Actually, it's pretty anticlimactic after all the votes are counted. There's a bit of a lull before I take office in January."

"Oh."

Ian looked back and forth at Miles and Lori. "So you came to visit Sissy."

Miles' grin grew broader at Ian's pet name for her, and Lori rocked back on her heels. Had he come just to see her?

"I did," he repeated as if to answer her silent question. Even in the fading light in the barn, she thought she detected a flash of something familiar in his eyes.

"Um, do you need a room? We're usually closed at midweek during the off-season, but I'm sure my mother wouldn't mind."

There was definitely a spark in his blue eyes when she mentioned a room. Lori huffed out a breath. Had he come to see her? Or to see her naked? Even more frustrating: Would she be able to resist him if that was his plan? Somehow she didn't think so.

Miles' chin went to his chest before he jerked it back up again. "Honestly, I hadn't thought that far ahead."

His admission caught her off guard. Miles was not one to go off script. Ever.

"Oh." Miles wasn't the only one repeating himself. Lori gestured toward the B and B. "Well, why don't we go inside and we can figure it out," she suggested. She'd be able to handle the situation much better if they were on her home turf of the kitchen. Lori felt off-kilter staring at a dressed-down Miles covered in kittens.

Ian put the kittens in an empty stall with their mother and the three of them headed toward the back door of the B and B. Miles' hand swung loosely at his side, unnerving her with its proximity to her body.

"Miles!" her mother exclaimed when they entered the house. "What a nice surprise."

Except her mother looked anything but surprised. Instead, she looked guilty. And excited. Lori stomped into the kitchen. Bruce was making himself a cup of coffee in the Keurig. He didn't look any more surprised at the sight of Miles than her mother did. Lori pulled a bottle of Riesling out of the fridge, uncorked it, and poured herself some. Taking a healthy swallow, she then surveyed the scene over the rim of the glass.

Her mother was handing Miles a set of keys to the Bordeaux Suite, one she traditionally reserved for honeymoons and anniversaries because of its double soaking tub and private balcony.

"I promised Ian a trip to the library if he finished all his schoolwork," her mother was saying as Bruce quickly tied the laces on his sneakers. "We'll probably grab a pizza afterwards. I'll text you when we get to the pizza place in case you two want to join us." With Tessa at their heels, they were out the door faster than if they were practicing for a fire drill.

Lori felt Miles' stare bore into her as she sipped her wine, but she refused to meet his eyes. Not when she doubted her own body's reaction to him. "Of all the places you could go to rest up after the campaign, I'm surprised you would pick the Oregon coast in November."

She watched out of the corner of her eye as Miles pulled off his jacket and draped it over the back of a chair. "Actually, did you know that as Gavin's best man, I'm responsible for the groom's cake?"

Once again, he'd surprised her and Lori coughed as she choked a little on her wine. Miles reached for her glass, taking a sip for himself, his blue eyes dancing.

"I had no idea," she said as she pulled another glass out of the cabinet and poured wine into it before refilling her own. Something told her she might need the fortification.

Miles leaned his elbows on the other side of the island. "Yep. And apparently, my brother has been spoiled for any other woman's baked goods."

She coughed to cover the laughter that bubbled up inside her at the absurdity of his statement. Her giddiness was followed quickly by a burst of anger. *Damn him for making me fall more in love with him.* She'd patched up her broken heart just fine these past few months. But seeing him again was chiseling it back into shards. Miles wouldn't understand the concept because he kept his own heart under lock and key.

"You didn't have to come all this way to ask me to make

a cake for your brother," she snapped. "An e-mail or a phone call would have sufficed."

He walked around the island and leaned a hip against the counter next to her. Her nostrils breathed in the achingly familiar scent of him, making her feel a little light-headed. She closed her eyes to steady her nerves, all the while willing her hand not to reach out to touch him.

"That's not the real reason I came," he said softly.

Slowly, she raised her eyelids. Miles pulled something out of his shirt pocket and began twirling it on his finger.

"My grandmother's ring!" she shrieked.

"You sure?" He held it up to the light. "Although it does match the description you gave Lamar."

Her anger evaporated and joy filled the space it left behind. Lori never thought she'd see her talisman again. "It is! Oh Miles, where did you find it?"

"Apparently, Emily has a penchant for sparkly things."

Understanding dawned on Lori. "Her sparkly box!" Lori laughed incredulously. "Emily couldn't resist anything that glittered. She was always digging through the drawers." Her hand shot to her mouth. "Oh my gosh, she used to play with Tessa in my room! The lure of a packed duffel bag had to be too much for an inquisitive six-year-old."

"Mmm. It seems my adorable niece might be leaning toward a life of crime." He laughed and the sound of it scraped against her lower belly, making her muscles clench. "My sister Kate is in for a rude awakening."

"Your poor mother, having to explain that to her guests."

"Nah." He winked at her. "I'm pretty sure she blamed the whole thing on Midas."

She didn't bother choking back the laugh this time. Lori was so delighted to see her grandmother's ring again. When she reached for it, however, Miles closed his fingers around it.

"Hey, do I get it back or not?"

Miles returned the ring to his front pocket. His face was enigmatic. "That depends on the answer to a question. You said you wouldn't leave Chances Inlet without this ring, but you did anyway. Why?"

Lori's cheeks burned and her chest grew tight. She felt like she was on the upslope of a roller coaster. Was he really here to rehash her embarrassing declaration of unrequited love? "I left to protect you from the scandal that surrounded me. But you know that already. Why are you here, Miles?" Her voice sounded hoarse as she pushed the words through her throat, now raw with emotion.

Miles placed a hand on the counter on either side of her, pinning her in. "Because I can't *not* be here." He took a step closer so his body was pressed up against hers.

She soaked in the warmth of him, trembling when his hard muscles came in contact with her traitorous body.

"A hundred and seven days ago you gave me the greatest gift one person can give another: unconditional love. And I didn't know what to do with it, so like a fool, I let you slip away."

She slid her palms up over his chest. "You counted the days?"

"And the hours, but I had to stop because that only made me more insane."

Wrapping her hands around his waist, she pulled him in closer. "This isn't just a Dudley Do-Right thing, is it? Because I understand why you can't love me back."

He lowered his forehead to her shoulder. "Yesterday was supposed to be a dream come true. To win an election was all I ever wanted. Except it wasn't. I kept thinking something was missing. And something was. It was you."

Lori didn't dare breathe.

"When Justine died, it was easy to wall up my heart because she was gone and she wasn't coming back. But you're still here, living and breathing, walking around this earth without me. It was making me crazy." He skimmed his lips along her neckline and Lori shivered. "I thought it was just because I didn't want you with someone else, but it really was because I can't live without you." Those gorgeous blue eyes she adored stared into hers. "I love you, Lori. I don't care who your father is or what he did. And I don't care what any voters might think. All I know is that I don't want to spend another hundred and seven *seconds* apart from you."

Lori's face hurt, she was smiling so broadly. She was glad

her body was pressed against the cabinet because her limbs had turned to jelly with his words. "That, Congressman McAlister, is the most beautiful speech you'll ever make." She reached up and pulled his mouth down to hers. Their kiss was raw and hot, and the room began a lazy spin as his hands roamed over the parts of her that had missed him the most. Tears leaked out of her eyes, but Miles kissed them away.

"I don't want this to be an intersection of our lives, Lori," he whispered. "I want our paths to merge forever. You and me. With kids and grandkids. Maybe even a dog or two. I know I'm asking a lot for you to throw yourself into the fish-bowl that is politics, but together, we can make it work. I know we can. I love you so much."

She smiled at him through her tears. "I love you, too, Miles McAlister." Lori kissed a corner of his mouth. "I really don't feel like meeting my family for pizza. Do you?"

"Why, Lori, are you asking if you can have dessert before your dinner?" he teased.

"Well, it has been a hundred and seven days."

His smile was wicked as he carried her up to the Bordeaux Suite, where he proceeded to give her more than one helping of dessert.

EPILOGUE

Miles charged up the steps to his Capitol Hill townhouse, eager to share the events of the meeting with Lori. His progress was halted in the narrow foyer by a traffic jam made up of the crew from the television cooking show that had been filming in the kitchen all morning. The audio technician gave him a wave as he maneuvered the big boom microphone out to the production van.

Rounding the corner into the bright sunny room that took up nearly the entire first floor of their century-old row house, Miles stopped short as he caught sight of his wife laughing with one of the producers. Dressed in a form-fitting purple sweater that would make most of her male viewers drool before she even started cooking, she boxed up the remains of a lemon tart for the crew, grinning as she teased the director about sharing it with everyone else.

Lori's smile still had the power to make him weak at the knees. She'd been stingy with it when he'd first met her, and now, he considered each one a gift. Her grin deepened when she caught sight of him leaning against the doorframe.

"Miles!" She hurried over, wrapping her arms around his neck. "How was your meeting with the president?"

The rest of the crew murmured their good-byes as they slipped out of the kitchen, leaving the two of them locked in an embrace. "It went well. Your cupcakes were quite a hit. She was wondering if perhaps you'd consider taking over the job as White House pastry chef." He nuzzled her neck.

"Mmm, I'm kind of busy with the gig I've got going as your wife," she teased. "But if she backs you in your Senate race, I might consider a guest appearance or two."

His wife of three years had become quite a celebrity in the cooking world with her weekly cable network show. Miles marveled at how the woman who used to hide in the shadows was now comfortable in front of a worldwide television audience. Lori was also the successful author of three bestselling cookbooks. The fact that she'd donated all her profits to a charity helping victims of her father's Ponzi scheme further endeared her to her legions of fans.

"I told the president that you'd just as soon wait until we're living there to take over the kitchen," he said.

"Astute answer, Congressman." She kissed him soundly, loosening his tie as she did so.

"We still have some time before we have to catch our flight to Chances Inlet," he murmured as he snaked a hand beneath her sweater. "How about you and I enjoy a little dessert to celebrate my successful meeting with our commander in chief?"

The sound of the back door opening stilled his roaming fingers. Lori laughed as she slapped his hands away. "That's going to have to wait until tonight."

"Dada," their son shrieked from his perch in the stroller.

"Hold on there, Donnie." Lori reached around the toddler's flailing hands and kicking feet to unfasten him from the stroller. Donnie's blue eyes sparkled as he stretched his arms up at Miles. Lifting his son to his chest, he breathed in the scent of baby shampoo and apples the boy had been munching while on his walk.

"I tried to tire him out," Cassidy said. "But now I think I'm the one who needs a nap."

"You're a trooper, Cass," Lori said as Miles snuggled their son. "Most college kids go to Florida on their spring break. You come to D.C. and get stuck babysitting."

"Spring break in Florida is overrated." Cassidy grinned. "Besides, I'd never get to see my little godson otherwise." She tickled the boy's thigh, making him giggle. "I'll take him upstairs and get him cleaned up. Ginger has texted me three times to make sure we don't miss our flight. My guess is she has a major announcement to make at Patricia's birthday dinner tonight."

Miles handed his son off to Cassidy, who had the boy chortling with glee by the time they reached the nursery upstairs.

Lori smiled slyly at him. "It'll be great having everyone together again for the weekend. I'm so glad your mother always includes my mom, Bruce, and Ian in the festivities as well."

"Yeah, but leave it to Gavin to upstage everyone." He pulled his wife back into his arms. "Something tells me my mother will be more delighted with the gift of another grandchild than the lace shawl we got her in Scotland."

"Actually, that's not the only gift we got her." Taking his hand in hers, she placed it on her belly.

A lump formed in Miles' throat as he looked down at his wife's midsection before meeting her eyes again. "Really?" He lifted his hand to brush the hair back off her face. "That explains the gorgeous glow." He pulled her in for a slow, deep kiss.

"Remember that when we're on the airplane later," she said.

"Have I told you lately how much I love you?"

Lori kissed his jaw. "Every day. But I never get tired of hearing it."

Donnie began wailing and Lori sighed as she headed for the back stairs. She stopped at the base of the steps and looked over her shoulder at him. "All those years I spent dreaming of something better—wanting more—I never imagined a life as good as this one with you, Miles. I love you."

As he watched his beautiful wife climb the stairs, Miles

thought back to that list of goals he'd written when he was ten years old. How naïve he'd been thinking ticking off items on a list would make him happy. All he ever wanted was right here in this house or waiting for him at his mother's inn in Chances Inlet. Lori's gentle lullaby drifted down the stairs. Miles grinned like a fool as he made his way to the nursery and the family that made his list—and his life—complete.

Turn the page for a look at

SLEEPING WITH THE ENEMY

the new Out of Bounds novel
by Tracy Solheim

Jay McManus had built his reputation—not to mention his fortune—in business by always keeping his composure and never letting his opponents see him sweat. That cool, ruthless demeanor had propelled him to the top of the dot-com industry before he'd even hit the ripe old age of thirty. It had also earned him enough begrudging respect and money to enable him to become, at thirty-five, the youngest owner of a National Football League team. Right now, though, he was beginning to sweat his decision to go public with his lucrative software company and sink his profits into the Baltimore Blaze.

"Let me get this straight—according to some obnoxious gossip blogger, the Sparks, our team's cheerleaders, are filing a lawsuit suing the team?" With two fingers, Jay pulled at the Windsor knot on the silk tie threatening to strangle him.

"As of this morning, there's only one cheerleader named, but it is a class action suit, which means any of the several hundred women who've cheered for the team during the past decade could potentially join in." Hank Osbourne, the team's general manager, looked way too relaxed for having just dropped a bombshell into Jay's morning coffee. Instead of being the cool one, Jay wanted to strangle someone. "These types of cases are springing up throughout the league," the GM said calmly.

Known as the Wizard of Oz throughout the NFL, Osbourne was a taciturn former military officer who'd been running the day-to-day operations of the Blaze football team for five years and was well respected among the players, the league, and other teams. Jay hadn't given a thought to replacing him when he'd taken over ownership from his godfather the preceding year. The guy had earned his pay and then some since Jay had arrived. As recently as this morning, the GM had been dealing with a kicker who'd been placed on suspension by the NFL after he'd violated the league's alcohol abuse policy one too many times. Unfortunately for the player—and the team—the guy had just been enjoying a beer while on a family vacation. Not that it mattered to the league. Now, besides needing a kicker before the season opener this week, the team was apparently about to get hit with a sensational lawsuit by scantily clad women waving pom-poms.

This kind of bullshit just doesn't happen in Silicon Valley, Jay thought as he stood up from the round table in his large corner office at the Blaze practice facility. He began to pace methodically in front of the room's long picture windows, scattering the dust motes floating in the bright morning sunshine as he did so. "How many people know about this?"

"You know as well as I do, Jay, that this blogger is followed by every media outlet," Hank said. "I spoke with Asia Dupree in our media relations office before I came in here. She's already fielding calls from all the networks and major sports sites."

Jay swore under his breath. The *Girlfriends' Guide to the NFL* had been a pain in the league's ass for over two years now. Unfortunately, most of what the anonymous blogger reported was true. It was the sensationalistic spin she put in her posts that aggravated him—and every other person who'd found themselves mentioned on her site. Lately, it seemed, the Blaze had taken more than its fair share of hits.

"Not only that, but Asia says some women's groups have been calling, too."

He turned to face the other men in the room. "You can't be serious?"

Hank nodded solemnly as the others looked everywhere but at Jay. "Which means the commissioner will likely want to be kept apprised of what we're doing."

Which meant Jay's day had just gone from bad to worse. The NFL commissioner, Reggie Austin, thought Jay was too young and too inexperienced to own the Blaze, and wanted one of his cronies to take over the team instead. But he hadn't had the power or the votes to block Jay's ownership bid. So instead, the man took every opportunity to say "I told you so" to anyone who'd listen. Now, thanks to a cyberbully, this was apparently going to be another one of those opportunities.

"The cheerleader, what do we know about her?" Jay directed his question at Donovan Carter, the Blaze's chief security officer, who was seated at the opposite end of the table. A former college football star, the stocky African-American with the shaved head had once been an agent with NCIS before joining the Blaze staff.

Don scanned his tablet. "Not much yet. Her name is Jennifer Knowles. She was a student at the University of Maryland, but she's not enrolled there this semester. She cheered for the Blaze for two years beginning with the Super Bowl season year before last. The roster doesn't list her as a member now. I have a meeting with Nicki Ellis, the coordinator of the Sparks, at ten. Hopefully she can shed more light on this."

"What does she want?" Jay asked. Someone always wanted something from him. Especially women. Usually it was Jay the women wanted, and if they couldn't have him, they wanted money. Lots of money.

Hank released a long-suffering sigh. "We won't know for sure until Art gets ahold of the complaint being filed." He gestured to the man seated beside him: Art Langford, a tall man sporting a bad combover, who served as the team's general counsel. "We've got someone at the courthouse ready to grab a copy when it reaches the clerk." Hank steepled his fingers and leaned back in his chair. "In all likelihood, she's jumped on the bandwagon of other cheerleading squads who've filed similar suits against their teams. Most have claimed wage discrimination. That argument won't hold up in our house."

"Explain it to me," Jay demanded. He made it a habit to know every detail of each business he owned, but it hadn't occurred to him when he bought the team that he needed to familiarize himself with the operations of the Blaze cheerleaders. Jay was angry at himself for the slipup.

"The Sparks generate their own income in the form of special appearance fees, as well as through other merchandising such as calendars and posters. Last year that amounted to just over one point three million dollars."

Jay's personal assistant, Lincoln Harris, interrupted Hank's explanation with a loud whistle before Jay locked gazes with the young African-American man. Linc quickly dropped his eyes back to his tablet.

"Most teams reabsorb that money into their own coffers, but we use it to ensure the young women are afforded a decent wage—keeping in mind this is only meant to be a part-time job." Hank continued. "The women sign a contract outlining what they're responsible for with regard to appearances, transportation, and practice time. All in all, the Sparks are among the highest paid in the league."

"Yet, according to some malicious blogger, one of them is filing a multimillion-dollar lawsuit against this team." Jay let out an impatient huff as he continued pacing. Something didn't make sense.

The four other men in the room were silent. Art squirmed a bit in his chair.

Jay pinned the lawyer with his gaze. "Out with it."

Art flinched slightly before pulling out a sheet of paper from a folder in front of him and handing it to Jay. "The suits pending haven't all been strictly about wage issues."

Jay scanned the sheet, his pulse squeezing at his neck despite his loosened tie. He lifted his eyes to the men assembled in the room. "For the love of Christ, tell me there is no one in this organization performing a *jiggle test* on the cheerleaders." Somehow he managed to push the words out through his tight jaw.

"Whoa," Linc said from beside Jay. "Is that really a job? Because if it is—"

Jay silenced his brash young assistant with a glare. Linc had been with him for four years. A three-time all-American wrestler from Duke, Linc had a sharp mind for software that usurped even his prowess on the mat. When Jay went public with his company, he'd intended to leave Linc in place to look after Jay's remaining shares. But Linc was an athlete at heart and the opportunity to work in the NFL was every boy's—and man's—dream, so he'd convinced Jay to bring him along. Up until this moment, Jay hadn't regretted that decision.

Linc gave him a sheepish look. "Not a joking matter. Got it." He went back to his job of taking notes of the meeting.

"Not as long as I'm managing this team," Hank said, his expression every bit as stern as Jay's likely was. "That behavior will not be tolerated."

Jay rubbed the back of his neck, feeling his tight muscles pinch beneath his dress shirt. He really needed a few rounds in the gym with a punching bag. But that would have to wait until this evening. "So how do we prepare and defend ourselves against this crazy case? I really don't want the added negative publicity going into the season. Art, can we hand this off to the league? With so many other similar suits clogging up the courts, surely they have a standard defense prepared."

"That's the problem," Art said. "Cheerleaders are not considered part of the NFL. Each group falls under the purview of the individual team. Even if the league comes up with some standard policy now, it would be too little, too late. The teams are on their own to defend this."

With a harsh sigh, Jay flipped the paper out of his hands and let it drift back toward the table. "Then do your best to make this go away, Art." He picked up his coffee cup for a fortifying sip of caffeine, which he now wished was laced with Scotch. Art deferentially cleared his throat, causing Jay to nearly choke.

Jay arched an eyebrow at the lawyer. Art shot a pleading look at Hank. The coffee went down Jay's throat painfully as he braced himself for what was yet to come, pretty damn sure that it was something he wasn't going to like.

"Art isn't exactly a trial attorney," Hank said unapologetically. "He handles the player contracts, issues with sponsors and the unions, but whenever we've had a trial, we generally hire out."

Swearing under his breath, Jay clunked his coffee mug back down on the table and resumed his pacing. "So we have a specious class action suit looming and—even if we can defend against the claims—I'm going to have to fork out a ransom for outside counsel?"

"Unfortunately, that's the way these things work, Jay," Hank said. "But I've already contacted our local counsel. Stuart and his firm have handled at least a dozen other court cases for the team with great success."

Jay jerked to a halt. "*A dozen other court cases?* How come this is the first I've heard of them? Why weren't they disclosed when I took over ownership last year?" If there was one thing Jay hated, it was being blindsided. He prided himself in having information long before his opponents—much of it information his business rivals wished he hadn't uncovered.

It was Hank's turn to arch an eyebrow. "I believe the words I used were 'with great success.' Stuart is discreet and very astute. He's the one with eyes on the courthouse. In fact, if this case comes to fruition, Stuart already has a partial strategy mapped out, including a whopper of a lawyer to represent the team in court. His firm just merged with a big firm in Boston. The same one that employs Brody Janik's sister. She just successfully defended a small Baltimore company in a major environmental class action suit. Between her trial success rate, her being a woman, and her connection to the team, Stuart thinks we'll have an advantage in the court of public opinion, which is half the battle here."

Jay moved to the large windows overlooking the Blaze campus, putting his back to the other men in the room because he wasn't so sure he could maintain a stoic expression any longer.

"I'm sure you've met Bridgett, at the very least at Brody's wedding this past spring," Hank was saying. "By all accounts, she's as brilliant in the courtroom as she is beautiful."

The tension that had been torturing his neck and shoulders since the meeting began settled uncomfortably in another part of Jay's anatomy as he thought of the "brilliant" and "beautiful" Bridgett Janik. She'd avoided him at her brother's wedding, just as she had every time their paths had crossed in the past eighteen months. Always impeccably dressed in some expensive, figure-flattering outfit, the petite blonde with the light gray eyes hadn't even graced him with a haughty look since he'd taken over ownership of the Blaze. It was as if he was invisible to the woman, while the short hairs at the back of his neck lifted *every freaking time* she entered the same room as him. Given his reaction to her, she couldn't be as immune to Jay as she pretended. He allowed himself a moment to admire her ability to remain aloof—it was a skill he'd cultivated for years. But he needed to discredit her as the Blaze's outside counsel. Because working with the alluring Bridgett Janik would be too much of a distraction for Jay, and he didn't need any more distractions in his life.

His eyes were still focused on the leaves changing color on the trees surrounding the practice facility as he spoke. "I'm sure that's a conflict of interest." He tossed the suggestion out, hoping Hank and Art would latch on to it.

"Actually, no, it isn't," Art piped up. "There's no prohibition on a family member representing another family member in a courtroom. Although, it's not always the best idea. I can quote several cases where it hasn't been effective." Hank cleared his throat and Art continued. "In any case, Ms. Janik will be technically representing you as the owner of the Blaze. Her brother's association with the team is irrelevant."

Great, Jay thought to himself, *the guy can't try a case in court, but he knows all the intricacies of conflicts of interest.*

"With any luck," Hank pointed out, "we won't need outside attorneys, but I think Stuart's plan is a good one. Having Bridgett in our corner will certainly give us some credibility with both men and women."

Jay hoped Hank was right, that this case would die out before the Blaze became the butt of jokes by late-night talk show hosts. More important, he hoped it would settle quickly so that he'd be able to keep his distance from Brody Janik's sister.

"Stuart is sending his team over this afternoon, as soon as they go over the court documents," Hank went on to say. "In the meantime, let's let Don see what he can find out about the Knowles girl. After that, we can come up with a defensive game plan."

He listened as the other men filed out of his office. All the while, Jay was formulating his own game plan on how to ensure Bridgett Janik would quickly recuse herself from the case.

The teakettle whistled with annoyance while Bridgett Janik carefully stirred the ingredients for chai tea into her cup. She tucked the cell phone between her ear and her shoulder and reached for the shrieking kettle.

"I'm sorry, Stuart, but I thought you actually said cheerleaders for a minute there." Bridgett stirred her tea before blowing carefully over the rim.

"That's because I did say cheerleaders, Buffy," the senior partner for her firm's Baltimore office, Stuart Johnson, replied on the other end of the phone. He'd dubbed her "Buffy the Class Action Slayer" two years ago when she'd persuaded the judge to quash half the designated class in a large environmental case weeks before the plaintiffs had even issued subpoenas. "Good to know you didn't leave your hearing over in Italy with all your hard-earned money. How was the shopping spree, anyway?"

Bridgett recognized a redirect when she heard one. And Stuart's were always among the best. It was what made him such a successful trial attorney.

"My trip to Italy was wonderful, Stuart. I slept until noon. I ate bread and pasta and I shopped like I had the money to spend. The best vacation a girl could want after eighteen months on a case. But you already know this because your wife was there for part of my vacation." Elizabeth, her boss's wife, had a bit of a shoe fetish. When Bridgett had mentioned she was headed off for a shopping vacation on the Italian coast, the older woman had looked so enthralled that Bridgett had invited her along. She hadn't minded the company because it gave her an excuse not to invite one of her interfering sisters. "Get back to the subject of stupid cheerleaders, Stuart."

"You say *cheerleader* as though it's dirty somehow." Stuart's tone was teasing. "Naughty even." He laughed at his words, and Bridgett let out an exasperated sigh as she carried her tea over to the large window in the living room of her condo in Boston's trendy Back Bay area. Sunlight sparkled off the dew still glistening on the rooftops in the early autumn morning. "What have you got against cheerleaders anyway?" he asked.

Bridgett blew on her tea. "Nothing."

"No, your tone says otherwise. Don't tell me you always wanted to be a cheerleader but you just weren't chirpy enough?"

"Funny." She took a sip, letting the chai mingle on her tongue. The Janik girls had all been cheerleaders—all except for Bridgett. She'd tried out, begging her friend Jessica to audition as well. Given that two of her sisters had preceded her on the squad, Bridgett figured she'd be a sure thing. After all, she had the looks and the requisite pom-poms to fill out the uniform. Jessica—the one she'd had to coax into trying out—got picked instead. Stuart was correct. It was the chirpiness. The cheer sponsor and the two captains thought Bridgett was too serious to be an effective cheerleader. Well, she was a serious person. A girl didn't get into Harvard without being one.

Apparently, the decades-old slight went deeper than Bridgett remembered, judging by her reaction this morning. She'd have to examine that little character flaw later, though. "Focus, Stuart. You said we're taking on a case involving cheerleaders. Can you give me more detail than that, please?"

Stuart laughed. "Usually you only get snippy when I mention *conscious uncoupling*. I'll have to add *cheerleader* to the list of words that make Bridgett lose her practiced cool."

Bridgett was glad Stuart couldn't see her bristle at the phrase *conscious uncoupling*. "Hey, Jimmy Fallon, do you want to call me back after you get finished with your monologue?"

He laughed again before sobering up. "I didn't say we were representing the cheerleaders. We get to be the bad guys and defend the party they are suing."

Now, that was more like it. Bridgett took another sip of tea as she considered the possibility of being retained by a school or a university against a bunch of girls in short skirts and ridiculous hair bows. "Oh, please tell me we get to defend against a group of helicopter parents who want their daughters to all win the first-place trophy?"

That got another laugh out of Stuart. "That tune will change when it's your little darling sobbing that some myopic judge robbed her of the blue ribbon."

Bridgett paused with her teacup poised at her lips. She wondered if Stuart was right. But then, she'd never know, would she? Somehow she doubted that, even if she had a child, she'd want him or her not to think they had to be winners all the time. How would that prepare them for life? Life could be cruel. Bridgett knew that firsthand. There was no use sugarcoating it. The point was moot, however, and Bridgett swallowed her tea around the lump in her throat.

"Actually, these are NFL cheerleaders," Stuart explained.

"The NFL has cheerleaders?" Of course there were the Dallas Cowboys Cheerleaders. They were practically icons. But, Bridgett wondered, did the other teams have actual cheerleaders? She'd never really noticed.

Stuart was silent for a moment on the other end of the line. "You can't be serious. Don't you go to your brother's football games?"

Bridgett's younger brother, the baby of the Janik family, was Brody Janik, a Pro Bowl tight end for the Baltimore Blaze and certified heartthrob to women around the globe. He was as much of an icon as the Dallas Cowboys Cheerleaders. In fact, her brother's new sister-in-law had once been on the Dallas squad. "Sure I go to his games, but I don't go to watch the cheerleaders." She mainly went out of family obligation and because Brody was the one member of the Janik clan who understood Bridgett for who she was. The rest of the Janiks wanted to make her over to be more like them: settled. "I didn't think the Blaze had cheerleaders."

"They do," Stuart said just as an ominous feeling settled in the pit of Bridgett's stomach. "And they're suing team management for alleged workplace violations."

"Oh no," Bridgett whispered.

"Oh yes," Stuart said. "And the Blaze have hired us to handle their defense. And you, Buffy, are the perfect person to take the lead. Not only are you a woman—although it would have helped tremendously if you'd been a cheerleader at one time—but you're also Brody Janik's sister. Score one for us in the headlines when this goes public later today."

With a less than steady hand, Bridgett set her tea down on the antique marble side table she'd bought in Florence a few years back. Stuart wanted her to defend the Baltimore Blaze in a class action suit? Against cheerleaders? If that wasn't too insulting, she factored in the team's new owner: Jay McManus. The man was insufferable, arrogant, obscenely wealthy, and sex on a stick. And he made her stomach crawl every time she got within fifty feet of him. She did everything she could to keep her distance from the man at all costs. Working for him on his defense would violate her own personal restraining order and Bridgett couldn't go there.

"I'm sure it's a conflict of interest somehow," she said, adding a silent prayer after the words left her mouth.

"Come on, Bridgett. Second year law school. There's no conflict here even if the Sparks were suing your brother directly."

Bridgett softly banged her head against the warm window, scaring a pigeon hanging out on the other side. Of course Stuart would have thought this through. He didn't make a move without carefully considering all the options. She tried another tactic. "I don't know. I've been in Baltimore for over two years on the Pressler case. I'd like to hang out close to home for my next case."

"Hang out at home? Bridgett, before you left for Italy, you begged me to staff you on a case that was anywhere BUT

Boston. Remember the nagging family whose radar you are trying to fly under? Brody's been married for six months. You're the only single one left. They're gunning for you, Buffy. But hey, if you want to deal with that, I've got an open-and-shut discrimination case filed by some fast-food workers in Worcester you can first-chair."

There's no such thing as an open-and-shut case that involved discrimination. With another headbang against the window, she cursed her entire family, including her not-so-favorite brother, Brody, and her sweet old Grandpa Gus, who had conspired together to marry her off to the first available orthodontist they could find. She'd be a sitting duck if she stayed in Boston.

"How long?" she said, her tone resigned.

"That's the can-do spirit," Stuart said. "I won't know the particulars until we pick up the filing at the courthouse. I sent Dan over there to get it."

Bridgett sighed. Dan Lewis had been her associate on the Pressler case. At least he was a good lawyer.

"That blogger who writes the *Girlfriends' Guide to the NFL* made a vague reference to the case late last night—that's what put it on Hank Osbourne's radar. Since then, the media have run with it." Stuart's chuckle sounded amazed and annoyed at the same time. "Believe it or not, several women's groups have already announced plans for protests of this Sunday's Blaze game."

Bridgett knew of the blogger. Whoever was behind the poison pen—or in this case, keyboard—had tortured her brother, Brody, last season, nearly causing him to lose his career and the woman he loved.

"I've set up a meeting for three this afternoon at the Blaze headquarters. Hank will be waiting for you. And, Bridgett, I don't have to tell you what a client as wealthy as Jay McManus could do for this law firm—not to mention your partner earning statements."

"Wait, you said Hank will be waiting for *me*. Just where exactly will you be?"

"On speakerphone. I've got to be in Manhattan to take care of another of those conscious-uncoupling cases you love so much. But I'll meet you back at the Baltimore office tonight and we can discuss strategy. Toni has you on the eleven o'clock flight, so you might want to pack those gorgeous Burberry bags of yours and hustle to the airport."

As she hung up the phone, Bridgett gave the window another thump with her forehead. Her options were limited, really. She could stay in Boston and suffer her family's futile attempts at matchmaking or head to Baltimore, where a meeting with the man she'd come to know as the Antichrist awaited her. Every nerve ending in her body screamed that she'd just made the absolute wrong choice.

ALSO FROM INTERNATIONAL BESTSELLING AUTHOR

Tracy Solheim

BACK *to* BEFORE

~ A Second Chances Novel ~

Chances Inlet, North Carolina, has a famous power for second chances. But its charms are lost on the town's favorite son—until *she* comes along…

When his father's sudden death puts his family's construction business in serious debt, architect Gavin McAlister is forced to put his dream career in New York on hold. Making matters worse, his fiancée calls it quits. Desperate to return to his big-city life, he discovers an opportunity to save his family, one that has him reluctantly starring in a home restoration TV show.

Former soap star Ginger Walsh hopes this job as a TV makeup artist will lead to better things. So far it's only brought her to a hamlet full of people who don't like her—except Gavin. After a wild night out leads to Ginger waking up in Gavin's loft—and the rest of town talking—the two of them soon wonder if getting back to before is what they want. Because being in each other's arms certainly feels like what they need…